ORDEAL

ORDEAL

Deanie Francis Mills

A DUTTON BOOK

DUTTON
Published by the Penguin Group
Penguin Books USA Inc., 375 Hudson Street, New York, New York 10014, U.S.A.
Penguin Books Ltd, 27 Wrights Lane, London W8 5TZ, England
Penguin Books Australia Ltd, Ringwood, Victoria, Australia
Penguin Books Canada Ltd, 10 Alcorn Avenue, Toronto, Ontario, Canada M4V 3B2
Penguin Books (N.Z.) Ltd, 182–190 Wairau Road, Auckland 10, New Zealand

Penguin Books Ltd, Registered Offices: Harmondsworth, Middlesex, England

First published by Dutton, an imprint of Dutton Signet,
a division of Penguin Books USA Inc.
Distributed in Canada by McClelland & Stewart Inc.

First Printing, May, 1997
10   9   8   7   6   5   4   3   2   1

ACKNOWLEDGMENTS
From *Voices of Our Ancestors: Cherokee Teachings from the Wisdom Fire* by Dhyani
Ywahoo, © 1987. Reprinted by arrangement with Shambhala Publications, Inc., 300
Massachusetts Avenue, Boston, MA 02115.

REGISTERED TRADEMARK—MARCA REGISTRADA

LIBRARY OF CONGRESS CATALOGING-IN-PUBLICATION DATA
Mills, Deanie Francis.
    Ordeal / Deanie Francis Mills.
        p.   cm.
    ISBN 0-525-94202-5 (acid-free paper)
    I. Title
    PS3563.I422964073   1997
    813'.54—dc21   96-49694
                                                                                    CIP

Printed in the United States of America
Set in Transitional

PUBLISHER'S NOTE
This is a work of fiction. Names, characters, places, and incidents either are the products
of the author's imagination or are used fictitiously, and any resemblance to actual persons, living or dead, events, or locales is entirely coincidental.

ORDEAL

This book is dedicated to Russell Galen,
visionary, dragon-fighter,
dream-maker, agent, and friend—
with respect, affection, and gratitude . . .

. . . And to my Cherokee grandmothers,
whose own voices have been lost.
May they speak again in these pages.

Mourn not the dead that in the cool earth lie—
But rather mourn the apathetic throng—
The cowed and the meek—
Who see the world's great anguish and its wrong
And dare not speak.

RALPH CHAPLIN (1887–1961)

"Disease of the ordeal" is believed by many Cherokee to have been sent to someone to test his or her endurance and courage.

Prologue

Southwestern Louisiana, 1980

*T*HE *ambush was unexpected.*

Ghost-gray morning mists veiled sweating SWAT team members, heavy-laden in full urban assault suits and body armor and armed with AR-15 rifles, 9mm semiautomatics, and Remington 870 pump shotguns as they labored silent as Ninjas through the thick underbrush and dense trees surrounding the "Community," a ragtag group of survivalists who had been holed up with their charismatic leader in the swampy thickets of the bayou for months.

Their mission was to serve the leader with a search and arrest warrant. Because he was known never to leave the compound, this was the only way. Reliable intelligence sources had reported an arsenal of weapons on-site, and though the inhabitants were trained in combat techniques and the use of firearms, resistance was not expected, though team members were fully prepared to neutralize the suspect if he took a hostage or fired upon them.

Fifty yards from the compound, they maintained radio silence, not even speaking quietly enough to hear one another on their earplugs, as they deployed two eight-man squads broken into teams of four and four tree-perched snipers to seize and control key terrain around the ramshackle buildings. Humidity thick enough to touch dripped off the leaves in the form of heavy dew and poured off the agents in drivels of sweat. To some of the veterans on the squad, it felt like Vietnam.

No birdsong pierced the eerie silence. It was their ultimate betrayal.

The squads emerged into a clearing which surrounded their objective for twenty-five yards in all directions. As they began moving rapidly on cat's feet across the clearing, all hell broke loose. The ambushers attacked from well-concealed positions with overwhelming firepower. The front units, trapped in a deadly kill zone in the near ambush, had only one course of action to adopt: they immediately launched a direct assault into the compound. The center and rear units, still sheltered by trees, went into a protective flanking position.

Putting maximum pressure on the compound, the teams maintained the momentum of the attack, covering one another and continuing the assault for a relentless twenty minutes before overcoming the key ambush positions and descending in full force on the leader and his closest defenders.

He quickly surrendered.

Everywhere was the hot sickening odor of fresh blood mixed with fired gunpowder. The carnage would haunt the nightmares of every person present that hellish morning for the rest of their lives.

Some would pay for it that long—two federal agents sustained career-ending wounds; they were not killed because of the bulletproof qualities of their Kevlar vests.

But the survivalists, who were not wearing protective armor, would pay a much dearer price. As the agents searched each building for casualties, adding up the body count as they went along, many of them would live to regret their own combat skills. Horrified at what they found, some of them would quit the SWAT team that day.

In the end, nobody knew exactly who shot the kids.

All any of the men ever saw were the M16s, sprouting through windows as they charged the buildings, aimed right at their heads.

PART I

A Dream Within a Dream

All that we see or seem
Is but a dream within a dream.

> EDGAR ALLAN POE
> "A Dream Within a Dream"

Our heart changes, and that is the
greatest cause of suffering in life.

> PROUST

A person's destiny stands not in the future,
but in the past.

> HAVELOCK ELLIS

A people without a history is like
the wind on buffalo grass.

> ANCIENT SIOUX SAYING

CHAPTER 1

"SLOW down, Daniel, dammit!" yelled Wren Cameron, jamming her right foot against the floorboards as if that would stop the car. "You're not ready for speed yet. Not till you learn control."

Daniel gave his mother a sideways, cocky grin and slowed the car down maybe five miles per hour. Handsome little devil. Since he'd gotten his braces off, he was becoming a real ladykiller. Maybe someday he'd figure that out. As it was, he was still too bashful for girls and spent all his spare time hanging out with his renegade friends.

"You were a real butthead in Mr. Rund's computer science class today," she said in her Straighten Up and Be Serious mother voice. "He dragged me out of my own class—*again*—and I had to deal with him and then with Mrs. Satterwhite, and now I've got to drive you to and from Saturday school for the next month, which means I get to be punished too!"

She glared at him even as he was rolling his eyes, and he glanced away.

"The Runt is a skinny little twerp, and I can't stand him," he muttered.

"You're right, Daniel. Mr. Rund is a skinny little twerp. But he thinks that stunt you pulled with the computers was, let's see, how did he put it? Oh yes, he said it was deliberate, malicious, and destructive."

"What? But I—"

"I know. I explained to him that you are a computer illiterate. And I think we both know that, for a computer teacher, so is he. But he is still your teacher, and you will do what he says and at least pretend to respect him, because I have *had* it with being lectured by other teachers because my own son insists on behaving like a preschooler!"

"Not really. I was a pretty good kid in preschool."

"Not funny."

As usual, Wren wanted to kill her fifteen-year-old son at the same time she was defending him. If he acted up only in Rund's class, her life would be so much simpler. But not a week went by that Wren was not summoned to the vice principal's office to deal with the overbearing Nadine Satterwhite, or ambushed in the halls by a semi-hysterical teacher, or even called up during her conference period by local police.

Daniel's offenses were never serious. He did not do drugs, stayed clear of what passed for gangs in a small Texas town and, so far anyway, had not indulged in the sort of gratuitous vandalism that had plagued schools in recent years.

He did drive his teachers to near dementia, make lousy grades in spite of an IQ in the "above average to bright" range, square off daily with his parents, antagonize his twelve-year-old sister, Zoe, to tears, hang out with emotionally troubled kids from dysfunctional families, carry an attitude around like a heavy backpack, and indulge in such behavior as riding around in the back of a pickup, smashing rural mailboxes with a baseball bat—which, the police had informed Wren, was a federal offense.

Wren and her husband, Harry "Cam" Cameron, a small-town defense attorney, had done everything two parents could possibly do to keep the boy from falling off the deep end. Their sixteen-year marriage was solid and loving, their parenting was consistent and firm, and they had always spent as much time as possible with their two children.

Daniel, hyperactive, stubborn, and prone to dramatics as a child, had never been particularly easy to raise, but he had always been cherished. And he did have his loveable side. He was funny, witty, bright, energetic, imaginative, and, when he wanted to be, affectionate.

Cam, who had spent half his life dealing with the criminal element, felt deep shame and an abiding horror at his son's behavior and attitude toward life. Daniel's apparent refusal to consider his "victims"—distraught teachers, rural families whose thirty-dollar mailboxes had been destroyed, and others—disturbed him greatly. His biggest fear was that Daniel would turn out to be no better than most of his clients.

Or even—perish the thought—that he might have to defend his son in a court of law someday.

Wren, who looked at her son through a mother's eyes, saw Daniel somewhat differently. She saw a scared little boy, trapped in the body of an almost man, who didn't want to grow up just yet. Peter Pan, trying to fly. Although his behavior worried her too, she believed in her heart that Daniel was essentially a good person who would straighten out with time and maturity.

He did seem easily susceptible to the influence of his friends, some of whom seemed not to possess that inner self-control that had, so far, prevented Daniel from taking that dangerous first step into real crime.

Wren—more than her son would ever know—understood what it meant to rebel against stultifying rules and regulations. She understood her son's frustrations.

She also understood how very easy it was to take that first perilous step.

After an uncomfortable moment Daniel said, "I guess Dad's gonna totally freak out."

"Your dad's just worried about you, son," she said. "He wants you to grow up with some integrity. But with the path you're on, he doesn't see that happening."

"Yeah, man, we shoot up like, every da-ay," he responded in his best junkie voice. "Then we pack a piece and, like, go cruisin' for some bruisin', you know what I'm sayin'?"

Wren rubbed her forehead. Another tension headache. She'd been getting them every day lately, thanks to being caught constantly in the middle of the tug-of-war between her son and her husband. After an endless minute of godawful heavy metal screeching on the car radio, she said, "By the way, if I ever catch you filching beers from the fridge again, I will step out of the way, Daniel, and let your dad do whatever he sees fit."

"I didn't—"

"Don't push it. Just don't."

They rode in sullen silence, both remembering the screaming fight that had erupted between Daniel and his dad when Cam had discovered the missing beers, while the radio blared from the car speakers. Finally, Daniel said, "So am I, like, grounded for the rest of my life?"

"Maybe." She glanced at him. "Depends on your behavior from now on. If you'll keep your ass out of trouble and make a few passing grades, I guarantee life will be a whole hell of a lot easier on you, kid."

"Uh-huh."

It was the wrong thing to say. The wrongest. The kid had a way of saying *uh-huh* that made Wren want to slap the shit out of him. It was only *uh-huh*, technically, but what it really said was *Fuck you*.

She felt the rage bubbling up inside of her. "Listen here, you little idiot—"

She stopped. She was too mad. She'd made a promise to herself never to call her kids names. "Okay. I shouldn't have called you an idiot, but you shouldn't have pushed me to it, Daniel. But I'm going to tell you one thing—" She glanced out the side window. "Park right here—" Pointing out a space, Wren waited until he'd turned off the engine, then turned to face her handsome sulk-faced son. "I know you think you've got a tough life, but let me tell you, the day will come when you would give anything—anything in the world—to have this life back again, and it will be gone, do you hear me? *Gone*. And I guarantee you one thing: that will be the worst punishment you can ever have."

Leaving him to think that over to the nerve-screaming sounds of his so-called music, Wren headed into the supermarket—her most hated chore. Yet more woman-drudgery. The few men who did shop were either divorced, widowed, or carried lists prepared by wives. The wives prepared the lists, of course, because they planned the meals, and made sure the bathrooms were stocked with toothpaste and that their daughters had enough tampons and their husbands weren't out of razor blades. Men, of course, weren't capable of thinking in such other-directed terms. Not if a woman was around to do it for them, anyway.

Unfolding her own list, she shoved the wobbly cart toward the meat department and was standing next to a freezer full of chickens, searching for the boneless skinless breasts, just like that, just like any other day, when the world opened up and swallowed her whole, when her life came to an end, when everything she had ever worked for or dreamed of was shattered, when everyone she ever held dear was ripped away, leaving her exposed, naked, vulnerable, and very, very alone.

CHAPTER 2

"H I, Lissie."

Two words. Two simple little words. And though the voice which spoke them was one she hadn't heard in more than sixteen years, it was as familiar and intimate to her as her personal brand of tampons.

Lightning bolts of shock jammed into the top of her head, zigzagged down her spine, and burned her feet to the floor. She grasped the shopping cart so that she wouldn't disappear in a puff of smoke.

He was standing behind her, and he stepped around in front, grinning like a schoolboy caught in a prank and God—God, his face and body and voice—sexier and handsomer than ever—both pulled and repelled her at the same time, like two magnets placed end to end.

He reached out and took a silky strand of her hair, letting it slip slowly through his fingers, and the gesture, so tender and sensuous, struck her like a slap.

Soft streaks of silver fanned out from his temples through thick, curly brown hair, but it was the only sign of aging she could detect. Though he was the same age as Cam, Jeremiah Hunter still had a belly taut as a drum. Veined forearms bulged from the starched camouflage fatigue shirt rolled tightly just above the elbows, leading to big, sensitive hands which had once made her pant. His jaw was square, his lips and chin chiseled, and those eyes—she couldn't look away from them—those same soulful dark eyes with thick bristled black lashes and decisive tangled brows. At six foot four, Hunter towered over Wren, and when he smiled at her, she remembered that Lucifer was the most beautiful of all of God's angels, before he tumbled down to hell.

"I believe the years have made you even more beautiful, Lissie." He stepped back, giving her body an admiring appraisal.

Go away! Get out! she wanted to scream. Instead, gripping the cart for support and forcing her tongue to move in her dry mouth, she said, "It's W-Wren now."

"I know, I know! I had a helluva time finding you. I don't know how I could have forgotten how smart you are; I mean, if the feds couldn't find you in sixteen years, what made me think it would be easy for me? But then, I always did love a challenge."

Her heart made painful little jerks in her chest. Wren glanced around to see if anyone was within earshot. An old Hispanic man was digging around in the fajita meat. Ungluing her feet, Wren shoved the cart around the corner and stood, staring blindly at cereal boxes.

It was the Apocalypse of her life. Nothing would ever be the same again. Of all the nightmares over the past years, of all the pains she had taken to reinvent her life and avoid capture by the FBI, it had never occurred to her—she wouldn't let it!—that Hunter would be able to find her.

That he would even get out of prison.

Jesus, didn't prison terms mean anything anymore? Didn't armed robbery, murder, and attempted murder of a federal officer deserve more than sixteen lousy years? A small cry caught in her throat and she stifled it. *How soon it all comes back to us,* she thought.

"I guess I taught you well," he said with a smile in that liquid bedroom voice. "I knew when you escaped during the raid that they'd never find you. Most people who create false identities make one stupid little mistake, like calling their parents, or using an alias that's too close to their real names, or making up a Social Security number that's out of sequence with the state of their supposed birth. But I knew my Lissie would outsmart the whole fuckin' world."

"K-keep your voice down," she said, betraying her nervousness. A frazzled young mother with a newborn in the shopping cart and a squalling toddler dragging at her leg yanked a box of Cheerios off the shelf and swerved past Wren and Hunter. Wren waited until the woman disappeared around the corner before speaking. "What do you want?"

He feigned hurt. "What do you mean, what do I want? I want *you*, of course. My little Lissie. I want us to kick ass again just like we did in the old days." He leaned closer, his face inches from hers. "We've got a new camp goin', Lissie. It's so much better than the last one. You won't believe it when you see it. A bunch of real, committed patriots who know what's worth fighting for in this life. I've been planning it for years." His voice quavered with the old excitement. She could remember when it once rang from the rafters, inciting otherwise sensible people to fight for . . . to fight for . . . what? Death?

She struggled to straighten out emotion-tangled thoughts. "I thought you were in prison."

"I was. Sixteen long, lonely years. But that's all over now."

"Did you escape?"

He laughed that loud, infectious laugh that had once made her laugh, too. "Naw, naw, nothing like that. I was paroled. All legal. It took me a while to get everything going and a while longer to find you and, boy, was the search worth it."

He touched her hair again and she flinched. He cocked an eyebrow. "What's wrong, love?"

Wren was shaking—hard—from head to foot. It took great self-control to hide it from his piercing gaze. "Hunter . . . I'm married now. I've got children—a whole new life. I can't just walk away from everything."

He nodded. "I know. That Zoe's a little doll, and Daniel, well, something tells me he's a bit of a handful." He grinned.

Her insides twisted at the mention of her children's names on *his* lips. How did he know? He must have been stalking her for a while, watching her family. The thought made her knees weak.

"Anyway, bring 'em along if you want. We can home-school 'em there at the base camp." He chuckled. "Pretty smart, Lissie, marrying a defense attorney. What a joke." He laughed out loud.

There was a roaring in her ears and she thought for a brief panicked moment that she was going to faint. She knew, now, how the

Jews must have felt when, after hiding out successfully from the Nazis, they opened the door one day to find the SS standing there, ready to lead them to their slaughter.

"No."

The voice came from far away, as if it were not her own, and yet it was. She forced herself to look into his eyes. "I can't do it, Hunter. Not anymore. Those days are over. I have a new life now. I can't . . . I just can't."

He smiled at her. It was a sweet, sad smile, a knowing smile. It said, *You'll never walk away from me.*

Cold fingers clamped over her heart. She shivered.

"*Mom?* I got tired of waiting in the car. Can we have some Cocoa Puffs? Who's this?"

When Daniel was little, she would have swept her child up in her arms at that moment and raced for the car to run for their lives. She would have protected him with her life. She would have fought for him to her death. But he was not little anymore. He was a gawky man–boy standing a head taller than she, staring in open curiosity at her past, waiting politely to be introduced to the one man she had kept secret for sixteen years, the one man who had the power to destroy them all.

Talk about living a lie.

One of the things Daniel hated about living in a small town was that there was never anybody new to meet, so he was surprised to amble into the supermarket and find his mom talking to this . . . guy. Daniel had never seen anybody quite like him and he wasn't sure why. Maybe it was the camouflage shirt he wore; it wasn't like what a hunter might wear, it had patches and stuff on it from the army. Plus he was a big tall guy and he was buffed, a weight lifter, no doubt about it.

"You must be Daniel," he said, engulfing the boy's hand in a grip so strong he couldn't help but wince.

"Yes, sir," he said, putting on his company manners.

"I'm Hunter. I'm an old friend of your mother's."

Daniel glanced at his mom. She was staring at her feet. "You knew her in college?" he asked politely.

Hunter chuckled. "Nope, not then. Before. I knew your mom when she was just about your age."

"I was eighteen," his mom said, and she sounded tense. Daniel wondered what he'd done wrong now.

Hunter smiled down at his mom, and Daniel couldn't help but think that he looked like a movie star or something. And the way he was looking at Daniel's mom was not the way a guy usually looked at a married woman with kids.

Daniel's friends sometimes gave him a hard time about how good-looking his mother was. She worked out and swam laps at the Y pool, and her hair—unlike every other mom and every other school teacher he'd ever known—swung down black to her waist. Her cheekbones were high, her complexion dark—especially in summer—but her eyes were, like, this startling blue. He knew she had a Cherokee grandmother, but not much else. Her folks were dead and she'd grown up in an orphanage, so she didn't talk much about her past.

Even Daniel had trouble understanding what his mom had seen in a guy like Cam Cameron. He was nice and all that, but, geez, the guy was boring! Daniel was already taller than his dad, who was almost completely bald, never worked out, and at forty-six—ten years older than his mom—was getting a gut. All he ever did was work to get his sleazeoid clients off and watch TV.

That was the problem with Daniel's parents. They had no life.

Daniel's greatest fear was that he would turn out like his dad. He just knew there had to be more excitement in life. When he got out of school, he wanted to go into the army and be a paratrooper. Or maybe a cop on the SWAT team. Or a race car driver. Anything but a small-town lawyer.

Anything but a boring bald guy with a gut, sitting in front of the TV while his good-looking wife graded papers.

The thing was, his dad had *never* done anything interesting. He didn't go to Vietnam or even the army because he had asthma or something. He never did anything wrong. Never got into any trouble. Made straight As. Went to college on a National Merit Scholarship. Hell, he was probably a fucking hall monitor or something.

"Yep," said Hunter, yanking Daniel's thoughts back to the present. "Your little mom was hell on wheels back then."

"She *was?*" Daniel glanced at her, and he could see the muscles working in her jaw. She was really pissed about something. It gave him an uneasy feeling.

With a sudden jerk she started pushing the shopping cart down the aisle at breakneck speed, swerving around other carts and tossing stuff in. Weird stuff. Like, she passed right by the Pop Tarts and threw oatmeal in instead. Daniel hated oatmeal. He grabbed a box of Pop Tarts and slipped them in the basket when her back was turned. Hunter, sauntering along behind her with his hands in his pockets, gave Daniel a conspiratorial grin and stage whispered, "I used to do the same thing to my mom."

She glared at them over her shoulder and hurried down the next aisle, passing right by the milk, when Daniel knew good and well they were out. Shit, *what had he done?* Had she found that joint in his desk drawer? Because it wasn't really his; it was Eric's, and anyway he didn't like the stuff, didn't see what the big deal about it was, but he kept it for Eric. He *knew* he should have done a better job of hiding it. They'd never believe him even if he did tell them the truth.

His dad had a real thing about lying.

At the beer aisle, his mother pulled down a six-pack of Miller Draft. "When I was a kid about your age," said Hunter, still smiling, "I used to snitch my dad's beer right out from under his nose."

Daniel's mom whirled, opened her mouth, shut it, then pressed resolutely on, throwing some Doritos in the cart when Daniel had specifically asked her to buy Cheetos. He boldly put some in beside the Doritos, but his mom didn't say anything.

To Hunter, he said, "Didn't you get into trouble?"

"For what?"

"Uh, stealing beer from your dad?"

Hunter chuckled. "Nah. He was always too sloshed himself to notice. I bet me and my friends cost the old bastard a fortune in beer."

Daniel gave his mother a nervous glance. If she'd heard the guy, she didn't act like it. It was hard to imagine that they'd once been friends. This guy was really cool, and his mom was so uptight. He didn't get it. He followed her to the check-out. The cart was half full.

Daniel pondered the situation. He decided that it couldn't be the joint, or she'd have said something in the car. He wondered if he'd said something wrong to Hunter, but he couldn't think what it could have been. Hunter was a nice guy, and he was just making small talk with him. What could be so bad about that?

"Daniel," his mother said suddenly, "go wait in the car."

"What for?"

"Just do it."

"Why?"

"*Daniel*—"

Hunter put a big hand on Daniel's shoulder. His touch was gentle, but firm. "Better do what your mom says, Dan."

"His name is Daniel."

Daniel looked from his mother to Hunter. What the hell was going on?

Hunter smiled at him. "Hasn't anybody ever called you Dan?"

Daniel shrugged. "Mom doesn't like nicknames."

Hunter threw back his head and guffawed, and for the life of him, Daniel could not figure out what was so funny. He smiled uncertainly and glanced at his mother. She was not smiling. "Well, kid, you look like a Dan to me," said Hunter. "You don't mind if I call you that, do you?" He gave Daniel a knowing look.

And Daniel, still worried about making his mom mad, and yet irresistibly drawn to the idea of finding yet one more way to get under her skin, smiled at Hunter and said, "No."

"Good." Hunter squeezed his shoulder. "Dan it is, then. We'll talk again, son. I've got to shove off myself, anyway. You better run on for now."

Without a backward glance in his mom's direction, Daniel obeyed immediately.

Cam and Zoe were laughing together at something on the television when they heard the car pull up into the garage. Cam got to his feet and headed for the kitchen to help bring in the groceries. He heard the back door open and his wife's quick step through the utility room. Then she sort of exploded into the kitchen and brushed past him, white-faced. She headed straight for the bedroom.

Had to be Daniel. What the hell had the kid done now? Cam walked straight into the garage, where Daniel was filling his arms with grocery sacks from the back end of the Blazer. "What did you do to your mother?" Cam demanded.

Daniel, sprouting about five plastic food-laden sacks and on the verge of dropping every one of them, pushed past his dad in the cramped space of the garage. "You tell me and we'll both know," he said in that rude way of his.

Cam raised his face to the ceiling and took a deep breath. It had been so pleasant, laughing at the TV and enjoying an evening at home with Zoe, his "good kid." Zoe never gave him anything but joy. If it wasn't for her, Cam would despair at his apparently dismal track record as a parent. Instead, Zoe gave him hope for Daniel. Sometimes.

But every time Daniel walked through the door he brought a thundercloud with him. The storm was sure to follow. Most of the time Cam didn't know what to do. If he'd dared to backtalk his dad the way that boy mouthed off at him, he'd have been picking himself up off the floor.

What the hell was it this time? Vandalism at school? Driving without a license? More failing grades? In some ways Cam thought Wren was too easy on Daniel. Too quick to be understanding when she should be strict. Too ready to talk when she should discipline. Still, there was no denying that Daniel was a complete mystery to Cam, and that was scary. He relied on Wren pretty heavily to be his map reader on this rocky journey of their son's adolescence.

He just hoped and prayed, more than anything else, that the trip wouldn't wind up at a dead end.

With a heavy sigh Cam stepped into the utility room, and engaged in a peculiar little dance with his son as they both jockeyed for space in that narrow room. Daniel tossed his head. The kid insisted on wearing his hair in that moronic part-down-the-middle hangdown style that made him resemble a puppy dog with floppy ears.

Cam was five eleven, not particularly short, but at fifteen, Daniel already outstood him by two inches. He wasn't the only father he knew whose son was taller. In fact, he'd hoped for a while that the boy might show an interest in basketball, but of course he should have known that Daniel wouldn't want to do anything that might require that kind of work. Still, it made him oddly uncomfortable, looking up into his son's dark and indiscernible eyes.

On the way through the den, Cam told Zoe to help her brother with the groceries and for them to put the things away, and he headed down the hall to the bedroom he shared with Wren. Opening the door, he stood still for a moment in the doorway, taking in the sight of his wife cowering under the blankets in the fetal position. She was fully dressed, all the way down to her shoes.

He hurried to the side of the bed and looked down at her. There was a sickly paleness beneath her dark skin, as though she were about to vomit. "Wren? Honey, what's wrong? Are you sick?"

Wren sat up, pulling the bedspread up to her chin and wrapping her arms around her knees. She began an odd sort of rocking motion. "He's here," she whispered. "He found me."

Cam had absolutely no idea what his wife was talking about, but the tone of her voice and the look on her face was enough to send a shiver down his spine. He sat down on the edge of the bed and took one of her cold little hands in his. "Who?"

For a moment she didn't speak, as though what she had to say was too awful to blurt out. Then she closed her eyes and said the one word Cam had hoped never to have to hear again in his lifetime: "Hunter."

She turned to him, then, with a face so full of despair and fear and anxiety, Cam knew, in that brief split second, that nothing would ever be the same again.

CHAPTER 3

WREN felt a mounting pressure behind her eyes and jumped up, dragging the bedspread with her and wrapping it around her shoulders. She must not cry. She *would* not.

Wren never cried. She did not allow herself. Even in the delivery room, when nurses placed her precious ones in her arms, she had swallowed the tears because she had not wanted to appear weak to the others.

She swallowed again and blinked a couple of times, her back to Cam. When she felt more composed, she turned to face her husband. "He came up to me in the grocery store. Just like that. He's been paroled."

"How did he find you?"

She shrugged. "What does it matter now? He did, that's all I know."

He nodded, then bowed his head in a gesture she knew well from watching him in court. The bedside lamp glowed off his dear bald head, and Wren felt a desolation of the soul. After taking another moment to bring her rioting emotions under control, she said quietly, "He's got another Community. He doesn't call it that. He just calls it a camp. But it's survivalists, just like before."

Cam raised his face to meet her eyes, and he was no longer a lawyer, but a vulnerable person who perceives a threat to his family but as yet has no idea how to combat it. "He wants you back . . . doesn't he?"

Wren took her bottom lip between her teeth. "How did you know?"

He shrugged. "Why else would he go to so much trouble to find you? You were his possession once, his property, and now he wants you back."

Wren felt a sudden, grasping panic. She began to pace back and forth, dragging the bedspread with her. "I don't know what to do. I don't know what to do!"

Cam reached for the phone.

"Wait—" She touched his hand. "What are you doing?"

"I've got friends on the police force. Some of them owe me a few favors."

She shook her head. "No."

He hesitated, then sat back. "Why not?"

"Well, for one thing, he's done absolutely nothing illegal. He didn't threaten me in any way—he's too smart for that. As for the other thing, well, you know that as well as I do."

"You're afraid they'll turn you in."

"I know they'll turn me in. What choice have they got?"

He nodded and said nothing. After a moment he said, "We've got to tell the kids."

"*No!*"

"Wren, this is a matter of their safety. They have to know to watch out for this guy."

Pacing, pacing, huddled beneath the blanket, she said, "I can't."

He sighed.

"I'm sorry." At the disapproving look in his eyes, she cried, "How can you ask me to do such a thing?"

"For them," he said quietly. "You'd do it for them."

"I can't protect them from Jeremiah Hunter! Telling them the truth about me is not going to protect them from Hunter! Surely you realize that." She tripped over the bedspread and flung it aside, kicking it for emphasis. Just talking about it, just *thinking* about the past threatened to send her emotions cartwheeling out of control. Wren knew this, and yet she could not stop herself.

"Wren, honey—"

"How can you ask me to do this?" she yelled. "I can't! I can't!"

"Okay, okay." Cam sprang to his feet and reached for her, but she eluded his grasp. "Calm down. It's all right."

"*It's not all right!*" she screamed.

"Shhh, do you want the kids to hear you anyway?"

She stood trembling in front of him, her eyes wide, hair disheveled and wild. In a dead quiet voice she said, "You cannot ask me to tell my two children that their mother is responsible for the deaths of thirteen people—including two kids."

She held shaking hands out in front of her and looked down unseeing at them. "I'll never get their blood off my hands."

Then she ducked into the bathroom, slammed the door, and vomited so violently that she could see, after all, the blood.

"Wren!" Cam pounded on the door. "Unlock this door!"

"Daddy? Is something wrong with Mom?" Zoe stood in the bedroom doorway, sensitive as always to any tension in the house.

"She's . . . she's not feeling well, sweetie. Don't worry about it."

She gave him an uncertain look.

"It's all right. Run on now."

She turned to go, and Cam heard Daniel's voice behind her asking, "*What'd he say?*"

Cam shook his head. Daniel was always sending his sister out to spy for him. He jiggled the doorknob and, in a somewhat quieter voice, said, "Wren, don't make me break down this door. I'll do it if I have to."

He heard the door unlock, and pushed his way in to find Wren stooped at the sink, her back to him, splashing water on her face. If she'd been crying, he couldn't tell. She never let him see. He knew she'd been sick, though, and he put his palm between her wire-taut shoulder blades. "You all right?"

She nodded, and then suddenly turned and buried her face in his chest, holding him tightly around the waist. He held her for a long time, soothing her and pushing her damp hair back out of her hot face. "Come in here and lie down," he said, "while we figure out what to do."

She nodded and let him lead her to the bed, where she propped herself up on pillows and tugged up the blankets. He removed her shoes, then picked the bedspread up off the floor and wrapped it around her, tucking it in as if she were a child.

He grimaced at the hollow-eyed look of her face and silently chastised himself for feeling helpless. Arranging himself on top of the covers next to her, he crossed his ankles, leaned back against the bedstead, and pulled her into the crook of his arm. "So what do you want to do? Move?"

She shook her head. "We can't do that to the kids. Besides, he'll find me wherever I go."

"Then let me talk to some of my cop friends. I'll get them to do me a favor."

"No. They can't aid and abet a federal fugitive, Cam, you know that. And once they turn me in, the FBI will show up and arrest me. I'll be taken away *in front of the kids*. Who knows how many years I'd have to serve."

Cam didn't say anything. They'd had this argument before, ever since she had revealed to him her true identity on the day he proposed marriage. He married her anyway, because he could not imagine life without her, but her past had cast a shadow over their lives ever since, even though they rarely discussed it.

For the first few months she had been nervous as a bird, looking over her shoulder almost constantly in a figurative as well as literal sense. When Hunter was convicted and sentenced in a highly public trial, she seemed to relax somewhat, though she was always ill at ease around strangers and did not make friends easily. What friends she did have, of course, had no idea.

Cam was the only soul in the world who knew, and it had forged a bond between them early on, based, he knew, on her trust in him. After all, she had not come to him as a client. They'd met in a park, where he went every day to eat his sack lunch and get away from the office. Their courtship progressed rapidly, mainly because Cam was the type of man who liked to take care of people, and Wren had seemed so in need of someone to care for her.

Hunter had left her badly scarred, but the botched FBI raid on the Louisiana bayou survivalist camp where he'd maintained a little kingdom of sorts—and the resulting violent deaths of people she'd lived with and loved—had shipwrecked her, the damage so deep that

Cam knew, when he married her, that there would always be a part of her missing.

He didn't care. He'd just wanted to be able to look at her every day for the rest of his life.

They'd built a good life together and, at least until Daniel had started getting into trouble, a reasonably happy one. With the passing of the years, Cam guessed, they'd mellowed somewhat. He no longer felt the ghost of Hunter's presence in bed between them when he tried to make love to his wife. She no longer flinched whenever he raised his voice, or feared his anger.

Jeremiah Hunter had been one brutal son of a bitch.

And now he was back.

What worried Cam the most was that his wife was not just worried or upset—she was terrified. He wanted to comfort her, but he didn't know how. She wouldn't let him call the cops and, he had to admit, there was a very real possibility that if he did, she would wind up in custody.

Who knew what this guy was likely to do? He was a certified terrorist. It never ceased to boggle Cam's mind, the way some of these cons could manipulate a system, tug on the heartstrings of a parole board, put on whatever performance was required for them to be considered good boys by the criminal justice system—so that they could be set free to go right back out and do the same thing they'd been doing before.

As a defense attorney, he did the best job he could to get his clients a fair trial, but he had lines over which he would not cross. He would not defend child molesters or any sex crime suspects. And he would not defend an accused murderer unless there was compelling evidence or at least a very strong suspicion that the guy was indeed innocent.

Which meant, basically, that Cam didn't make a whole hell of a lot of money. Not as much as he could make in corporate law or defending the high-profile guilty.

So where did he, Harry Cameron, stand with Hunter? Here he was, middle-aged, out of shape, a lawyer who fought against the death penalty and had a real problem with killing even animals, who didn't own a handgun. And here was Hunter, a killer without conscience, well armed and well trained, and, Cam suspected, quite muscle-bound from years of lifting weights while on the inside.

What could they do? Get an expensive home-security system installed? What about when they were at work and at school? Hire bodyguards? With what? They didn't have that kind of money.

"I could go back."

"What?" Cam gave himself a mental shake. He'd thought Wren was asleep, she'd been so still against his chest.

"I could go back to him. Then the kids would be safe."

He gathered her close to him and held her in his arms. "I'll never let you go back to that guy," he said. "I'll die before I see that happen."

Cam's words chilled Wren, and she shivered against him. "Don't say that," she said. "The *ravenmocker* will come."

"The ravenmocker?"

She nodded. "My grandmother used to tell me that in the Cherokee legends, the raven is a spiritual guide and healer. But when someone is sick or in danger, sometimes the evil spirits take on the shape of the raven, and come to suck out the life of the weak."

He squeezed her. "I like to hear your grandmother's stories. I wish I could have known her." It was a classic courtroom ploy, a distraction to keep her from thinking morbid thoughts.

"She was an extraordinary lady. A spellbinding storyteller. I only got to spend two summers of my life with her in the Oklahoma Cherokee country when I was a kid, and yet her stories are still such a part of me."

"You should share them with the kids, Wren. All I've ever heard you tell them is how she gave you your name, Little-Wren-Who-Chases-the-Big-Hawk. They loved it."

She shook her head. "City kids. They've never seen how those little tiny birds badger those big old hawks away from their nest. Like an elephant running from gnats."

"But you should tell them more. It's a part of their heritage, too."

"I'd like to," said Wren sadly, "but I'm afraid that if I go into too much detail about my grandmother, I'll somehow let it slip that Mother and Dad are still alive, and that I haven't seen them since I was eighteen years old . . . since I got involved with Hunter. It's unforgivable that they have grandparents they've never met. I'm sure my sister's married by now. She must have kids. Cousins they don't even know! How can I possibly tell them those things without them finding out *why* I haven't seen my family?"

She sat up, pulling away from him. "If my kids ever find out the truth about my life, they'll hate me."

"Don't be ridiculous."

"I'm not. They'll know that everything I've ever told them about myself is a lie. How could they ever have any respect for me after that?"

"Wren—" He reached his hand out for hers, but she didn't take it.

"I'm sure Mother and Dad have long since given me up for dead," she said. "It's best just to let the past bury its dead."

She said it, and she heard herself saying it, even as she felt herself thinking, *Until the ghosts rise up to haunt you.*

CHAPTER 4

WHEN the bell rang at the end of the school day, Daniel did not
bolt out of his seat, as was his custom. He wasn't ready to go
home yet, and he did not want to see his mom at all.

He wished he knew what the hell was going on. For the past week
his mom had been totally weirded out. And it was getting worse.
Talk about paranoid. She'd always been a little overprotective, but
this was outrageous. Even Missy Prissy Goody Two-Shoes was getting PO'ed about it.

He took his own sweet time getting to his locker. Eric passed by.
His hair was purple today and it looked really cool. Old Satterwhite
had nearly kicked him out the day it was green. Apparently she
thought purple was more natural.

"Hey, Eric."

"Hey, dude."

"You gotta save me, man. My mom's gone psycho on me, and I
gotta get out of that house before somebody gets killed, man."

Eric grinned. His purple shirt wasn't the same kind of purple as
his jeans, and neither one matched the shoulder-length hair. He was,
like, clash city. Good old Eric. You could always count on him to
make a real fashion statement. Eric put a hand on Daniel's shoulder.
"What seems to be the problem, my good man?"

"I wish to hell I knew. She's totally freaked."

"Okaaay. Sounds to me like what's called for here is a good party."

"You are so right, my friend. The question is: how?"

"Ah, but a simple problem. Leave it all to me, the Beav."

They'd reached the top of the stairs and were just heading down to his mom's schoolroom when she started up the stairs. As usual lately, she looked pissed. "Where have you been?" she demanded. "You were supposed to meet me fifteen minutes ago."

Daniel exchanged glances with Eric. He stopped, clicked his heels together with a dull rubber sneaker thump, and shot out his right hand in a *Heil Hitler* salute. "*Mon Commandante!*" he cried. Eric snickered.

His mother was not amused.

"When I say three-thirty, I *mean* three-thirty, Daniel."

Daniel's face flushed. What was the *matter* with the woman? Here she was treating him like a baby in front of one of his buddies. Daniel had opened his mouth to cuss her out when Eric stepped ahead of him and said, "It was my fault, Mrs. Cameron. See, I've got this big paper due in history, and I just don't know where to start with it. Since Daniel, here, flunked history last year and is now taking it again, I figured he would be the ideal student to help me with my paper."

Daniel's mom scowled.

"I was just asking him if he could go to the library with me after school and work on the paper, see, but Daniel was telling me that he didn't think he could go because, uh, you've been . . . not feeling very well lately and he was thinking maybe you might need his help around the house."

Daniel sighed. Eric always started out with these great plans, then he got carried away with himself and went too far and blew it. He glanced at his mother. She was standing at the bottom of the stairs, her fists on her hips, looking up at them. "Eric, that's the biggest load of bullshit you've ever come up with."

Daniel snorted. He couldn't help it. It just came out.

"No lie, Mrs. Cameron. Honest. I've got a paper due in history. You can go ask Coach Thurber, if you want."

She shook her head, bringing one hand up to rub her forehead. She looked like hell. Daniel wondered suddenly if his parents were going to get a divorce. All his friends' parents were divorced. Even though they seemed to get along all right, hell, you never could tell what went on in your parents' bedroom.

Yuck. He didn't like to think about it.

"That's okay, Eric. I know you guys have a paper due in Coach Thurber's class. I don't suppose *Daniel* has gotten started on it yet?" She turned hostile eyes toward her son.

He shook his head. Best not to say too much just now.

To his shock, she slowly nodded her head. "All right. All right. But *I* will take you to the library and *I* will pick you up, is that clear?"

"Yes, ma'am," they chimed.

"Let's go. I'll come get you at five-thirty."

"*No!*" cried Daniel. "I mean, it's open until eight-thirty."

"Yeah," added Eric. "Could be we could actually get finished with it altogether. You never know."

Daniel glared at him. He reached up to push his hair out of his eyes, and behind his wrist, mumbled, "Shut up, man."

His mother was watching them suspiciously. "Where are your books?"

"Huh?" That was Daniel's standard answer when he wanted to buy some time.

"Your books. I would think that if you were going to the library to work on a paper, you'd want your notebook and, oh, I don't know, maybe a pen?"

"Yeah, right!" said Eric. "How stupid of us. We forgot." He bumped into Daniel in their scramble to get back up the stairs to their lockers before ambling on down to his mother's car, where Zoe was waiting for them.

Nobody spoke much in the car. Usually his mother tolerated his favorite metal radio station out of San Antonio, but today—like every day for the past miserable week—she seemed to be in a daze.

Maybe his parents *were* getting a divorce. Daniel was surprised at how much that thought scared him. On the one hand, it would give him something in common with his friends. Hell, Eric's mom had divorced three or four different so-called dads. On the other hand . . . what would happen to them? Would he have to move? He'd spent his whole life in this town, and although he hated living in a small town, he did have a lot of friends. He didn't want to have to start over in a strange school.

Staring out the car window, he gnawed on a roughened fingernail. For once he wished Missy Prissy Goody Two-Shoes would do her usual nonstop babbling about her straight As and her awards and her teacher's pet stories. Anything to cut the silence.

Eric farted.

They glanced at one another and doubled over in the backseat, snorting desperately to keep from howling. Eric farted again. "And that's all I'm going to say about it," he choked.

Missy Prissy Goody Two-Shoes looked over her shoulder where she sat, as usual, in the front seat next to Mom. "Eric, that's gross," she said.

They couldn't help it. They howled.

Daniel glanced at his mom. To his surprise, her shoulders were shaking. He hadn't seen her laugh in a week.

Greatly relieved, as they scrambled out of the car at the library steps, Daniel hesitated by his mom's car window. "Uh, see ya," he said. It was his way of saying, *I'm glad you're feeling better.*

She smiled at him. Good old Mom. She never had any problem translating his shorthand. "I'll be back at eight-thirty sharp," she said, but she was not looking at him. She was looking all around, up and down the street, as if she expected IRA terrorists to come jumping out of the bushes and mow him down with Uzis.

He and Eric bounded up the library steps. As the glass door closed behind him, Daniel glanced back. His mom was still sitting there. He stepped back where she couldn't see him and waited. It was about a half minute more before she finally pulled away.

Paranoid.

"Let's go," said Eric, tugging at his arm. They hurried through the stacks and out a rear exit, where they took off at a dead run, taking great leaps now and then on the sidewalk, just to see if they could hit the trees.

Eight thirty-five. The library was closed and there was no sign of Daniel or Eric.

Oh, God, thought Wren. *I never should have left him alone.*

She'd thought they'd be safe in the library. She hadn't thought Hunter would try anything in such a public place. Daylight Savings Time was still in effect, but a golden haze covered everything under a hot blanket of clouds in the humid Indian summer, setting the still-green leaves of the hill country trees alight like translucent empty Coke bottles. The clouds were haloed bloodred with the dying glow of the sun, like a violent memory.

She'd had that stupid faculty meeting at four-thirty, and then there was Zoe's piano lesson at five-thirty, and then she was so far behind in her paper-grading because she'd been so distracted lately, so she thought it would be all right to sit at home working next to Cam while the boys were at the library.

Hunter had vanished as mysteriously as he had appeared, and his continued silence had only served to unnerve her. It was so tempting to think—to dare hope—that he might have taken her refusal to go with him at face value and left town.

She knew better.

Maybe Cam was right. Maybe she should call the police and take her chances with the FBI. Nothing was worth risking the lives of her kids.

Eight forty-five.

Idiot! She'd been so stupid! How could she have thought they could handle this on their own? How could she have forgotten just how dangerous Jeremiah Hunter was?

Wren leaped from the car and raced up the library steps, jiggling the door. Nothing. No one.

She ran around the building like a fool, as if she might find the boys hiding somewhere in the bushes like they used to do when they were little.

Then she jumped back into the car and peeled rubber for home.

Cam and Zoe were, as usual, sitting in front of the TV together, like two peas in a pod. Wren burst into the den. "They're not there!" she cried. "They're not at the library!"

Zoe glanced over her shoulder, then went back to the program. She was used to her brother not being where he said he was going to be and didn't see it as a crisis. Cam got instantly to his feet, glanced at Zoe, then steered his wife into the kitchen.

"Did you go inside?"

"At eight twenty-five. I couldn't find them, so I just waited out in the car for about twenty minutes."

"Did you talk to the librarian?"

"Yes. She said they were never there in the first place."

Cam's face and the dome of his head turned a bright pink—a danger sign if there ever was one.

"That little shit. I should have known, as soon as you told me the term paper story, that he was conning you *yet again.*"

"Cam . . ."

"He manipulates you, Wren. Plays you like a well-tuned guitar. What is it with sons and their mothers?"

She sighed. "I don't know. Even Ted Bundy's mother loved him at the end." She rubbed her aching head, and reached for some aspirin.

He strode over to the window and parted the curtains. "It's getting dark. I guess I'd better start looking for them."

"Where would you look?"

"Well, we'll start by calling Eric's mom."

"Yeah right. I might as well pass the time making origami."

"You gotta start somewhere."

Wren swallowed the headache remedy with a glass of water, then called Eric's house. As expected, no one was home, so she left a message on the machine. "Now what?"

Neither of them said what they were really thinking: if the boys were wandering around town on foot, as they were prone to do, they were fair game for Hunter.

Wren kept a list of numbers by the phone. Most of Daniel's friends had, not only their own telephone lines, but their own private answering machines as well. America in the nineties. She left three or four messages.

"They must all be together somewhere," she said, and the thought was a bit of a comfort. She didn't think Hunter would do something so bizarre as kidnap a whole group of gangly teenage boys. Though one never knew. "What now?"

"I'll get in the car and go driving around. I might spot them."

None of Daniel's friends had their driver's licenses as yet. They tended to roam the streets like a restless pack of young dogs, jostling and joking and looking for mischief. Once Wren had discovered a massive supply of toilet paper in Daniel's closet. She had pretended not to notice, thinking there was far worse trouble the boy could be into than papering people's trees. Besides, she was halfway tempted to paper Rund's house herself.

Cam left and Wren waited stiff-backed next to Zoe, who was steadfastly ignoring the general tension in the air. She was weary of her brother's escapades and not eager to set off a tirade by asking about his latest.

Still, her presence had a calming influence on Wren. At twelve, she was already inching taller than her petite mother, and though they shared the same blue eyes, Zoe resembled her father far more in looks and temperament. From potty training to report cards, everything had been easier with Zoe. Just being around her was sometimes a comfort.

Wren tried to tell herself that she was being foolish. After all, this was by far not the first time Daniel had pulled a stunt like this. But Hunter's unexpected presence in their lives had lent a terrifying edge to even the slightest mishap; what once might have been greeted by frustration and fury by his parents was now a black hole of fear.

At nine-thirty, just as a gentle mist began collecting at the darkened windows and Wren heard Cam's car pull into the garage, Daniel sauntered through the front door. She sprang to her feet—wanting to hit him, wanting to hug him.

Zoe, like a deer startled by intruders in the woods, sprang off the couch and left the room.

Cam came into the kitchen.

For a moment everyone stood awkwardly. Then Daniel blurted, "I'm sorry I had to leave the library, Mom. See, Eric got one of his migraines. I tried to call, but you weren't home, so we just left. He took some medicine and I stayed with him a while, and then Meshack came by and we decided to go shoot some hoops at the park. Gosh, I didn't realize how late it was. I was planning on getting back to the library in time to meet you."

Wren was shaking from head to toe. She couldn't trust herself to speak. When Daniel told her these stories, he was so convincing. So sincere. Many times, in the beginning, she had believed him, had trusted him. Until she stumbled across the first lie. Then the second. Then she lost count. Now, she had trouble believing anything the boy said, and it sickened her. She *wanted* to believe him. He was her *son*.

He gave her a rueful smile.

Cam's fists were clenched at his sides. With a trembling voice he said, "You're lying, Daniel."

"No! Really! Those migraines are a bitch. He pukes his guts up."

"I said, you're lying! Don't lie to me, Daniel. Do not lie to me!"

It was Cam's most electrifying courtroom voice. When they were first married, Wren would go catatonic at the sound of it.

Cam's upper lip curled into a snarl. "I saw Meshack at McDonald's. He told me you guys had gone to the pool hall to hang out." He took a step toward Daniel. "I am warning you, my son, don't you dare bullshit me. I've been lied to by the pros."

"So what are you saying?" cried Daniel. "Are you saying I'm one of your psycho defendants? That's all the hell I am to you, aren't I? A criminal."

Cam's voice was deadly quiet. "If the shoe fits, son."

Something snapped in Daniel's eyes. Wren could see it from across the room. His voice rising to an out-of-control pitch, he screamed, *"That's just your problem, you son of a bitch! You think everybody's a criminal! You think I'm a criminal! Maybe that's why I act like one."*

"How dare you speak to me like that!" shouted Cam. "You selfish, spoiled little shit! You have no idea what you put your mother through tonight." He moved toward his son and the two angry males squared off. "If you gave a damn for anybody in this world besides yourself, you'd see she's going through hell right now—"

"Cam—" said Wren, moving toward the two.

"Yeah, right! That's it! I don't give a damn about *anybody!*"

The boy, his face suffused with unshed tears and frustrated rage, whirled and threw back the front door, which banged against the wall with such force the doorknob broke a hole in the sheetrock, and dashed out into the murky, wet night.

Wren sprinted over to Cam and stopped him from following. "I'll get him," she said. "You need to calm down." His arm was shaking under her hand, and she looked up into his puzzled, heartbroken eyes. "It's okay, Cam," she said. "He didn't mean it. He's just all mixed up right now."

Assuming her usual peacemaking role, Wren hurried out the front door and squinted into the hardening rain. Daniel was stalking off down the glistening sidewalk, his hands jammed into his pockets, his hair already plastered to the back of his neck. "Daniel!"

He didn't stop. She ran after him and tried to take his elbow. He jerked it away from her. "Get away from me!"

"Daniel, stop! You can't be alone out here right now."

"You've all gone psycho," he cried. "I'm getting out of here."

"Daniel, no, wait—" She struggled to stop his headlong gait, which wasn't easy, considering the difference in their sizes. For the first time in her life, Wren felt a vaguely unsettling fear toward her son. She wondered if he was going to hit her.

"It's not safe out here, son. Come back in the house."

He turned to her, his young face anguished. "Don't you hear yourself? Don't you see how paranoid you sound? I can't take it anymore."

"You don't understand. You have to trust me—"

He shook his head dismissively, and so intent was Wren on making her son listen to her and come back into the house that she did not notice the white windowless van creep slowly past. Only when it stopped and the back doors swung open did it register in her brain: *DANGER.*

"Daniel—" She grabbed her son.

Four big men dressed all in black, including black ski masks, poured out of the van like some evil potion.

Hopelessly she tugged at her son, as if running would save them.

He stood heavily rooted in shock.

Iron arms clamped around her body; a suffocating hand gripped her mouth. Two men overtook her son. She struggled mightily, screaming her husband's name with all her strength, but there was no sound save the scrape of the van door, the soft tumble of their bodies to the van floor, and the *shhhhh* of tires on wet pavement as they drove away, gathering speed in the moist, gloomy night as home and everything dear receded far into the distance.

It was all over in seconds.

As three of the men worked rapidly in the back of the Stygian-dark van to bind and gag Wren and Daniel, one of the men crouched in front of them and yanked the ski mask off his head.

It took a moment for her eyes to adjust. What little illumination there was came from the light of streetlamps rolling over the rain-speckled front windshield. The man's face was shadowed, but Wren would know that husky silhouette anywhere, and when he smiled, his teeth gave off a fiendish gleam.

His voice shimmering with triumph, Hunter spoke but one word: "Perfect."

CHAPTER 5

I T took Cam less than five minutes after Daniel left for him to feel that sickening lurch to his stomach that signaled something was wrong.

Two minutes. Maybe three.

Fights with Daniel always clouded Cam's thinking and pushed every other consideration out of his mind. Any other time he would have been sharp to the fact that Wren had no business outside the house alone, even if she was just standing in the front yard—especially not after dark.

Scrambling up from his chair, he jogged for the front door and flung it open, switching on the porch light as he did so, silvering the rain into steel spikes on black silk.

He called to his son. Then his wife.

No response.

Fully alarmed now, Cam ran outside across the lawn to the sidewalk and looked up and down the street.

Gone.

Babbling, panicked thoughts urged him to race for the car and take off in search of them, but realization, like a sucker-punch to his gut, brought him to his knees in the soaked grass.

No.

He'd lost them. Because of his stupid temper he'd lost them, because of his stupid carelessness he'd lost them, because, because . . .

Burying his face in wet hands, an involuntary moan escaped him and was quickly squelched by the heedless rain. "I'm so sorry, Daniel," he cried. "Please, please forgive me."

Wren. What was going to happen to her?

He couldn't think. Couldn't get himself together.

Help. He had to get help. A name from the past flashed into his terror-struck and grief-watered mind, and he grasped at it like a drowning man.

"You stupid fucking idiot," he said to himself as he struggled to his feet. "Why in the name of heaven didn't you think of this before?"

The report did not look good.

On-site survey of the physical facilities and offices of the Leatherwood Building in Midland, with regard to access control, fencing, lighting, alarm systems and evacuation plans—particularly establishment of plans for dealing with bomb threats—read like a how-to spy manual for assassins.

Steve Austin, retired after twenty years of distinguished service with the Federal Bureau of Investigation, was a tall, attractive fifty-something black man. (He hated the politically correct term "African–American," mainly because his people came originally from Jamaica, not Africa, and because it was so damn much trouble to say, much less write out. Hell with it anyway.) A confirmed Type-A with high blood pressure and a wife who worried too much, Austin had just married off his last daughter and was looking forward to finally enjoying his retirement.

Someday.

For now, though, he was too busy running Guaranteed Security Associates, Inc., a private full-security company based in Dallas he had started five years before. Guaranteed Security had a small but very exclusive clientele of extremely wealthy and highly visible Texans.

And none was wealthier or more visible than Buck Leatherwood.

Shit. He almost forgot. Swiveling in his chair, the report still clutched in one hand, Austin fumbled for the remote control he kept on his desk and switched on the small color TV set on a mahogany bookcase behind him. The newsmagazine program which was featuring his famous client was already into the segment. Austin grabbed a blank videotape, plugged it into the adjoining VCR, and pressed "record" on the remote.

"... *A self-made billionaire who got his start by oilfield wildcatting, Buck Leatherwood is an audacious risk-taker and bold decision-maker—a natural in business. When everybody else was living lavishly on oil prices of thirty-five dollars a barrel, speculating their substantial fortunes on junk bonds and real estate, Leatherwood bailed out and invested in the communications industry."*

Several of Leatherwood's television and radio enterprises flashed onto the screen, as well as an imposing shot of the Leatherwood Building itself.

"*A couple of years later,*" continued the smooth voiceover, as shots of depressed oilfield businesses appeared onscreen, "*oil was selling for eleven dollars a barrel, savings and loans were going belly up, Texas land couldn't be given away and oil magnates were filing for bankruptcy, while Leatherwood was richer than ever.*

"*But that isn't why some people want to kill him.*"

Austin cringed. What a nightmare. Now they'd have copycat loonies to contend with. Some of their threats were worse than the originals.

"*—It isn't even because of his natural flamboyance,*" the reporter was saying, displaying footage of vintage Leatherwood: jingling silver spurs on his handmade snakeskin cowboy boots, sporting thousand-dollar Stetsons and custom-made lambskin Western-cut jackets. To Austin, he looked like a frontier outlaw with his thick, downturned pewter-streaked moustache, craggy face, and sharp-eyed gaze.

"*—Nor do most people mind his colorful stunts, like the time he crashed a ritzy lobbyist dinner at the governor's mansion by riding a horse straight into the formal dining room.*

"*After all, this is Texas.*"

Austin grimaced.

"*Granted, he can get on some people's nerves,*" the reporter said slyly, cutting to one of Leatherwood's frequent appearances on talk shows and newsmagazines. Of course they picked the worst one, a situation in which Leatherwood's big mouth almost got punched by

one of his fellow guests. Austin sighed. In his youth Leatherwood
had once made a living as an auctioneer at cattle sales, and he loved
nothing better than launching into a streaming set of invectives
against someone who might be opposing his point of view, the words
so fast and hypnotic that all other voices were instantly silenced.

"*Even that isn't the problem,*" the reporter was saying. "*Some
people actually like it.*

"*No, what makes Buck Leatherwood such a natural target is that he
is a man with a mission. A very controversial mission.*"

Austin leaned forward. The manner in which his loudmouth
client was handled in the media had a direct bearing on the death
threats. Not that Austin could blame him. Hell, he had kids himself.
They were grown now, but he could understand, and that was one
reason he had taken on this walking headache as a security client.

The newsmagazine was displaying gory footage of the carnage
which had resulted five years before, when Leatherwood's only—and
much beloved—daughter was gunned down at a fast-food restaurant
where she'd stopped for a milkshake after school with some friends.
The assailant was dressed in combat fatigues and loaded down with
several assault rifles and thousands of rounds of ammunition.

By the time he'd used up a hundred rounds or so—putting the
last one in his own head—seventeen people were dead, including an
infant, a pregnant woman, and three small children. The sole sur-
vivor—a cook who'd barricaded himself in the meat freezer—said
the guy laughed at his victims as they screamed in panic and tried to
get out of the door, cover their loved ones with their bodies, or hide
under the plastic tables.

Melanie Leatherwood was shot in the back as she scrambled for a
rear exit.

The camera was unflinching. Depending on what he said when he
opened his mouth, this could be a good thing. They'd get far more
sympathy mail than death threats.

"*Since that tragedy,*" the reporter was saying, "*Leatherwood has
been a tireless, even obsessive, gun-control advocate. It is no secret to
other proponents of gun control that Leatherwood's fortune and considerable influence had a big impact on getting the hotly contested
Brady Bill and the Crime Bill of 1994 passed in Congress, as well as*

the ban on several types of assault weapons, including the one which caused his daughter's death."

Leatherwood's crinkled cowboy face filled the screen. Off-camera, the same reporter asked, *"Are you finally satisfied with the way things are going?"*

Austin's colorful client shook his head. *"I'm far from satisfied,"* he said. *"I remain convinced that America's climbing violent crime and juvenile crime rate is directly attributed to the easy availability of firearms. I'd like to see much stricter governmental controls over their sale and purchase."*

"You know your opponents are adamant that the possession of firearms remains a Constitutional right."

"Certainly. I own firearms myself. But I don't think the Constitution gives us the right to amass arsenals, and the only purpose for weapons of war is warfare. The wholesale slaughter of people. You can't tell me the founding fathers had that in mind back when they gave people permission to keep their single-shot muskets."

The camera focused on the handsome young reporter's face. He gave Leatherwood an insincere grin. *"You sound suspiciously like a politician,"* he coaxed.

But Leatherwood wasn't biting. He shrugged. *"Waste of time and money,"* he said.

"So I take it," pressed the reporter, *"that you prefer to use your affable eccentricity as a gimmick to draw more and more public attention to the issue, which will, of course, put increasing pressure on lawmakers."*

Austin's client gave the man a stare that had withered many a hotshot before him, and said simply, *"Whatever it takes, son."*

The interview continued for several more minutes, but the reporter asked Leatherwood nothing more provocative. When it was over, Austin turned off the set and swiveled back to his desk. Leatherwood was tireless. He stumped endlessly and never turned down a television appearance, even when he hated the program's host.

Most interviewers, and most of the viewing public, remained sympathetic to the grieving father. But he had enemies . . . deadly enemies who feared encroaching governmental controls on their Constitutional right to bear firearms, and considered Buck Leatherwood nothing less than Satan himself. There were threats—lots of them. And the people making the threats were highly capable of carrying them out, as far as Austin was concerned.

Austin finally scanned the report, which had been prepared by his able assistant, Sandra Dodge:

"Client refuses to establish a program of security training for all employees, maintaining that such a program would frighten the employees and make them feel as if they were working in a fortress. He concedes to the establishment of a program to handle his mail, and to a program for handling bomb threats. However, he refuses to instigate a hostage survival program. (See above.)

"At the corporate headquarters, Client refuses to install a metal detector at the front entrance. He has read our report on information collection and analysis of domestic and international terrorist threats and the establishment and maintenance of effective liason with all appropriate law enforcement agencies.

"He is willing to instigate some measures of our travel control program, but refuses to reroute various choke points.

"This investigator recommends tightening personal security around Client as added precaution against possible assassination; however, our hands are tied with respect to corporate security."

Austin rummaged around in his desk for some Rolaids and thoughtfully chewed two. First-line security measures included the participation of the individual who might be targeted. Total protection was impossible—it wasn't cost effective and was too prohibitive for the lifestyle of most American executives—what Leatherwood liked to refer to as "fortress mentality." So there would always be some risk, but Leatherwood would make their job as security providers a whole hell of a lot easier if he would meet them halfway. About the only thing they could do to protect themselves in such a situation was get the guy to sign a release.

Austin could sympathize with him, but hell, how could they *guarantee* security for someone who insisted on refusing their suggestions? He'd drop Leatherwood altogether as a client, if it weren't for the fact that he also insisted on paying them twice the usual (hefty) fee. And it didn't hurt that he was, by far, their best advertisement.

That is, if they could keep the man alive.

Austin glanced at the clock. Getting on toward ten. Shit. He'd get another lecture from Patsy on working too much. She was always after him to get his cholesterol checked. Like he gave a shit.

He stood up and was shrugging into his suit jacket when his private line rang. He picked up the phone and said, "I'm on my way, dear."

There was a hesitation, then a voice which sounded vaguely familiar said, "Mr. Austin? Your assistant said I could use this number if I had an emergency."

There was a muffled sob, and then the distraught man said, "I'm Harry Cameron, sir. Do you remember me?"

As his life telescoped sixteen years, Austin sat straight down in his chair. He'd gotten better at blocking out the memories through the years, but Harry Cameron's voice brought it all back to the day he had lived to regret more than any other in his life, to the day hell had erupted from out of the steaming bayou bowels of the earth and he had come face to face with the devil himself.

He cleared his throat. "Yes, Mr. Cameron. I do remember you. How can I help you?"

"He's got her," came the answer in a rapid flow of words he could hardly follow. "Hunter. He's out, and he's got Wren—I mean, Lissie—and my son, Daniel. He's got 'em both, and I don't think I'm ever going to see them again. Please help me."

With that, Harry Cameron broke down and wept.

PART II

MATERIALISTS AND MADMEN

Materialists and madmen never have doubts.
                                                    G. K. CHESTERTON

For wicked men are found among my people.
They watch like fowlers lying in wait.
They set a trap.
They catch men.

                                                    JEREMIAH 5:26
                                    New American Standard version

There is nothing so extravagant or irrational which some
philosophers have not maintained for truth.
                                                    JONATHAN SWIFT

Terror is on every side.

                                                    JEREMIAH 6:25
                                    New American Standard version

CHAPTER 6

A CIGARETTE lighter flashed in the dark van, highlighting Hunter's face. In the brief red glow Wren made out the outline of an AK47 cradled in his lap. She glanced over at Daniel. Though her eyes still saw red spots from the flame of the cigarette lighter, she could see the whites of her son's terrified eyes. Wren pulled her feet up close to her butt and scooted over close to the boy, shoving a guard's leg out of the way with her sneakered foot and glaring at him defiantly until he moved. She pressed her body up close to Daniel's and could feel him trembling.

Hunter's voice was warm and intimate as he said, "Sorry about the gag and all, babe. Gotta do it until we clear the city. Once we get on the road heading west, I'll give you some room to breathe."

Wren angled her body so that one cuffed hand could reach out behind her and pat Daniel's arm. The guards had all removed their ski masks, and the one closest to her raised the barrel of his AK47 so that the watery light from the front windshield would reveal it. A warning. She stared directly into the man's eyes and kept patting her fingertips on her son's arm.

Hunter shook his head. "Didn't I tell you guys? She's a regular little spitfire, isn't she?"

The man staring into Wren's eyes didn't blink. Neither did she.

"Ah, don't worry about it, Kicker. She's too smart to try anything here. Wouldn't want to risk the life of her baby now, would she?"

Grinning behind the red glow from his cigarette, Hunter stretched out a long leg and kicked at Daniel's foot. Daniel jerked his leg away.

"Now. I think the first thing we'll deal with is that hair, what'd'ya think, Kicker?"

Breaking his gaze with Wren, the man called Kicker returned Hunter's grin and nodded. In the deepest voice Wren had ever heard, he said, "Wouldn't want any of the army to mistake him for a girl or nothin'."

The men all laughed. One of them ran his fingers through Daniel's hair and he tried, futilely, to duck his head out of the way.

"I think maybe a Keanu Reeves kinda look. You know. Like in the movie *Speed*. That was one cool movie, wasn't it, Daniel?" Hunter's voice carried no trace of a threat. He might as well have been starting a conversation on a train.

Wren moved closer to her son and closed the fingers of one hand around his shaking arm. *Dear God*, she thought, *I just thought he wanted me, really. If I could have guessed one of my young ones would wind up in this situation, I'd have turned myself in to the FBI and been done with it.*

Regret, sharper and more vicious than any which had cut into her after the raid, pierced her heart. Thoughts of Cam and Zoe, bereft and frightened at home, made her want to die.

It had occurred to her that Hunter might approach one of the kids, but only as a ploy to get near her. She'd never seriously considered that he might involve one of them.

The acid bitterness of hindsight.

She wondered what Cam was doing to deal with it. She was certain none of the neighbors had heard or seen anything in the dark wetness of the night. Like everything else Hunter did, it had been smooth as a liar's charm. She doubted the whole thing had taken as long as thirty seconds.

Her fault. Once again. All her fault.

Wren gave Daniel's arm a final squeeze, then maneuvered her body so that she could still be close to him but lean back against the side of the van. To her surprise, he folded his body over and leaned his trembling head on her shoulder. She rested her face on the side of his head, and in a few moments he finally stopped shaking.

Not a big tough baddie anymore. Just a horrified kid.

Oh, Daniel, I am so very sorry, my sweet boy.

Rubbing her chin absently against her son's silky hair, she had a sudden vision of him, dressed in his Superman costume that she'd made out of some blue long johns, a pair of red knee-high socks, and a length of red cloth. He'd run around the yard for months with that tattered piece of crimson flying from his neck, fighting many valiant battles—complete with noisy sound effects—with the bad guys.

Back then Daniel/Superman had always won. Now here were the real bad guys, and Wren knew down deep in her soul that with these people, there could never be a clear win.

"I can't wait till you guys see the base camp," said Hunter, as if they'd been chatting together for a while. "It is so far superior to the one back in Louisiana. Better armed. Better manned. Better stocked. And our cover is foolproof. The bastards'll never find the Armageddon Army, will they, guys?"

The other men nodded or voiced their agreement.

"See, Daniel, the thing is . . . I asked your mom nicely to come back with me. She said no. And I can understand that, after what happened before. When you lose your buddies in combat, you don't necessarily want to return to that same battlefield, right, guys?"

"You got that right," rumbled Kicker.

"Amen," added the one they called Preacher.

Daniel sat straight up, swiveled, and stared at his mother.

Oh God, shut up, Hunter.

"But *this* place . . . ahhh . . . wait till you see it, Lissie." His voice rang with all the old charisma and power. "I *had* to get you back. I *had* to—you don't understand. We're gonna wreak vengeance on those assholes once and for all. For all our dead buddies. *Revenge . . .* you will see just how sweet it can be. And you're gonna help us do it."

Hunter beamed at Wren. Her vision had fully adjusted to the van's shadows, and she could clearly see the fire in his eyes.

When she was young, he had set her aflame with his passions, had ignited her to leave home, school, friends, everything familiar—just to follow him.

Another lifetime ago.

Glancing over these many years later at her young, pinched-faced, panicked son, Wren squeezed shut her eyes and forced down the raw fear from the back of her throat. Although Jeremiah Hunter wasn't twenty-eight years old anymore, either, he was still a towering, formidable presence.

Only now, eighteen years after she had first laid virgin eyes on this charismatic man with the magnetic voice, Wren knew that he was much, much more dangerous.

CHAPTER 7

"**O**KAY, Mr. Cameron. The first thing you need to do is gather your nuts up under you. Calm down."

"I know. I know. I just don't know what to do."

"Well, you did the right thing calling me. Have you spoken to the police?"

"No! I didn't . . . I didn't want them to track my wife down like she's some kind of criminal. I don't know . . . Do you think I should?"

Austin hesitated. The local police were in no position to find a chameleon like Jeremiah Hunter. They would have to call in the FBI. And Cameron was right. As soon as she turned up on their fugitive list, the bureau would probably assume that she went with Hunter voluntarily. It could be very dangerous for her, especially if Hunter put up the kind of fight this time that he'd put up in Louisiana.

Plus, there was that little matter of Austin's part in this whole thing. Since he was no longer working for the FBI, there was little they could do to him in a disciplinary way, but as a retired agent who occasionally consulted on various cases, Austin still enjoyed a certain access to the almost limitless facilities of the bureau through his old contacts. If his part in this whole thing busted wide open, he'd almost certainly lose that access.

If he could call in some favors, he might be able to ascertain Hunter's whereabouts on his own. Maybe then he could make some kind of trade: a mother of two who'd led an exemplary life for the past sixteen years after serving as a key informant on one of their most high-profile cases of domestic terrorism and bank robbery and had committed no known crime against the government—in exchange for Hunter. It was possible he could arrange to have her officially removed from their federal fugitive list.

In any case, there was a good chance they wouldn't shoot her.

She could be returned to her family. Then he and Harry Cameron wouldn't have to share any more little secrets.

"Mr. Cameron, if you are willing to trust me, I think I can help you find your wife without directly involving the authorities. But you've got to do your part—"

"Anything."

"You've got to come up with some kind of convincing cover story for the absence of your wife and son from work and school. Do you think you can do that?"

There was a brief silence. "I didn't even think about that."

"Can you do it?"

"Yes sir, I think so."

"I'll be sending someone down to talk to you. Tell them everything you can remember—write it down if you have to. I'll need your full cooperation in every way."

"You've got it."

The man's pathetic eagerness wrenched Austin's heart. He couldn't imagine what the guy must be going through. It made him want to go home and hug his wife. "I'll do everything I can to find her, but I can't make any guarantees."

Cameron sighed. "I don't think anybody can, Mr. Austin. Not where this animal is concerned." His voice broke.

"Hey . . . if he wanted her dead, she'd be dead. I think you can be reasonably assured that she's alive and well at this point. Your son, too."

"You think so?"

"I do."

"God . . . it's my only hope."

"You cling to it, Mr. Cameron. Call me if anything out of the ordinary happens, all right?"

"Okay."

"And I'll call you at least once a day to keep you apprised."

"I wish there was a way I could thank you—"

"Forget it. I'm doing this for Lissie. I owe her that much."

An awkward pause stretched between the two men. Finally, Cameron said, "I don't think she ever blamed you for what happened, Mr. Austin. In fact, I know she didn't. She blamed herself."

Austin pushed his glasses up and pinched the bridge of his nose. Funny. It seemed that everyone blamed himself for what happened on that day except the one man who was most responsible.

"I'll get that son of a bitch," he mused aloud, "if it's the last thing I do."

Cam replaced the telephone receiver and put his face in his hands. Austin was right. He had to get himself together. He'd be no help to Wren otherwise.

He wished he felt better about calling Austin. But he was beginning to realize that this was the kind of situation in which, no matter what he did, he would not feel better. Not until Wren and Daniel were home safe.

Something told him they were in for a long siege.

It had taken five or six years of faithful marriage before his wife had trusted him enough to reveal the details of the raid. He could still remember her voice when she talked about it, how it droned on in a monotone curiously blank of emotion.

"Hunter always had guards posted, from first light to around midnight. That morning one of the guys—they called him Samson because he was so strong and wore his hair in a long ponytail down his back— anyway, Samson grew up in the bayou and knew every animal and bird. He was really a very gentle man. I loved him.

"That morning, Samson was on duty, and he noticed immediately when the birds grew quiet. He knew right then that someone was in the woods. It took him a while to find them, but when he did, he notified Hunter immediately, and Hunter set this whole silent alarm system in motion. Before ten minutes had passed, he had the entire camp armed and ready, poised like hunters in a duck blind. Those poor agents.

"I didn't know what to do. I was so naïve. Such a stupid kid. See, I was still very idealistic, and I had this idea that when Hunter saw the feds coming, he would surrender rather than risk one precious life.

"I was wrong.

"There were other things I didn't realize until it was too late. See, I didn't know how deep the Community's loyalty was to Hunter. We had camp meetings every day in which he talked about how the feds were the enemy and they would come to take away our freedom to live as we chose and that they would be taking part in this big world conspiracy to enslave us. As blindly in love as I was with the guy, even I didn't buy everything he said. If I had, I never could have betrayed him like I did.

"I mean, it just did not occur to me that these people would fight to the death. To the death! That they would risk the lives of their children!

"Even after everybody took up their positions, I thought that Hunter would get into this, thing, you know, where he took advantage of the situation. I mean, he was nothing if not theatrical. I figured he'd get into some kind of standoff, using us as bargaining chips, that he'd hold out for the media attention. And that, gradually, we'd all leave except for Hunter, and then they'd get him.

"I know it sounds incredible now, but that is what I actually believed. I was so young and stupid, I guess I thought that wishful thinking would count for something.

"Besides, Agent Austin promised me. He promised! He said nobody would get hurt.

"It's the only way I would cooperate with them. The only way I'd give them the information they wanted on the bank robberies Hunter had committed and the arsenal he had stored at the Community. And that man he killed. Without me they'd never have been able to find the body.

"Even so, I never, never would have done what I did if I'd had even the remotest idea of what was going to happen.

"I don't know who fired the first shot. I'm pretty sure it was Hunter. And just like that, man, we were in a war!

"Oh, God. Bullets flying everywhere, glass breaking, people screaming that they'd been hit. If you've never been in battle, or even a military exercise—and I'm not criticizing you because you haven't— I'm just saying that you can't begin to imagine how loud it is, and how confusing and terrifying.

"Samson was shot right in front of me. His whole sweet face just exploded. Blood went everywhere, all over me and all over the room. And I just stood there, staring at him. I could hear the bullets

whistling. You know, when a bullet flies close by your head, you can hear it.

"I thought I was going to die. But I couldn't move. I think maybe a part of me wanted to die. Wanted to get hit. I was armed, of course, but I never fired my weapon. How could I? By that time I knew some of those agents who were storming us. It was, like, who deserves to die?

"Then I heard Richie crying. He was in the next room. It kind of unstuck me. I ran in to his room, and it looked like a battlefield. His mom and dad and brother were all dead. He was still holding his gun, pointing it out the window, and I pulled him down to safety. At least I thought I did.

"That was before I saw the blood. He'd taken a direct hit to the chest, and, and . . . he was crying, just like a ten-year-old will do when he's fallen off his skateboard, you know? I think he was in shock. I don't think he'd realized yet just what was happening.

"I tried to save him. I tried so hard. I held him so tight my arms went numb, but the blood just kept coming and he was choking on it and I couldn't help him. I just rocked him back and forth until he stopped breathing.

"I wanted to sit there until somebody killed me, you know? But suddenly one of those agents hit the wall of the house—he was trying to climb through the window.

"And I ran. I knew where the trapdoor led to the tunnel. I'm convinced Hunter was planning to take it himself, but he was pinned down by heavy fire. I remember slipping through the trapdoor and pulling it down over me. And it was pitch dark in there. I'd forgotten to bring a flashlight or anything else, really.

"There were scorpions down there, and worms and cockroaches—you can't imagine. But I didn't think about any of that because Richie's and Samson's blood was all over me. I could smell it. It overpowered even the smell of the earth.

"And I crawled like a blind mole. Just crawled until I came out the other end, which was about fifty yards, I think. The snipers never saw me, because they were focusing on the camp and I came out behind them.

"I was covered with dirt and blood and filth, but the thing is, something happened to me down in that tunnel. Something happened to my mind. Because I can't remember anything else after that. I don't know what I did or where I went. I don't know how I found a change of

clothes or managed to elude the authorities. I've tried to remember, but it's just gone.

"For weeks I couldn't even remember the raid. Couldn't remember anything except in nightmares. I think they call it a fugue state. It slowly came back to me, in bits and pieces, over the years. But I still don't know where I went or what I did after I came up out of that tunnel like some sort of bloody monster in the mist.

"I don't remember anything until I got off a bus here and took a walk in the park while I waited for the next bus. You were there.

"Something about you made me stop running.

"But it seems that all I have to hear is a firecracker, or a car engine backfiring . . . and I can still smell the blood on my hands."

"Daddy?"

Cam looked up, blinking at the sound of his daughter's voice. He was still sitting on the edge of the bed where he'd placed his panic call to Austin, his elbows on his knees, his face in his hands.

He stared blankly at his little girl, standing there in the bedroom doorway looking at him with Wren's eyes. Wren was so strong in so many ways and so fragile in others. If Austin found her and brought her back home, what would she be like?

She'd never be able to stand another shoot-out. And if anything happened to Daniel . . . it would probably kill her.

"Daddy? What's wrong? Where's Mom and Daniel?"

I don't want to do it, he thought. *I don't want to shatter that sweet innocence. I want to keep her safe and sheltered for just a few more years.*

But they didn't have a few more years. Not anymore. Not like the years they'd had.

Struggling to hide the utter bleakness and despair that he felt, Cam patted the bed beside him. In a careful voice he said, "Come over here, honey. We need to have a talk."

Her stare sliced through his precarious self-control like a scalpel. Gingerly, as if the bedspread were breakable, she sat next to him, her hands folded primly in her lap. He put an arm around her shoulders and drew her close.

"Something's wrong, isn't it?" she said. "Did Daniel and Mom have a bad car wreck?"

Where in the world do I start? he thought. Then he seemed to hear

Austin's voice, sharp and commanding in his brain: *Just gather your nuts up under you and begin.*

After a moment, he said, "Daniel and Mom are going to be away for a while."

Twisting around to look at him, she said, "Are you and Mom going to get a divorce? Daniel said he thought so."

"What? No! That's not it at all, sweetie."

Tension leaked from her body like air from a balloon. "I didn't think so," she said. "But Mom's been acting so weird lately and everything, well . . ."

He shook his head. This was going to be harder than he thought. It was hard for him to believe that a divorce would actually be good news compared to what he was going to have to tell his child.

The one fact he could cling to was that his Zoe was an extra-ordinary child, and they had a special relationship. Wren called Zoe an "old soul." She seemed to have the meaning of life all figured out before she even started school. Possessed of an amazing maturity, her biggest problem in school was that she was, emotionally and mentally, too old for her friends. Making friends had been a struggle all her young life. Wren and Cam had hopes that when she started the ninth grade the year after next, she might be able to find some kindred spirits in older friends.

Lord knew, she was far more sensible than Daniel.

"Well then, is Mom sick or something? Ariel's mom has breast cancer." She looked at him with worried eyes.

He gave her a squeeze. "No, she's not sick. Just give me a minute, Zoe, so I can best think how to tell you this."

"Just tell it," she said, "and we'll sort out the rest later."

He nodded, amazed as usual at her insight. There was nothing else, after all, that he could do.

He began by telling her all about a little wild child named Lissie, and about how all she ever wanted was to be free.

CHAPTER 8

HE gags were removed about two hours after the kidnapping. Daniel looked like what the paramedics would refer to as "shocky"—his complexion pale and sweaty, his expression fixed and dazed. He sat in a sprawl on the floor of the van and said nothing.

Immediately, Wren got to her knees and crawled over to where Hunter sat leaning against one of the front seats. "Please," she said, just loudly enough for him to hear, while looking him straight in the eye where she knelt before him, her hands still cuffed behind her back, "let my son go."

He stroked her hair. "Can't do it, babe," he said.

Steeling herself not to flinch under his touch, she said, "He's no use to you. He's just a kid. And he doesn't know anything. I've never told him . . . anything."

He smiled that beautiful smile. "Now, why doesn't that surprise me?"

"Hunter . . . I'll do anything. Anything you want. I'll help you rob a bank—I don't care. Just let Daniel go."

He glanced over to where the boy cowered against the side of the van under the watchful eye of his guards. "I've got big plans for my man Dan."

"No."

He quirked an eyebrow. "What'd'ya mean, *no*?"

"Leave him alone."

"Oh, but, see, you don't seem to understand, Lissie. You no longer have any say-so as to what happens to the boy." Reaching around behind her, he lifted her hands by the chain that connected them. "He's in my hands now." He dropped them and placed the warm palm of his hand against her arm.

It made her flesh creep.

"Oooo . . . goose bumps. I see we've still got that old spark." He winked at her.

Narrowing her eyes at him, Wren clenched her jaw, then, slowly and clearly, she said, "You lay one hand on my son . . . you hurt him in any way . . . and I'll kill you."

Feigning shock, he drew back under the intensity of her gaze and returned the stare thoughtfully for a moment. Then, digging slowly though his pants pocket—while never once taking his eyes from hers—he reached around her back, yanking her close against him.

They were close enough to kiss. She could feel the muscles of his chest bunching as he manipulated the cuffs, but she never blinked. There was a metallic *chink*, then her hands fell free.

Pulling back, still watching him, she rubbed her wrists.

To the astonishment of everyone watching—and no one more than Wren—he placed the stock of his AK47 in her hands. Still holding onto the gun, his eyes boring into hers, he said, *"Do it."*

Simultaneously, behind Wren's back, came the distinctive *clack-clack-clack* of three safeties being released on three AK47s. "Hunter!" cried Kicker. "What the f—"

Hunter raised a hand in a holding gesture. Then he let go of the thumbhold stock and released it into her sweaty grip.

"Mom!"

Wren dared not drop her gaze. It was amazing how familiar the heavy weapon, most likely Chinese-manufactured, felt in her arms again. She ran her hand forward of the trigger and felt of the magazine. The semiautomatic center-fire rifle was fitted with a 75-round drum magazine. And a scope. She hefted it.

Of course. Nothing but all-out everything for Hunter. Overkill was his middle name.

Her heart was pounding so hard it shook her body.

Hunter was giving her one of those mirthless grins she remembered so well. "Go ahead," he said. "You want to kill me? Do it."

Lifting the weapon until it was aimed squarely at his head, she didn't bother to sight. They were too close.

Tilting her head slightly, she continued holding his gaze by looking at him around the scope. Eye to eye.

One shot.

That's all it would take.

"*Do it.*"

"*Hunter!* Man, don't—"

He smiled wider.

All she had to do was release the safety and pull the trigger.

That awkward safety that was positioned over on the right side of the rifle. The one with the distinctive *clack*.

She'd be dead before she could pull the trigger. And that would be the death of Daniel.

The bastard knew it, too.

Wren lowered the rifle. Her arms were aching, more from adrenaline rush than from the weight of the rifle. She'd lifted lots heavier at the Y. Shoving the rifle back into Hunter's arms, she turned away in defeat.

All three guards had their weapons aimed straight on her. They did not lower them until she'd sat back down next to her horrified son.

"See?" said Hunter with an arrogant laugh. "I was never in any danger. I knew I wouldn't be. Dan—let that be your first lesson in learning to handle firearms. It's all about mental conditioning." As he raised his gaze to Wren's, the smile vanished, and in a deadly serious tone he added, "Never point a firearm at anyone unless you are fully prepared to pull the trigger."

She couldn't look into those cold, empty eyes anymore. Glancing at Daniel, she found him looking at her with . . . what? Disappointment?

With a slight shake to his head, he turned away from her.

He thinks I blew an opportunity, she thought, frustration spurting through her body with every rapid beat of her heart. *He thought I'd be Rambo and blow them all away with one Hollywood sweep of my big gun, and we would escape without a scratch.*

And how was he supposed to know any better? It happened in the movies all the time.

What did this child know of the smell of blood and the screams of the dying?

She felt Hunter's stare lingering, and she boldly met his gaze, as though false bravado would hide her nervousness and anxiety. She could read his expression like a headline. It said, *Fuck with me? You'll lose every time.*

"Federal Bureau of Investigation, San Antonio."

"Agent Martinez, please."

"May I ask who's calling?"

"Steve Austin."

"One moment, please."

Austin took his glasses off and put them on his desk. The room went blurry. He hadn't slept all night.

"Steve Austin, you old fucker! What's goin' on with you, man?"

"Nothin' much, Mike. How's it going down there in Margaritaville?"

"Typical madhouse shit. Bet you miss it, huh?"

"Well, I don't know. We never had any of that kind of nuthouse crap when I was there. Nothing but sane people would do for the FBI back then. We handed all the loonies over to you guys who were left behind."

Martinez laughed. "You grizzle-headed pickaninny."

"Greaser burrito-eater." Martinez had finally made Austin smile. When working long, frustrating cases together in the old days, they'd let off steam by trading ethnic slurs. It went without saying that either one of them would kill anybody else they heard make such remarks about the other. No two men could respect one another more.

"What can I do for you, buddy?"

"This is absolutely unofficial, okay?"

"Goes without saying."

"Yeah, well, this is *really* unofficial. Major big-time unofficial."

"Got it."

"I'm looking for Jeremiah Hunter."

"Aren't we all? He skipped out on his parole a few months ago."

"He's doing bad things again, Mike."

There was a pause. "What kind of bad things?"

"Let's just say the same kinds of bad things he did before."

"You were the case agent on that Louisiana raid on the Community, weren't you?"

"A fact I shall regret to my dying day."

"Hey—you won't find anybody around here throwing stones."

"I've got to find him. Fast."

"Steve . . . you know I'm your man, but I gotta ask here . . . are you about to put me in some kind of godawful compromising position?"

"I don't think so. If I did I wouldn't have called. Let's just say—for now—that we have a mutual interest in finding this guy."

"Are we talking bank robbery again, or could it be . . . maybe a little domestic terrorism?"

"Well, my middle name is *Guaranteed*."

"Okay. You got a starting point?"

"Informant says he's got another survivalist camp going."

"I was afraid you were going to say that. Should we notify the ATF?"

"Possibly. Not yet."

"Okay. I love playing twenty questions. You gonna give me a hint as to where?"

"I don't know."

"Aw, c'mon man. A state? How about a region of the country?"

"That's all I know."

Martinez groaned. "I can't believe this. Do you know what you're asking me?"

"I have a pretty good idea."

"Shit, man. There's hundreds of them psycho groups all over this country. They call themselves fucking patriots."

"Aren't they concentrated mostly in the Pacific Northwest?"

"There's a lot of them up there, because of the thick forests, but there's just as many now in the desert Southwest. Also some in the deep South and some in the Northeast."

"None in the Midwest?" joked Austin.

"Not many. Too flat," answered Martinez seriously. "They're too paranoid about not being able to hide out in the plains from us big bad government troops when it's time to mount their civil war."

"You got anybody infiltrating the Aryan Nation?" That was the white supremacist umbrella group for most survivalist organizations.

"Of course. What, you kidding?"

"Tap some of your sources. See what they've heard about Hunter. Somebody's got him holed up somewhere."

"I'm telling you, man, it seems like the satellite picks up a new camp every goddamned day. It scares the shit out of me. Every fuckin one armed to the teeth, and those assholes know how to use their firepower, too."

They paid a silent moment to fallen agents who'd learned that lesson the hard way.

"Mike—listen up. This needs to be top priority."

"What're you telling me, man?"

"I'm telling you that if we don't rush this thing . . . it could be shaping up to become a second Community. It could make that whole Louisiana raid look like a practice run."

"*Madre de Cristo*," muttered Martinez, and Austin knew he was crossing himself.

CHAPTER 9

A JOLT and sudden stillness awoke Daniel from a terrible night-mare in which he'd been kidnapped by—he opened his eyes, blinked, and squinted into the shadows. His head was resting on his mother's leg, and in a confused rush-and-jumble of thoughts he realized that he'd been having no nightmare at all, that this was real. The gag had been removed, but he was still handcuffed. As he struggled to sit up, his mother said, "Don't be frightened. We've just stopped for gas."

He couldn't believe how soothing her voice sounded. Leaning close to her, he whispered, "Mom, I gotta pee bad."

She patted his numbed hands. "Hunter," she said, her voice still reasonable and calm, the way it was when she once took Zoe's temperature when she was little and it was way high and she didn't want to scare her. "It's been a long trip. We need to visit the restroom."

There was a moment of tense silence, and then Hunter gave a slow nod. "All right," he said. "But you go one at a time. Kicker will go along. If either of you so much as sneezes for help, or does anything stupid, I'll kill whoever's left behind. Understood?"

"Yes," she said. "We won't do anything stupid, will we, Daniel?" Her eyes blazed into his.

Daniel's head was clearing from sleep. To him this looked like the perfect opportunity to escape. She squeezed his wrist so tight he almost yelped. There was something about her face in the dim van shadows and oily gas station light that was almost scary. He'd never seen her like this before. "No . . . sir," he said.

"Good." Hunter signaled to Kicker, who handed his assault rifle over to another man called Smithy and opened one back door of the van partway, slipping out of the gap as quickly and quietly as a snake. While Hunter removed Daniel's handcuffs, Smithy trained his weapon directly at Daniel's mother. Preacher kept an eye on everybody.

Daniel's hands fell free, and he felt a shove between his shoulder blades.

"Hurry up," said Hunter, his voice creepy at the back of Daniel's neck. "And don't forget about your mom."

Daniel's whole body felt stiff as he climbed out of the back of the van and looked around with disappointment. It wasn't the humongous truck stop he'd been hoping for—just one of those dot-on-the-map country fillups.

In the next island over, a cowboy leaned against a filthy pickup, waiting for the hose to kick off. Standing at the back of the van, flanked by Kicker, Daniel gazed yearningly at the cowboy, shooting mental *help me* messages at the guy, but he just nodded lazily in Daniel's direction before glancing back down at the hose sprouting from his gas tank.

Kicker nudged Daniel's elbow. Moving almost in lockstep, the big man and Daniel walked around to the side of the building, where a door to the men's room stood ajar. Daniel couldn't believe it. Any other time the door would be locked and they'd have to go inside for a key. Just his luck.

With a rough assist from Kicker, he stumbled through the door. When he pushed it shut, it jammed onto a huge booted foot. "No need to close it," rumbled Kicker. "I'll watch the door."

Daniel fumbled with the zipper of his jeans with shaking hands. Once he finally got his pecker out, nothing happened. He needed to go so bad, but nothing would come out. Maddening. Eric would say, *They scared the piss out of you, man.* A nervous laugh escaped Daniel in spite of himself, and it loosened the tension enough that he was finally able to relieve himself.

Daniel's brain worked furiously as he took his time washing his hands. He wished Eric were with him. Eric was the idea man. If Eric was along, he'd have a plan. Some way to attract attention. To escape. To knock the guys out. *Something.*

In the streaked, rust-specked mirror over the sink, Daniel drew back in surprise at his reflection. The sputtering greenish overhead fluorescent light brought out the olive in his complexion, giving his skin a sickly cast. His hair stuck out all over the place.

But his eyes. They'd turned almost completely black with fear, and Daniel found he was holding them so wide open that the whites showed all around. He splashed cold water on his face and plastered down his hair. *Do something.*

"Hurry the fuck up," barked Kicker. Daniel jumped, stuck his trembling hands in his pockets, and trailed out of the restroom. *Run.*

He could do it. Glancing nervously around, his heart pounding so hard it felt as if it might jump right up out of his throat, Daniel thought he could maybe make a break for it. Could run screaming for the guy at the cash register. Could dash madly for the highway, maybe flag somebody down. Could start a fire with the gasoline. Could spray the guys with it—

"*Don't forget about your mom.*" Hunter's final words rang in his mind.

They'd kill her. Daniel had no doubt about that. He couldn't take the chance, after all. Hanging his head in defeat, he allowed his guard to deposit him back into the rear of the van, where his mother, visibly anxious, surprised him with a hug.

It was her turn next. For the first time Daniel was left alone in the van with Hunter, Preacher, and what's-his-name—Smithy—while the driver filled up the tank and messed around under the hood. Daniel hadn't expected to feel so . . . bereft . . . without his mother. Hadn't realized how much he'd depended on her to reassure him. Staring at one of his big shoes, he gnawed on a fingernail.

"Your mom says you're probably hungry," said Hunter. "That true?"

Amazingly, it was. Still, he didn't want to give the guy the satisfaction of knowing it. Daniel shrugged.

Hunter chuckled. "Tough guy," he said to Smithy.

Daniel wondered if his mother would try anything. She seemed to know how to act around these guys. Maybe she would think of a way to outsmart them. Maybe she would get away.

But would she abandon him?

You almost abandoned her, came a guilty thought. *That's different,* he figured, *she's my mom. Moms don't leave their kids.*

Do they?

She was gone, it seemed, a very long time. Daniel tore the fingernail down to the quick and it started to throb. What if she didn't come back? Would they kill him? Would they kill her?

Was that guy Kicker . . . messing with her?

For the first time Daniel thought about his dad. Would he ever see him again? A fierce longing flooded his heart. More than anything in the world, he wished he could say, *I'm sorry, Dad.* At that moment he'd give everything he owned just to be home again.

If you'll just get me back home, God, he prayed, *I'll never get into trouble again.*

There was a thump at the rear of the van, and Daniel's mother climbed back into the vehicle. He was so glad to see her he almost cried. With her sitting next to him, thoughts of hope came tumbling back. His dad would be on it, Daniel knew. Cops all over the state would be looking for them. Their pictures would be on TV, and that cowboy would see them, and he'd call in to this hotline like they had on that TV show, *Unsolved Mysteries,* and the FBI would come find them.

"It's going to be all right," murmured his mother, and with all his heart he wanted to believe her.

Each of the men took a turn in the restroom, and when Hunter returned to the van, his arms were full of Coke cans and candy bars, which he dumped out on the floor. They left the cuffs off of Daniel and his mother. Everybody took a candy bar and a Coke as the van lumbered back out onto the highway and gained speed. Daniel wolfed down his candy.

"Here, take mine," his mom said, pressing her unopened candy bar into his hand. "I don't want it."

"No—"

"It's okay. Really. My waistline," she added, her lips stretching into a weak smile.

Reluctantly he took the candy, intending to save it, but as usual his stomach overruled his brain and he ate most of it, insisting that she eat some. She took two small bites and left the rest for Daniel.

The drive was interminable and dragged on most of the night. Daniel dozed off and on, until the wheels crunched onto what must have been a very rough dirt road of some kind, so rough that they had to go very slowly, and even then they were all jounced around a good bit.

For some reason this part of the drive frightened Daniel more than any other. His mother took his hand, and he clung to it. The bouncing and grinding seemed to go on forever. Where the hell *were* they?

How would anybody ever find them?

All that time in the van—the men with the guns, even the stop at the gas station—had seemed unreal somehow, but there was something about this nerve-jangling part of the trip that had an air of finality to it. The front of the van took a sudden, steep plunge, and Daniel had to brace his legs to keep from sliding forward toward the driver's seat. Then the van leveled out and finally jolted to a stop.

The driver, Hunter, and two of the guards got out, leaving Smithy once again to aim his rifle at Daniel and his mother.

Dead silence.

No traffic noises. No distant sirens. After a long moment Daniel's rattled sense of hearing picked up a muffled thrumming that he finally identified as the wind whipping against the sides of the vehicle.

The rear doors suddenly banged open, and Smithy gestured toward his two prisoners with his rifle. Daniel made his stiff, clumsy way to the rear and out onto the ground. To his city-boy eyes, the darkness was absolute. He was grateful for his mother's hand when he felt the deadly prod of a rifle barrel in his back and he stumbled forward.

"There's an open doorway in front of you," muttered Hunter. "Watch your step."

"Could we have a flashlight?" asked Daniel's mom.

"No lights. Your eyes will adjust. There are two sleeping bags on the floor, a bucket in the corner for a pot. See you tomorrow."

Daniel, stepping tentatively after his mom, entered the blackest black-on-black he'd ever known, but before he could turn around he heard the decisive *clang* of a door slamming shut behind him.

He stood stock still, his body weak and drained. His mother put her arms around him and he did the same to her. For a long moment they just held onto one another. It seemed to Daniel that she might be shaking, but he couldn't tell because he was quaking like a rabbit.

"I'm so sorry, Daniel," she said. "You'll never, ever know how sorry I am."

"For what?"

"For getting you into this. For everything."

"It's not your fault."

"Yes, it is, honey. It's all my fault." Her voice broke, and to his dismay, he wondered if she might be crying. Daniel had never seen his mother cry, and it unsettled him, like the feeling he got once during a vacation trip to California, when the floor beneath him trembled during a mild earthquake tremor. He didn't know what to do. He patted her hair awkwardly.

She pulled away from him suddenly, cleared her throat, and said, "Let's find our sleeping bags and get warm."

Bewildered, he crouched down near her and groped around until he found a bag to squirm into.

"Take your shoes off first," she said, her voice once more under control.

"Oh." He fumbled with the long laces on his hightops.

"Let me help you with the bag."

"I can do it, Mom."

"Okay." She climbed into her own bag and scooted up next to him. "Have you got it?"

"Yeah."

"Let's get some sleep, then."

Daniel burrowed into the warm folds of the bag, arranging his body first one way and then the next. The floor seemed to be concrete and it was hard.

And his mind was exploding.

"Mom?"

"Can't sleep, huh?"

"What's going on? What's with this Hunter guy and you? What was all that stuff he was talking about in the van?"

The silence stretched out so long that Daniel, fearing she was asleep, said, "Mom?"

"I'm here."

"Where are we? What are we doing here? What was he talking

about—the Armageddon Army? And what did he mean by revenge? When did you know this guy? I just want to know."

She sighed. "I was hoping you would never have to know any of this, Daniel."

"Any of what? And why did he call you Lissie?"

"Because . . . Lissie is—was—my name."

"What do you mean?"

"I was born Elizabeth Montgomery. My parents called me Lissie."

"Was that before they died?"

Silence.

"Mom?"

"Daniel . . . I just want you to listen, okay?"

"Okay."

"You have to understand that when I was young, I didn't under-stand a lot of this myself. It took me a long time, distance . . . and years . . . to finally realize why my mother was the way she was."

"What was she like?"

"Beautiful. Just about the most beautiful woman I ever saw."

To Daniel, his mother's voice became disembodied from her, floating into the velvety night like fireflies on the dark wind, as if it were independent of her, speaking of its own free will. It was a strange, spooky sensation, like fainting.

"My mother's name was Margaret. She was born in the Cherokee territory of northeastern Oklahoma during the depths of the Great Depression to a full-blooded Cherokee mother and a white father. Back then Native Americans were hated by many people. People like my mother were called half-breeds. Signs on restaurant doors often said: NO DOGS OR INDIANS ALLOWED. You know those old Westerns your dad likes to watch?"

Daniel nodded. "Yeah. He likes John Wayne and all those macho men."

"Well, if you pay attention, you can see that the movies back then almost always depicted Indians as bloodthirsty savages or cartoonish buffoons."

"What's a buffoon?"

She didn't answer. "You can't imagine the poverty my mother knew as a child. They had no electricity, no indoor plumbing. They had to haul water to the house to bathe and heat it on a wood stove.

Food was often squirrels or rabbits, whatever they could shoot in the woods. Most job opportunities for Native men and women were usually restricted to the dirtiest, hardest jobs. It just . . . it twisted her mind."

"Like how?"

"It made her hate who she was. It made her hate herself, you see. Then, when my mother was a teenager, the government moved her family away from their lands, all the way out to California. She was forced to attend an all-white school, where the kids laughed at her and made fun of her clothes and her ways. You have to understand, she was in high school and didn't even know how to use a telephone."

"You're kidding."

"Think about it. They didn't have a phone back in Oklahoma, and none of their close friends or relatives had one, either. I'm just saying, she was like this alien creature to the kids in that big modern high school. All she had to fight back with was her beauty, and she used it to win the most promising young bachelor in school."

"Your dad?"

"That's right. Daddy was from a prominent family, and they disapproved of Mother so much that when Daddy married her, they moved to Texas to get away from it all. I think his parents disowned him, because I never knew them."

"He must have loved her a lot," interrupted Daniel.

His mother hesitated. "You're right. He always loved Mother. I think he liked to think of himself as her savior, in a way. He saved her from grinding poverty and gave her this whole new life. He liked to do things for her and buy her things. Anyway, Mother worked as a waitress to put Daddy through college, and he went into banking after graduation. She never told anyone in Texas that she was half-Indian. From that point on, Mother did everything in her power to reinvent herself."

"What do you mean?"

"I mean she tried to become something she was not."

"Like what?"

"Like high society. It became Mother's driving force in life that we would live in the right neighborhoods and attend the right schools and drive the right cars and do all the right things."

Daniel pondered this. "So you're saying she was a snob."

"Very much so. But not because she thought she was better than everybody else."

"Because she thought she wasn't as good as they were."

"Oh, Daniel. I wish I'd had your wisdom when I was your age. It took me twenty years to figure that out."

"So you guys were rich?"

"I guess some people would think so. I'd call it more like upper middle class. But we were certainly rich by Cherokee standards. We lived in a part of Dallas called Highland Park, which is a very exclusive area—to this day."

"So she was a soc."

"A what? A *soash?*"

"You know. Social climber."

"Oh." She gave a small laugh. "Yeah, you could say that. She wanted me to learn all the social graces—ballroom dancing and charm school manners and deportment and elocution."

"What's that?"

"It's how you carry yourself and express yourself."

"Oh, I get it. She didn't want people to laugh at you the way they'd laughed at her."

His mom was very quiet for a while. Finally, she said, "Where'd you get so smart?"

"It's easy when you're not living in the middle of it."

"You're right."

"So . . . when did your parents die?"

A deeper silence set in, so deep that Daniel worried he'd gone too far. They'd been having a nice talk, and he wondered if he'd upset her.

The silence was uncanny. It wasn't total, because the wind never seemed to stop whispering and thudding against the sides of the building, like the muffled noises of someone trying to get in. It was such a lonely, scary sound. He shivered.

When his mother finally spoke, he jumped. "Daniel . . . they're not dead."

Tingles of shock shot through Daniel's body. All his life he'd been led to believe his grandparents were dead. "You mean . . . that whole story about the orphanage . . . was a lie?"

"Son, this is my greatest shame. I don't know how else to tell you but just to tell you."

"Where are they now?"

"I guess they're still living in Dallas."

"You mean you don't *know*?"

"I mean . . . I haven't contacted them in eighteen years."

It was Daniel's turn to be silent. He lay flat on his back and stared up into the empty blackness of their prison, trying to imagine what it would have been like to have had two sets of grandparents instead of just one. Someplace else to go in the summer. More Christmas presents. And they were supposed to be *rich*. Eric would shit bricks.

His mother began talking a little faster, her words assuming an urgency he didn't entirely understand. "I hated all those society games that my mother wanted to play. You cannot begin to imagine how bad I hated them. We had terrible battles, Mother and I."

So, his mom had fought with her parents, too. So why did she give *him* such a hard time? "What did your dad think?"

"He thought that child-raising was woman's work. He'd come home from the bank and hide behind his newspaper while Mother and I fought. All that time I was happy only when I was at my grandmother's." Her voice grew warm and happy. "See, when I was a little girl, once when I was nine and then again when I was eleven, I was permitted to spend a whole summer with my grandmother, Ahw'usti. That means—"

"Little Deer. They're spirits who impart wisdom and knowledge." He yawned.

"Daniel—how did you know that?"

He shrugged within his sleeping bag. "You told me once when I was a little kid." He was beginning to feel drowsy.

"I did?"

"I was sick. You told me some stories to help me sleep."

"That's right, I did. Huh. I'd forgotten all about that."

"So you got to stay in the woods with your grandmother?" Daniel began to drift toward sleep.

"She still lived in that little house without plumbing or electricity. She cooked and heated the house with a wood stove. And it was *wonderful*. Daniel, I wish you could have known her—"

"Is *she* dead?" Daniel couldn't hide the sarcasm in his voice, and he regretted it instantly, because when his mother spoke again, he could hear the hurt.

"She died when I was about your age. But when I stayed with her, I could run barefoot like a little wild creature through the woods and wade in the streams. There were animals all over the place. It was beautiful."

"No TV?"

"Honey . . . there was no electricity . . . remember?"

"Oh." It sounded boring to Daniel.

"But it was okay, because Ah'wusti was all the entertainment I needed."

"But without lights—" Jeez. No Nintendo. No CD player. No comic books. No MTV. Talk about *prison*. "Weren't you bored?"

"Oh, Daniel." She chuckled. "You're such a spoiled city kid. We used kerosene lamps. And by the light of the fire and the lamps, she would tell me wonderful stories of the Cherokee way, the legends and animal stories and myths of our blood and heritage—she was a true Cherokee storyteller. I would sit entranced for hours and beg for another story."

"Why didn't your mom let you go back more often, since you liked it so much?"

"She thought my grandmother was corrupting me. I'd come back with feet hard as shoes and my face nut brown from the sun. It wasn't ladylike. She kept trying to force me into these frilly dresses when all I wanted to do was play softball outside."

"No wonder you ran away." Daniel's grandmother didn't sound like a very nice person. Maybe it was just as well he didn't know her.

"I didn't run away."

"So what happened?" Daniel yawned again, loudly. Sleep tugged at him. He closed his eyes.

"I met Jeremiah Hunter."

The man's name, said aloud in the intimate darkness, poisoned the very atmosphere. Suddenly Daniel wasn't sleepy anymore. He rolled over, trying to bunch up the edge of the sleeping bag for a pillow on the hard floor. For a while there, it had been kinda cool, like he and his mom were out camping or something. All they needed was a campfire. But as soon as she brought up the guy's name, the reality of their situation came whooshing in on Daniel with all the force of the wind that pounded against the building.

They weren't camping after all. They'd been kidnapped. They were being held hostage in some godforsaken place.

And he was scared.

As if she hadn't noticed the change in him, his mother went on. "I was eighteen years old. A freshman at SMU. I wanted to go to college as far away from home as I could get, but Mother insisted on keeping me right where she could keep an eye on me."

It was cold. Daniel's sleeping bag was warm enough, but fear was an icy companion, working its way across his flesh like a frigid draft. He tried to focus his mind on what his mother was saying. The past he could handle. "SMU's in Dallas, right?" He burrowed deeper into the bag, drawing his knees up to his chest, and closed his eyes.

"The SMU campus is located just a few blocks from our old house. Mother wanted to make sure I pledged the right sorority. Lucky for me, I had a little sister by then, and she *loved* all that ribbon and lace—"

Daniel's eyes flew open. "I've got an *aunt*? I mean, on your side of the family?"

His mother's voice sounded infinitely weary as she said, "Abigail. We called her Abby. I was nine when she was born—that would make her twenty-seven years old now."

"Do I have any cousins you haven't told me about?" Daniel couldn't keep the bitterness from his tone as he yanked at the zipper on his bag.

"I don't know, son. The last time I saw Abby, she was nine years old."

Daniel couldn't imagine life without his little sister. Most of the time he wanted to smush her like a bug, but she was his *sister*; if anybody else tried it, he'd cream 'em. It occurred to him that if he had to be away from her for very long, he would miss her. "Mom?"

"Yeah?"

"Do you ever miss your family? I mean, do you ever get homesick?"

"Every day of my life, sweetheart. Not a single day goes by that I don't think of them and miss them."

"So . . . why don't you call them up? I mean, they'd be mad and all, but they'd be glad to hear from you."

"I can't."

"Why not?"

This time the silence was very long. The air seemed charged with it, and the encroaching wind, began to whistle urgently through the narrow gap between the walls and the roof of the building. Daniel shivered, but not from cold.

"When I first met Hunter, I was a silly, rebellious, restless college freshman. I wanted to feel like that kid again—the one who ran barefoot through the woods. I wanted that part of me that had been buried in all my mother's pretensions. So I attended a meeting one night of the environmentalist club—"

"*What is that?*" Daniel sat straight up.

"The environmentalist club?"

"*No. That noise.*" He was whispering.

After a moment of silence his mother said, "I don't hear anything."

Daniel strained to hear. "I did. A noise like . . . I don't know what. Like something . . . out there." Shuddering, he bundled the sleeping bag around his ears.

"It's probably a critter of some kind, honey. This is the country."

A bleakness of sorts settled over his soul. Again in a whisper he said, "Do you think they have a guard posted outside?"

His mother hesitated. "Maybe."

"Could he be listening?"

"I doubt that anyone can hear us, sweetheart. Don't worry, okay? It's all right."

But it wasn't all right. Nothing was all right. How could she say that? In the darkness her hand found his head and stroked his hair. Daniel lay back down and, in spite of himself, relaxed a little.

"I know this is scary," she said. "I'm scared, too. But nobody's going to hurt us."

"How do you know? Every time we move they threaten to kill us. These guys are freakin' crazy." Just talking about it made him feel colder than ever.

She patted his head and he pulled away. "I know it looks bad, Daniel. But if Jeremiah Hunter wanted us dead, we'd be dead by now. I don't know how else to say it. He's got something else in mind. If we just do what he says, we'll be all right."

"I don't see how you ever got involved with a creep like him," Daniel said.

"That's what I'm trying to tell you." Her voice was soothing again. "The environmentalist club, remember?"

He sighed. *Think about the past,* he thought. *The past can't kill you.* Or could it? After all, it was his mom's past that had gotten them into this whole thing in the first place.

Okay. He would try to understand. It wasn't like he had anything else to do or anywhere else to be. "That's when all the college protests and stuff was going on, wasn't it?" he asked politely.

"Well . . . that's a good point, Daniel, because you see, all those antiwar and civil rights marches and things were going on when your *dad* was in school. I came along ten years later. It was a whole different group in the late seventies. The Vietnam war was over, John and Bobby and Martin were dead, Nixon had resigned, that boring Jimmy Carter was president, and the whole hippy scene had basically collapsed under its own weight and too many drugs," she said dreamily. "There weren't many places for the rebellious young to go. No great causes left to embrace. But that night Jeremiah Hunter blew the top off the joint."

His mom's voice became electrified at the memory. Something about it made Daniel uncomfortable. He punched his sleeping bag. "So what was so great about him?"

"Hunter was a twenty-eight-year-old Vietnam combat veteran attending school on the GI bill, and he was so . . . so rugged and virile—"

"What does 'virile' mean?"

"Sexy."

"Oh." He was sorry he had asked.

"Well, he took over that podium and whipped our little apathetic student crowd into a frenzy. It wasn't so much what he said—I couldn't even remember a few days later—it was the way he said it."

"Huh?"

"He was just so . . . forceful. I guess you'd call it manly."

"You mean macho."

"Not necessarily, Daniel. To me, macho is a negative word. Pretending to be something you're not. But a manly man is just . . . masculine. Sexy in a very manly way."

"So he was hot."

"Well . . . yeah. I went up to him after the meeting, and there was something about the way he focused his entire attention on me while I was speaking, as if every word I said was the most important thing he'd ever heard before. And his eyes . . . they had a kind of excitement and a little danger lurking just behind them."

Daniel wasn't sure he wanted to hear this. After all, this was his *mom* talking.

"He took me out for coffee afterwards," she said, "and he talked to me about living off the land, independent of intrusions by arbitrary rules and regulations, carving out an existence where you were true to yourself and no other, whittling life down to its raw basics—and I tell you, I was just absolutely smitten. I mean, it's like I'd been waiting my entire life to hear this."

She paused. Daniel said, "So what happened?"

"He had this . . . group of people who were living literally back-to-nature down in the Louisiana bayou. And the way he talked about it, it just seemed like exactly what I'd been looking for my whole life. So . . . I dropped out of school and followed him down there to live."

"What did your parents do?"

"What could they do? They were horrified, of course. Mother had no idea what I was into until it was too late. I think she figured it out when they got my report cards in the mail and found out I was flunking out of school."

"*You* flunked out of school?"

"It's not my proudest memory."

"I can't believe it."

"Neither could my parents."

"Couldn't they, like, come and get you or something?"

"I was eighteen. A legal adult."

Daniel thought this over. Then he said, "So okay. It didn't work out. You broke up. Why didn't you go see your folks then? They'd have forgiven you, wouldn't they?"

"Well, son . . . it wasn't that easy. Hunter . . . he wasn't what I thought he was."

"Why? Was he into drugs or something?"

"No. But . . . let's just say that he was into some things that I didn't find out about until it was too late. Some illegal things."

"Like what?"

"I'd really rather not say." The tone in her voice sharpened, like it did when she looked at *his* report card.

"Why not?" Daniel prodded, his interest in what she was saying suddenly intensified.

"I just don't want to get into it right now!" she snapped.

Daniel, almost consumed with curiosity, wanted to egg her on, but he knew it would only make her mad. He decided to leave that touchy subject alone for the time being. "So what happened?"

"The FBI moved in. There was a very bad . . . scene. I ran away."

Daniel sat back up and peered at his mother. His eyes had adjusted to the darkness. Her voice was no longer disembodied, but her face was ghostlike.

"You mean . . . you're wanted by the FBI?"

She said nothing.

"You're . . . a *federal fugitive?*"

"It's not what you think, Daniel."

"Then what is it?"

"I don't want to get into it right now, I said. It's extremely late, we're both exhausted—"

"Is that what Hunter meant when he was talking about revenge? He wants you to help him get revenge on the *feds?*"

"I don't know what he wants to do," she said evasively.

"Mom . . . *what did you do?*"

"I made a terrible mistake, Daniel. That's what I did."

"But what did you *do?*"

"Son . . . I didn't do anything wrong. And that's all I'm going to say about it right now. We've got to get some sleep."

Her sleeping bag rustled as she settled in, and Daniel knew from her tone of voice that she would say no more. He laid back and stared blindly in the direction of the ceiling. Unbelievable. He had grandparents on his mother's side. An aunt. Maybe a cousin or two.

And his mom, *his* mom, a high school chemistry teacher . . . was a federal fugitive.

They'd been kidnapped by some psycho freak she used to know and dragged out to some kind of prison in the middle of nowhere by a bunch of macho thugs with big guns.

Suddenly Eric, school, and that paper he had due in Coach Thurber's class seemed like something from a different universe.

But it was his own mother who was the alien.

And now Daniel was beginning to wonder if he would ever be able to find his way back home again.

CHAPTER 10

IT was *yippety-yip-yap* cries of a pack of coyotes that brought Wren fully awake from a fitful doze in the sunless dawn of their cinder-block cell. They sounded disturbingly close.

Tricksters, all of them, was her first thought. With her brain scrambled by fear and fatigue, it took a moment to get her bearings and fully face their situation. It was still too dark for her to see Daniel, but she could hear his breathing as he slept beside her. She needed to go to the bathroom, but she knew that would awaken him and she was anxious to let him sleep as much as possible. Soon enough he would be awake, and afraid.

In spite of the horror of their circumstances, Wren couldn't help but feel they'd had a major breakthrough in their relationship the night before. Telling her son the truth about her background had been somewhat of a relief for Wren.

Although she had left out quite a lot.

Thinking back, Wren wondered if she should have gone ahead and told the boy everything. She'd hesitated more out of concern for him than embarrassment for herself. After all, he'd endured a shocking trauma which was still, essentially, ongoing. At the time Wren had been worried that if she revealed too much too soon, he would somehow snap under the pressure of it all.

I'll tell him everything in time, she thought, *when he's ready for it.*

For the time being, Wren had to concentrate all her faculties on the realities of their situation: they were being held hostage at a survivalist camp in a remote wilderness location. She knew these people. They would be heavily armed and well trained, and the compound would be under guard. The wary edge of fear had placed all her senses on alert: ever vigilant for the first signs of danger, ever watchful for a way out.

She listened now for any muffled sounds of life outside their small prison. She'd already crept around the sides while Daniel slept, measuring the room's dimensions with her hands, feeling for a window, a crack, anything she could use to their advantage.

The room turned out to be solid, barely big enough to hold the two sleeping bags. Wren wondered if Hunter used it as a sort of holding cell, a disciplinary measure to keep his troops in line. It was clean and bare: simple cement block construction on a concrete foundation. She couldn't reach the ceiling or see it yet, but she assumed it was something like corrugated tin.

A colorless strip of pearlescent dawn was just beginning to be revealed along the inch-high gap under the door and along the tops of the walls just under the roof when Wren heard the first crunch of footsteps outside and an accompanying cadence of voices. She tensed, trying to make out what they were saying, but the people were too far away and they were only passing by, not approaching the hut.

Driven at last by discomfort, Wren crawled out of her sleeping bag and made her way over to the five-gallon bucket in the corner. Her only privacy was to turn her back and rely on the room's natural darkness to cover her embarrassment while she urinated.

As expected, the noise awoke Daniel. She could hear him stirring around behind her and she hurried to pull her jeans back up. There was no toilet paper. They were going to make her ask for it.

The room was unheated and she scooted back down into the sleeping bag to warm up.

"Mom?"

"Yeah?"

"What's going to happen to us?"

She hesitated. "I can't say for sure," she answered truthfully.

"Are they going to kill us?"

She could hear the fear vibrating throughout his voice, and it made her chest ache. "I don't think so, sweetheart. Not as long as we cooperate with them."

"Do you think they want a ransom or anything?"

In other words, *Are they going to contact Dad? Are they going to let us go?*

She couldn't lie. "They didn't kidnap us for money."

"He wants you, doesn't he?"

"Yes."

"Then why did he take me, too?"

"You're . . . a way for him to control me."

"Oh."

"He knows that as long as he's got you, I won't try anything foolish."

"So it could have been either me or Zoe, then."

No, thought Wren, *Hunter never does anything that haphazardly. He wants my son for something else, and I can't even bear to think what.*

"Mom?"

"What?"

"Why does he need you to get revenge on the feds? Can't he do it on his own? I mean, with Kicker and them?"

"I'm not sure, Daniel." Wren had a pretty good idea of what Hunter wanted with her, but she wasn't prepared to explain it to Daniel. At least, not yet. Not until he'd had some time to adjust somewhat to their situation.

What Wren didn't know was how Hunter *knew.* That he had found her at all had been enough of a shock, but Wren knew Hunter too well to think that his interest in her was purely sentimental. He must have been stalking her for weeks. Their mailbox stood at the curb. It would have been easy for him to examine her mail while they were all at work and school. From the books, catalogues, and magazines she ordered, he could have figured out easily enough that in spite of Wren's name change, marriage, and motherhood, she had not completely abandoned certain . . . fascinations . . . with her old life.

Wren sighed. What had she been thinking all those years? She'd told herself the publications enhanced her teaching, gave her ideas for chemistry experiments.

Indeed.

"Does he want you to be his girlfriend again?"

The question startled Wren. The plaintive note in her son's voice pierced Wren's heart. She said, "I'll never be his girlfriend again. I love your father too much."

"Did you love him?"

"Who?"

"Hunter."

"When I was young . . . I thought I did. But it wasn't love. Not really. It was more like the blind adoration of a puppy. Once I started to grow up, I could see it for what it was. I could see *him* for what *he* was. And then I met Cam. Your daddy's ten times the man Jeremiah Hunter will ever be."

Daniel said nothing, and Wren wondered if he was doubting the wisdom of that last statement. He was young yet. He would learn, just like she did.

A *thunk* at the door startled them both, and when it swung open, the sudden flood of light blinded them. A woman, her body trim in desert-tan camouflage fatigues, her face hardened and suspicious, set down two metal trays with a *clunk* on the floor by the door and straightened quickly, her hand on the grip of a holstered 9mm. She stepped back without a word and slammed the door.

The smell of scrambled eggs, greasy hash browns, and pungent coffee almost overpowered Wren, whose stomach was queasy from nerves. But Daniel, she knew, would be starving, so she handed one of the trays to him and took for herself a metal cup of coffee which was still surprisingly hot and bracing.

"Aren't you going to eat?" he asked, the words barely discernible around eggs and toast.

"Maybe a piece of toast," she said, nibbling on one to please him. "Why don't you have my eggs and potatoes?"

"Mom, you gotta eat."

He was right. "Just toast for now, honey. You have the rest if you want it. Really. My stomach's a little upset this morning, is all." She took two limp triangles of toast from the tray and handed him the rest.

It was like chewing Play-Doh, but she forced herself to do it for Daniel's sake. He didn't need to be worrying about her on top of everything else.

"I thought maybe they might be going to starve us," he said, his mouth still full. "I didn't know what they were going to do."

"That wouldn't serve any purpose," she said. *We'll need our strength for whatever Hunter's got in mind,* she thought. *And I'll need my strength to get us out of here.* She swallowed another half-chewed bite of toast.

Daniel cleaned both trays, and she stacked them neatly by the door. The glow of daylight seeping into the room seemed to reassure Daniel, and they listened in silence to strange new sounds: the moan of the wind, distant shouts as the camp apparently went through morning calisthenics, Preacher's incantations of some sort of prayer, the drone of Hunter's voice and the answering shouts as he led them in a gathering that seemed to Wren to follow the rhythms of the daily camp meetings she remembered from Louisiana, and the constant crackle of gunfire from the firing range.

As the hours passed, Wren felt a bond forming with her son at once as delicate and as strong as the filament of a spider's web. She had always felt closer to Daniel than Cam did, but puberty had thrust a sort of invisible crevice between them that threatened at times to become a chasm.

During many a long and sleepless night, she'd tangled more than a few blankets with her restless little mother-fears, thinking up ways to cross over to the other side before the cleft widened into a canyon. Sometimes she would dream that she was grasping for her son and he was always just out of reach. She would awaken gasping and sweating because, somehow in her dream she knew that if she couldn't grab him, he would die.

How ironic that it took the realization of her worst, most basic and profound fear to belay her son to her over that imaginary ravine. The problem now was in knowing just how much rope to give him.

As the day crawled past, Daniel spoke to his mother about many things: the sadistic basketball coach who drove him off the court even though he loved to play the game; the pretty blonde who sat next to him in history class, but who wouldn't go out with him because she assumed that Eric-of-the-purple-hair was on drugs and therefore so was he (he wasn't, he assured her, and neither was Eric, though Eric had been known to take a drag of weed now and then);

the bad habit he had of letting his temper rule his mouth; big-brother worries about Zoe.

His talking was compulsive and, Wren knew, fear-driven, but it warmed her heart all the same. *So much of our children's inner lives are hidden from us,* she mused, *simply because we are too busy to sit down in one place and listen to them talk about themselves for any length of time.*

The same stern-faced female guard brought them a dinner tray late in the afternoon and emptied the yellow bucket. Two meals a day was hardly enough to sustain a fifteen-year-old boy, but Wren didn't mind sharing most of her food with him. The truth was that her stomach was constantly upset, much like when she was pregnant, and she didn't feel any more like eating than she had then. But she would pick out just enough to keep Daniel from worrying about her.

The fact that Hunter did not visit them at all that first day set Wren even more on edge. Clearly it was no oversight; he had some sort of master plan, and it made her feel like a chess piece, being shoved around on a board with no will of her own and no idea what the game strategy was.

Daniel relaxed a bit more the second night and slept somewhat easier, but for Wren the wind-driven lonesomeness of night was almost unbearable. Ghosts of family and home haunted the inky blackness, and every fear—both real and imaginary—crept down the back of her neck and crouched in the shadows of her mind like roving lunatics.

On the third day of their captivity, when they had just begun to adjust to the metronomic monotony of routine, two guards—Kicker and the wordless woman who brought their food—flung back the door to their cell and, silhouetted in the sunlit glare of the open doorway, announced that Daniel and Wren were to be taken to the showers and given a fresh change of clothing.

Daniel glanced toward his mother in alarm. She understood his anxiety; as a prisoner, he'd gotten used to his prison. Any change in routine or surroundings would bring on an attack of insecurity.

Wren felt no such qualms. This would be her first chance to get a look at their surroundings, and she intended to take full advantage of it. In particular, she wanted to get an idea as to where they were located and to perhaps estimate the size of the encampment. She gave Daniel a reassuring nod and gestured for him to step outside ahead of her.

Both their guards were armed with shotguns as well as their holstered sidearms. "Head for those buildings over there," indicated Kicker, pointing vaguely toward the right and prodding the boy with his shotgun. "Walk slowly, and if you try any stunts whatsoever, I'll kill you."

Wren waited, trying to suppress the sudden fear she felt as she listened to her son's footsteps crunching on hard, dry earth, moving away from her to a place she couldn't reach. Keeping her face carefully devoid of expression, she stared into the narrowed eyes of her captor until the woman gestured for her to leave.

Wren moved tentatively out the door and stumbled to an almost immediate halt as she took in her first full daylight look at their surroundings.

The first sensation she had was of everything inside her sinking, sinking into a quagmire of doubt and desolation. The first word which popped into her mind was: *moonscape.*

Everything, from the vast, bleached-out blue canopy of sky overhead to the anemic, chalky soil underfoot, echoed a kind of bleak, barren emptiness. The compound was secreted down in a rocky bowl-like draw, surrounded by inhospitable treeless hills littered with stark boulders that stood out like gravestones. Barbed wire stitched the ridges above the camp, where she spotted at least one armed guard patrolling on horseback.

Prodded by a shotgun barrel against her spine, Wren almost staggered in the direction her son had taken. Even the stunted plants were unwelcoming; everything that grew in the dusty, dry dirt was hazardous with thorns or spikes or leaves as hard and jagged as a serrated knife blade.

Everywhere were rocks; the soil itself was as hard as stone. Mesquites grew here, but they were too dwarfed to be called trees and many of them looked dead. The only sound over the incessant distant crackle of gunfire was the moan of the wind and the answering lonesome soporific groan of a nearby windmill.

The buildings were unadorned cement block structures painted pale tan with camouflage splotches of brown and green to match the ground cover. Even the roofs were covered with great stretches of camouflage netting. The exhaustive attempts at camouflage puzzled Wren, but there was no time to think about it just then. She assumed from her previous experience that the various buildings made up a mess hall, a meeting hall, dormitory-type sleepers, and military-style showers and latrines divided into men's and women's. There were a few small trailer houses scattered about that Wren figured must be reserved for married couples and, of course, for the Armageddon Army's exalted leader.

The shower was a simple affair, much like one at a girl's gym or a campground. No concessions had been made to modesty, and Wren tried to forget about the armed woman guard who sat in a folding chair, smoking a cigarette and watching her as she quickly bathed and washed her long hair. There wasn't a great deal of water pressure, but it was hot and felt so good that Wren almost forgot where she was. Shampoo, soap, towels, and the like were laid out on shelves for communal use. While Wren was combing out her snarled hair with a wide-toothed comb, her silent companion handed her a set of clean desert-cammie fatigues, which she quickly donned, along with a pair of lace-up boots that were close enough to the correct size to be comfortable.

On the return trip to the hut, Wren took note of something she hadn't really noticed before: it was surprisingly warm for October, and the sunlight was unforgiving. Judging from the landscape as well, she knew without a doubt that they were located somewhere in the desert Southwest, but beyond that she didn't have a clue, except for the long drive it had taken to get there. Far western Texas, then, or New Mexico. Maybe even Mexico.

The only thing she did know for sure was that Hunter could not have picked a more remote spot for his base camp, and that realization, more than any other, punched gaping holes in the flimsy structure of hope Wren had constructed for herself during the past three days.

The woman shoved her the few remaining steps into the hut and slammed the door behind her. The silence was almost palpable.

Daniel was not there.

When he did not return after a few minutes, the few remaining props that had kept Wren going wobbled dangerously close to collapse. Pacing the floor like a caged lioness, she circled the tiny cell with an increasing sense of urgency, her fear stripped raw and pulsating like an open wound.

Panic began to seep toward the surface, like blood.

I'll go mad, she whispered silently. *I'll go mad.*

Her thick hair dried; likewise the damp spot it had made on the back of her fatigue shirt.

Her legs gave out and she plopped down on her sleeping bag. She reached for Daniel's bag and wadded it up in her arms, burying her nose in his scent while panic oozed out of the torn part left by his absence.

She couldn't breathe. She couldn't think. Every now and then her heart would tumble in a sort of somersault within her chest, and she would gasp at the shock of it until it got itself under control again and beat in a rhythm at once rapid but steady.

If he didn't come back, would her heart stop beating altogether?

A *thump* at the door sent a shock wave through her system as it swung open and a tall young man, familiar yet strange, stepped through the doorway, backlit by the arid, blanched afternoon light.

His hair had been completely shorn, down to a half inch on top and sidewalled over the ears. Like her, he was clad in camouflage fatigues of tan and brown and lace-up boots. If it hadn't been for the awkward, angled, adolescent posture and set of his shoulders, she might not have recognized him at all before the door was closed and they were once again doused in darkness.

"They shaved me like a poodle," he said, his voice cracking on the first syllable of "poodle," and she laughed and laughed with relief and the release of tension.

"I look like a bowling ball," he moaned.

"Actually, I thought you looked kind of hot," she giggled.

"*Mom!* I can't believe you said that."

"Silly boy. Don't you think moms know when their sons are gorgeous?"

He made an unflattering noise.

"Actually, now that I can see your eyes again, I like it."

"Well, I don't."

"You will," she said. "It'll be much easier to keep." It's what she said, but the new relief had already whooshed out of her and been replaced by the hollowness of the old fear. She knew what was happening. They were being stripped of their identities and molded into the likeness of their captors. Shaving Daniel's hair was not just a practical thing to do; it was also highly symbolic. Armies all over the world followed the same principle.

The act had also telegraphed a silent but powerful message to Wren: *You're not getting out of here. Might as well join the program and get used to it.*

She'd die first.

That night, as she lay awake trying to find some way to shield herself from the relentless onslaught of hopelessness that threatened to overpower her, she resolved to tell Daniel everything about her past.

He would need to know so that they could not use it as a weapon to harm him. She would wait until after breakfast. He would be able to listen better then, when he wasn't hungry. But the next morning, before she had a chance to bring it up, they had their second surprise: a visit from Hunter. His presence filled up the cramped room, and he leaned against the wall, arms folded across his chest, while Kicker waited just outside the open doorway, shotgun in hand.

"How're you guys doing?" he asked politely.

Sitting Indian-style on his sleeping bag, staring at his boots, Daniel shrugged. Wren said, "We appreciate the showers and the clean clothes." She knew that the price for not being appropriately grateful could be high.

"Good," said Hunter, seemingly preoccupied. "Good." Rubbing his chin, he glanced over at her. "What do you think of the layout?"

She thought rapidly, then said, "Impressive."

He grinned. "I knew you'd like it. I'll show you around tomorrow. You'll be amazed at how much better it is than the Community."

Keeping her voice carefully steady, she said, "I'm sure I will."

"Dan, wait'll you see your mom in action. You'll see what a crackerjack she really is."

Warning bells clanged in Wren's brain; sirens screamed and red lights flashed STOP STOP STOP.

Daniel looked from his mother to Hunter. "Huh?"

"Well, you've had a long time to visit in here, haven't you? A long time for you to get to know your mother a little better. I'm sure she's taken the opportunity to tell you all about herself."

Wren caught Hunter's eye and gave him a desperate little warning shake to the head, realizing instantly that it was the wrong thing to do. It was the kind of signal she was always giving Cam over the heads of the kids.

But this wasn't Cam.

"Yeah," said Hunter, smiling at her as he said to her bewildered young son, "I guess she's maybe too modest to tell you about how she used to be the best explosives expert—bar none—I ever saw."

"*Explosives?*" Daniel swiveled and stared at his mother.

"Aw, man—you should have seen her! Thanks to your mom, we were able to make off with more than twenty-five thousand dollars once from this supposedly uncrackable bank safe! She blew that fucker right in half—and the cash didn't even have so much as a *scorch* mark."

With a chuckle and a shake of the head, he added, "We were an unbeatable team, your mom and I. But I guess you already figured out how sharp she is; shit, sixteen years on the run from the feds, setting up this nice suburban life. Jesus—teaching *chemistry?* I laughed right out loud when I found that one out. No wonder the stupid government bastards never suspected a thing. I tell you, I feel real lucky to have her back. Together, we'll blow those sons of bitches to kingdom come."

Hunter's handsome face took on a pensive cast, and his voice quieted. "It's the least they deserve for killing so many of our brave and valiant buddies in that raid. The one where I got caught. Sixteen years I spent in prison. Anyway, you don't know this, but you're lucky, too, Dan. If your mom hadn't known about the trapdoor, they'd have probably killed her, too. But she got away, thank God. Believe me, they'll regret that to their dying day."

Wren, her cheeks tingling hot, dared a quick glance in her son's direction. He was gaping at her. The color had drained from his face. Without all that hair, his stupefied expression seemed as open and exposed as that of a child who accidentally stumbles upon his parents setting out toys on Christmas Eve, realizing for the first and last time that there is no Santa. That there never was a Santa.

That it was all a lie.

"Well, it's time for our daily devotional," said Hunter, his demeanor once again chatty and cheerful. Smiling, he stood away from the wall and turned toward the door. "A few more days and you guys will be taking part with us. But for the time being, I hope you are comfortable. Let me know if there's anything you need. Oh, and Dan—your hair looks great."

The closing door eclipsed Daniel's face in the room's customary gloom. Wren could hear the raspy sound of his breathing. It sounded as if he were about to hyperventilate.

"I was going to tell you," she said. "I was planning to tell you—"

"*Liar.*"

The word struck her like a slap; it knocked the breath out of her. She wanted to say something, but she could not.

"You said you didn't do anything wrong."

"Daniel, let me explain—"

"You didn't tell me there was a raid," he said, his voice curdled with disgust. "You *ran!*"

"Daniel—"

"You blew up a safe, and you stole the money, and when the feds came, you ran away and left people to die!" He was sobbing and he didn't even know it. "You *lied* to me!"

"I never lied to you. I—"

He sprang to his feet, all misdirected energy. "*You hypocrite!*"

Wren tried to get to her feet, but the sleeping bag was tangled around her legs.

"I sneak out of the library to hang out with my friends, and you guys act like I'm some kind of *criminal!*"

Those damn boots. Those damn fucking boots. She couldn't get disentangled.

"I swipe a couple of beers from my own refrigerator, and you act like I'm *Satan* or somebody!" He was panting; the air crackled with his rage.

Wren kicked loose from the clinging tendrils of the bag and stood up, facing her son in the unlighted little hut. She could smell his anger. It towered over her and she cringed.

"Does Dad know? *Does he?*"

Summoning up the tattered fragments of her ragged courage, Wren said, "Son, I want you to calm down. There is a lot you don't know. A lot I haven't told you."

He gave a mirthless laugh. "Oh, I'll bet *that's* the truth." In the murky shadows she could just make him out shaking his head. "But then . . . what *is* the truth? Huh? Let's see . . . my mom is a bank robber, and a coward, and a federal fugitive, and a liar, and a hypocrite."

A great yawning cavity of despair opened at Wren's feet. Of all the disasters she had feared, none could have been as horrible as this. That fragile bond between her and her son that had been slowly strengthened day by day, braid by braid, now lay severed.

And she couldn't fix it.

She reached for him. Her fingers brushed his sleeve, and he cried out as if they had scalded him, drawing back from the acid that was his mother.

Her chest hurt. She couldn't breathe.

"Does Dad know? And could you tell me the truth this time? Please?"

She swallowed. Her throat burned. "Yes."

He turned away from her and leaned his face into the wall.

"Daniel, you have to let me tell you what happened. It's not what you think. You've got to believe me, son—"

He mumbled something against the cold, hard wall.

"What?" Silence. "What did you say? Daniel?"

"I *said* . . . it's too late."

CHAPTER 11

C AM stood in the middle of the supermarket junk food aisle, trying to remember which one it was who liked Doritos—Zoe or Daniel? One liked Cheetos and one liked Doritos, and he couldn't remember which was which. He grabbed a bag of Cheetos and threw them in the cart, took three steps, then stopped. If it was Daniel who liked the Doritos, he'd gripe to high heaven and drive them all crazy. Cam took the Cheetos out of the cart and put Doritos in.

Then he remembered that Daniel wasn't there anyway. He put the Doritos back on the shelf. And what if Zoe didn't like Cheetos after all? They wouldn't get eaten and it would be a waste of money. He put the Cheetos back.

Picking up a six-pack of Coke, he hesitated. Didn't Zoe like Diet Pepsi, or was that Wren?

A powerful, almost irresistible urge possessed him; more than anything else in the world at that moment, Cam wanted to jerk the scarlet cans off their little plastic rings and hurl them, one by one, as far down the aisle as he could.

Abandoning the cart, Cam stalked out of the store and got into his car, slamming the door after him. For a long time he sat there, shaking off the insanity and staring unseeingly at all the other weary ones—the people who'd put in full workdays and still had to wander supermarket aisles, searching for food, when all they really wanted to do was sit at home and watch TV.

Wren usually shopped for groceries after school. Since her workday ended at three-thirty, Cam had always assumed it couldn't be that hard. That was three—or was it four now?—days ago, back in that other time, when they still had a family.

He'd thought a lot of things then that he didn't think anymore.

Go home, check out the cupboards, talk to Zoe, make a list, he told himself. *Grow up.*

Cam didn't realize until she was gone how many little everyday things Wren did that he depended on her to do to keep a household running. With the initial shock of her and Daniel's disappearance, he and Zoe had stopped functioning. He took a couple of days off work and she stayed home from school. They clung to one another and dove for the phone every time it rang.

Basically, they were waiting for a miracle.

But by the third sleep-deprived night and restless free-form day, the numbness began to wear off. The dreamlike quality of their living nightmare took on a sharpened focus at the edges, a hardened sense of reality. Cam and Zoe had to face the fact that this was not a situation which would resolve itself overnight.

That it might not resolve itself at all was a horror they were not yet ready to absorb, preferring to simply let that possibility lurk in the unexamined background for the time being.

"You've got to resume your normal life," Steve Austin had said during their last phone conversation. *"People will start to ask questions."*

But what was normal about this? How could they possibly keep up the charade? How was Cam supposed to work when he couldn't even decide which chips to buy, for Chrissake? His whole world had been set on its edge in a dizzy tailspin, upsetting his center of gravity; he couldn't hang on much longer.

Cam pressed the remote garage-door opener and wondered how on earth he had gotten home. He had no memory of driving. All he could think about anymore was Wren and Daniel and what was happening to them and Zoe and himself and what they were going to do. Driving was a secondary, habitual thing; it was a goddamned miracle he hadn't wrecked the car or killed somebody.

He found Zoe in the kitchen, concocting some sort of goulash in a frying pan with hamburger meat and onions and beans. It smelled surprisingly good, and Cam felt a guilty hunger. It shamed him to think of eating when he didn't know if Wren and Daniel were able to, but he always ate anyway. Starving himself would serve no real purpose. It wouldn't get them home any sooner.

"That smells good," he said with false cheeriness, planting a kiss on her upturned cheek. "Have we got any tortillas?" He opened the refrigerator door and dug around in the contents.

"I thought you were going to buy groceries," accused his daughter with a smile.

"I didn't know what we needed," he said truthfully.

"I'll make you a list, Daddy." She bustled about with a wooden spoon in one hand and a bottle of hot sauce in the other. "The tortillas are on the bottom shelf, but Daniel never closes the bag, so they're probably dried out by now."

Cam found the tortillas, half in and half out of the bag, as crusty as saucers. A wave of customary annoyance at Daniel surged through him, followed by a wake of grief. *I was always on his case*, he thought, *about stupid little things that don't matter.* He stared at the tortillas in his hand through blurry eyes.

"Mom says you can soften them up if you put a few drops of water on them, wrap them in paper towels, and put them in the microwave for a few seconds." Zoe removed the tortillas from his hand and set them down on the counter. "If you want to make burritos out of this, I can grate up some cheese." Pushing him gently out of the way, she rummaged around in the refrigerator. "Here's some. Oh! That butthead! I can't believe Daniel put this cheese in here without wrapping it up first. Now we can't use it."

In the next moment she was flinging the rock-hard cheese into the sink with a loud *clunk* and crying, "Why does he always have to ruin everything?" Then she ran from the kitchen, and Cam heard the door to her room slam shut.

With a heavy sigh Cam turned the stove off. It made sense to him that Zoe would blame her brother for their situation. After all, it was Daniel who had skipped out of the library, come home late, lied, provoked an argument, and stomped out with his mother in hot pursuit. So it was Daniel, to Zoe's twelve-year-old mind, who had gotten himself and their mother kidnapped. To her way of thinking, if they'd just all stayed cozy together in this house, they'd have been safe from Hunter.

She couldn't be expected to understand that there was no place safe from Hunter—not for Wren, anyway. And apparently not for Daniel, either.

He was going to have to talk to her. On his way to her room, he passed through the den, where piles of neatly folded laundry were lined up with military precision on the couch. The vacuum cleaner was standing in the hall, and the bathroom nearest Zoe's room gleamed. He knocked at her door, waited a moment, then entered, expecting to find it looking the way it usually did: like the site of a bomb explosion. Instead, he found everything in it compulsively organized—right down to the perfect positioning of her unicorn posters. She had even rearranged the books on the shelves into alphabetical order.

Zoe was sitting in the middle of the bed, her body folded up into a tight ball, arms wrapped around her knees, clutching her battered and beloved stuffed toy, Fluff Dawg, face turned toward the wall and hidden beneath a curtain of shining chestnut hair.

"The house looks really nice," he said awkwardly. When she didn't respond, he said, "It's okay for you to be angry about what happened. It's normal to feel mad at Daniel, even though it wasn't really his fault that he and Mom were taken away."

"She shouldn't have gone after him," Zoe muttered. "Then Hunter would have just taken Daniel and not her, too."

Cam sat on the edge of the bed. "I thought we talked about this," he said. "I thought you understood about the relationship between your mom and Hunter. You know he wants her to help him again for a while. He didn't really want Daniel, you know. He just didn't want Mom to try to escape from him. But it's okay. Mr. Austin is going to help us find them and bring them home. You'll see."

"But he hasn't found them yet," she said quietly, revealing the true reason behind her anxiety. "Why hasn't he found them yet?"

"Because . . ." Cam hesitated a moment, then said, "He's got to check out the whole country. It's going to take some time."

"But Daniel's going to miss too much school. He'll never catch up!"

"Don't worry about that. We'll help him get caught up." He stroked her hair.

In a barely audible voice she whispered, "I miss him. He always tells me who the geeks are so I won't make the wrong friends at school."

"I know. He loves you in his own funky way."

Suddenly, she sat up and pinned him to the wall with those blue eyes. "You need to go to the store and buy some Diet Pepsis. I want Mom to have plenty of Diet Pepsis when she gets home."

With that, she burst into tears and collapsed in his arms, the sobs wracking her with such strength that she almost lost her breath.

Helpless rage flooded through him, but there was no place to go with it. He had failed to protect his family, and now here he was, barely able to hold the remnants together. He never should have listened to Wren in the first place. He should have called out the goddamned National Guard, if that's what it took to defend them from this threat. He should never have let his family out of his sight.

Zoe's tears were subsiding somewhat. Her face puffy and miserable, she said, "I think I'd like to take a shower now."

"Good idea." He patted her wet cheek.

"Daddy?" Chewing on her bottom lip, she looked away. "Is that guy . . . going to kill them?"

"No, no! He needs them. He has plans for them. And don't be afraid for your mom. You don't know how tough she is. She's lived with these people before and she knows how to handle herself. She'll keep Daniel safe until Mr. Austin can find them."

He wasn't too sure about all of that, but it seemed to reassure his shaky little girl somewhat. Leaving her to prepare for her bath, he wandered into Daniel's room and closed the door quietly behind himself. Colorful comic book hero posters lined the walls, their impossible muscles bulging from bizarre costumes, their faces looming fierce over the room. A shelf in one corner held his old Ninja Turtle action figures collection; notebooks stuffed with comic book trading cards lay scattered over the desk and dresser. Clothes and chaotic plastic CD covers littered every available surface. Cam picked up a psychedelic T-shirt in neon colors that shouted the superiority of some obnoxious heavy metal band. It still smelled of Daniel.

His knees weakened and he sat down hard on the edge of the rumpled bed, the T-shirt still bundled in his arms. A mysterious lump under the covers drew his attention and he groped around, finally closing his fingers over something fluffy. With growing disbelief Cam withdrew Daniel's battered old stuffed bear, its head and arms hanging by threads.

Cam had given him that bear when he was two years old; they'd been inseparable for years after that when he was little. Cam hadn't even known Daniel still had the bear, and he'd have never dreamed that the boy had secreted his old friend away under the covers.

Why, he's still just a big kid, he thought. *Hell, I was treating him like a man because he was bigger than me.*

Some father.

He couldn't stand his own thoughts. Springing up from the bed, Cam hurried from the room and into the kitchen, where he finished cooking whatever Zoe had started and made himself a couple of cheeseless burritos out of it. The phone rang and, as usual, he had it answered before the second ring.

"How are you doing, Cam?"

"Not too well, Mr. Austin," he answered truthfully, "but we're coping. We made it through one more day, and that's about all I can handle at a time."

Zoe materialized at his elbow, hair still dripping from her shower, her face questioning. He mouthed *Austin* at her, but when he had nothing new to relate to her after a moment, she made herself a small plate of supper and carried it into the den to eat in front of the TV.

"Have you spoken to the school officials yet? I mean, with any kind of fallback plan for an extended absence for Daniel and Wren?"

"Not yet."

"Cam. You've got to take care of this."

"I know." He was embarrassed. It was a silly thing, really, putting off the inevitable in some wild superstitious hope that the impossible would occur.

"Have you at least decided what you're going to tell them?"

"I think so. I mean, I'm going to tell them that we're having marital problems, brought about mostly by the constant tension over Daniel, and that Wren has taken him out of state to attend a special school for emotionally troubled kids."

"Good. That sounds good. And what about Wren's absence? They can't keep calling in substitute teachers to cover for her."

"I'm going to tell her principal that she's going to stay with Daniel for the first month or so, to see how the new school is working out and to give us some . . . space, I guess."

"Not you guess. You have to be firm here. No indecision."

"Okay. Right. I'll see if they can put her on a leave of absence and hire a substitute to take over her duties until she's able to get back."

"What about Zoe?"

"What about her?"

"They'll wonder why Zoe didn't leave with her mother, won't they?"

"Oh." Cam felt a little flurry of panic, then said, "I'll say that Wren didn't want to disrupt Zoe's life any more than was absolutely necessary, and so she left her here with me until we decide what to do about . . . everything."

"Excellent. Tell you what. Let's say the school is in Dallas. I'll have an associate call and request that Daniel's records be sent to our post office box here. That will add a certain legitimacy to your story."

Cam said, "What if they say they grew up in Dallas or something and they never heard of this school?"

"Tell 'em it's new. Experimental. A change of scenery for Daniel, at any rate."

"All right." Cam felt a surprising sense of relief. Once they got this unpleasant detail out of the way, he and Zoe could concentrate on, well, surviving. "Mr. Austin—I'd like to get my daughter some counseling to help her deal with all this."

There was a pause. "I can understand your desire to do so, Cam, but I'd have to advise against it for the time being. The story sounds far-fetched at this juncture. Either a counselor would fear that the child was making this whole thing up—in which case she *would* be disturbed—or even worse, they could fear that you'd chopped up your wife and your son and buried them in the backyard or something."

"What?"

"I'm just saying that without appropriate media attention, your story about the kidnapping could never hold up to scrutiny. A counselor could cause all kinds of problems for us."

"What if I went with her? Explained things?"

"It wouldn't help. And even if you did manage to convince a therapist, there would still be that strong temptation to alert law enforcement in a misguided attempt to help."

"But I thought patient–doctor stuff was confidential."

"People are human, Cam. I really think that, under the circumstances, it would be best if you handled this situation on your own. For the time being, anyway."

Lowering his voice and turning his body away from the den, Cam said, "I don't know what to say to her. This is terrible for her."

"I know. And I'm sorry. But if you just listen to her whenever she wants to talk, and love her, and give her plenty of support, she'll probably turn out to be tougher than you think."

Cam heard footsteps behind him and was surprised by a tight, one-armed hug from his daughter, who'd brought her still half-full dinner plate back to the kitchen. Transferring the phone to his other hand, he wrapped an arm around her and hugged back. "She's a pretty tough kid," he said aloud. Zoe smiled up at him and returned to the den.

He didn't say what he was really thinking: that without Wren, he was merely shadow-boxing at life, that more of his strength came from her than he had ever imagined, that he needed her with a ferocity that took his breath away, that he could not imagine himself managing all this without her, that he was ill with worry over her and missing her, that it was *he*, Cam, who wasn't very tough at all.

CHAPTER 12

F OR twenty-four almost unendurable hours, Daniel did not speak to Wren. Again and again she tried to explain to him why she hadn't told him everything in the first place, but he would only pull his sleeping bag up over his ears and ignore her. At other times she would try to justify her participation in the bank robbery Hunter had referred to, but he would only set his shoulders and mumble, "Uh-huh."

She wanted to scream.

At some point in the windy, well-black depths of night, it occurred to Wren that her son still did not know the whole story, that if she could just make him understand, it would repair the terrible gaping hole Hunter had made in the tapestry of their relationship. As it was, Daniel was seeing things from the underside, like a garbled mass of threads and knots; if she could only show him the picture those threads wove, it would restore his trust in her.

The decision helped her sleep a little.

But as the nocturnal gloom of their cell faded to the gunmetal gray of dawn, Wren found herself strangely reluctant to reveal to Daniel the complete solution to all the mysteries of her past. She wasn't sure why. Maybe it was the unfamiliar profile he presented in his desert cammies and buzzcut. Maybe it was the stubborn set of his jaw. Or his relentless silence. Or maybe it was her sudden certainty that there was nothing more she could say to her son that would make any difference in his attitude toward her; from now on, he would judge her strictly according to her actions.

After all, hadn't his parents said the same thing to him, once he'd damaged his credibility to them by lying? In one particularly dramatic confrontation with Daniel, Cam had dashed his empty coffee cup to the kitchen floor, shattering it. *You've smashed our trust in you*, Cam had said, *as surely as this coffee cup. Even if you glued it back together, it would still be cracked. If you want us to believe in you again, you've got to prove yourself to us by what you do, not what you say.*

They ate their breakfast without speaking.

When they had finished, Hunter, once again shadowed by Kicker, paid them a visit. "Let's go take a look around," he said. "I want to show you the base camp." He stood back to allow them to walk out. Kicker, waiting outside the door, stepped back, hitching up his shoulder sling and cradling his shotgun.

This time Wren gave Kicker's weapon more than just the cursory glance she'd given it while anxiously following Daniel to the showers. It looked like a Mossberg 500—probably chambered with double-aught bucks—and had one of those mean pistol grip pumps which had been banned by Congress. He had probably taken out the so-called "hunter's plug," which limited it to holding only three shells, so that it could hold up to eight, which was also illegal. A person couldn't run fast enough to keep from getting shredded by that gun, and Wren figured this particular shooter would take great pleasure in the shredding. She glanced up and met his eyes just in time to catch a fleeting grin fading from his face.

Sadistic bastard.

"Let's go." With a courtly gesture Hunter indicated that they head toward the largest of the buildings in the compound, which was directly across from the tiny building which had become home to Wren and Daniel. Glancing around at the lonesome landscape while the dusty wind whipped her long hair across her face, Wren noticed that there were no large crowds of people outside the buildings, either. They tended to move separately or in small clots. She saw no Blacks, Hispanics, or Asians.

They passed a pavilion of sorts, constructed of a wire-mesh roof covered with camouflage netting and suspended on poles and open on all four sides. Beneath the pavilion a group of about twenty physically fit men and women were doing calisthenics, led by the guy she remembered as Smithy. There were only five or six women, but everyone wore desert cammies and had hair either cut short or pulled back in neat braids and ponytails. As they passed the pavilion, Wren studied Smithy. Like Hunter and Kicker, he wore his cammies rolled up tight around muscled arms.

On one arm, just above the roll of the sleeve, Wren spotted a black armband. Nobody else seemed to be wearing one. Surreptitiously, she glanced through her veil of windblown hair at Hunter and Kicker. They, too, wore black armbands. Up close, she spotted the design of a gold lightning bolt on the armbands.

So the guys who kidnapped Daniel and me must be part of some elite inner circle, she surmised, *like a police SWAT team or the Navy SEALS or Army Rangers.*

She wondered what you had to do to make that inner circle.

They reached a cinder-block building that was the size of a cafeteria in a large high school. Hunter, who always did have the manners of a gentleman, held open the door for Wren and Daniel, while Kicker, the shotgun resting casually in the crook of his arm like a harmless toy, followed.

"This is our meeting room and mess hall," said Hunter.

Wren and Daniel stumbled to a halt at the same time, mesmerized by the beautiful and ferocious mural which covered the back wall: An armor-clad skeleton, empty eye sockets glaring starkly from the skull, sat astride a raging, ash-gray stallion, its nostrils flaring bloodred, eyes full of fury and muscles rippling with virile power. In one bony fist the warrior clutched a flying guidon, black, upon which were emblazoned the Greek symbols for Alpha and Omega in crimson, separated by a gold lightning bolt. In the rider's other hand, upraised like a triumphant sword, flashed another lightning bolt.

Beneath the image, with flawless calligraphy, the artist had rendered the following message in black: BEHOLD A PALE HORSE, AND HE WHO SAT ON IT HAD THE NAME "DEATH."

Wren stifled a shiver. Something about the painting was profoundly disturbing to her. There had been nothing like this at the Community. The symbolism was so . . . *warlike.*

"Isn't it magnificent?" said Hunter. "One of the girls painted it. I liked it so much, I had a tattoo of it made." He rolled up the sleeve on his right arm as high above the elbow as he could and displayed the tattoo to an astonished, and obviously impressed, Daniel.

Shyly tapping Hunter's arm on the tattoo of the guidon, Daniel said, "What does this mean?"

"Alpha and Omega," said Hunter. "The first and the last. Who is and who was and who is to come." He grinned at Daniel's puzzled expression. "It's the symbol for the Armageddon Army's Alpha/Omega Strike Force." Rolling down his sleeve just a bit, he indicated the black armband. "Best of the best; better than all the rest—isn't that right, Kicker?"

Kicker grunted assent.

Forgetting for the time being that he was a hostage to this man, Daniel said, "What does the Strike Force do?" His face, freed of its hairy hiding curtain, was animated.

Hunter, quirking one eyebrow and cutting a glance in Wren's direction, said, "Special missions."

Like kidnapping, you son of a bitch, she thought.

Something was wrong here. Way wrong. There had been no "Strike Force" at the Community, and nothing comparable to it. Although they'd all been given paramilitary training, the gentle people she remembered from those days seemed more like a hippie commune than hardened soldiers.

This so-called Armageddon Army, and in particular the Strike Force, seemed to Wren to be much more aggressive. During the long drive after their capture and the days of their imprisonment, Wren had yet to see a spark of warmth and kindness in anyone's eyes, with the exception of Hunter himself, and she didn't trust it.

She gazed uneasily at him as he flexed his biceps for her son, causing a slight rippling motion in the tattooed guidon and provoking a laugh from the boy, who was clearly fascinated with the strange and beautiful.

Uk'ten, she thought. That mythical dragon-sized rattlesnake of Cherokee legend, the splendid Uk'ten, so hypnotic in all his glory, could strike his admirers with lightning speed. It was said that even to follow in the footsteps of Uk'ten would lead to death.

In an attempt to distract Hunter from Daniel, she feigned interest and asked, "How many Strike Force members are there?"

"Seven." He looked up at her. "Including myself." Rolling the sleeve of his fatigues back down to his elbow, Hunter indicated the door. "Let's go down to the range," he said.

Wren and Daniel, with the ever present Kicker bringing up the rear, followed Hunter along a barely discernible trail through scratchy catclaw bushes, spiky yucca, and dried-out prickly pear cactus. The trail slanted downward, and they had to watch their steps on the rocky, crunchy soil. Occasionally, Wren would glance around the surrounding hills, trying to spot any sort of characteristic that would distinguish one of them as a landmark, but they all looked the same to her.

A *person could get lost out here*, she thought, *and never turn up save for the buzzards*.

As the gun range came into view, the loud *crackle-pop* caught in Wren's throat like the bad memory it provoked. Once a crack marksman, she had not picked up a gun since the FBI raid on the Community, although she had a secret habit of drifting through gunshops now and then, keeping an eye on the newest makes and models. Since most gunshop employees tended to ignore, overlook, or patronize its female customers, she was seldom approached or hassled.

She never told Cam about those ventures into the world of firearms. It was a guilty secret, like drinking alone. Probing too deeply into the whys of it would only reveal certain aspects of her nature that were perhaps best left unexamined.

Like why she'd chosen to go back to school after Daniel was born and major in chemistry as opposed to, say, elementary education or some such thing. She'd told herself at the time that her earlier experience of studying the various chemical compounds used in explosives had rendered the subject easy for her. That's what she'd told herself, anyway. The fact that explosives still fascinated her was not something she liked to think about.

Then there were the underground press publications she followed, not to mention certain bulletin boards she liked to browse on the Internet. They featured the latest developments in explosives, among other things. If Cam had wondered about her subscriptions to such information, he never said anything. It was as if her husband thought that if he ignored such things, they would go away.

But they hadn't gone away. Jeremiah Hunter had seen to that.

This gun range was set up much like the one she remembered from the Community. The smell of gunpowder assaulted Wren's senses. It made her want to run. It made her want to get her hands on one of those guns and fire until the target was obliterated.

The open-sided corrugated tin shelter, covered as usual with camouflage netting, faced simple plywood man-sized targets, rectangular in shape, with smaller head-sized rectangles on top. Distances were not marked off, nor were scoring points designated on the targets. Learning to shoot here was not about winning contests in marksmanship. It was about killing.

A half dozen men and one woman practiced firing a dazzling array of weapons, from semiautomatic shotguns to the Colt .45 pistols favored by the army to various 9mm handguns, as well as a number of automatic weapons she recognized such as the Heckler and Koch MP5 and the standard AK47s and M16s. A few of the individuals who were practicing at the stationary targets glanced over with distracted curiosity, then went back to their firing. A big muscle-bound man Wren had not seen before, his shaved head glistening with sweat above glittering mirrored sunglasses, supervised. He, too, wore a black armband.

"We teach an enhanced form of the Weaver stance here," shouted Hunter over the incessant gunfire. From a gun-loaded table, he selected a TEC22T pistol with a Ram-Line 50-round extended magazine—all part of the banned list—and handed the assault pistol to Daniel.

He looked immediately toward his mother, his face all but screaming, *What do I do?*

"It's okay," said Hunter, his voice ringing over the surrounding gunfire. "You've got to learn sooner or later. Here, hold it like this."

Wren, trapped beneath Kicker's watchful eye and a dozen assorted loaded firearms, could say nothing. She felt her heart crack open and silently screamed, *Leave my son alone! Don't do this, please.* She beseeched Hunter with her eyes, but he ignored her.

"It's heavy," said Daniel as the gun barrel dipped toward the ground.

"Wait, wait, wait."

They all looked up as the big man with the shaved head approached. "Hunter, man, you lost your mind? Can't you tell this baby hasn't ever held a gun in his hand before?"

Hunter looked at Daniel. "That true, kid?"

Daniel glanced at his mom.

Hunter said, "Didn't your daddy ever take you hunting?"

Daniel, glancing toward the ground, mumbled, "No, sir."

Kicker shook his head. "What's his problem?" he rumbled. "He one of those gun grabbers or somethin'?"

Hunter shrugged. "Aw, he's a wuss accountant or some such thing."

Wren's cheeks burned. *You'd be thrilled to have my husband defend your ass in a court of law,* she thought. *Too bad he's got too much integrity to even consider it.*

"Besides, this so-called weapon is a piece of shit, Hunter. The only reason you keep it around is because it looks mean, but it's worthless. I'd as soon have a TEC9—also useless—as this."

Hunter grinned. "Now, John, there's no need in taking somebody's taste in weaponry as a personal insult." He took the weapon from Daniel and handed him one of the army-issue Colt .45s, this one outfitted with a laser sight.

The man shook his head. "Hellfire, man, let's start him out on something that doesn't scare him half to death." He took the pistol from Daniel.

Hunter held his hands up. "You're the expert." To Daniel he said, "Dan, this here is Big John. Best firearms instructor and gunsmith I know." He stepped out of the way.

Big John sorted through the weapons on the table and selected a Smith & Wesson .38. "This one's loaded with wad cutters," he said. "It won't have as much kick as it would with hollow points."

Hunter rolled his eyes. "It's a cap gun, for God's sake. Absolutely no knockdown power."

Big John ignored him. "He's gotta start small. We'll work him up to the mean guns. But don't you be givin' him that cannon you carry to shoot. Not yet. The recoil alone would knock his skinny ass to the ground."

Kicker chuckled.

"It's a stainless steel Desert Eagle, chambered for the .50-magnum cartridge," stage-whispered Hunter to Wren. "I've got a spare fourteen-inch barrel mounted with a scope for it that'll take down a bear," he added. "If I take it out and show it to you, it'll only scare you."

The men giggled.

Wren stopped herself just short of rolling her eyes. This was so typical of Jeremiah Hunter. The bigger the gun, the more impressed he was with it. The truth was that a .50-caliber cartridge, while formidable in a sniper rifle, was hardly worth using for close-range self-defense. Not to mention how heavy it was to carry. *But if I see a bear,* she thought sarcastically, *I'll be sure to call on you, asshole.*

Big John placed the .38 in Daniel's hand. Daniel gave an uncertain nod.

"Oh, for God's sake, John, I can show him how to shoot that pea-shooter."

Big John stepped back. "Be my guest."

"You right-handed or left?" Hunter asked.

"Uh . . . right."

"Good. It's easier for me to teach right-handers. Okay, stand with your feet about shoulder width apart. That's good. Now, step back with your right foot—not that far back, Dan. You want to be comfortable, like this, see?"

Wren watched in much the same manner one might observe a car wreck. On the one hand, she was grateful to Big John for intervening—the .38 revolver was much smaller and more lightweight. It would fit his hand more comfortably than the TEC22T and have much less recoil than the .45. It would also help him acquire the necessary confidence a beginner sorely needed.

On the other hand, she did not want Daniel down here at the gun range like one of the guys. That's where it all started.

At least, that's where it had started with her.

"Now. Keep your body aligned over your feet. Good. Face the target. No, the target, not the gun. Okay, now bend slightly forward from the waist. You a jock?"

"Not really."

Hunter chuckled. "Good. You watch a lot of movies?"

Daniel gave a nervous shrug. "I guess."

"Well, a lot of actors do it wrong in the movies. Bring your left hand up, but keep that elbow bent, see. It's only the right arm that locks at the elbow." He positioned himself behind Daniel, taking gentle hold of the boy's shoulders, just as he had done to Wren so many years ago. She could still remember the thrill it had given her, and from one glance at Daniel's face, she could see that same controlled excitement.

"Now, bring the right arm around to meet the left, but keep the left arm at a comfortable angle to your body."

Daniel complied, with assistance from his friendly instructor.

"Put your hands like this around the pistol grip—loosen up, son! This is just a practice." He laughed at the furiously blushing boy. "Lay the fingers of your left hand in the grooves of the fingers of your right hand. No, like this." He pried the gun from Daniel's hand and showed him, then handed it back. Daniel complied perfectly. "Good! You're doing great. Now, the trick is to bring the gun up to eye level. See the sight right here? Okay, align your eyes with it. You can close one eye if it helps. Wait now—you're about to clutch that trigger like it's a girl's tit. I told you, you been watching too many movies. Just use the tip of your trigger finger, not the whole knuckle. That's right. Now, aim for the body mass. When I give the signal, squeeze the trigger slowly—don't jerk on it, okay?"

Turning away from Daniel, Hunter fished around on the table for a pair of ear protectors, which he placed on the boy's head himself. Wren stared with a sort of macabre fascination. The revolver quivered in the boy's trembling hands.

Hunter motioned to Daniel, and the gun fired, its barrel swinging upward. Wren's entire body jerked.

Involuntarily, she glanced at the plywood target. There was a hole in the upper right-hand corner.

"Not bad!" cried Hunter. "A little more practice, you'll be an expert."

Daniel's whole face grinned.

Wren's stomach squeezed in on itself, forcing bile up into her throat. She gave a mighty swallow and struggled not to throw up.

"Lissie, next time it'll be your turn," said Hunter as he replaced the revolver on the table along with the ear protectors. "You could probably handle our advanced course," he added, referring, she suspected, to their running course, night course, and pop-up targets. He was smiling at her. She wanted to rip his eyes out.

As they trudged back up the incline toward the base camp, Daniel asked Hunter where they stored all those weapons. Grinning over his shoulder at Wren, he said, "Secret hiding places, Dan."

In other words, buried underground. There was no telling the size of the arsenal he had amassed during his months with the so-called Armageddon Army. Or what he intended to do with it.

Along the winding trail, while the wind tangled her hair, catclaw barbs, cactus spikes, and mesquite thorns caught at Wren's clothes and scratched her boots. She felt grudgingly grateful for the fatigues and furious that she had to feel that way. Hunter's manipulation of them was already well underway, and there was absolutely nothing she could do about it. As the trail leveled out, Hunter asked Daniel if the boy would care for a soda, and the delight on her son's face frustrated Wren even more.

Homesickness overwhelmed her.

They entered the mess hall, and Hunter indicated that they should sit at one of the cafeteria tables. Kicker pulled a folding chair out from the table, turned it backward, and straddled it, the shotgun resting in his lap.

"What's your poison, Dan?" called Hunter from the kitchen. Daniel asked for a Coke. Hunter brought the Coke and handed Wren a Diet Pepsi. She glanced up in surprise and he winked at her as if to say, *Hey, I know everything there is to know about you.*

She did not return his smile.

"I guess you're wondering what all this is about," Hunter said to Daniel as if Wren already knew. He took a seat across the table from Daniel, his body uncomfortably close to Wren's.

"I know you want my mom for something," said Daniel, staring at his Coke can as if he were afraid to look his captor in the eye.

"I want your mom for a lot of things."

The intimate tone in his voice brought a flush to Wren's cheeks and a quick glance from her son. There was nothing she could say. He looked away.

"I *need* your mom, Dan, to fight with me in the war against the Gestapo government traitors who would goose-step all over my rights—and your rights, as guaranteed by the United States Constitution—to carry firearms for protection against the predators who would betray my birthright, come into my home, take away my weapons, and enslave me. We have the right, guaranteed by the Second Amendment to the Constitution, to form a militia, because our founding forefathers realized that an armed citizenry is the best deterrent to totalitarianism." He smiled at the boy. "Do you understand what I'm saying, son?"

Daniel shrugged. "Not really."

"Okay. Let me put it this way. The lying, thieving, scumbag politicians are in the process, as I speak, of selling out our rights to those Nazis in ninja costumes who would break down our doors under the guise of the federal government, seize our property, and murder our women and children." He leaned forward. "They spy on us, you know. All the time."

Doubt flickered in Daniel's eyes.

"Why do you think we have to camouflage our buildings?" He waited.

Finally, Daniel said, "I don't know."

Pointing a forefinger ominously upward, Hunter stage-whispered, "Satellites."

Wren turned her face and rolled her eyes.

"That combined FBI–ATF raid on the Community I've been talking about? They murdered children there, you know. Shot them down in cold blood."

Daniel turned a horrified gaze in his mother's direction, as if expecting her to refute what Hunter had said. She didn't dare. She tried to communicate her helplessness to him with her eyes, but, like most teenage boys, he was oblivious to subtleties. He shook his head in disgust.

"The fat fags of our charlatan government, backed by their Gestapo, the FBI and the ATF, are already passing laws in this United Social States of America that steal our freedoms from us, little by little, weapon by weapon. And they've got their puppet mouthpieces, don't think they don't. Like that asshole, Buckwheat Peckerhead."

For a moment Wren was stumped, then she thought, *Oh Lord, he must be talking about Buck Leatherwood.*

"And when they've finally torn this country apart, with the help of Lucifer Leatherwood and his filthy money, they will use the National Guard against us—don't think they won't—and when that time comes, you better believe there will be holy warriors armed and ready for battle, freedom fighters and patriots like the Armageddon Army who aren't afraid of ninja suits, and *you*, my son"—he pointed a dramatic finger at the spellbound boy—"will be damned glad on that day that you're on the right side."

"*Amen, brother*," cried Kicker.

But Wren hardly noticed. She was staring in horror at the rapt face of her son as he watched Hunter evangelize. She'd seen that look before, many times, on the faces of others who'd been caught in the filmy web of his rhetoric.

But they were dead now. All dead.

CHAPTER 13

A s the sleek black limousine maneuvered its smooth path through bumper-to-bumper Dallas traffic, Steve Austin secured his earpiece and spoke into the radio. "Number Two, your delivery should arrive any minute now."

"Good. We're looking forward to receiving it, Number One."

Although, as owner of Guaranteed Security, it was not essential for Austin to provide hands-on security to his high-profile clients himself, he liked to do on-site work occasionally in order to keep his staff on its toes, reassure the client, and make sure that too much desk work didn't rob him of his edge. He'd seen it happen, plenty of times before, when he worked for the Bureau. A crackerjack street agent would leave the bricks to get on the management track, and after a few years of supervising investigations from behind a desk, would wind up virtually helpless out on the street.

Austin had preferred to remain "just an agent," passing up lucrative management-track transfers in order to work cases. As a result, he had built up an extensive network of informants, made valuable contacts in every branch of law enforcement, learned to think like a cop, put lots of bad guys away, and retired with a whole hell of a lot less money.

Now he was making more dough than he'd ever imagined while in the Bureau, and was working too damn much to spend it. His wife was disappointed, but he couldn't give it up. He loved it too much. He'd make it up to her. Someday.

The limo pulled up to the curb and Austin sprang out, his eyes automatically searching the buildings opposite for any open windows high above which could provide a prop for an assassin's rifle. His team should have already secured that building, but he wouldn't be much of a supervisor if he didn't double-check.

Scanning the sidewalk to make sure no one was approaching, and glancing at the front door to ascertain if Number Two was standing there waiting, Austin swung open the back passenger door closest to the curb and stood opposite the open car door, positioning himself as a shield as Buck Leatherwood unfolded his wiry body from the backseat and headed into the building. As they entered the lobby, Austin nodded at Number Three, who was standing patiently by the elevator, making sure no one used it.

"Mr. Leatherwood!" cried a petite, sharp-faced black woman who was approaching them with her right hand extended. Elegantly dressed and attractive, she glanced at Austin, then took Leatherwood's hand. "I'm Sabrina Cross, the producer for *Dallas Unplugged*. We are so honored to have you on our show."

Austin had met Cross before, and had run a check on her. She was clean.

"Thank you, Miz Cross," drawled Leatherwood. "It was nice of you to invite me." He stepped genially through a metal detector frame. Austin displayed his gun and private security ID for the bored rent-a-cop standing by and followed his client at a discreet pace behind.

"Makeup is just down the hall here," Cross said warmly, linking her arm through Leatherwood's. Austin glanced into each open doorway as they passed. This particular studio had pretty good private security of its own, a company he had worked with in the past, but he remained vigilant all the same. His wife claimed he never relaxed, not even in his sleep.

When Leatherwood had been properly pancaked, and his cowboy hat carefully replaced on his head, Austin and the little producer escorted him into the studio, where they stepped over jungle vines of cables to a simple set consisting of two chairs adjacent to a small round table which held a pitcher of water and two glasses. Behind the chairs hung a heavy blue drape. Austin peeked behind the drape and waved at Number Four, who lifted his hand in return.

Then, while Cross briefed Leatherwood about the upcoming show's format, Austin turned and glanced out over about a hundred empty seats, arranged in slightly elevated rows behind the cameras. Each member of the studio audience and stage crew would be hand-checked for weapons by his staff, but it didn't help Austin's nerves. The more people present in a room with his controversial client, the less control he had.

Austin's biggest fear was explosives. Naturally they'd already brought the dogs in for a routine bomb check, but against explosives—that favorite weapon of the terrorist—there was no real protection. He often had a recurring nightmare about what he called "Murphy's Security Check," in which everything that could go wrong, did. Key people turned up missing, the dogs weren't available, the client refused to cooperate—and then, as soon as the key lights were struck for his client's speech or talk show appearance or banquet presentation or whatever—Austin would spot the explosive device just as it was about to detonate. He'd wake up in a cold sweat every time.

Leatherwood was graciously deposited in the green room by the very efficient Ms. Cross, and Austin waited with him, standing by the closed door.

"Wonder why they call these places green rooms?" pondered Leatherwood. "I never been in one yet that was green." He looked around the small, impersonal room containing a vinyl couch, a television set, and a table with a coffee pot and a box of doughnuts. He began to pace.

Austin knew that Leatherwood, contrary to his relaxed persona on-screen, was actually nervous every time he had to make a television appearance. He thought of himself, first and foremost, as a businessman, not a media darling. And he never forgot—not for a moment—his reason for appearing on the program in the first place.

"They're talkin' on the Hill about repealing the assault weapons ban. Again." He glanced in Austin's direction. "The gun folks say they like to use them for hunting. Now, what kind of animal could people possibly be interested in hunting with a weapon capable of shooting bullets at speeds in excess of two thousand feet per second and discharging up to fifty bullets in a spurt?"

Austin shrugged. "Humans."

Leatherwood tugged at the knot on his necktie. It was handsome navy silk with silver stripes, and blended beautifully with his pearl-gray suede Western-cut suit jacket. He shook his head. "When they get me, that's probably what they'll get me with."

"They're not going to get you. Not if we have anything to say about it." Austin crinkled his brow. Leatherwood was showing signs of fatigue. It wasn't like him to be so fatalistic.

"The hate mail's still comin' in, isn't it?"

"Some," Austin hedged. If Buck Leatherwood ever saw some of the demented ramblings and vicious threats—some of them embroidered with scriptural references—that arrived in his mail every day, he'd never sleep again. "Don't worry about it." He waved a hand dismissively.

"I guess that's your job, right?" Leatherwood jingled the change in his pocket.

"Right"

As he reached the closed door where Austin was standing, Leatherwood pivoted and paced back across the room. "You know I'm doing the *Doug Richards Show* in a couple of weeks."

"I know." Doug Richards was a world-famous American journalist who conducted a popular late-night current events interview program.

"They've asked that prick Paul Smith to do it with me."

Austin grimaced. Richards did like to go for the oil and water. Paul Smith was the fresh-faced, thirty-something president of the well-known Christian fundamentalist political group, USA, or United for a Stronger America. The organization had gained great power in recent years by raising millions of dollars from various church groups and other right-wing organizations to defeat various "targeted"—meaning liberal—congressmen, senators, and governors. USA had publicly taken a great deal of credit for the Republican landslide midterm elections of 1994.

Their stand on gun control was well known: they were vehemently opposed to it.

It would make a lively debate, all right. It would also double Leatherwood's hate mail and death threats.

"I wouldn't mind the little twerp so much if he weren't so god-damned sanctimonious," complained Leatherwood. "He acts as though, if you don't agree with his point of view on a given subject, then you're going straight to hell."

"Maybe that's why so many folks have joined his organization," said Austin with a quiet smile. "They just want to cover their bases."

Leatherwood came to a stop in front of the little table and stared pensively down at the coffeepot. "I hear he's got a little girl of his own," he said, his voice roughening. "I wonder how he'd feel about the subject if he found himself standing in the morgue one day, looking down at her bullet-riddled body."

Austin, thinking of his own two daughters, said nothing.

Through his earpiece, Austin's man who was posted just outside the door warned him that Sabrina Cross was about to enter the room. The door swung open. Her smiling face appeared in the doorway. "Do you need anything, Mr. Leatherwood?"

In an instant his brooding features had stretched into his trade-mark grin. "Call me Buck."

She smiled back. "Okay . . . Buck. I'm sorry our host is running late today. He'll be in very soon to meet you and chat with you a little before you go on the air."

Austin's phone rang. With an apologetic glance in his client's direction, he pulled the cellular device from his jacket pocket and pressed the button. "Yes?" He turned away slightly.

"Steve. Mike Martinez here. I know you're busy but this couldn't wait."

The producer was still talking to Leatherwood, who had inclined his head toward her in that charming way of his that never failed to work on women. Taking a step back for a little more privacy, Austin said, "Go ahead."

"I think we got a lead on where Jeremiah Hunter's holed up." Austin spun toward the door as though their quarry were in the next room. Cross and Leatherwood stopped talking and stared at him. "It's okay," he assured them, trying in vain to settle the surge of adrenaline that was tingling throughout his body. Like his client before him, he began to pace.

"And hang onto your hat, buddy," said Martinez. "It's a biggie."

Leatherwood was watching him. Austin stopped pacing, covered the mouthpiece, and said, "It's about another case. Nothing to worry about." Leatherwood gave him an uncertain nod and returned his attention to Sabrina Cross, who was in the process of introducing the show's host, who had just entered the room—Wade Garrett, a past-his-prime pretty boy pseudo-journalist who was lucky to have a local talk show, because his chances of attracting New York's attention were long gone.

The babble of voices was making Austin crazy. "Speak up, beaner boy," he muttered.

"Glad to, Sambo."

Austin grinned in spite of himself.

"Okay. We got a call from this sheriff's deputy we've worked with before. Seems the deputy hauled in a guy on a parole violation, and he claimed to be working as an informant for us."

"Was he?"

"Not at the time, no. But we'd used him in the past, so when the deputy called our office, we took it as a signal that he had something for us. Couple of our guys went down to talk to him, and we hit pay dirt, man."

Wade Garrett was laughing. It was a phony laugh, and the sound got on Austin's nerves. He scowled.

"Seems this guy knew Hunter in the joint, down in Huntsville. Hunter was recruiting short-time cons to join him at a new survivalist camp he was going to form when he got paroled. Our guy said what the hell and joined up."

"Same as the last one?"

"Not exactly, and this is the good part. Our guy says the place is state-of-the-art. Weapons, facilities—everything top-notch."

"Gun running?"

"Maybe. Drugs, possibly, though they're not allowed to use them at the camp. Only beer and cigarettes."

"He's a regular Boy Scout, isn't he?"

"Yeah. But there have been a rash of bank robberies in Texas and New Mexico that are still unsolved."

"But your guy didn't know for sure?"

"Not yet. We're keeping him on the inside for now. We're gonna see what he can find out."

Austin thought rapidly. "How often do you make contact?"

"Once a week. He makes a supply run into town."

"I need to talk to him."

Martinez hesitated. "I don't need to tell you how risky that is. You know how paranoid these people are. If they even suspect he's a snitch, they'll kill him. You know that."

"They won't suspect."

"You sure?"

"My middle name is—"

"I know, I know. Guaranteed."

"Mike, I've got to talk to the guy as soon as possible. It's a matter of extreme urgency." Sabrina Cross caught Austin's eye and tapped on her watch. "Look, I gotta go. How soon can you set this up?" He nodded at her.

"A week from Friday, I guess." Martinez's reluctance oozed from the phone. Austin well understood the feeling. They had a hot lead on a delicate operation, and here he came, ambling into things, messing stuff up.

"I won't blow it for you," he said.

"Hope not," said Martinez. "We've already paid the guy ten thousand."

"*What?*" Austin knew as well as Martinez that the federal budget for informants was virtually limitless, but this seemed extreme, even to a former fed.

"We want Hunter bad."

As his client prepared to leave the room with the talk show host and the show's producer, Austin said, "Not half as bad as I want him, old friend, and that's a fact."

They agreed to arrange the details later. As Austin followed Leatherwood into the studio, he struggled to keep his attention on the job at hand. It was a Herculean task, because all he really wanted to do was race for the airport and catch a plane for the boonies.

No. That wasn't right. All he *really* wanted to do was get his hands on Jeremiah Hunter, so that he could personally tear the man from limb to limb.

Then all he *really* wanted to do was call up Harry Cameron and say, "We've got 'em, buddy, and they're coming home."

But instead, he positioned himself behind and to the side of Buck Leatherwood, facing the audience just out of range of the television cameras, and prepared to wait.

CHAPTER 14

"**H**E'S not what you think he is, Daniel."

It was late, and Daniel was tired, and he was trying to go to sleep in that crappy sleeping bag on that shitty hard floor, and the last person he wanted to talk to was *her*. He turned away from her and said nothing.

"You're beginning to think he's kind of cool, aren't you?" his mom coaxed. "I mean, I know that what happened out on the gun range today was exciting and all, but it's not what you think. You've got to remember that, son. *Nothing is what you think it is.*"

"How come Dad never took me hunting?" he blurted in spite of himself. "All dads take their sons hunting."

"That's not true, Daniel."

"In Texas it is."

She was quiet a moment. "Your daddy doesn't like guns," she said, and added, "Neither do I."

"But Hunter said you used to be a good shot."

"Used to be. Not anymore."

"I don't see what's so wrong with just firing at a stupid target. It's not like we're killing anybody or anything."

"But you might have to . . . someday," she said.

He snorted loudly. "Aw, *Mom*! You are so paranoid! It's just ridiculous. All we were doing is a little target practice. It's no big deal." His voice reflected his scorn. She was getting to be so lame.

He punched his sleeping bag. Hunter said they might be getting out in a few days, might get to join the others. Maybe then he'd get to sleep in a real bed and eat off a table instead of on the floor. And maybe then he'd get to get away from *her*.

Ever since Hunter had told him the truth about his mother, Daniel had lost all respect for her. To think she had lied to him all of his whole entire life. Who knew what else she was lying about? He'd never be able to trust anything she said anymore.

But that wasn't the worst thing. Every time he thought about all the lectures he'd suffered through about stuff like *integrity* and *honesty* and *doing the right thing*—when all along, the whole thing was just so much crap!—it made him want to puke.

At this point—and Daniel had to admit that he felt a little guilty about it—he didn't really care if they got to go home or not, because he didn't really want to see his dad right now, either. Because if his dad knew, all along, that his mom was lying, then that made him a liar, too.

"Daniel?"

"*What?*"

"I love you, son."

"Yeah, right." Whoops. Maybe he went a little too far with that one, but he was pissed. He didn't really care if he hurt her feelings. After all, *she* had hurt *him*. If nothing else, she could have told him the truth while they were stuck in this shithole for the first three days. Like, he was pouring out his guts to her, and she never said a damn thing.

If it wasn't for Hunter, he probably never would have known the truth.

Daniel rolled over on his back, folded his arms behind his head, and stared up into the blackness. He was starting to get used to the constant bluff and bluster of the wind. It wasn't so bad out here, really. He didn't have to go to school, and it was getting kind of interesting. It's not like they were being tortured or anything.

He thought about what Hunter had said about the government. A guy'd have to live in a cave not to know about some of the more spectacular blunders that had been made in recent years by the ATF and the FBI during raids on survivalists. Everybody was at least a little disturbed by it.

Not everything the guy had said made sense to Daniel. He had no idea what the Second Amendment was. Still, Hunter *had* said that they killed kids when they raided the Community. And Daniel's mom hadn't argued with that.

What kind of people would *do* a thing like that?

And if it was true, then shouldn't somebody, somewhere . . . fight back?

So much hard thinking was making Daniel tired. He yawned, rolled over on his side, and went to sleep.

Sometime in the depths of the night, Daniel was awakened by an outcry. Drowsy and confused, he thought at first that it might be Zoe, but once he became fully conscious, he realized that it was his mom, having some kind of nightmare. He could just make her out, thrashing around in her sleeping bag and making little frightened sounds.

He reached over and gave her head an awkward pat. "It's okay, Mom," he said. "It's okay."

She sat up, breathing hard as if she'd been running, her face ghosty in the gloom of their little room. "*Daniel?*" Her voice was raw and heartbreakingly vulnerable.

"It's okay. You had a bad dream."

"Are you all right?"

What a strange question for her to ask. After all, it was she who'd had the nightmare. "Yeah. Everything's all right."

Reaching over to him, she caught his hand in hers and pressed it against her cheek. It was warm, as if she had a fever. He didn't pull his hand away.

After a moment she lay back down and was quiet.

Daniel had never seen his mother truly scared before. Even on the night they got kidnapped, he had to admit she'd been really brave. The incident disturbed him deeply, and it was a long time before he slept.

The next morning, as they went about their embarrassing little morning rituals, Daniel's mom did not mention the nightmare, so he decided not to, either. Maybe she didn't even remember.

After another strained and silent breakfast, Hunter again showed up in the doorway, as cheerful and courteous as ever. Daniel found it a welcome relief from the tension. He noticed that Kicker did not accompany Hunter this time.

"You guys have had enough of a vacation," he said. "There's lots of work to be done around here, and everybody does his part. Lissie." He turned to Daniel's mom. "You'll work with the other women in the garden. Jennifer'll show you where it is. Dan, you come with me."

Daniel had only a moment to catch a glimpse of his mother's alarmed face as the tight-assed bitch who'd been bringing them their meals hauled her off toward the mess hall. He felt briefly sorry for her, then apprehensive about his own fate as he left the building with Hunter.

As they passed the pavilion, Daniel stopped to stare at a group of men and women who appeared to be in training for hand-to-hand combat. He'd never seen it close up and found it fascinating. After going ahead a few paces, Hunter glanced over his shoulder, spotted Daniel watching, and came back.

"Look interesting?" He smiled.

"Sure," Daniel said. "I've always wanted to learn how to do that stuff."

"Well, now you can," he said. "You'll be learning self-defense, lifting weights and getting into shape, and spending more time down at the gun range."

"Really?" Daniel couldn't help the eager tone in his voice. Without his mother around, watching every move he made, he felt himself relaxing a little. Hunter seemed like a really nice guy. "Cool," he added.

Hunter laughed and slapped him on the back. "C'mon," he said. "Got something I want to show you, kid."

Daniel followed him across the barren campground, his boots crunching on the rocks and hard dirt. A dust devil whipped past, stirring up a miniature funnel cloud of chalky dust. In the distance he could hear the crackle of gunfire from the range; it was a sound that went on until dark, every single day.

Five or six men, looking like hard-bodied soldiers in their desert fatigues and boots, jogged in front of Daniel and he waited for them. Kicker was the last to pass by. He nodded at Daniel as though he were a regular person or something instead of a prisoner. Bewildered,

Daniel nodded back as the men took off in unison into the hills behind the camp.

Hunter reached the steps of a small trailer house and motioned to Daniel. "Come on in," he called. "I'll show you around the place." Without his mother there to watch for clues as to how to behave, Daniel was uncertain what to do. He hesitated, then followed Hunter up the steps and into the trailer.

"Make yourself at home," Hunter said. "I'll see if there's any coffee."

A beautiful redhead with a long French braid down her back, a creamy freckled complexion, and eyes made greener by the small bits of green in her starched, trim cammies, emerged from the back of the trailer. "I'm almost finished cleaning," she said. She saw Daniel then and broke into a smile that made his knees weak. "So who's this beautiful boy?" she asked.

"Hands off," Hunter said, laughing. "A woman can get arrested for statutory rape, too, you know."

Daniel's cheeks burned at the remark. He wanted to disappear through the floor.

"This is Dan. He's going to be staying with us for a while. Dan, this is Meghan."

"Hi, Dan." She extended her hand.

He knew his hands were sweaty. He could tell. Wiping his right hand on the leg of his pants, he took her small one and shook it. She had a surprisingly strong grip.

"I guess I'll be running along, then. Looks like you want to have some guy talk. Hunter, let me know if there's anything more . . . I can do." She gave Hunter a warm, intimate smile.

Daniel stared at his feet. He had huge feet. His feet were an embarrassment. He wished he could sink through the floor.

"Don't worry," Hunter said. "I'll be in touch." They both laughed.

After she had gone, Hunter said, "I was terrified of girls when I was your age, too. Never fear. You will get over it." He went into the small kitchen and began to bang cabinet doors open.

Daniel stuck his hands in his pockets and looked around the cramped living room. Right beside the front door was a poster depicting a terrifying SWAT team guy all decked out in a gas mask and a black bodysuit, sprouting weapons of all kinds and aiming an

Uzi toward whoever was looking at him. There was a caption that read, *"Hi. I'm from the government and I'm here to help you."*

On top of the television set rested a human skull wearing a cocked U.S. Army green beret. Tentatively, Daniel touched the skull. It was not plastic. Recoiling, he blinked and glanced up at the picture frame which hung on the wall above. It contained a map of Vietnam with a pair of jump wings positioned above it, a Special Forces patch depicting a skull wearing a green beret with the letters MACV-SOG beneath, the Combat Infantry Badge, and other insignia he didn't know. (The only reason he knew those was because one of Eric's dads had the same stuff in their den. Before the divorce.)

In a red velvet shadow box was a Silver Star and a Purple Heart. Hadn't his mom said something about Hunter being a Vietnam veteran? She hadn't said anything about this, though.

Above the couch were a couple of crossed samurai swords.

There were books crammed in every nook and cranny. Daniel scanned some of the titles: *Methods of Long-Term Underground Storage; The Survival Armory; The Anarchist's Cookbook; How to Build Your Own Bazooka; FUGITIVE: How to Run, Hide, and Survive;* and *Principles of Quick Kill.*

There were many books on the Vietnam War, books on explosives, on hand-to-hand combat, and on all sorts of weaponry, from machine guns to combat knives. And there were stacks of magazines: *Soldier of Fortune, American Survival Guide,* and *Fighting Firearms.* A table against the wall held a short-wave radio and, beside that, a computer.

Daniel was studying a *Playboy* centerfold calendar which was tacked above the computer when Hunter came in and handed him a cup of coffee. It was black. Daniel had never had coffee without adding cream and sugar before. He took a sip and pretended to like it.

"What'd'ya think?" Hunter asked.

"About this?" Daniel pointed at the calendar.

Hunter guffawed. "Naw, not that. I *know* what you think about that. I mean, my digs. My place. What'd'ya think?"

It was a whole new world, is what it was, but Daniel couldn't say that. He said, "It's really cool. I didn't know you were in the Green Berets."

"I was one of the Lurps," said Hunter, his eyes darkening.

"What's that?"

"LRRP. It stands for Long-Range Recon Patrol. Special ops. Did a lot of missions deep in enemy-held territory, the kind where you didn't have the luxury of being able to call in artillery support— something the fag hippie protesters never knew about. Laos, Cambodia. Lost a lot of good men." He cleared his throat. After a moment he dug through a stack of papers near the short-wave radio and pulled out a yellowed photograph, which he handed to Daniel. "That was my welcome home parade," he said.

Daniel stared at the picture. "But . . . it's just a snapshot of an empty airport terminal."

"Exactly." Hunter's face cracked into a sad smile. "Just thought you might appreciate the irony of it. I wasn't but a few years older than you when I first went over there. None of us were, really."

The photograph made Daniel feel bad. He laid it gently on top of some magazines. He gave Hunter a shy glance.

"What? Go ahead and ask."

"I just . . . I was just wondering if you had . . . you know . . . any of that trauma stuff."

"Oh, you mean PTSD?"

"Huh?"

"Post-Traumatic Stress Disorder."

"Yeah, that's it. My friend's step-dad . . . had some problems with it."

Hunter nodded sympathetically. "The nightmares are the worst. But these guys"— he said, gesturing vaguely out there somewhere— "this Armageddon Army and these Alpha/Omegans . . . well, they've given me new reason for living. They've pulled me through it. I owe these guys my life."

Daniel gestured toward the shadow box. "You won the Silver Star."

Hunter shrugged. "No big deal."

"What happened? Can you talk about it?"

"It's nothing, really. I dragged a wounded buddy to a hot LZ and held off the enemy with cover fire until he could be loaded onto the medevac chopper. Got a little souvenir." Tugging at the shirt of his fatigues until it came loose from the belt, Hunter pulled the shirt up to reveal a nasty scar jagging a white path across his abdomen.

"*Jesus,*" breathed Daniel. "I mean . . . wow. I mean . . ." He didn't know what he meant and covered his embarrassment with a slurp of scalding hot coffee. He'd never met a real war hero before. Eric's step-dad had a bronze star, but he said they practically all got one of those, just by showing up and staying alive.

Man. He was beginning to see now what his mother must have seen in this guy back in the early days.

"I was just doing my job, son," insisted Hunter. "No more and no less than any other brave heroes of that war. We served our country when they asked us to, when just to go around wearing a uniform was to invite some longhair dope-smoking hippie scumbag to spit on us and call us *baby killers,* and how do they reward us?"

Daniel didn't know.

"They reward us by sending us down the long, slippery path to slavery. They reward us by taking away from us the freedoms we fought for and died for." He put a hand on Daniel's shoulder. "I wanted you to see this, Dan. I wanted you to know that while what we did to you and your mom may have been hard to understand at the time, well, I want you to know that I'm not some kind of raving lunatic or anything, okay?"

Daniel nodded. "Okay."

"I want you to understand that you have been *honored.*"

"Honored?"

"Recruited. You're a patriot now, a member of the Armageddon Army, a true freedom fighter. You're one of the elite now. Your training is just beginning, and I want you to know that it's a privilege. I don't want you to take it for granted."

Daniel shook his head. "I won't."

"Good," said Hunter, giving his shoulder a squeeze. "Good."

PART III

TWO PATHS

There are two paths to take:
one back toward comfort and security of death,
the other forward to nowhere.

HENRY MILLER

We hold in our hands the power to end sorrows,
and he who is willing to die
can brave any calamity.

PIERRE CORNEILLE
seventeenth-century French dramatist

. . . with the exercise of self-trust,
new powers shall appear.

RALPH WALDO EMERSON
"Self-Reliance"

It is the business of the very few
to be independent;
it is a privilege of the strong.

NIETZCHE

CHAPTER 15

WREN made up her mind to escape while she was digging up rocks from the garden and depositing them onto a large pile to the side. There wasn't a great deal of gardening work to be done in October; canning and freezing and planting of certain winter crops such as onions and radishes was already done. Hunter was just trying to get rid of her so he could start brainwashing Daniel.

Shouldn't be too hard of a task, she reflected bitterly, *now that Daniel's no longer speaking to me.*

It was worse than her worst nightmare. Wren could not have guessed the immensity of the despair which pressed against her shoulders as she mindlessly pried stones of all shapes and sizes from out of the irrigated soil beneath a vast, faded denim sky. They'd given her a pair of work gloves, but painful grass burrs jabbed into her knees, and there was simply no position to get into that did not result in a collection of stickers on some part of her body.

As she labored, she observed as many details as possible about the encampment. For one thing, it occurred to her that in all their days at the camp, she had never heard the high drone of an airplane flying overhead. Nor was there any traffic, save for camp vehicles, on the single well-guarded road leading out. From what Wren could tell, power was provided by electricity that had been run down the road, probably before the permanent buildings were constructed. The camp residents would read the meter themselves. She'd noticed that while on her way back from the shower.

From past experience she knew that water would be provided by wells they had dug, trash hauled to a private landfill, and sanitation made possible by septic tanks. Supply runs, she guessed, would be made once a week, and mail delivered to a remote post office box held in a fake name. She'd seen a satellite dish outside Hunter's trailer, which probably meant that he possessed the only television set.

The population of the camp was harder to figure, but judging from those she'd seen so far and the size of the facilities, Wren estimated the number at about fifty. The facilities themselves, however, were a complete puzzle to Wren. The Community had been a purely ramshackle affair, constructed of a tumbledown mismatch of shelters. It was primitive, too, with no indoor toilets or electricity. Furnishings and tableware had been provided by Community members who had moved out of their homes and brought them along. They drove mostly beat-up old pickup trucks, and many of the weapons they practiced with on the gun range and used in the FBI raid were secondhand, stolen, jerry-rigged, or otherwise haphazardly collected.

But this place, with its concrete foundations, solid cement-block construction, modern plumbing and wiring—not to mention the late-model four-wheel drive vehicles, the costly fatigues, camouflage netting and other military accoutrements, and the high-priced weaponry—was obviously well planned and well funded.

Where the hell is he getting the money?

Although Hunter did not use drugs, and never allowed anyone around him to, either, Wren was certain that he would not be above trafficking in them. Or perhaps he'd gotten into something deadlier, like gun-running across the Mexican border. He could still be robbing banks, but Wren doubted he would try anything so public and risky now that he was out on parole.

And who owned the land? The chunk of forest dominated by the Community had been donated by a faithful follower. Was that the case here? And if so, weren't there any neighbors, anywhere, who might question the comings and goings of a bunch of beefed-up men in camouflage fatigues?

"Let's knock off for now. It's time for lunch."

Wren jumped, every nerve ending in her body on edge. Jennifer, the blond hard-ass who'd been guarding her, gestured toward the mess hall. She was wearing a sidearm, of course, but kept it holstered as Wren struggled stiffly to her feet and tossed aside the rock she was holding. *So I get to sit at the grownups' table,* she mused, tucking her sweaty hair behind her ears.

"Here." Jennifer handed her a cloth-covered rubber band.

"Thanks," said Wren, feeling ridiculously grateful as she pulled her hair back into a ponytail at the nape of her neck.

Everyone who had not already had the opportunity washed up at a set of deep stainless steel sinks near the door, then Wren got in line along with the others, ignoring their curious stares as she searched the crowd for Daniel. There was no sign of either Daniel or Hunter, which agitated Wren so much that she had to be prodded into collecting a tray and tableware and moving down the cafeteria line for beef stew, corn bread, and peach cobbler.

It was a surreal experience. One minute it seemed she was being held prisoner, and the next, she was in the army, loading up her tray in the mess hall along with a few dozen other people all dressed alike. Although Jennifer kept a sharp eye on her, she was left pretty much to her own devices as she took a seat and fussed with a butter patty. Of course, since every single person in the room except for Wren wore holstered firearms of differing sizes and power, the message was clearly telegraphed that for her to make a break for it now would be, as Daniel would say, *like, duh.*

She sat alone at a long cafeteria table, in a little island of empty folding chairs. No one approached her, or spoke to her, nor did she encourage anyone to. Instead, she used her loneliness as a listening device, eavesdropping on conversations going on around her while keeping her face carefully impassive.

"Have you talked to Dave and Meredith?" a stunning redhead asked Jennifer.

"You kidding? I haven't seen them in two weeks."

With her peripheral vision Wren could see the redhead nod. "It's because it's October, you know."

"Oh, yeah. Hunting season goes into full swing now, doesn't it?"

"Deer. Elk. Quail. You name it."

"*Good.* Maybe Hunter'll loosen up and let us come and go a little more freely now."

Wren blew on her soup spoon. She thought she saw the redhead shrug.

"It depends. Dave and Meredith pretty much control who comes and goes through headquarters. They don't want to attract the attention of the game warden."

"Are some of us going to have to move up there and pose as hunters?"

"Probably. Some of the guys will, anyway."

So that explains it, she thought. Oh, it was brilliant. They had a front business, a ranch that supposedly leased hunting rights to visiting businessmen. That way no one would question the comings and goings of men driving dusty, gun-racked Suburbans and Jeep Cherokees and outfitted in camouflage fatigues. Wren knew people in the hill country of Texas who had done the same thing when the oil money started to peter out. Bored city boys looking for adventure often flew in from all over the United States and were absolutely thrilled if they could take home a trophy from so much as a three-point buck. They gladly paid thousands of dollars for the privilege.

Could that be where the money comes from? she wondered, then quickly rejected the idea. Too many pains had been taken to camouflage this camp; there was no way Hunter would risk strangers stumbling onto it while hunting.

She couldn't suppress the shudder which shook her body at the flashback memory of the poor man, lost while hunting, who had accidentally trespassed on Community property. The FBI would never have found his body if . . .

Giving herself a mental shake, Wren tuned in once more to the conversations around her but could learn nothing new. As she got to her feet with her tray, Jennifer appeared at her elbow. "I'll show you your bunk," she said, then caught the eye of the redhead. "Meghan? Come meet the new girl. This is Meghan."

Wren nodded. Meghan smiled at her with hard green eyes.

"Uh, what's your name?" asked Jennifer.

As the women turned expectantly toward her, Wren felt her cheeks flame hot. *I am not Wren,* she thought. *Not here. Not in this place. And I will be damned if I go by Lissie.*

"Don't you know your own name?" teased Meghan. "Or are you trying to come up with an alias?"

"Call me Elizabeth," said Wren finally, and almost said, *Call me whatever the hell you want; just don't call me Lissie.*

"Elizabeth sounds so formal," complained Meghan as they left the mess hall and headed toward the women's barracks. "We ought to come up with a nickname for you. Practically all the guys have one, and some of the girls, too."

What is the matter with this stupid woman? seethed Wren. *Doesn't she know that I'm a hostage? That I don't give a flying fuck what they call me, I just want out!*

She glanced all around for Daniel as they crossed the compound, but there was no sign of him. Either he was still with Hunter in his trailer, or they'd taken him down to the gun range again. As she was escorted into a one-story dormitory-style building, she felt the suffocating clench of hopelessness around her heart. They would be separated now. Her son was, essentially, lost to her.

As Jennifer indicated a narrow bed and accompanying footlocker (as if she had anything to put in it), Wren felt a bizarre wash of homesickness for the little windowless building where she'd spent so many days and nights alone with her son. Even when they had quarreled, they'd at least been together. She could remind him that no matter what, she still loved him. He could comfort her when she had a bad nightmare—his adolescent-angry way of loving her back.

No matter what happened, they'd been together.

But from this point forward, mother and son would remain apart. Hunter would see to that.

Tossing a pile of scratchy linens onto the footlocker, Jennifer retreated to her own corner, where she buried her nose in a romance novel and waited for Wren to make up her bed.

Dumbstruck, sheets pressed close to her chest, Wren thought, *What a difference a week makes when Jeremiah Hunter is around. Here you are longing for a goddamned prison instead of thinking about what your life was like, say, two weeks ago, when all you had to worry about was grading papers and keeping Daniel from smart-mouthing you too much.*

"You gonna stand there all day or get busy?" snapped Jennifer. "Hunter says you gotta take your turn at KP like everybody else."

And so she did KP and laundry duty—shit jobs, most of which were handled by the women, she noticed. So some things never changed, not with survivalists, anyway. It was a white Anglo-Saxon, Protestant, paramilitary, male-dominated culture. The men were simply more comfortable in the company of other men. They regarded women as falling into one of three roles: sex object, wife, or mother. The women, though trained in combat and survival techniques, would always be expected to be submissive to and care for the men and look after the children. They would never achieve any positions of real power in the organization, except as the girlfriend or wife of a powerful man.

For their part, the men tended to treat the women with protectiveness and certain Old World manners—twice during the course of the day, men apologized to Wren for using rough language around her.

At dusk, as Wren and her ever present guard, Jennifer, were making their way over to the mess hall, Hunter came toward them, his handsome face creased into a congenial smile. Daniel was not with him.

"You're just the person I wanted to see," he said to Wren. "Let's go for a walk. I want to show you something."

All afternoon long, Wren had waited for the dinner hour, in hopes of at least catching a glimpse of Daniel. Now she was going to be denied even that. Pierced through with disappointment, nerves stretched thin as old rubber bands, Wren had a hysterical urge to start running and keep running until somebody finally shot her dead and she wouldn't have to think anymore.

His hand closed gently over hers, and it was all she could do not to cringe as he led her through the brush and brittle dying mesquites. There was no birdsong, and the thundering wind had slowed to a breathless whisper.

They began to climb, and Hunter dropped back behind her as the rugged cantilevered incline became somewhat trickier to navigate. At times they walked on slabs of solid rock, other times they worked their way around squatting junipers or boulders standing stark upright like unmarked tombstones. By the time they reached the crest of the ridge, Wren was out of breath.

Hunter held apart two strands of barbed wire for her to step through, and they walked along the summit while the horizon slowly caught the clouds on fire and the relentless white of the alkaline soil gradually pinkened.

Still, the landscape was not softened.

When they turned to look down upon the camp, as Hunter chattered on about the mighty Armageddon Army and the distinctive base camp of which he was so proud, Wren craned her neck in all directions. Finally, abandoning all pretense of actually listening to him, inch by growing-horror inch, she turned her body. Three hundred and sixty degrees. She squinted. She shaded her eyes.

Down below, the road sliced through the valley like a jet stream through a camouflage sky.

But there was no sign of civilization.

No distant twinkle of house lights. No car headlights beading along the road. Not even the faraway glow a town might make on the horizon.

For maybe twenty miles in all directions, for as far as the eye could see in the dying light, there was nothing. There was nobody.

Monotonous lookalike rolling scrubby hills stretched out endlessly.

But there was no help to be found.

Not anywhere.

CHAPTER 16

O N the way home from work three weeks after Wren and Daniel
disappeared, Cam stopped off at the supermarket. He'd
noticed an empty box of Kotex in Zoe's bathroom and knew
she would be far too shy to remind him to buy some. He would trade
boxes quietly and save her the embarrassment. He also needed
tomato sauce for the chicken cacciatore he was planning for supper,
and they were out of Zoe's favorite cookies.

When he walked in the back door with his arms full of groceries,
Cam noticed that Zoe had allowed the house to grow dark again. It
was one of many subtle differences in her behavior that disturbed
him. Flipping light switches as he went, he moved through the quiet
house in search of her, and found her, as usual these days, in Daniel's
room, playing Nintendo.

Because her brother had always given her such a hard time about
playing with his Nintendo video game system, Cam had not minded
when she first ventured into the forbidden territory. It seemed like a
good way to get her mind off their troubles. He had even played with
her a time or two.

Standing in the door frame of Daniel's shadowed room now,
watching his daughter's intense face, the noisy colors of the game
reflecting off the glasses she always wore at home, Cam worried over
the difference a few weeks had made in his daughter. Zoe now

seemed to be losing interest in many of the things that had once given her pleasure. She never seemed to read books anymore and TV bored her. Cam suspected that she headed straight into Daniel's room as soon as she walked in the door from school. She stayed there, most nights, until bedtime.

"I got a call from your choir teacher today," he said.

As her thumbs worked the buttons like a telegraph operator relaying an emergency message, to a background concoction of musical notes surely devised in some Far Eastern torture chamber, Zoe ignored him.

"Zoe. Put it on pause or something. I need to talk to you."

With a heavy, long-suffering sigh and accompanying roll of the eyes, she pushed a button which froze the frantic action on the screen and turned to him in the sudden welcome silence, her face etched with annoyance.

"She says you've missed three after-school practices in a row and that you may lose your solo over it."

Zoe made a scornful noise that sounded alarmingly like Daniel. "I don't want to sing a stupid solo."

"But, honey! You were so excited about it."

She shrugged, again seeming to mimic Daniel. "So? I changed my mind. What's the big deal? It's not like it'll keep me out of Harvard or anything." She turned back to the game.

"Turn that thing off! I said I wanted to talk to you."

"*What!* If you make me turn it off, I'll lose my points. What do you want?"

Kneeling down in front of her so that they were at eye level, Cam took one of her limp hands into his. "I want my old Zoe back," he said. "I want to know what's wrong. This isn't like you. This isn't even healthy. A girl your age should be talking on the phone to her friends, hanging out at the mall, bugging me for money. You shouldn't be sitting here alone in the dark, obsessing about a video game. Talk to me. Let me help you."

"You can't help me, Daddy," she said, her voice wooden. "Just leave me alone." She pulled her hand out of his.

The gesture stung, but he hid the hurt. "Honey . . . I know this is hard on you, not being able to talk to people about Mom and Daniel. I know you're worried sick about them and it seems like you're never going to see them again. But they're going to come home again, you'll see. Mr. Austin will—"

"Mr. Austin is *useless*, Daddy. When are you going to get that through your head? They've been gone for weeks now. *Weeks!* He doesn't have a clue about what happened to them. Nobody does. It's like they're dead and I can't even go to the goddamned funeral."

Cam recoiled as if he'd been slapped. He'd never heard Zoe use language like that, never seen her so . . . defeated. "There won't be any funeral," he said firmly. "No matter what happens, we can't give up hope. Do you hear me? Zoe?"

"Just leave me alone, Daddy. I don't want to talk about it anymore." With that, she released the pause button and continued with the game, her eyes glazed, body tensed, thumbs blurred.

He didn't know what to do. Finally, he got to his feet and wandered back into the kitchen to put away the groceries. The sink was full of dishes. So was the dishwasher, and it had not been run. Crumpled chip sacks and empty soft drink cans littered the cabinet. In the laundry room there were damp, wrinkled clothes in the clothes dryer, sopping wet clothes in the washer, and piles of laundry everywhere else. On a hunch, Cam checked the dining room table, where Zoe usually piled her books and did her homework after school. At least she used to, back in their other life. Now there were no books of any kind on the table. There hadn't been for at least five days. He liked to think that his A-student daughter was completing the assignments in class, but he was beginning to wonder.

As he poured dishwashing detergent into the dishwasher and turned it on, Zoe's words haunted him. In a way, Wren and Daniel *were* dead to them. There was no exchange of mail, no phone calls, no weekend visits. There was not even any positive indication that they were alive.

Vanished, like ghosts.

How could he pressure his little girl to rehearse for a solo that, in all probability, her mother would never hear? How could he nag her about doing homework when he himself had turned down two major cases simply because he knew he'd be unable to afford them the concentration they deserved?

Every single day he questioned the wisdom of his decision to put everything in Steve Austin's hands and trust the man to find his wife without getting her into any more trouble than she was already in with the FBI. Maybe if he'd gone public with this whole thing in the first place, that national network of law enforcement would have found his wife and son by now.

Hell, even if they arrested her as soon as they found her, at least she'd be alive. At least she'd be safe.

Zoe could see her mother—who gave a damn if she was in jail?

If it weren't for the extraordinary trust he had in Austin, he'd have blown the whole thing wide open days ago.

He'd give it a little more time, Cam reflected. But not forever. His little girl could not hold on that long, that's all there was to it.

He wasn't sure he could, either.

There were other, trickier issues, things he didn't like to think about, but real life gave him no choice. Wren's leave of absence was not granted with pay. Without her income, half of their livelihood had disappeared, literally overnight. Right now, they had a little savings, and he was using that to cushion the blow, but that wouldn't last indefinitely. Either he would have to dip into the kids' college fund or . . . or . . . he didn't know what.

He really had no idea what they were going to do—one of the scarier realities of being a grownup. Sometimes he was tempted to sit in front of the Nintendo himself and veg out, but he didn't have the luxury of that option.

He prepared their meal and called Zoe to the table, a ritual he insisted upon, even though their conversation usually consisted of such fascinating tidbits as Cam asking Zoe, "How was school today?" and her answering, "Fine." And him saying, "How's your friend Missy getting along? I haven't seen much of her lately," and Zoe snapping, "Missy's a dork and I hate her guts now, okay? Why do you keep prying into my life?"

That kind of conversation.

On this night, the phone rang during dinner, but Cam no longer dove to answer it. As news of his and Wren's "separation" got around, Cam had been bombarded with calls from well-meaning friends expressing shock and sympathy, offering marital advice or the phone numbers of good divorce lawyers, and asking how to get in touch with Wren. Daniel's friends were even more bewildered; Eric called every single day.

So now they waited for the answering machine to take a message before deciding whether or not to answer it.

"*Cam? Steve Austin here. I have some news that might interest—*"

"Hello? This is Cam."

"How ya doin', buddy?"

"All right, I guess. What news?"

"Well, I hesitated even to tell you, Cam. If it doesn't pan out—"

"Tell me anything. Anything." Zoe glanced up at the urgent note in her daddy's voice. He tried to give her a reassuring smile, but she wasn't fooled, and continued to watch him like a cat about to pounce.

"Okay. I think we might have found the camp where Hunter took Lis—I mean, Wren and Daniel."

Cam's heart surged; his whole body tingled and his hands started to shake. "Where?" he said. "T-talk to me."

"I'd rather not say where just yet, Cam. I think it's best you not know until this thing goes down."

"What thing?" His heart was pounding so hard it made his chest ache.

"We found an informant, a guy who says he's staying at the same survivalist camp as Hunter. Seems he knew Hunter while they were both inside. Got recruited by the man there. Couple of days ago, I got a chance to question this guy. He was real jumpy, and when I asked him about your wife and son, he just about came unglued on me. Wouldn't admit to anything. Didn't want to talk about it at all. I think he had something to do with the kidnapping."

"Didn't want to implicate himself, then," said Cam, lowering his voice so that his vigilant daughter couldn't hear.

"That's the way I call it. I mean, if he didn't know anything at all about it, then why would he get so upset? He'd just say, No, I haven't seen them, and that would be that."

"So what're you going to do? Do the authorities know Daniel and Wren are in there?"

"Not yet. They are planning a raid, but these things take time, Cam, you know that. You're going to have to be patient here."

Cam began to pace back and forth, stretching the phone cord as far as it would go. "You don't know what you're asking."

"I know, I know. But this isn't TV—you ought to know that as well as anyone. People have a legal right and the constitutional freedom to live their lives any way they see fit in this country, as long as they obey the laws. We need concrete proof that laws are being broken before we can make any move on that camp."

Cam sighed. "They *are* breaking laws, goddamn it! They've kidnapped my wife and son, and they're holding them hostage."

"Do you want me to tell them that? I can do it if you want. They'll mount the raid ASAP if I do. Of course, I'd have to reveal the hostages' identities as well, and I have to tell you, once they found out your wife is a federal fugitive, it could change everything. They might even suspect that she was a willing participant in the kidnapping. Cam, I know this is difficult on you and your daughter. I'm just telling it to you like it is. But you make the call. Hell, it's your family."

Cam wound the phone cord around his fist. "Do you think they're all right? I mean, do you think that psycho Hunter is hurting them?"

Austin hesitated. "I can't say for sure, and that's the honest truth. It probably depends upon your wife. If she cooperates with him, they'll probably be all right. She's a very smart lady. I don't think she'd take any chances that could get the boy hurt."

"You're right." Cam untangled the cord. "It's just, I don't think any of us can wait a whole hell of a lot longer."

"We're not talking months. I can guarantee you that. We're talking weeks. Your wife is very strong. She's dealt with these people before. I think she can hold out as long as you can, don't you?"

Cam sighed. "I guess, yeah, but—"

"It's making you crazy. I can understand that. But don't forget that we have to do what would be best for Wren and Daniel in the long run. If we go storming in like an Old West posse, guns blazing, they could wind up dead."

"Okay. Okay, but let me ask you this. What about when they finally do move in? When they find Wren and Daniel, they'll ask questions for sure—"

"You let me handle that."

Cam nodded. It felt as if his heart, his body, his mind . . . would explode, would vaporize, would cease to exist in this time, this *eternity* between hearing this news, this joyful, this terrible, this nerve-wracking news . . . and finally holding his wife and son in his arms once again.

"I'll keep you posted," said Austin, his voice at once soothing and sympathetic—Cam's lifeline, his one link to sanity. "You hang in there, okay?"

"Okay," said Cam, studying his daughter's expectant face. "We will."

As he hung up the phone, Cam stood there a moment, staring at his daughter and yet not seeing her. He was trying to figure out how in the world he was going to be able to dangle hope right *there* in front of her eyes like a hypnotist's watch, and yet keep it always just barely out of reach. . . . How could he explain to her that, if they grabbed this delicate hope now and held onto it too tightly, it might suffocate and die, right there in their hands?

CHAPTER 17

T HE moment Steve Austin stepped into the smoke-laden bar, he started to crave a cigarette. He hadn't smoked in fifteen years, not since Patsy had gotten all bent out of shape about some article about the death rate among black men with high blood pressure. Stopping smoking was one of the few things he could do to make her happy; it seemed like a small price to pay for all the sacrifices she had made to his job through the years. For the most part, he didn't miss it; he'd never been a heavy smoker anyway, but walking into a room full of smokers never failed to make him want a cigarette.

Martinez was waiting for him in a corner booth and waved him over, his big grin lighting up the dim shabby recesses of the place. This was not a noisy cops' hangout, or a boisterous singles bar, or a cutesy-theme prowling ground for slick Yuppies ordering white wine. It was one of those quiet, smokey, nondescript no-cover-charge kinds of places where serious drinkers came to nurse their pain, play bad music on the jukebox, and be left alone. Hard-eyed hookers sometimes came in to warm up between tricks and keep their senses numb, and nobody bothered them.

It was a good place to have a couple of beers and talk business without anybody eavesdropping. Sliding into the tattered red vinyl booth, Austin ordered a Bud Lite. The world-weary waitress brought it over in a cold, sweaty bottle without a glass. Austin took a grateful swig and pressed the bottle against his burning eyes.

"Tough day?" asked Martinez.

"Cigarette smoke."

"Oh. Sorry." He stubbed out his cigarette before Austin could protest. "Life can't be that tough. How much you clearing these days? A hundred grand? Two hundred?"

"Don't know," said Austin with a wicked grin. "Never have enough time to count it."

"Boo hoo. Be glad to trade with you."

"Yeah? Spend one day chasing around after Buck Leatherwood and see how you feel."

"That gun-grabber? I'd probably feel like shooting him myself."

"Strange point of view for a fed."

Martinez shrugged. "I like my guns, just like anybody else. I've got a collection of my own at home. The only difference between me and the guys I go after is that they don't think they've got to follow the same laws as I do, and they're willing to go to war with our government for the privilege of doing whatever they damn well please."

He took an angry swallow of beer. "Don't get me wrong. Some of these people are sincere and they mean well. They're voters, taxpayers, veterans. But some of them are screaming nutcases. They're dangerous and they scare the shit out of me."

"Speaking of. What's the latest on our subject?"

Martinez gave a frustrated gesture of dismissal that made Austin's heart sink. "It's going slow. The informant's terrified, and we're having to promise him the moon to keep him cooperating."

"And?" Austin drained his beer and signaled the waitress for another.

"It seems that all this military downsizing and the closing of army bases all over the country has led to some major breaches in munitions security. Our guy thinks the in crowd of this camp is involved in the trafficking of stolen military weapons and ammo to other survivalist outfits around the country."

Austin winced. Getting proof would be tricky. Gun shows and army surplus stores everywhere often offered such things for sale. Serial numbers would have to be traced, and an evidence trail established through a tangled network of survivalist contacts who were savvy enough to use computer bulletin boards, among other things, to cover their tracks. They could even have sympathizers in the military who were already camouflaging the trail at its source.

Images of a long-term government sting operation involving undercover agents and the whole nine yards sprang into Austin's mind and almost paralyzed him.

"If you don't move soon," he said carefully, "then someone other than your informant could die."

Martinez gave him a sharp glance. "Like who?"

Austin hesitated. "Let's just say innocent bystanders."

"You gotta level with me, man. Can't keep me in the dark like this. It ain't right, and you know it." Martinez lit another cigarette.

"I know, and I will in time. But I'd rather not do it just yet."

Snapping the lid back onto his Zippo lighter and shoving it into his pocket, Martinez said, "Why not? Who're you protecting?"

Austin picked at the label on his beer bottle. "Let's just say a client."

"Information between you and a client is not privileged, Steve, you know that. You're not a shrink or a goddamn lawyer." He blew smoke out over the tops of their heads. "I could have a judge subpoena you and your records if I had to and find out whatever the hell I needed to know."

"I know that," Austin said, trying to still the sudden racing of his heart. "I'm trusting you not to, okay? For the time being."

"But you're still asking me to rush an operation that's not ready yet. I'm not even sure I've got the power to do that. We can't fart around there without having to go up the chain of command first and ask permission."

"And there's always some asshole up there willing to say yea or nay depending strictly on how it will impact his career advancement. I know. I remember."

"Then let me handle this in my own way."

Austin opened his mouth to tell Martinez everything, from the kidnapping all the way back to the raid on the Community, when Martinez said, "We may be able to move before long anyway. Our informant tells us they're expecting a big shipment soon."

"How soon?"

"I'm not sure. I'll know more after our next contact. Still, the

Assholes from On High may not want to move even then. They may want to find out who the supplier is first. You know. Keep going after bigger fish."

"Did you ever stop to think that this may well be the biggest fish in the sea?"

"I have, yeah. But what I think and two bits'll buy you a cup of coffee."

"Not in New York."

They grinned and the tension Austin had felt building between them eased somewhat.

"How'd you catch our subject in the first place?" Martinez asked suddenly, careful, like Austin, not to mention Hunter's name publicly. "I know all about the raid, but I never knew how you found him and knew when to move on him."

It was all Austin could do not to yank that cigarette from his friend's hand and take a drag. Not a single day of his life had gone by, not in sixteen years, that he had not thought about the raid. It was worse, somehow, whenever he tried to relax, to go fishing or putter around the house. Then all he did was brood. Which was one reason he worked so much. Even then, thoughts of that day, of the wounded agents, of the dead women and children . . . of everything, ghosted him. They haunted his dreams. They stalked his conscience.

"Are you all right? I didn't mean to—"

"No, it's okay. I'm all right." One thing for sure, he wouldn't be able to talk about it without another beer. He lifted his hand and caught the waitress's eye. She brought it over, and he swallowed about half of it at once. Just enough to have a little buzz, a little dulling of the pain, a little loosening of the tongue.

"We couldn't have done it without our informant," he said.

"Who was he?" Martinez finished his cigarette and, thankfully, did not light another.

"It was a she. Guy's girlfriend. A very young, very brave lady by the name of Lissie Montgomery."

"How'd you turn her? Promise of immunity? Cash?"

Austin picked up the beer bottle and stared into its amber depths. "We didn't have to turn her. She came to see us of her own free will. Wouldn't accept any money. Said her boyfriend wasn't who she thought he was when they got together. Said she'd seen him kill a man and that he was planning another job that would wind up killing more." He sighed and put the bottle back onto the table, turning it around and around on the wet ring it had left on the formica table. "Said all she wanted in return was my promise that nobody would be hurt. And I promised her."

"Jesus, Steve. What happened to her?"

"She disappeared during the firefight. We think she slipped through a trapdoor and took a tunnel out behind the snipers. I never got a chance to say I was sorry. Never got a chance to say thank you."

"Hey, man, it wasn't your fault."

"Whose was it, then?" said Austin. "I was the case agent. I was in charge of the raid. If it wasn't my fault, then who the hell's was it?"

The cry of his heart, over and over again.

"Well, I can tell you the first person who pops into my mind."

"I know." Austin drained his beer. He started to signal for another, but Martinez stayed his hand.

"You're driving, remember? Slow down a little. Let's get something to eat."

"Patsy tells me the same thing. How this guy had those people brainwashed. How he got them to put up the fight."

"Damn right." Martinez called the waitress over and ordered some nachos and water. "Too bad this place doesn't serve any real food."

"But he didn't shoot those kids," insisted Austin, lowering his voice to a near whisper. "We did. Ballistics proved it."

"They were shooting at you, right? And from what I understand, nobody knew the kids were the ones firing those automatic weapons. It's over, man. It's ancient history. We all learned from it, so stop beating yourself up over it. Let the dead past bury the dead. Or is it, let the dead past bury the past? Something."

But it's not past, protested Austin silently, anguish clutching at him. He'd drunk the beers too quickly on an empty stomach, and a fierce headache had set in. *It's not past. It's now, this minute. It's every day that Lissie and her son are held captive by that bastard. Every day that her family suffers. It's every day I stole from her by breaking my promise. If the raid hadn't turned so bloody, she wouldn't have fled in panic. And if she hadn't run, the FBI wouldn't have put her on its wanted list. I'd have gotten her immunity, even though she never asked for it. She was the only informant I ever had who never asked for a damn thing. She only trusted me, and look where it's gotten her.*

If he let her down again . . . if anything happened to her or her son, he'd never be able to forgive himself.

Their blood would be on his hands every single day for the rest of his life.

CHAPTER 18

AFTER the devastating discovery Wren had made during her sunset walk with Hunter along the ridge above the camp, she felt herself spiraling into depression. To keep from going nuts during the endless days and empty nights that followed, she played little escape games with herself. *I could jump into that Jeep,* she would think while doing morning calisthenics, *bust through the guards and haul ass down the road for the highway.*

Yeah, would come the inevitable devil's advocate thoughts, *and if you weren't shot to death, Dave and Meredith and their troops would be waiting for you at the pass.*

Once, while on her way to what she called the rock garden, she spotted phone lines snaking down the outer wall of Hunter's trailer and then underground—the only evidence of a telephone she'd seen in the whole camp. For a few days afterwards she was obsessed with the idea of sneaking into his trailer and calling for help. *I could call the operator,* she thought, *and give her a quick description of the surrounding geography for her to tell the FBI. They would find us and rescue us.*

Uh-huh, came the inevitable sensible argument, *and how do you propose to get away from your death camp watchers? They never let you out of their sight. Never. And what makes you think that der Führer, Mr. Paranoia himself, doesn't have some kind of device to prevent unsolicited use of his telephone without his knowing it?*

Amateurs die, you know.

At night, to keep from stuffing the corner of her pillow into her mouth and screaming, she would play the escape game.

I could sneak out tonight, she'd think as she listened to the soft snores of the other women blending with the rushing tides of the relentless wind. *I could climb the hills and slip through the barbed wire and just take off cross country.*

Yeah, right, would come the snide little voice, *and which way would you head? You have no idea in which direction the nearest town lies or how far away it is. You have no compass, no supplies. You would wander, lost in the desert. If you didn't die, they'd catch up to you. They'd kill you. And what about Daniel? Could you honestly leave him behind? He wouldn't go with you. Not now.*

Daniel. That of course, was the protest of her heart. *If you leave, and you die, he will surely be lost forever. As long as you stay, there's a chance he can be saved. Isn't there?*

She was divided against herself. More and more each day, it seemed, Wren suffered proddings of conscience, as if her grandmother were gently scolding her. *The Tsalagi,* she would probably say, using the Cherokee form of the word "Cherokee," *would say you have the illness of being two-hearted. You must bring all things into balance. You must be of one heart.*

But as the soul-withering days drifted like brittle autumn leaves into weeks, she continued to play the escape game, because not to play the game was to think of home, and to think of home was to sink into utter despair. But not to think of home was to think of Daniel, and to think of her son was to teeter slowly on the brink of madness.

He had become a stranger to her. A pod person, occupied by Hunter's mind-robbing mutants.

They never let her talk to him, not alone, anyway. If she had KP duty, he was working out with his new hero. If Daniel, as the camp's youngest and newest member, was peeling potatoes, she was assigned to the laundry. During the so-called prayer meetings—Hunter's indoctrination sessions—Daniel sat with Kicker or one of the other men, smoking cigarettes now like a bigshot, avoiding the pleading of her steadfast gaze.

Once, when she was serving dinner in the mess hall, he came

through the line. She'd wanted to leap over all the trays and fling her arms around him, or grab somebody's gun and start blasting away until only she and her son were left alive. She wanted to speak to him of Cam and Zoe and Eric, of home and school and life as a fifteen-year-old boy should live it.

"*Daniel,*" she'd said, spooning a deliberately small portion of mashed potatoes into his tray. "It's so good to see you, son."

"Hi." He took the tray. He did not call her Mom. He did not look her in the eye. He did, however, step back and hand her the tray again. "Gimme more potatoes."

Hunter, who had already eaten in his trailer and was standing just off to the side, watching, said "Dan!"

The boy snapped around, and Wren halfway expected him to salute.

"Show your mother some respect, boy."

With a sheepish glance in her direction, he mumbled, "Gimme more potatoes, please, uh, ma'am." He glanced over his shoulder at Hunter.

Hunter gave him an approving nod.

"Want some gravy, Daniel?" she said, joining in the psychic tug of war for the boy's attention. "I know you love gravy." It was a stupid thing to say, but it kept him close to her for just a few more seconds. She was desperate to be close to her son.

In a cold, stilted voice, he said, "I don't want any gravy, *ma'am.* And call me Dan, *Elizabeth.*"

Jerking the tray from her outstretched hand, he spun on his heel and stalked over to one of the tables, where he plunked down in the midst of a group of men, muttering something. They all laughed.

Her eyes met Hunter's. *Just shoot me in the heart right now and be done with it,* she said to him in her mind, *you've already killed me.*

He wasn't able to hold the fierce and accusing gaze of a mother wronged, and turned away.

If she'd had a gun, or a knife, or so much as a baseball bat in that moment, she'd have killed him.

Oddly enough, considering all the trouble he'd gone to to get her there, Hunter seldom approached Wren personally. He preferred to play a few games of his own. If he caught her staring at him, he would begin flirting with other women. Sometimes Meghan would visit him in his trailer, and the next day, he would catch Wren's eye and give Meghan a kiss, as if he expected Wren to be jealous. As if he *wanted* her to be jealous. The colossal arrogance of the man's ego, in any other circumstance, would have been laughable.

Cam, it seemed, had never existed, anywhere.

Wren never said his name aloud, or Zoe's. To speak their beloved names in this place would be to profane them. Every day her longing for them, her yearning for home, increased by geometric proportions. No penitent saint ever dreamed more of heaven.

She became a robot, a mindless masked face. No one ever saw into her mind. No one could touch her there. Cam and Zoe and Daniel, her beautiful boy Daniel as he once was and could be, she was sure, again, resided there.

It was a sacred place.

In a sense, it was as if Wren's soul had detached itself from her body. Her grandmother would call it *uhisoti*, an otherworldly melancholia, a numbed drifting, a yearning for that which she could not have.

Part of the problem was simply having to deal with sheer boredom. Although Hunter permitted her to participate in the morning workouts, she was not allowed to take part in any of the training exercises, such as hand-to-hand combat or firearms instruction. Though she'd been well trained sixteen years ago, it *had* been sixteen years. Methods change. But Hunter still did not trust her.

And there was little intellectual stimulation for Wren. There were few books unrelated to survival, and no newspapers or TV. So, she played mind games.

When the escape game was thoroughly exhausted, she started to play the *Why am I here?* game.

There was no need for Hunter to drag a terrified child off the street in order to convert him into another fawning sycophant. Plenty of those surrounded him already. No, Daniel was just a toy to Hunter, an amusement. People, to Hunter, existed to be used.

So what was her use?

A mission, he'd said. To get revenge for the fallen dead of the Community; translation, to get revenge for getting caught and imprisoned.

It had to be more than that; she was sure of it.

Money.

Of course, Hunter never did anything without the promise of profit attached. Every day she played the game, trying to figure out what her part was to be in the grand scheme.

And every night, she set herself adrift on a sea of longing.

One evening, through a complicated hookup of extension wires and other electronic whatnot, some of the men set up the TV at the front of mess hall on a table. Eating tables were cleared, and the folding chairs arranged so that most everyone would be able to see. As Wren filed in with the others, she craned her neck, as usual, for a glimpse of Daniel. He came strutting in with a couple of Alpha/Omega Strike Force men, a cigarette pack rolled up tightly in a sleeve of his fatigues. He was filling out in the shoulders, she noticed, and he laughed a little too loudly in a pathetic attempt to make the others notice that *he* was included with the *elite.*

Wren remembered how dismayed she'd been when he started wearing his hair long and listening to heavy metal music, mimicking the adventurous skateboarders he admired. *It's a phase,* she'd told herself, *he'll outgrow it.*

Kicker spoke around a cigarette dangling from one corner of his mouth. Daniel mimicked him, squinting just like Kicker did through the rising stream of smoke.

Now look.

She wanted to go grab him by the arm, scold him, drag him home, and ground him. Cheeks burning with impotent outrage, she watched her son, and spotted something she hadn't noticed before: *he was wearing a holstered gun.*

A chill set in, deep within her bones, moved icy through her veins, and crawled over her skin in goose bumps. *Hunter, you bastard, you've gone too far.*

No, not Hunter.

Daniel had gone too far. He'd stepped through an invisible portal, gotten himself caught up in some sci-fi wormhole that had whisked him into the nether reaches of the point of no return.

He was a boy no more.

Now he was a man. Armed and dangerous.

Trembling possessed her. She grabbed her elbows and squeezed them tightly to her body in an attempt to stop. Somebody turned on the TV, but Wren had learned the prisoner's art of being present-but-not-present, of showing her face but not her thoughts. It was the crowd who pierced through the crust of her preoccupation, making boisterous pep rally cheers and boos as they watched the program.

People who walk with a noisy step, said her grandmother in her mind, *are angry, dangerous people.*

The buttery smell of popcorn wafted over the room; bowls of it were being passed down each row of seats until everybody in the room had access to some. Mechanically, she put some in her mouth. It was good, but she was soon thirsty. She stopped eating and focused her attention on the TV.

"Here in our studios in New York, I'd like to introduce our first guest, Mr. Paul Smith, chairman of the popular grassroots organization, USA, or United for a Stronger America," said the program's host. She recognized Doug Richards, the award-winning network journalist. Thunderous cheers shook the room.

"And joining us from our affiliate in Midland, Texas, is Mr. Buck Leatherwood, who has gained fame in recent years—"

Almost immediately, Richards' voice was drowned out by a wave of boos and shouts of "There's ole Buckwheat Peckerhead!" Leatherwood's face soon disappeared beneath a snowstorm of hurled popcorn. Somebody hollered, "Shut up! We can't hear," and the crowd gradually settled down.

"Mr. Smith, polls show that a substantial majority of your conservative membership favors the lifting of all congressionally mandated forms of gun control. You have the endorsement of the National Rifle Association and the support of a number of Republican senators and congressmen, as well as that of some conservative Democrats. And yet crimes by firearms have risen drastically in recent years. What do you think is the solution?"

Smith gave the host an ingratiating smile, and Wren found herself unreasonably disliking the man on sight. *"First of all, Mr. Richards, let me correct your assertion that crimes by firearms have risen drastically. Although violent crime has risen, it was not committed by firearms, but by people, some of whom used firearms."*

In the pause that followed, the crowd burst into more loud whoops and cheers.

"The problems that have provoked these crimes began in the home

and in the drug-ridden streets. We need to support our families and increase the strength of law and order on our streets. Lock these savages up and throw away the key."

"Why bother? Just shoot 'em all!" yelled Kicker, followed by assenting applause from the audience.

"If the government insists on taking away the people's constitutional right to bear arms, then the only ones left who will be well armed will be the criminals, who can always get their hands on guns, and the army, which any former Communist will tell you, is the way to control a population."

Richards gave a thoughtful nod, although as far as Wren was concerned, the man had said nothing new. *"Mr. Leatherwood, how do you respond?"*

Leatherwood's worn and craggy Texan face was juxtaposed on screen beside the faintly smiling, young-eyed Paul Smith. Next to his energetic opponent, Leatherwood appeared battle-weary. *"Well, I'd just like to say that these problems within the family and on our streets with the drug trade are not restricted to the United States alone. They are worldwide problems,"* he drawled, sounding vaguely like former president and fellow Texan Lyndon Johnson. *"But our country is the most permissive of any Western nation as to the easy availability of firearms, and yet our crime rate, particularly that of homicide and other violent crime, is many times that of any other nation in the world. Japan and England, for example, have very strict gun control laws, and their crime rates are much lower than ours. Allowing people the right to amass arsenals for so-called self-defense has not made our cities any safer."*

One of the men in the room leapt to his feet. "You freakin' faggot!" he cried. "You want my guns, you can damn well come and get 'em!"

Massive cheers rocked the room.

"Then you can get the hell out of our country, and go live with those yellow slant-eyed creeps, where you can feel *safe!*" screamed the woman next to Wren, a short, stocky brunette with muscular legs, eyes of steel, and the ironically gentle name of Mary. Leaning toward Wren, her voice still loud and angry, she said, "That whole story about the murder of his daughter was just a hoax, you know." When Wren didn't say anything, she added, "It was cooked up by the government to whip up sympathy and cow Congress into making it legal for them to move in and take over."

"Are you saying the assault on that fast-food place never happened?" Wren couldn't resist asking.

Mary shrugged. "Either it never happened, or even if it did, Leatherwood's kid was not involved. They can do all kinds of crap with computer graphics now."

Shaking her head in disbelief (which Mary took to be amazement), Wren looked around at the crowd. What she saw was the most disturbing thing she'd witnessed since her arrival at the so-called "Armageddon Army" base camp.

The entire room was charged with a kind of fury, a rage that crackled in the air and seemed, by its very own living dark power, to dim the light.

Behind the rage, Wren knew, lurked its shadow: fear.

The TV debate continued, but it became increasingly difficult to hear over the curses and shouts of the crowd every time Leatherwood's face appeared. Satan himself could not have provoked more hatred. Wren strained to hear.

"*I have a hard time understanding the hostility of many of the gun proponents,*" he was saying.

"Understand this, buddy!" hollered Mary.

"*—former press secretary nearly got his head blown off in an assassination attempt against President Reagan, and all the hell the guy is asking is for us to take a few days to make sure somebody's not insane or a criminal before they buy a gun. What is so wrong with that?*"

"I'll tell you what's wrong with it," muttered Big John, who was sitting next to Wren, "it's just the first step toward the national registration of all firearms. Soon as they know who owns which weapons, they'll know where to come and find 'em."

By the time Wren could hear the program again, Doug Richards was saying something about death threats against Leatherwood. A film clip showed Leatherwood fighting his way through a hostile crowd who was picketing a studio where he had appeared on a talk show.

A tall, handsome salt-and-pepper-haired black man had formed a wedge with his body and literally pushed through the noisome protestors like a juggernaut, Leatherwood following in his wake.

Wren knew that man. She hadn't seen him in more than sixteen years, but she would know him until her dying day.

A high-pitched ringing muted Wren's hearing as she felt the blood rush from her head and her hands start to tingle.

You're going to faint, warned a voice from somewhere deep within. *Put your head down in your lap for a moment.*

She obeyed instantly. Her hearing swooped back in a rush of obscenities from several people around her, then faded again. The tingling edged away. She sat up.

Hunter had stepped in front of the TV, but she didn't see him at first. All she could see was Steve Austin, Special Agent Steve Austin of the FBI, the same Steve Austin who had mounted the ill-fated raid on the Community so long ago.

He had promised her no one would be hurt. He had promised to protect her, too, but in the end he wasn't able to. No one was, really.

Just as no one could protect her now.

But here he was, trying to protect Buck Leatherwood against the forces of such overwhelming wrath that Wren doubted there would be much defense against it, because those who allowed their dread to run rampant and primal in the disguise of rage knew how to fight with only one weapon: fear.

Such was the basis for all acts of terrorism: to coerce by acts of violence and terror. She'd looked it up once.

"*We know who this man is*," cried Hunter, his voice ringing in that commanding tone she knew so well. "He is an operative of the New World Order, a standing foreign army sent here to infiltrate our government by means of disinformation and media manipulation. These operatives are here now. Witness their success in brainwashing the American people into believing that guns are responsible for our so-called crime wave."

Loud cheers followed his words.

"We know that these people, these foreign operatives, communicate with one another, among other ways, by means of secret markers left on the back sides of road signs so that those who can't speak English can navigate their way around our country."

Preacher got to his feet and turned to face the room. "Right now the former leader of the Soviet Union, Mikhail Gorbachev," he interjected, "is holed up at the Presidio, the U.S. Center for Military

Intelligence west of the Mississippi, supervising the closing of U.S. military bases!" He sat back down to audience outcries.

"The government knows this," Hunter called over the crowd hubbub. "Yet they do not want the American people to know it. Not only that," he added with a dramatic pause, "but check out what happens whenever United States citizens try and arm themselves. *Remember the Community!*"

The Texans who rallied at Goliad against Santa Ana's forces to win their independence from Mexico could not have been more inspired by a call to *Remember the Alamo!* than Hunter's audience was by his battle cry. They roared.

Wren stared open-mouthed, aghast at what could happen when crowds of paranoid people allowed themselves to believe the most rampant rumors and pernicious myths, and who permitted themselves to be manipulated by a madman.

Hunter made quietening motions with his hands. "The objective of this New World Order is clear," he said, his eyes lit by an inner fire, "to strip the United States citizenry of their ability to protect themselves; weapon by weapon, encroaching law by encroaching law . . . and ultimately, to send its armed forces into the streets of our country to take control over all of us, our families and our children."

"I knew it," Mary said with a knowing nod. "The New World Order is already undermining the world economic system. Soon the whole thing will collapse and send our economy into chaos. The only currency that will be good then is gold."

"If we don't fight for our rights now," Hunter yelled over the riotous racket of the room, "we won't have any rights left to fight for."

"*Amen, brother,*" cried Preacher.

"If the Armageddon Army is not willing to act, then all the brothers who gave their lives in Vietnam and Desert Storm and Iwo Jima and Normandy will have died in vain." At the sudden hush in his voice, the room quieted. "When I was carrying around my seventy-pound rucksack on the killing fields of Vietnam, I watched buddies bleed. I held them in my arms as they gave up their lives for our country." Raising his voice level to a hoarse shout, he cried, "Are we going to stand for such a tragic waste?"

"*No!*" the crowd screamed.

"Are we gonna fight?"

"*Yes!*"

"Are we gonna fight?"

"*Yes!*"

"Are we gonna fight?"

"*Yes!*"

"Are we gonna fight?"

"*Yes!*" And a beat later, came another voice, young and proud, hollering, "*Hell, yes!*"

It was Daniel.

As the room erupted into an almost lunatic chaos of fanatic cheers, Wren went deaf.

All she could hear was her son, the stranger.

And all she could see—superimposed over everything—was the sad, worn-out face of Buck Leatherwood.

Then suddenly everything began to make crazy sense to Wren; she could see it all in her mind's eye: the hell and the hatred, the glory and the dream, the madness and the nightmare.

CHAPTER 19

STEVE Austin picked up the remote control and pressed the "mute" button, drowning out one of those nerve-jangling, strident pickup truck commercials. He wondered if other parts of the country were deluged with as many pickup commercials as was Texas. Did the advertisers think that potential pickup buyers wouldn't listen unless they were shouted at?

"Mr. Leatherwood looks tired," mused Patsy from her side of the bed. "Is he ill?"

"Not that I know of," said Austin, pushing up his glasses and rubbing the bump they'd formed on his nose. A fast-food taco place was now being hawked. The ad depicted someone racing for the joint in a Cadillac with a giant pair of longhorns affixed to the front bumper. "I think the man's just tired. Here he is running this multinational conglomerate, while lobbying for gun control at the same time. It's like holding down two jobs."

"So, why doesn't he quit one or the other?" She yawned.

"I don't think he knows how. It seems I'm not the only workaholic around." He grinned at her. With her milk chocolate skin and jet-black hair, his wife still looked like a schoolgirl to him, even after twenty-five years together. "And as for the lobbying . . . well, you couldn't understand what drives him if you hadn't seen how much he loves his daughter."

"She's been dead now, what? Two years?"

He nodded. "Something like that. Just a few days ago, he told me that it just gets harder as time goes on. He said Melissa was the only pure heart he ever knew."

They were quiet a moment, and then Austin said, "And as for the issue of gun control, it almost seems like a moot point to me, anyhow."

"Why?"

"Because, for one thing, the federal law has a loophole in it. The ban does not apply to guns or ammo manufactured before the law was put into effect. The gun-makers could see the handwriting on the wall ahead of time, and so manufactured hundreds of thousands of those weapons and millions of rounds of ammunition, which gun freaks were only too quick to snap up."

"You're kidding!"

"Shoot, that's not the half of it. Once the law did go into effect, they just started making the same guns with only one or two little changes in them, so that, technically, they're not the same gun, so it's legal to sell."

"I didn't know that."

"Oh, yeah. Take the TEC9 assault pistol. That's been banned, so now they've got the AB10. You know what the 'AB' stands for?"

"I'm afraid to ask."

"After the Ban."

"I can't believe it!"

"And that's not counting all the parts you can buy at gun shows; parts which, once a gunsmith assembles them, can be made into weapons which have been banned by the government."

She stared at him. "And this is legal?"

"Perfectly."

"So what in the world is all the fuss about?" She fluffed her pillow.

"The fuss is about the constitutional right to bear firearms, and whether the slightest congressional control over that right would only lead to more control, and more and more . . . until they've got all our guns locked up or incinerated."

"So they're afraid that Buck Leatherwood is going to take away their right to own guns, if not the guns themselves."

"Correct. And the rise in violent crime has gun enthusiasts as scared as it has the rest of us; more so when you factor in the paranoia. They're really afraid of being defenseless against criminals."

"So am I."

"Well, I'm afraid for you when I'm not around to protect you."

Snuggling up close, she hugged him around the waist. "At least I've got you here with me tonight. So I'm all safe and sound."

"I don't know," he teased. "Second watch is looking after the man tonight, and they're one short. Parker's out with the flu. Maybe I ought to catch a plane for Midland and help out."

"Over my dead body." She kissed him, once for fun and once with passion. Over the top of her head, Austin glanced at the TV. The program was back on. He couldn't resist it and released the "mute" button. Leatherwood's drawl filled the room.

With a melodramatic sigh Patsy pulled away from him and flopped back on her pillow. "Here I am in my prime, wasting away," she griped. "I guess I'm just gonna have to go find me some young guy who can keep up."

He shushed her. Pulling a pillow over her face, she made muffled screaming noises. Austin turned up the volume.

"*. . . just think some of you people are paranoid,*" Leatherwood was saying.

"*Oh yeah?*" said young Smith. "*I'm sure that's what many German Jews were saying back in the 1930s. 'So what if they make us sew the Star of David on our clothes? That's no reason to move out of the country. You're just being paranoid.'*" He gave the camera a smug smile.

"*You are such a little twerp!*" cried Leatherwood. "*That has nothing to do with . . .*"

"Uh-oh," said Austin. "The man's losing it."

"*Mr. Leatherwood, I don't think name-calling is going to help you make your point any better,*" interjected Richards.

The phone rang. Austin had seen all he needed to of what he was sure would soon turn into a debacle for his client. He snapped off the TV with the remote and picked up the phone from the bedside table. "Austin. I mean, hello?"

"Mr. Austin? Sandra Dodge here."

"Yeah." Austin swung his legs over the side of the bed and put his feet on the floor. "What's up?"

"The switchboard is jammed here, and I'm concerned as to how to best get our client home."

"All right. Reroute various choke points, as we discussed."

"The client won't like that."

"I don't give a damn if he likes it or not. Our job is to keep the man alive, and if he's going to do shit like call one of the most popular men in the country a little twerp on national TV, then he's just going to have to put up with the inconvenience while we save his ass."

"All right, sir."

"If he gives you any flak, tell him I authorized it. Only don't mention the other stuff I said."

"Right."

"Good call, Dodge," he added.

"Thank you, sir."

He could still feel her smile as he hung up. This was Dodge's first foray into the field, doing actual client protection. Always before she'd done groundwork, interviews, and stuff. He knew she was nervous, but he also knew she could handle the job.

Still, he'd feel better when he got the all-clear.

"Damn Leatherwood," he mumbled, stretching back out and pulling the covers over his legs. "He *can* be a peckerhead sometimes." When Patsy didn't respond, he glanced over at her. She was asleep.

Story of his life.

When the phone rang again, he pounced on it to keep it from waking her. "Austin here," he said in a low voice. There was no need to whisper or leave the room. His wife was used to his receiving odd-hour phone calls.

"Steve. Mike Martinez here."

"What's going on?"

"Got an update for you. This line safe?"

"No, it's a portable. Let me switch phones. Call me at my second number in five minutes."

"Your office number?"

"No. It's a second private line."

"Okay."

Austin got out of bed and padded into the adjoining office.

Closing the door, he fidgeted as he waited. When exactly five minutes had passed, Martinez called back.

"It's getting weird, man."

"What do you mean?"

"The closer we get, the more paranoid they get, and the more paranoid they get, the more suspicious we get."

"Like what?"

"Like we tried to send an agent in undercover to back up our informant."

"And?"

"No dice. Couldn't get him past the gate. Then SOG made plans to send in a sound man to bug the joint. That's when we found out that *nobody* gets into that place, man. No UPS guys, no meter readers, nobody. SOG sent back to their playroom for some high-tech toys so we wouldn't have to go inside, but it seems there's a waiting list and this case isn't considered priority. At least, not yet."

"What about the shipment? Won't that be delivered? You couldn't waylay it?"

"Shipment's going down in a week, but we don't know where it's coming from. We're trying to get the details now, but our informant's spooked and lying low for the time being."

"What spooked him?"

"No telling. We haven't been able to make contact."

"How about a brush contact, next time he comes to town?"

"He's not coming to town. If he is, he's not telling us."

"Aren't you guys watching him?"

"We've set up picket surveillance, yeah, but we haven't seen our guy specifically in a while. We do have a dead drop in town, and we're hoping he'll furnish us the necessary documents there pretty soon. Jesus, you wouldn't believe it, man, that place is a fucking *fortress.*"

"You think they smell you? Could be they made him."

"Could be. Hope not. We're planning to use aircraft with thermal imaging to detect hot spots next."

"Won't that tip 'em off?"

"National Guard says it sometimes conducts training exercises in that area, so we hope not."

"So what's next?"

"We're setting up an offsite for the field commanders. Word from on high is we hit with the shipment, informant or not. ASAC's taking over. You wanna be SSG on this?" Martinez was referring to the Special Support Group of nonagents who sometimes consulted on intelligence operations.

"You twisted my arm." Austin breathed a sigh of relief. More than anything, he wanted to be there, but there was only so much he could ask of his old friend. Although Austin would not take part in the actual raid, he would be at the offsite with the field commanders— plenty close enough to handle the situation with Wren and Daniel. "Tell me when and where."

"Seven days from tonight, man. Get a pencil and I'll tell you where."

Cam and Zoe Cameron sat side by side on the couch in the den of their home, holding hands.

"Daddy, do you think Mr. Austin is really going to be able to find Mom and Daniel and bring them home?"

Cam let go of his daughter's hand and put his arm around her shoulders. "I think he's working very hard, and I think it's very possible."

She sighed. "It's really hard, having hope."

"What do you mean, honey?"

"I don't know. When you don't think there's any hope, you kinda give up. You get used to things the way they are, sorta. But when you start to hope, then you start hating everything like it is. You want it to happen *now*. It's so much harder to wait."

He squeezed her shoulder. "That's true."

"Daddy?"

"Yeah?"

She hesitated. "I just wanted to say that I'm really, really sorry about the way I've been acting. I've just been . . . scared."

"I know." Cam nodded.

"I mean, I was just thinking about myself. I know you're having this really hard time and everything. I'm gonna try and help you a little bit more, okay?"

Pulling her close, he took a moment to collect himself. "We'll help each other, sweetheart." Staring over the top of her head at a framed family portrait that hung on the opposite wall, everybody smiling, everybody happy, Cam said, "We have to stay strong for Mom and Daniel. They really need us to be strong right now."

She nodded and said, "I know. It wouldn't be very good if they finally came home and here we were, basketcases."

He chuckled sadly. "No."

As he knuckled her on the chin, she smiled at him with her mother's blue eyes and said, "Don't worry, Daddy. We'll help each other."

Then they clung to one another for a long time and didn't say anything more, while darkness crept into the corners of their home and the night shadows menaced.

Wren waited for at least an hour after lights-out before pulling her blanket around her shoulders and slipping out of the women's barracks. She had to think and she couldn't do it in that place.

Behind the squat building rested a flat white rock, flush to the ground and free of scrub brush. It was relatively easy to find in the dark, and she sat there, drawing her knees up to her chest and swaddling herself in the blanket against the chill air. Everywhere was the spectacular night sky, unhindered by city lights, not just overhead but all around, filling her senses with its familiar comfort, and she wrapped herself in it like she had the blanket.

A crescent moon offered just enough light to give the landscape a ghostly glow. Gauzy curtains of cloud played hide-and-seek with the constellations, but Wren was able to make out the Pleiades. The Cherokee believed that human beings were created when Star Women fell to the earth from the Pleiades, whom they referred to as the Seven Dancers. It was a graceful story about life and death, light and dark, good and evil.

Wren shivered. Drawing the blanket closer, she tried to clear her head from all the confusion brought about by the cacophany of the meeting earlier that evening, when they had all watched Buck Leatherwood square off against Paul Smith on television and Hunter had made his call to war.

The louder the voice, Ahw'usti would say, *the weaker the man.*

But Ahw'usti wasn't here now. There was no one to share the

burden of Wren's knowledge. She'd figured it out at the meeting. They were going to assassinate Buck Leatherwood.

It would be a perfect one-two punch: get rid of the loathed gun-control advocate, and humiliate Steve Austin. Maybe even kill him, too.

Wren knew that acts of terrorism were not so much about killing someone as they were about theater, and the bigger and more telegenic the target, the better. So here was Buck Leatherwood, a high-profile, controversial, filthy rich, liberal gun-control advocate and media personality. Who better for the Armageddon Army to blow away?

Their cause would be doubly promoted when the media got wind of the connection with Steve Austin and began reeling out film clips of the bloody scene at the Community back in 1980. Even more perfect revenge.

This had to be what Hunter was referring to in the van the night he and the Strike Force had kidnapped her and Daniel. The fact that he apparently needed Wren to succeed could only mean one thing: he intended to use explosives.

Bombs were the terrorists' favorite tool. Assassinations, particularly bombings, usually resulted in media extravaganzas, which not only served as a forum for the terrorists' cause, but also afforded them power through fear.

But in this case, Wren figured, they weren't interested in just *any* explosives. Making explosives was usually such a simple procedure that teenagers could do it.

There had to be something more.

Expertise must be needed for this mission, special expertise. Apparently he didn't want just a crude bomb. He must want something more . . . selective.

Which got right straight down to the real nitty-gritty of Jeremiah Hunter: his primary motivation in life was always money. Somehow, he intended to get a great deal of money out of this situation, and he needed Wren to help him get it. How, she didn't know yet.

There was only one thing of which she could be certain: *innocent people were going to die.*

In a nightmare twist of fate, Wren found herself back in the same spot she'd been in so many years before. If she didn't do *something*, tell *someone*, people were going to die.

There was no telling how many people, either. Hunter would certainly have no compassion for bystanders. He and his followers in this so-called Armageddon Army were no gentle back-to-nature hippies. Most of them were ex-cons, she now knew, and the Alpha/Omegans, for sure, were cutthroat, lawless fanatics, probably after a cut of the take for themselves.

People were going to die.

I can't stand by and do nothing.

The old dilemma. And yet, once before, she had acted; once before she had told someone. And people died anyway.

You can't be sure people will die if you act, but you can be sure they will die if you do not act.

But what about Daniel?

It seemed to Wren that, if she went for help, she had no choice but to hike out alone in the night and head across open country. She might make it. She might not. Either way, Daniel would never go with her.

I don't mind risking my own life for the good of the many, she thought. *I did it before and I can do it again. But can I risk the life of my only son?*

Once she was discovered missing, there was a very real possibility that Hunter would kill Daniel in revenge.

I can't bear it.

And what about Cam? And Zoe? How could she face them again if anything happened to Daniel?

I can't bear it!

But what if she did nothing? What if she not only stood by and allowed these people to die, but actually participated in their murders? Daniel would see this thing that his mother had done, and in seeing, would suffer a soul-death, she was sure of it. The fact that she did it to save his life would be lost on him. He would probably die young anyway, or wind up spending the rest of his life in jail.

In many ways, Daniel was already a lost lamb. Hunter had severed the line to home and family and all that was good and decent in his boy-life, and had set him adrift, forcing Daniel to cling to Hunter as a pathetic lifeboat.

Illusion.

It was all clever illusion; smoke and mirrors; magic too quick for a boy's eyes. He would not know it was a trick until he found himself drowning.

Hunter the Uk'ten had poisoned the boy by a single swift bite. As the poison spread through his blood, Daniel would grow more confused, more deceived, more blind, until eventually, he would die.

And what hope did her precious son have here in this place, this Unuk'sutii, this den of the rattlesnake?

But I am weak, she thought. *I can never make this journey through the wilderness; I don't know how; I could die. And then how can I help my son? How can I help Mr. Austin and those people then?*

Quietly, drifting soft in her mind like thistledown on the wind, she heard her grandmother say, *"It is not you who are weak. Weakness itself is the illusion."*

"But I don't know what to do," she whispered. "Ahw'usti, I don't know what to do!"

"The knowing is within you," came the still, small voice she wanted so much to ignore. *"Fear is the ripple caused by winds of confusion on the pool of your mind."*

"Yes . . . I do know in my heart," breathed Wren, "but in my mind, it all seems so crazy and hopeless. How can I possibly survive out there? I don't know my way; I won't have any supplies. They will surely come after me—how can I elude them? And Daniel, my beautiful boy, how can I leave him? How?"

"To the Cherokee, granddaughter, the heart is the mind. You know already. You know."

"Damn the old woman!" murmured Wren, her head in her hands. "Why can't I get her out of my head? Why does she haunt me like the evil spirit of an old dead crone? It's aggravating!"

Pushing herself to her feet stiffly, she huddled beneath the blanket and stared up at the wild night sky as the wind whipped the single long braid into which she had plaited her hair. To her grandmother's people, life and death, history and new beginnings, all traveled through time in a circle, like the crescent moon. The dark side of the moon was that part of the circle hidden from view, that time yet to come. The journey started at the top of the crescent and worked its way around.

Ahw'usti had taught her granddaughter that a single thought set the journey in motion.

"*You know.*"

So many years had gone by during which Wren had seldom given her grandmother a thought at all, especially in the years since she had reinvented herself. But the longer Wren remained in this desolate place, the more Ahw'usti seemed to intrude into her mind.

"*You know.*"

"All right! All right, you old witch. Your sorcery has enchanted me. And I know, okay? I *know* already. So. The question is . . . when? You know so much, tell me when."

"*Seven is the most sacred number to our people.*"

So be it then. In seven nights, she would leave on the journey.

As the moon dipped below the horizon, the base camp buildings cast long and utterly black night shadows in the dim starlight. The distant howl of a lone coyote floated to her on the wind. Cold and bone weary, Wren suddenly felt more alone than at any other time during her lonely life. Turning her face at last toward the pitch-dark silhouettes, she headed inside and was soon eclipsed.

CHAPTER 20

T HE sheriff's department chosen for the briefing was located in a tiny, isolated town not far from the Rio Grande River. Even though they'd carefully chosen to meet two counties over from the survivalist camp, in order to avoid alerting sympathetic local citizens who might warn the camp residents, the sheriff's office was still too small for a briefing room. Austin met Martinez and his team in a remote rural barn the day of the raid, which was scheduled for that night, a Saturday.

Many briefings in a number of other locations had already been held: briefings for the forward observers (a typical bureaucratic term for snipers); briefings for the intelligence team, which included Martinez; briefings for the "dynamic entry" teams (tactical, or SWAT, teams); briefings for the ancillary and support teams; for the tactical EMS teams, for the commanders, and briefings in Washington, D.C., for all sorts of various directors and assistant directors.

The barn, which was normally used to store equipment, was huge. It had a concrete floor and was wired for electric lights. A nearby field was to be used for the staging area from which the various teams would depart. By the time Austin arrived, the barn, which had been set up as a command center, was swarming with local law enforcement officers and federal agents. Thick extension cords snaked everywhere, hooking up computer terminals, FAX machines, copiers, and safe-line telephones. Everybody looked terribly busy. It brought back bittersweet memories.

Austin spotted a couple of guys he knew from the FBI's crack Hostage Rescue Team, otherwise known as "Super SWAT," but they were occupied with something and he decided to speak to them later. Apparently they preferred to hide all their high-tech doodads in the vans he'd seen parked outside. Most of the support teams would arrive in incremental groups, riding commercial or otherwise disguised buses. (There were some inglorious raids, Austin could remember, in which the entire retinue had arrived at the site in lengthy caravans of various federal and otherwise official vehicles, creating a menacing and unplanned parade aimed right toward their "secret" target.) Fortunately, OPSEC, or Operations Security Process, had made some changes.

If the HRT had been in existence back in 1980, he reflected with that same nagging sadness, things might have been different.

Martinez was standing in front of the stage, talking to an agent Austin didn't know. He looked up, waved, and walked over, as usual, with that shit-eating grin all over his face. "What are you doing here, man?" he cried. "We don't have any watermelons around."

"Yeah? Damn Meskins probably stole 'em all," said Austin. The two men shook hands warmly. "What the hell's going on here?"

Martinez rolled his eyes. "It's like the goddamned flesh-eating virus, man. One minute it's my little team, stumbling around in the dark with our thumbs up our butts, and the next minute, the whole goddamned government's come flying in to play hero and save us all from ourselves."

"I already noticed the HRT."

"That ain't the half of it. We got your ATF SRT," he said, referring to the organization's crack Special Response Team. "We got your CMT—"

"Oh no! They called Crisis Management? We're doomed."

"Then we got your federal marshals, who have a vested interest in finding Mr. Hunter."

"Uh-huh." Austin glanced at the man pointed out by Martinez. He didn't know him. Not good. It was an unknown equation regarding the future of one Lissie Montgomery, alias Wren Cameron, federal fugitive. He'd have to plan his strategy carefully.

"Then we got your TRAC."

"What the fuck is that?"

"What, you never heard of the Terrorist Research Analytical Center? Where you been, man, a cave? Then we got your JTT."

"Pardon my ignorance. They've gone and changed the letters on me since I got out. What be the JTT?"

"Why, I refer to the Joint Terrorism Task Force. Keep up. Then we got agents in charge and assistant agents in charge and dumb fucking flunkies like me."

"Well then, what the hell do they need me for?"

"Don't you know?" Martinez feigned horror. "You're the—"

"I know, I know. The SSG. How could I forget."

"We wouldn't start without you."

"Yeah, right."

"Then you got your local gendarmes here, your sheriff, your sheriff's deputies, a few local curious po-lice, and of course, life would not be complete without the Texas Rangers."

Austin quirked an eyebrow at him. "Well, I guess *so*! Who the hell do you think is supposed to keep all *these* guys in line?"

Martinez laughed. "That's truer than you think."

Austin shook his head. This was a classic government operation: overwhelm them with superior manpower and firepower. The theory was that fewer people would get hurt that way. Sometimes it worked. Sometimes it didn't.

"*Okay, everybody, listen up!*" A prim, balding man in a brown suit stood on stage and clapped his hands, looking every bit the high school assistant principal. "We're ready to start the briefing now. . . . If you will all please find a seat. . . . Gentlemen? Oh, and *ladies*, of course! Let's get started. There's coffee and doughnuts over here on the table. . . . Could we . . . please be quiet!"

Someone handed him a microphone, which he tapped. High-pitched feedback made everyone wince, but at least it got their attention, and gradually the room came to order. "I'm Special Agent Burt English from the Del Rio resident agency of the FBI. These are kind of my stomping grounds. I'd like to introduce the Texas Ranger for this county and the sheriff."

While introductions were being made, Austin leaned over to

Martinez and whispered, "I always wanted to be an RA. Almost total independence. No daily bullshit from on high."

Martinez nodded, but they both knew that sometimes the small satellite offices were used as punishment for agents who'd screwed up at one of the big-city field offices, and that to be assigned to one basically meant your career would stagnate. Some agents liked bringing up kids in small towns, liked the autonomy of the situation, or planned on using the assignment as a phasing-out stop before retirement, leaving the ambition for the whiz kids. But just as many chafed at the more boring cases usually found at an RA and only stayed as long as they were forced.

The category which fit English could be critical; if he was a go-getter, he'd have a network of informants already established, a positive working relationship with the state and local law enforcement, well-written 302s from each case he'd handled, and a good general feel for the rhythms of criminal life in his division. He could be a crucial link between the agents and officers who'd been working the case for weeks and dealing with the informant, and all the outside agencies called in for the big bust.

It was a sensitive matter. Egos got stepped on. Offend somebody too much, and a crucial piece of evidence just might turn up missing, or a 302 written excluding something important. Worse came to worst on a big case like this, and careers could go down the tubes.

So. If he was an asshole, they were all screwed.

Martinez elbowed Austin. *"English is a worthless prick."*

They were screwed.

". . . and I'd like to introduce the agent in charge of this case, Special Agent in Charge Elliot Sizemore from our San Antonio field office. He will be the incident commander for this operation."

As Special Agent Sizemore climbed the three wooden steps leading to the stage, Austin murmured, "I thought you were the case agent on this one."

"Technically, I am. But he's my boss, so he gets all the glory."

Austin grinned. "Well, speaking on behalf of all retired federal agents, it's nice to know that some things never change."

Special Agent Sizemore had a polish about him that bespoke experience and ambition. The crowd grew much more attentive when he spoke. "As many of you have figured out by now, I guess, this case has been given top priority from Washington. They *do not* want a repeat of some of the tragic mistakes made during federal raids of survivalists in the past. It's my job—and all of our jobs—to see that doesn't happen."

He gave the audience a stern look, as if expecting defensive protests from the group, but nobody said anything.

"Okay. Good, solid intelligence from several sources reports that this particular compound, made up of a group of well-armed and well-trained paramilitary survivalists, has engaged in the theft of weapons and explosives from various National Guard and army base locations around the country; to wit—" at this point, he pulled a pair of reading glasses out of his breast pocket, put them on, and consulted a sheet of paper "—C-4, nerve gas, machine guns, rifles, ammo, dynamite, grenades, mortars, and grenade launchers."

Ripples of talk moved over the room, like the treetop chatter of a flock of birds.

When the crowd had settled down, Sizemore said, "During the robbery of a National Guard armory in Louisiana, members of this organization fired upon a guard, wounding him slightly in the hand.

"Since the leaders are never seen leaving the camp, the decision was made to make a dynamic entry as opposed to a Contain and Call-Out, or a siege and negotiate operation. For this reason we have called in our high-risk control teams."

He paused, as though expecting argument, and when none was forthcoming, went on. "It will be our mission to deliver indictments on seditious conspiracy, the interstate transportation of stolen property, illegal possession of certain automatic weapons, and the attempted murder of a federal official."

Putting away the paper, he quieted the crowd with his hand, smiled, and said, "Also, it would appear that there is an obscure Texas statute which forbids the forming of private armies."

A wave of nervous laughter swept over the room.

"So either way, I think it's a good bust." When the second, more polite, ripple passed, he said, "I'd like to introduce our domestic terrorism expert from TRAC. Debbie? Would you come up here? This is Debbie Wong."

A short, trim Asian woman with an impossibly tiny waist, great legs, and glossy black hair, ascended the stairs and took the mike, adjusting it down at least a foot to her height.

"Nice split-tail," mumbled Martinez.

Austin scowled. "Martinez, you're crude."

"I know. Rude, crude, and socially unacceptable."

"Can you hear me? Okay. I'm Special Agent Wong," she said, gently correcting the gaffe made by Sizemore in introducing her. Although she spoke with a slight lisp, her intelligence was razor-sharp.

"These types of groups are made up of secret, isolated cells throughout the country, whose members take part in guerilla tactics, survivalist training, self-defense instruction, weapons training, and various religious activities." As everyone in the room considered the implications of that statement for all the federal agents who would be putting their lives on the line that night, the room grew very quiet.

"Most of the people in these organizations believe in what is loosely referred to as the Christian Identity Movement, that we are in the end times, that the second coming of Christ is imminent, and that racial and social upheaval will precede that event. Entire families live in these camps, preparing for Armageddon.

"To be fair," she emphasized, "not all survivalists are criminals. Some of them mean well and, for the most part, mind their own business. They are deeply independent and believe in living off the land." As she spoke, she gestured gracefully with her pretty hands. "However, they all believe that the federal government is their enemy. Some even adhere to the theory that the United States government is being taken over by a sort of foreign cartel they refer to as the 'New World Order.' "

She paused, then said, "Which means, basically, that they can kill you and not feel bad about it." Uncomfortable murmurings spread through the group.

Quietly, Mike said, "Some of these nutcases, like the Posse Comitatus, believe that any government over the county level is unconstitutional. I mean, there's a *bunch* more out there now than when you were in the Bureau, Steve. Some of 'em have got assassination target lists. They've been known to kill off IRS agents."

Austin said, "Well now, we can't fault them for a little, teeny mistake like that, can we?"

Grinning, Mike shook his head.

Special Agent Wong daintily cleared her throat. "Recent legislation banning various weapons and so forth has sent many borderline wannabes over the edge into full-fledged paramilitary survivalism. They call themselves Patriots, or sometimes, White Patriots.

"The problem is that these isolated, armed encampments can be a hotbed for criminal activity. Sometimes the members participate in crimes such as armed robbery, arson, bank robbery, and murder, as well as the assassination of various government officials. They fully believe that everything they do—no matter how aggressive the crime—is *defensive*, and that they are justified in doing it. And they can be violently racist."

"Aw," whispered Austin, "and I was really wanting to join up."

She waited for the resulting restlessness in the crowd to pass. "Now, if you think all these boys are dumb rednecks, think again. Some are well educated. Some are war heroes. Some are mercenaries. We—meaning agents of the federal government—are considered their enemy and they believe themselves to be at war with us. I know I've said that before, but I can't emphasize it enough.

"And they have access to computers like everybody else. Computer bulletin boards connect some of these groups in a sort of web—and they occasionally help one another, especially if they hold an allegiance to a charismatic spokesman. And there are conventions, believe it or not. The Aryan Nation holds one every year."

She paused. "Are there any questions?"

One ATF agent asked, "Can you automatically assume that everybody in the compound is committed to die?"

Wong considered her answer carefully. "Terrorists have a saying: 'To join costs nothing, to get out is impossible except by a coffin.' "

"So you're saying they are committed."

Wong nodded. "What I'm saying is that, in a closed combat situation, it could be only the leaders and a few die-hards who are literally willing to die for the cause. Most of them live this way because they dig the life, not because they're all that committed to whatever cause the leader espouses. But the leader may have convinced them that they have no choice. Any more questions?"

"Who's establishing perimeter security?" yelled a guy from the back of the room.

Special Agent Sizemore quickly stood and turned to face the group. "Uh, I'll handle this one, Debbie."

Everyone in the room could hear the condescension in his tone, but Austin had to give her credit; she never blinked.

"HRT will establish perimeter security," said Special Agent Sizemore. "They will also breach and secure the compound, with backup from the San Antonio field office SWAT team and ATF SRT. Then other agents will be permitted to enter the compound to present the indictments, help conduct building searches, and collect evidence."

And track down the Camerons, please God, thought Austin.

There were a few more questions for Special Agent Wong and then she relinquished the mike to Sizemore. "I was going to have a profiler from our behavioral science services unit come down and talk about the typical leader of these groups, but then I realized that former Special Agent Steve Austin is here," he said. "Mr. Austin was the case agent on the Community raid and personally arrested Jeremiah Hunter."

Austin, who was muttering some wisecrack to Martinez about ninja wannabes when he heard his name, looked up in surprise just in time to hear, ". . . retired now, but he can tell us what we need to know. Mr. Austin? Where are you?"

Reluctantly, Austin got to his feet. The Community raid was not exactly his greatest moment of glory with the Bureau and he sure didn't want to do any bragging. But he did know Hunter.

Making his way to the stage, he took the mike and looked out over the group assembled before him, who comprised some of the sharpest law enforcement personnel in the world. "Well, first thing I want to say is that I sure wish some of you guys could have been with us that day."

There was a grateful laugh, followed by a smattering of applause.

"Uh . . . I guess they faxed in his mug shot and you've all got copies? Okay, that mug shot is sixteen years old, which would make Hunter, what, forty-four now? Forty-six? So I'm not sure—"

Martinez signaled him. "Steve? Do you mind?"

"Not at all." Austin gestured for Martinez to stand. "This is my very good friend, Special Agent Mike Martinez of the San Antonio field office. He's been case agent on this for several weeks now, and he's interviewed the informant."

Mike got to his feet and addressed the crowd. "We're still waiting on the computer-enhanced aging on that mug shot, but our informant served time with Hunter, and he says that the guy really hasn't changed all that much. Got a few smoking wrinkles and gray hairs, like the rest of us." He grinned. "But he's a lifelong weight lifter and in excellent shape, so you shouldn't have any trouble recognizing him."

"What about a beard?" somebody asked.

Martinez said, "Informant says no." He sat back down.

"Thanks, Mike." Austin paused, thinking. "Okay. I guess the *second* most important thing you need to know about Jeremiah Hunter is that he is a coward. Oh, he talks the talk, but he never really did walk the walk. Strictly a wannabe from the word go."

Some of the agents who'd confronted Hunter types before were nodding. Encouraged, he went on. "You can't believe anything the guy says. He'll sit right there and tell you war story after war story, and every goddamned one of 'em is fake. The truth is, he was dishonorably discharged from the army after only six months of service, and he never did go to Vietnam. And if you wanna know the down-and-dirty truth, a whole hell of a lot of these so-called survivalists fit that description."

Some of the group looked surprised.

"Oh, yeah. Anybody can order any patches, insignias—whatever they need, from catalogues which service the *real* veterans. All you need is a credit card. They don't ask to see your DD-214. And you can get all kinds of military crap at gun shows anywhere in the country."

Looking out over the group, Austin said, "Do me a favor when you take down this son of a bitch. Ask him to show you his Silver Star that he supposedly received for valor during combat in Vietnam. Truth is, he bought it from some homeless guy."

Austin waited for the outraged crowd comments to fade. When the group was once again quiet, he said, "Hunter likes attention, and he can seduce a whole crowd of people faster than you could get a whore's panties down in New Orleans during Mardi Gras." After the laughter passed, Austin said, "My apologies to the ladies of the bunch." Some of them nodded, some shrugged.

"He's always got to have the biggest dick in the room—oh, sorry again. There weren't that many women in the Bureau when I was there." A couple of them smiled at him. "But I mean, the thing is, it's all show. When you make the arrest, you'll see he's carrying the biggest damn piece he can find. I believe he'd carry a bazooka if he could find a way to make it portable." More snickers.

"*What's the first most important thing?*" hollered somebody from the middle of the group. "You started with the second most important."

"The first most important thing to know about Jeremiah Hunter?"

With a heavy sigh Austin scanned the faces of all the bright young men and women watching him, and said, "The most important thing to remember . . . is that he will kill you just as soon as look at you."

CHAPTER 21

S HE was almost undone by Daniel.
There was no proper way to say good-bye to him, of course.
No way to let him know all that was in her thoughts. She dared
not trust her own son.

But she could not leave without seeing him one more time. For
seven days she watched for an opportunity, but he was never alone.
She was beginning to despair when, on the evening of her departure,
at dinner, the other men at his table finished eating before he did
and left him by himself for a few precious minutes.

Heart in her throat, she went over to his table and sat down next
to him. He looked at her with surprise but no particular resentment,
and went on eating as though she were simply not there. She noticed
a pimple on his chin, and it hurt, seeing him still a teenager in so
many ways.

As she opened her mouth to speak, a sudden rush of emotion
caught her off guard and she had to struggle not to break down, to
act as though nothing were wrong. She cleared her throat. She took a
drink of water. Daniel fidgeted, already impatient to leave. Impulsively, she reached out and caught his hand in hers.

"No matter what happens," she said, "I want you to know that I
will always love you."

Before he could say anything, she was already on her feet and rushing for the door. Once she was outside, she sprinted for the women's showers and shut herself into the latrine, which contained little cubicles privately marked by curtains. Pressing her hands tightly against her mouth so that no one could hear, she wept at last, the tears flooding silently from her as if they had no end.

What good will a mother's love do this boy if Hunter kills him? she thought. *Kills him because his mother chose to leave? I can't do this. I can't do this.*

Wren, a person normally of strict self-control, had never experienced emotions this powerful, this wrenching, this overwhelming. It was a ripping open of her while still alive, a plundering of her beating heart.

It was frightening.

The temptation to cancel her plans was almost irresistible. After all, the whole crazy enterprise was real only in her mind. It would be so easy to forget the whole thing, return the water bottles and beef jerky she had stolen from the mess, take a shower and go to bed early. No one would ever be the wiser, and in the morning Daniel would still be alive.

Granted, he could be alive anyway, but there was that very real risk that Hunter would avenge her escape by taking the life of her son. Whether they eventually found Wren in the desert or not would make no difference to him; the point would have been made to the others.

If she stayed, Daniel's survival would be guaranteed, at least for the time being.

But Steve Austin, Buck Leatherwood, and who knew how many others would die, and they would probably die by her hands.

As the surge of tears gradually ebbed, Wren remembered that killing Leatherwood—even killing or publicly humiliating Austin—could not be the sole purpose for Hunter; money had to be involved, *had* to be. Any of the guys could probably blow up Leatherwood, but not all of them could crack a safe in half without even scorching the cash.

He needed her. Without her there was a chance he might scrap the plan altogether.

The Cherokee believed that all human beings, indeed, all living things, were connected by the same spirit. All living things, in effect, were one. To stand by while others suffered was to hurt oneself; to desecrate the environment was to foul one's own nest.

If you do nothing, and people die, came the thought, *you will have no right to grieve for those who died in the Community raid.*

Gathering a handful of toilet paper to blow her nose, Wren thought, *Who do I cry for, then? Do I cry for my son? Do I cry for myself?*

And then, *You mourn for all who face the fire of the dragon.*

The dragon. An ancient symbol—even among the Cherokee—of the untamed energies of human fear and anger. The symbol of evil.

The voice of her grandmother came again to Wren as the night shadows gathered and darkness descended: *"If the little wren refuses to chase the big tawodi—hawk—from her nest, he will surely go on to rob the nests of others. Fear is real only in the mind. Have courage."*

Resolve came to her then, like a gift. Peace washed over her like the warm fluid of a mother's womb.

The truth was that Wren could not, after all, protect her son. Not anymore. If he wanted to be a man, it was time he learned to protect himself.

She could, however, do the right thing. Even little wrens had power against the great tawodi when they set their minds to it.

Emerging from the darkened cubicle, she washed her face at one of the sinks, took a deep breath, and headed to the barracks to make her final preparations.

From that point on, Wren did not look back.

The offsite, which would now serve as the Forward Command Post for the raid, was set up to look like a hunting camp. A collection of vans and trailers, many of them disguised with camouflage paint, were clustered together, along with pickup trucks outfitted with hunting chairs and various other four-wheel-drive vehicles. Austin was wearing some clothes Martinez had secured for him: baggy camouflage pants and coat, a goofy cap, and a T-shirt that depicted a picture of the world and carried the words: "EARTH FIRST. WE'LL HUNT THE OTHER PLANETS LATER."

Soon after he arrived, Austin sought out Jeb "Bulldog" Porter, the tactical commander for the operation, and the agent in charge of the HRT, who was setting things up in one of the disguised vans.

Although prematurely silver-haired, Porter had that SWAT team hawkeye look about him and was remarkably fit for a guy at least fifteen years older than the young hard-body crackerjacks working under his command. Austin had met him once at Quantico, where they were both taking classes in updated crime scene investigative technology, such as laser fingerprinting and the use of Luminol to detect blood which had supposedly been cleaned off of furniture, floors, and walls.

Fortunately, there was absolutely no bullshit about the man, which could not be said about very many federal agents.

Porter welcomed him with a distracted handshake. "I need to talk to you about a matter of extreme urgency," said Austin, "and it's classified." Porter gave him a long, keen appraisal, then sent everybody else out of the van.

"I'm working privately for a family," Austin said, choosing his words with care. "The wife and son were kidnapped a few weeks ago by Jeremiah Hunter, and I have good reason to believe he is holding them hostage at this camp."

"Jesus." Jeb looked at him in genuine shock. "A few *weeks* ago, and you didn't tell anyone at the Bureau?"

"The family was afraid, given how paranoid these people can be, that even the slightest risk of a media leak could put their loved ones in extreme jeopardy." Austin didn't blink. It wasn't a lie, anyway.

Porter withdrew a small notebook from one of his many pockets. "Description."

"White female, age thirty-six, five-four, one hundred fifteen pounds, brown hair, blue eyes. Name of Wren. Like the bird." He waited while Porter jotted down the information. "White male, age fifteen, six-one, approximately one hundred sixty pounds, brown hair, brown eyes. Name of Daniel." Groping around in his coat pocket, Austin produced a school photograph of Daniel and a snapshot of Wren.

Porter examined the pictures. "Last name?"

Austin hesitated. "Cameron."

"Okay." Snapping shut the notebook, he pocketed the photographs. "I'll brief the guys on the raid force teams and show them these pictures." He frowned. "Do you think Hunter could have them dressed in cammies like the others we've seen?"

"Highly possible. I'd look for whoever's not armed."

Porter nodded, already heading out the door. "I copy." Looking back, he said, "I assume the SAC knows nothing about this."

"You assume correctly. Or anyone else, for that matter."

For a long moment Porter gazed directly into Austin's eyes. "I'll let you know as soon as we've got 'em."

"Thanks, Bulldog. I knew you would."

After that there was absolutely nothing else for Austin to do but wait and try not to think too much.

Wren waited for two full hours after lights-out while the camp settled down and her eyes adjusted fully to the darkness. Then she slipped out of the women's barracks in the velvet depths of the hushed night like the shadow of a shadow, unseen and unheard. Knowing there would be a guard posted at the gate and another one at a fence point on the east ridge, she did not carry a light of any kind—not even matches.

Fixing her position by the North Star, she chose the planet Jupiter to guide her out of the camp. A star, she remembered from the night-tracking instruction she'd received at the Community so many years before, could be followed for about fifteen minutes before it would begin to lead her too far off her course as the earth revolved on its axis.

But she'd forgotten so much.

She'd forgotten how the absence of light would bleed out her depth perception; even her feet seemed disembodied and remote. Rocks appeared flat. Bare branches disappeared altogether.

And the noise. Sound, she remembered, drifted far on the night air; each foot had to be placed solidly under her, and each step weighted carefully, heel first, before being completed. Otherwise, not only might she stumble over a flat-looking rock, but the crunch of her footfall could alert someone to her nocturnal presence.

But as she made her painstaking way out of the base camp grounds and up into the surrounding hills, memories began flickering back. *Hold your head at a forty-five-degree angle to the ground. Look ten percent to the side and let your peripheral vision make out the details of what you see. Just don't stare at it. Keep your eyes moving.*

The new moon afforded her no helpful light, which was a good thing, or else the guard on the hill to the east might spot her. Movement, she remembered, was the easiest thing for the eye to see.

It was not a straight path, by far. Boulders, brush, junipers and scrubby mesquites blocked the way every few steps. *If you detour to the right around an object, detour to the left the next time.* Otherwise, she might find herself wandering in a great circle, probably to the right, since she was right-handed.

If it could be that simple. If a boulder looked like a boulder and a juniper, merely a juniper. But under the disguise of darkness, every bush and every rock appeared sinister.

Monsters lurked everywhere.

Her watch, thankfully, could be read by night, and when fifteen minutes had passed, she chose another star from her limitless selection and followed it. Repeatedly, she checked her position by the North Star—the one stable marker in the night sky. It soon became her friend, the one thing in the world she could count on.

Urgency loomed behind at every step. *Hurry. Hurry.*

It was not possible; the slightest rushed foot placement could cast her to her knees, or send a rock echoing to the base of the ridge.

The silence was absolute. On a November night there were no insects humming, no birds chattering, even the wind seemed to be whispering rather than howling.

Night silhouette.

Wren froze. She'd forgotten that, even by the faint glow of starlight, objects made silhouettes on the crests of hills or even along the sides.

She had to keep going. There was little she could do about the possibility of being spotted as a night silhouette, at least, not at the moment. All she could do was keep creeping along and hope that nobody followed her.

Moving with stealth across an open landscape in the black of night with the possibility of pursuers at her heels required intense concentration. Soon everything in Wren's life vanished, save for her guiding star and the next step.

Never in her life had she been more terrified.

Daniel lay awake for a long time, trying to find a comfortable spot on his bunk, trying not to think about his mother.

Something wasn't right. He couldn't put his finger on it, but her coming up to him at dinner like that was weird. She'd never done it before. What did she mean, *no matter what happens?*

What was she planning?

With a brief flash of fear he wondered if his mom was thinking about killing herself. Maybe they didn't get along all that well, but he sure wouldn't want her to do anything like that. She was his mother, wasn't she?

He knew she was unhappy, but Hunter said it was just a matter of time before she got used to things and settled down. He said that this mission the Alpha/Omegas were planning would get her excited.

Pounding on his pillow, Daniel decided that his mom really wasn't the kind of person to take her own life. As he flopped onto his back, the answer came to him like a thunderbolt: *She's planning to escape.*

Oh man! What . . . how . . . It all made sense! How could she do it, though? If she stole one of the rides, the guard at the gate would shoot her before she got ten feet. He was armed with an M1 and plenty of rounds of ammo.

Would she try to hike out? She wouldn't do something that crazy, would she?

She would.

He was right, he knew he was right. His mom was going to try to sneak off in the night, take off across the desert, and . . . and what?

Tell somebody.

Natch! That's *exactly* what she would do! She would keep on until she found a house or a store or something, and then she would call the *feds!* He knew she would; she wouldn't care if they arrested her; she'd send them back here to get Hunter.

Oh, shit.

Then here they'd come in their stupid ninja suits and crap, just like they did to the Community! Hunter said they hadn't been doing anything wrong at the Community, just minding their own business. He said the feds made up all this shit about weapons and stuff that was all lies just to cover their asses, that the real reason they raided the Community in the first place was because they'd bought a whole bunch of SWAT team crap and they needed to justify the expense. Hunter said the feds just did not want anybody to have guns, and that they'd killed *kids!*

It must be true. His mom hadn't said Hunter was lying about those kids so Daniel figured the whole thing must be true, just like Hunter said.

Hunter'd been good to Daniel, just like a father. He'd taught Daniel how to shoot and how to defend himself—that's something his so-called dad never did! All *he* ever did was bitch, bitch, bitch.

Hunter talked to Daniel, and he really listened to what Daniel had to say; he wasn't always criticizing him and stuff. He accepted Daniel for who he was and wasn't always trying to change him.

Shit, she could get them all killed.

He couldn't let her do it. And anyway, what if something happened to her out there? She could get snakebit or who knew what. She could get lost. She didn't need to be out there wandering around in the dark.

The way Daniel saw it, he didn't have any choice. It was for her own good; it really was.

He was going to have to tell Hunter. They'd wake everybody up to search for her. Like, *now*.

CHAPTER 22

THERE was no room to pace in the cramped van where Austin stood, feeling like an idiot in those oversized pants and cornball cap, and it was driving him crazy. But they couldn't have budged him out of there with a concussion grenade.

It had begun, and everyone was waiting tensely for the first radio com on a secured channel.

Martinez had set it up so that Austin could watch one of the countless rehearsals earlier, which had been conducted at the Ft. Hood Military Operation Urban Terrain training facility (with the help of one of the army's crackerjack Special Forces teams), so he could see now in his mind's eye what was happening. (MOUT had been chosen so that a reasonable facsimile of the camp could be constructed and outlined for indoor operations.)

While they waited, a high-flying FBI airplane (called a "Bubird") had already discharged seven crack HRTs in a silent parachute drop. Three of them were to secure the helicopter landing zone, while four snipers, using night-vision goggles and tranquilizer pellet guns (which only made a muffled *thud* when fired), were to take out any guards who might be posted on the two highest hills surrounding the survivalist camp. From there they would train the starlight scopes of their high-powered rifles on the encampment as cover for the infiltrating agents.

"*Red Team One, this is Red Team Six. Over.*" Austin jumped in spite of himself. Red Team Six was the agent to secure the east hilltop.

"*Go ahead, Red Team Six. This is Red Team One. Over.*"

"*The package is tucked away. Over.*"

"*Roger Red Team Six. Out.*"

Austin breathed a sigh of relief. By eavesdropping on the communication between the men on the ground, they now knew that one hilltop was secure. It took a while longer to hear from the other hill, agonizing moments for everybody in the van.

"*Red Team One, this is Red Team Four. Over.*"

"*Go ahead, Red Team Four. This is Red Team One. Over.*"

"*Nobody home. Over.*"

"*Roger Red Team Four. Out.*"

Austin exchanged glances with Martinez, who'd been standing silently in the corner, biting his nails. What they'd just heard was interesting. Red Team Four was telling them that there had been no guards posted on the other hill.

"*Bulldog, this is Red Team One. Over.*"

Porter, his face lined with concentration as he listened in on the exchange, quickly answered, "Roger, Red Team One. This is Bulldog. Over."

"*Baby's bed is ready. Over.*"

Now the landing zone was secure. Austin and Martinez exchanged a silent high five.

Porter nodded and said, "Roger Red Team One. Bulldog Out." Then he said, "Charger, this is Bulldog. Over." He was contacting the assault team leader, waiting in the first helicopter.

"*Bulldog, this is Charger. Over.*"

Leaning forward in the intensity of the moment, he said, "The cradle is ready. Over."

"*Roger, Bulldog. On our way. ETA two-zero. Over.*"

"Roger, Charger. Good luck."

Austin was dying to pace the floor. The choppers were estimating twenty minutes to the LZ.

"*Red Team One, this is Charger. Over.*"

"*Go ahead, Charger. This is Red Team One. Over.*"

"*The baby's ready for bed. Over.*"

"Roger Charger. Lullaby on Frequency Two. Over."

"Roger that, Red Team One. Music loud and clear. Out."

So far so good. The chopper pilots would now be receiving a homing signal, which would lead them to the LZ like a screech owl diving for a hapless field mouse.

Fifteen sweaty, endless minutes crept by like the hands on death's watch. Finally came the welcome crackle: *"Bulldog, this is Charger. Over."*

"Go ahead Charger. Over."

"Baby's getting sleepy. Over."

Austin couldn't stand it. This was the final approach of four Huey UH-1H helicopters, each containing six HRT assault team members whose job it would be to secure the camp from the north. Flying at high speeds below the ridgeline, they would come in around the base of the ridge downwind, in order to muffle their sound as much as possible.

He remembered Vietnam . . . how it felt to come swooping into a hot LZ, poised and ready for God knew what, the ground coming up faster than he would ever want it to, feeling the tail drop and his stomach along with it, the *whupwhupwhup* of the helicopter engine straining to make the tactical landing, leaping for the ground just before the chopper skids touched down, sprinting hellbent low and away from those deadly helicopter blades, his brain on high speed, his heart in his throat, his eyes looking in all directions at once, trying to keep alive, trying to stay alive. . . .

It was tough, standing there.

"Bulldog, this is Charger. Over."

"Go ahead, Charger. Over."

"Babes in bed. Providing air cover. Over."

"Roger Charger, Bulldog out."

Austin started to bite his own nails. Each of the four teams had a different color designation, and each had a highly specific objective. The Blue Team would hit the eye of the dragon: the leader's trailer. Simultaneously, the Green Team would secure the men's barracks and the White Team the women's barracks. The Black Team would secure the perimeter and take out the guard on the road.

"Bulldog, this is Gray Team One. Moving out. Over."

"Roger Gray Team One. Bulldog out."

Fifty more agents, many of them ATF SRT, made up the Gray Team. As soon as the choppers touched down, they had started drag racing in vans down the caliche road leading into the compound. Since the road twisted around for three bumpy miles, it would take them about five minutes to reach the camp.

For the people asleep in the compound, it was the beginning of the Apocalypse.

Wren had traveled only a couple of painstaking miles when she heard something, a sound carried to her in the clear, windless fingers of the crystalline night, a distant grumble like the sound of vehicles being started. She looked back, but the camp was not visible from where she was now, on the far side of the northwest hill.

She'd been found out!

They were coming for her for sure.

From the black hulks lurking on the ghostly crest of the ridge in front of her, Wren knew another ravine loomed, possibly a creek bed. Hiding down in it was her only hope.

Heedless of noise or leaving any sort of trail which would be easily trackable at dawn, she scrambled up the slope, stumbling, scraping her hands and knees, snagging her coat sleeves on clutching thorny plants, heart pounding, breath rasping in her throat, hands grasping, senses tumbling.

The ravine was deep. Black-on-black shapes, crouching and watching her with shadowed eyes, turned out to be junipers and gnarled mesquites. She picked out what path she could make out by starlight and slid down it into the jaws of the beast, on her butt.

She was swallowed up. The sky was completely blotted out, all stars instantly obliterated by the thick brush and tangled trees overhead. It was a world of infinite darkness and all-encompassing primal fear.

Blindly blundering, trying not to whimper like a shot deer, she groped her way into a thick tangle of juniper branches and brush, where she curled her body into as tight a space as possible, and waited.

Steve Austin, Mike Martinez, Jeb Porter, and several other men rocketed along the rugged twisting road down which the Gray Team had just traveled. As soon as the compound was secured, they would enter, along with various other agents and SSG personnel. Adrenaline tingled through Austin's veins like whiskey, and he remembered all over again why he had joined the FBI in the first place.

The rush, pure and simple.

Next to war, there wasn't anything like it, and any veteran who didn't admit that was a damn liar.

White chalky dust churned out behind them, glowing bloodred in the taillights. Everyone listened in tense silence as various team leaders checked in on the radio with Bulldog Porter, their words crackling out in staccato code.

And then, almost as swiftly as it had begun, it was over.

The Gray Team leader couldn't hide the triumph in his voice as he announced what they would later ascertain had been a textbook success: bloodless and efficient. Unlike the army, who trained soldiers to go in firing and kill or be killed, the purpose of the FBI's Hostage Rescue Team was to complete a mission with as little bloodshed as possible. Though they were highly capable of killing everyone there, if necessary, it was not the primary objective.

They were there to serve warrants, make arrests, and seize stolen property, and were trained not to fire unless fired upon or in defense of fellow agents. The night raid had been deliberately planned in hopes that these well-armed, well-trained people would simply not have enough warning time to respond in force.

There was no time for jubilation, however. A building-to-building, room-to-room search still had to be conducted and any hiding camp members flushed out. A massive cache of weapons which fitted the description spelled out in the warrant had already been discovered.

But as they were waved through the gate at last, Austin had only one thing on his mind: finding the Camerons. As if reading his mind, Porter directed the driver to take them to the head trailer, where the organization's leader awaited them, under guard and in handcuffs. As they passed knots of stunned compound people either lying prone on the ground or being cuffed and frisked, Austin started to tremble. Some of it was adrenaline mixed with a hint of fear, but most of it was rage.

How many lives was this man going to destroy before his career was over?

Thoughts of Lissie Montgomery drifted through his mind like

stardust, so young when he last saw her, so scared. Every single time she met with him, she'd been risking her life. Every time she sketched out the details of a proposed Community bank robbery for them, she took a terrible chance. Every time she gave them a name or described weapons in the Community armory, she risked death.

From the beginning, the only thing she ever asked for was that no one get hurt, and yet she had been hurt the most deeply of all.

Some agents, over a long period of time, grew dangerously attached to their informants. Informants were, by nature, criminals and liars. To seriously befriend one was to flirt with the devil.

But this girl was different; she had been then, and she still was. There was something about her that made him feel fatherly toward her, made him want to protect her. But in the end, it seemed, nobody had been able to protect her from Jeremiah Hunter.

More than anything in the world, Austin wanted to shake this brave lady's hand and tell her that she was going home.

Austin was armed, of course. He carried his favorite SIG-Sauer P228 9mm in a shoulder holster. As they made the final curve leading to the trailer, he fantasized about lining up those gun sights right in the middle of Jeremiah Hunter's arrogant, handsome head and pulling the trigger.

Austin was the first one out, but he waited for Porter to lead the way into the trailer, his impatience coiled within him like a cobra as Porter made final radio instructions to someone. Two HRTs, armed with the FBI's Remington model 870 shotguns, guarded the door.

"Good job, boys," said Porter as he ascended the steps.

"Stand proud," agreed Austin, following Porter so close on his heels he almost stepped on them. The small aluminum house trailer had a squat door, and Austin ducked his head as he walked in. Black ninja suits were everywhere. Some of the guys still wore their hoods, and they were all heavily armed. Parting the sea of black like Moses, Porter approached the sofa, where a man sat quietly. Austin shoved his way through and joined the field commander.

It wasn't Hunter.

"Who is this guy, Charlie?" Porter asked one of the black suits.

"It's a guy named Pete Stanley. I already called it in, and he turned up loud and clear on NCIC and TCIC computers. Weapons violations, armed robbery, attempted murder—a real charmer."

"Where's Hunter?"

"We've been asking around since we got here, sir," said a bulky man in black who was standing nearby. "Nobody knows what we're talking about. They say Hunter never was here. Most of them never heard of him."

"Is that right."

"Yes sir."

"Thanks. Good job, son."

"Thank you, sir."

"Now, Mr. Stanley, let's have a little chat, shall we?"

Austin jostled for position next to Porter. Pete Stanley, with tattoos on both arms and a scowl on his ugly face, looked like a mean son of a bitch.

"You have a family, Mr. Stanley?"

"I do. A wife and three kids. They're outside now, being terrorized by your glory boys."

"I'm sure they are," said Porter with a wicked little smile. "Would you like to see them before we leave? Because, otherwise, it could be a while. You know, what with paperwork and all. Could be days. Maybe weeks."

Stanley glanced toward the door.

Austin studied one of the tattoos; it depicted a skull with a snake crawling through one of the eye sockets.

"Tell me where Jeremiah Hunter is," said Porter.

The man clenched his handcuffed fist, and the snake undulated. "I will tell you the same thing I told your mutant robots: I have absolutely no idea where Jeremiah Hunter is. I knew him briefly in the joint, years ago. But even if I did know, I would not tell you greasy government sons of bitches if you *killed* my wife and kids." He turned his head and spat on the floor.

That's when the first fey flicker of doubt took flame deep within Austin's gut, in that place where a man *knows* a thing but doesn't want to face it yet.

It took a few hours for that little flame to assume wildfire status, take hold, and finally consume him. He gave it that long.

Long enough to search every square inch of that camp. Long enough to interview people and more people. Long enough to realize that the informant who had made this grand bust possible in the first

place had disappeared—probably around the time Martinez had lost contact. Long enough to figure out that although the bust was good, the informant (true to the nature of most informants) had lied about Jeremiah Hunter as soon as he caught wind of how valuable information on Hunter could be.

Long enough to realize that Lissie Montgomery and her son, Daniel, were not to be found anywhere in the camp, had never in fact been near this particular survivalist enclave at all.

Long enough to face the gut-burning blow that he was going to have to face Harry Cameron and his little girl Zoe and tell them that he had blown it again, that their wife and mother, son and brother, were still lost and would not be coming home after all.

They were lost, lost . . . and he didn't know where to find them. Didn't even know where to look.

Or even, for that matter, if they were still alive.

In the chilly predawn hours, finally frustrated beyond imagination and filled with impotent, exhausted rage, Austin eased himself into the backseat of a Suburban as tired federal agents labored around him, talking quietly and occasionally laughing softly together out of earshot. For a long time he sat staring at nothing. Then Steve Austin leaned his weary head facedown onto the back of the front seat, and wept.

CHAPTER 23

DANIEL was surprised that Hunter didn't get mad when he told him about his mom. He acted as if he'd been expecting it all along. "You did the right thing, son," he'd said, "and don't you worry. We'll find her."

Within five minutes the whole camp had been alerted, and five minutes later they were assembled in the mess hall. Hunter divided everyone up into small squads of four each and assigned them sectors to search, advising them to put small pieces of fluorescent tape on their backs so that they could keep track of one another in the dark, and to make sure their weapons had glow-in-the-dark night sights. The Alpha/Omegans took four-wheel-drive Jeeps outfitted with two-way radios and rode two apiece. Daniel rode with Hunter.

Because they didn't know if Wren was armed or not, they each carried weapons of choice. Daniel was now carrying the Colt .45 Hunter had wanted him to shoot that first day on the range so long before. The truth was, it had a little more kick than Daniel would have preferred. His wrists were always killing him after target practice, but he didn't want to be called a sissy by the other guys. Or worse.

Although Hunter didn't require the uniformity, most folks in the camp carried the Colts or various 9mm's; the Colts because they were used so successfully by the army, and the others because they could exchange ammunition if need be, like in a shoot-out. Most of the Strike Force members preferred combat shotguns or Heckler and Koch M5 submachine guns.

Hunter, of course, was carrying his "bear gun." Daniel noticed he'd exchanged the barrel for a longer one and that it was fitted with a scope. Hunter also brought along a pair of night-vision goggles, all of which made Daniel uncomfortable. He didn't think Hunter would hunt down his mother like a deer or something, but why else would he have brought the stuff? Daniel started to ask Hunter about it, but something about the fierce intensity on his face as he focused on his driving while they bounced along in their four-wheel-drive across rugged open country made Daniel decide against it.

Everyone had been ordered to use lights very sparingly. Game wardens tended to check out unexplained lights in this remote, open country. In fact, they didn't even use lights at the base camp at night unless they had blackout shades, and no lights were ever used on the exteriors of the buildings.

"We'll get out and walk now," Hunter said as he brought the Jeep to a stop. "And I'll teach you some things about night patrolling." He started rummaging around for something in the backseat.

This was so cool. This was by far the coolest thing Daniel had ever done in his whole entire life. Eric and Meshak and all the guys back home seemed so far away, like memories of childhood. He'd been so bored with life and school, and Hunter had, like, *rescued* him from it all, and Daniel was grateful for that.

Hunter was his own man in every way. That was one thing Daniel liked about the guy: he didn't need *anybody*. He could take care of himself in every situation, man—that's what Daniel hoped to be someday.

"Okay. Let's go." Hunter and Daniel got out of the Jeep, and when Daniel closed the car door and the little dome light went out, they were plunged into instant, unfathomable darkness. It reminded him of the little room he and his mother had shared their first few days at the base camp.

Only this wasn't a little room. This was a vast and unforgiving land. And his mother was all alone out there.

Then, for the first time, Daniel began to be afraid.

*   *   *

Wren waited, cramped beneath the tangled, prickly arms of the gnarled juniper, for what seemed like hours. She was just about to stretch her legs and get out when she heard the crunch of boots on rocks and the scratch of brush against sleeves. It sounded incredibly loud, almost right next to her, but she knew the dark was playing tricks on her again.

Scarcely daring to breathe, she waited. Soon came the unmistakable racket of someone sliding down into the dry creek bed, probably in much the same way she had. Muffled curses let her know there were two men, but she couldn't tell who just yet.

"Christ. It's blacker'n a witch's pussy down here."

"*Shshsh.*"

"What?"

"Did you hear something?"

Smithy. One was definitely Smithy. The other was no doubt a fellow Alpha/Omegan, since the elite seldom mingled with the masses. Big John maybe. Not Kicker. She'd know Kicker's deep bass voice anywhere.

What did it matter? If they saw her, they'd shoot first and ask questions later. Wren's heart jerked her whole body with each beat; she was *sure* they could hear it.

Suddenly, just to the right of Wren's sheltering juniper, a brilliant light glared. Instantly she squeezed shut her eyes.

"Oh, Smithy, you dumbass! You shined that light in my eyes and now I'm completely blind. Shut it off, idiot. *Dammit!*"

"Sorry."

"We're not supposed to use lights. Hunter specifically instructed—"

"Yeah, and I noticed the *great man* took along a pair of night-vision goggles himself."

"He did?"

"Damn right he did. What, you think he was going to stumble around here in the dark like the rest of us?"

Interesting, thought Wren. *It would appear there might be trouble abrewin' in the ranks. Well, what'd'ya know.*

"Anyway, I was only trying to help."

"The light just makes it worse, you moron."

"Let's just get the fuck out of here. This place is giving me the creeps."

"Lead the way. I'll just follow the elephant noises."

Some night search. Ex-cons, reflected Wren wryly, made lousy soldiers.

With infinite slowness she let out her breath. She was shaking so hard she feared the tree might give her away.

As the men moved down the empty creek bed that formed the ravine, Wren heard, "—Damn fool to think we could find her out here in the boonies in the middle of the night with no lights. Buncha crap. Dan should have just keep his mouth shut. She'd have turned up missing in the morning, and she won't get all that far in the dark anyway."

They moved farther away. Wren, her stomach turning in on itself, strained to hear what they were saying over all the racket they were making in the brush. She barely made out, "—kid had to kiss butt. It's his mission in life."

"Yeah, like somebody else I know—"

Finally, they were gone. Wren didn't move. Not for a long time. It just didn't seem worth it anymore, somehow. Then, heartsore and stiff, cold and dejected, she unfolded from her hideaway. A sip of water relieved her fear-parched mouth. Movement helped with the cold.

There wasn't any medicine for a weary heart.

Pulling herself blindly out of the ravine, hand over hand, Wren finally emerged into the night, panting and lifting her face automatically toward the heavens.

She had to find the North Star again. It truly was her only friend.

When Cam opened the door to Steve Austin, he knew right away there was bad news.

"Just tell me one thing," he said, still clutching the door-knob. "Are they dead?"

For a split second, time vanished. There was no past, no future, just Austin's exhausted, sad-eyed face. Then Austin shook his head. "No," he hesitated. "At least, as far as I know, they aren't. I can't promise anything, but as far as I know they're still alive."

"They weren't there, then? What happened?"

"May I come in? I think we should discuss this inside."

"Of course. Yes, of course, come in, Mr. Austin. Please." Cam held open the door. He stepped back with one foot and held onto the door with one hand, and Austin walked across the threshhold, but none of it was happening. None of it was real. It was a dream. Not real. A bad dream. He would wake up. One of these days, he was sure of it, he would wake up.

Zoe came scampering into the room, and with one look at her face, Cam's numbness went cold, then hot.

"Where's Mom and Daniel? I thought you were going to bring them home, Mr. Austin."

"Both of you. Come in here and let's sit down. I'll tell you everything." Austin took a step toward the den.

"Dad?" All the hope of the world was in her face, and he felt himself going cold again. She turned to Austin. "Mr. Austin? What's wrong? What is it?"

"I'll tell you—"

"*Tell me now!*" Zoe screamed, her voice as high-pitched as a two-year-old's.

Austin froze. Cam stared at his feet.

"We didn't find your mother and brother at the camp," he said. "We searched all night. Everything was as the informant had told us it would be. We made numerous arrests. We confiscated stolen military armaments. But Jeremiah Hunter was not there. He had never been there. Our informant lied."

"And you *believed* him?" said Zoe with a hysterical little laugh. "I mean, he *is* a criminal, isn't he?"

"Zoe—"

Austin raised his hand. "No. She's right." He rolled his eyes. "From out of the mouths of babes."

After an awkward silence, Cam said, "I think I need to busy my hands, Mr. Austin. Please, come into the kitchen and I'll make coffee."

He and Austin turned toward the door, almost forgetting about Zoe, who asked plaintively, "Can I have cocoa?"

Cam gave her a tight hug. She was shaking like a leaf. "Sure, honey. Cocoa it is. I'll make you my special blend."

While Austin and Zoe sat at the counter on barstools, Cam made them something to drink and dug out some cookies. Austin talked for a long time, his voice shadowed with self-recrimination and regret. Cam felt sorry for him. "You did the best you could, Mr. Austin. I couldn't have done anything different."

"Well, that's what I want to talk about," said Austin. "I think that I've done everything in my personal power to get your family back, and it's not enough. I also think that the time has come for you to go public about this and let the chips fall where they may. The FBI will mobilize, then, and everyday people will be on the lookout."

With a sigh Cam nodded. "What do you think, Zoe? This should be your decision, too."

"Well, when Mom got into trouble, it was a long time ago, and she really didn't do anything wrong, did she, Mr. Austin?"

He paused. "I have to tell you, she did assist in a bank robbery. But the bank was unoccupied at the time. No one was hurt. Still, she should be granted immunity because she cooperated fully and voluntarily with us."

"This guy Hunter . . . he made her do it, didn't he?"

"Probably."

"Couldn't we, like, get a lawyer or something? Somebody who could help Mom?"

Cam smiled. "Yeah. We could get a lawyer or something."

"But as long as she's with Hunter, he could hurt her, couldn't he? Or Daniel?"

With a grimace Cam said, "He might."

"Then let's go for it."

Austin said, "You must be prepared—this is going to be very high-profile. You'll be swamped by media. They can make your life miserable."

Cam shook his head. "Not any more miserable than it has been." Zoe caught his eye and gave him a little, *We're in it together, Dad*, half smile.

"Let me ask you this," said Cam. "Couldn't *you* get into a lot of trouble? I mean when I asked Wren to marry me, and she told me about her past, well . . . it's hard to explain why I called you. It's not that I didn't love her anymore or that I was afraid or anything."

Austin touched his sleeve. "You are a courageous man who knows

that to do the right thing—just simply *do the right thing*—can sometimes be the hardest thing."

"I guess," said Cam doubtfully. "I've felt guilty about it for sixteen
years."

"I can understand that. She's your wife and you love her, but in a
way, doing the right thing forced you to betray her."

"She never knew about it, thanks to you. And I'll be grateful to my
dying day for what you did, Mr. Austin."

Austin shook his head. "Don't you think it's time you started
calling me Steve?"

Cam grinned. "Probably not."

"Anyway. That girl had been through hell. Not only that, but we'd
never have caught Hunter without her. As it was, we found so much
incriminating evidence at the compound that we didn't need her
testimony to make our case anyway. Besides, there was no evidence
that she fired on any federal agents during the raid on the Community. My guess is she panicked and slipped into the tunnel pretty
quickly, so all in all, I figured the United States government *owes*
her, you know? They had who they wanted. She was never really
important, not from the beginning."

"So why didn't you turn her in? Let her take her chances with the
system?"

Austin shrugged. "She had a whole new chance at life, a new
beginning. I was afraid that if for some reason she wound up
spending time in prison, she'd lose that chance. I just couldn't stand
to see that happen. Not after giving her my word before."

"Aw, I'd have hung around," said Cam.

"Yeah. I know that now."

"I've always wondered . . . what did you tell your superiors?"

"Nothing," said Austin. "I never told them a damn thing."

"So . . . you aided and abetted a federal fugitive while you were a
federal agent."

"That about sums it up, uh-huh."

"Could you get in any trouble now?"

"I don't know. And I don't really care. Not anymore. All I want is
to get that lady and her son back home where they belong. And I'll
do everything in my power to see to it that happens. For what it's
worth, you have my word."

"I never doubted it."

Nobody said anything for a while. They all knew what each of them had to do, and each dreaded it in his or her own way. At the same time, each knew that it was the only way, the only hope remaining.

And time was running out.

CHAPTER 24

G RADUALLY, Wren became a creature of the night.
As the wind gathered energy for the dawn, so did she. It enfolded her within powerful wings, cloaking her footfalls and confusing her pursuers with phantom sounds. Eventually they all fell away and returned to their beds, but she kept walking, camouflaged by the wind, which loved nothing better than to confound the predator with mixed scents and hidden sounds.

The wind, however, was capricious and couldn't always be trusted. On some nights it did just the opposite.

But on Wren's first night in the wild, the wind was her friend and teamed up with the dark to disguise her progress. Eventually, the stars provided all the light Wren needed. Still, she had to step carefully, for a hole could look just like a dark stone or deadwood, and a twisted ankle at this point could prove fatal.

Her journey fell into a survival rhythm. She would first set her course by the stars, then glance down to place her feet, then cock her head to watch forward with her peripheral vision; back down to her feet, overhead again to check the star map, down to her feet, tilt her face to see up ahead. Right around this obstacle, left around the next. Glance at her watch, find the North Star, choose another guiding star.

The Cherokee believed that after death, the very wise could join the stars. Wren liked to believe that her grandmother was up there somewhere, guiding her and making sure that she did not select the wrong star.

Sometimes she wondered about the mysteries of DNA and the cosmic spiral of time and space. Were the instincts of her ancestors imprinted boldly on her cells, teaching her skills long since forgotten? Or was the spirit of her grandmother living within her own soul, speaking to her in her greatest time of need?

Were the answers to be found in the stars, or in her own heart?

Then, to her extreme consternation, the stars began to fade. Panic set in. What would she do without them?

But it was only the dawn. She decided to choose a hiding place before the *nutawa*, the rising sun, illuminated the earth and led her captors to her. She would sleep a while there. Down in a draw, three juniper trees hunched together like gossiping old women, the arms of their branches reaching all to way to the ground as if working the soil with their fingers. Hidden within the skirts of the itchy evergreen needles, she discovered a soft bed—shelter, perhaps for a doe and her fawn. She crept into the secret room and curled up, using deadwood and the sleeve of her coat for a pillow.

Somehow, she remembered one last thing to do: position a stick on the ground, pointing north.

At last, exhaustion possessed her, and she gave herself up to it. She was asleep almost instantly.

Breakfast was served an hour early at the Armageddon Army base camp, so that the soldiers could be ready to leave at first light in the search for Daniel's mother. They were ordered to concentrate on a two-mile perimeter of the camp, and to thoroughly search every dry creek bed, every tree, every hole in the ground which could be providing a hiding place.

At the headquarters, Dave and Meredith had already been alerted. The moment Daniel had told Hunter of his mother's escape, the headquarters team had been mobilized to post round-the-clock guards on the road leading to the highway and with the vehicles parked at the phony hunting camp. The electric wires, strung from base camp along the road to the south and onto the highway, were given special attention, in case she'd used them as guideposts to lead her out. So far, though, there was no sign of her.

Daniel hadn't slept much. As the hours passed, he worried more and more about his mom. He didn't see how she could have armed herself; Big John kept a close count of all the weapons and who carried what at any time. Still, Daniel knew for a fact that some of these people were trigger-happy; they'd probably shoot her first and find out later whether she was armed or not.

And nobody, in this place, would shoot to wound.

Meghan especially gave him pause. She was pretty and sweet and all, but he'd noticed a dark side to her. She was fiercely possessive of her position as Hunter's woman; the fact that he'd gone to so much trouble to bring an old girlfriend to the camp didn't set well with her. She never said anything to Daniel about it, but he could see it in her eyes whenever his mom was around Hunter.

It was weird, seeing a girl jealous of his mom.

Still, he wouldn't put it past her to blow his mother's head off if she had half a chance.

Why did his mom have to go and do this? Hunter hadn't done anything to her; he'd never even made a pass at her.

Shadows of his dad and Zoe, looming ever larger day by day in the corners of his mind, whispered guilty thoughts in Daniel's ear, but he wasn't ready to face them yet; he didn't want to think about it.

Strapping on his nylon camouflage holster, Daniel remembered what Big John had told him; if Hunter was going to insist that he carry his .45 cocked and locked, then he needed to keep the flap down to protect the hammer mechanism from dirt. He did so, but he didn't snap the flap in place; after all, you never could tell what might happen out there.

Furious hunger and a disarming need to pee awoke Wren from a dream-chased sleep. Her head hurt and early morning cold had seeped through her pants and coat and skin directly to her bones. Peeking out from her screen, she could detect no signs of anyone nearby and so crept off to relieve herself, catching her breath in the cold wind. Scampering back to her refuge, she gnawed on one of the beef jerkies and drank some water. Then she combed her hair with her fingers and rebraided it.

The temptation to stay in her little sanctuary was strong. Like a child who thinks he can't be seen if he hides beneath a blanket, she could almost convince herself that if she were only very quiet, they would never find her.

But they would.

They would track her down just like a deer. Her only hope was to keep going until she reached a phone or a vehicle or a pack of deer hunters—*something*, whatever she could find that might bring help.

As Wren emerged from the junipers and gazed around, she could see nothing but a dusty, green-mottled tawny sea of emptiness. The khaki soil beneath her feet was hard as concrete.

It was vast and lonesome, featureless as the bleached-out sky above.

After checking the position of her stick and aiming herself due north, she started walking.

Close up, the rocks were not all alike. Some were scarred with rusty stains, like spilled blood. Deformed scraps of deadwood littered the land, as if dropped behind by careless adolescent trees while on their way to some watery place.

As time passed, she would fix her position by the sun and keep walking. Her only company was the ancient lamentation of the wind and the crunch of her own feet on the gravelly ground. Because the terrain was not flat but marked by swells of rolling ridges, she found herself trudging up inclines frequently, and so broke off a steep smooth spike, which Big John had told her was a *sotol* cactus, for a walking stick. The word for the spearlike plant was Spanish, he said, and early white settlers had actually constructed houses of them since there was no wood or even the kind of sod which had been used by prairie newcomers.

When the sun was straight overhead, she stopped in the lee of a draw and rested in the shade of a massive boulder, taking more water and jerky. Tiny little purple and yellow flowers seemed to be growing out of sheer rock here and there; it was nice to know that, even in this bleak place, there could be found a certain natural beauty.

When she alarmed herself by dozing off briefly, she struggled to her feet and continued on, her stick moving in rhythm with her left foot. There were little hazards to watch out for all over the place. One plant, in particular, which was called the "allthorn" because that's what it was, all thorns; it could be nasty for stumbling into. Occasionally she would come upon wads of grass, but they were never green, always gray-brown in color.

The sun, even in November, was relentless, and she pulled a desert cammie cap out of one of the side leg pockets of her fatigues and socked it down low over her eyes. Eventually she began to sweat, so she took off her coat and tied the sleeves around her waist, but the wind was too sharp and she had to put it back on.

Every so often she would pause to survey, squint-eyed, the horizon in every direction, searching for her searchers. Only when she had satisfied herself that no one was approaching would she move on. Binoculars would have been a good idea, had she thought of it.

Hunger gnawed at her, but the worst thing to deal with was the thirst; her throat was parched all the time, her eyes grainy and her skin leathery to the touch. Back at the base camp, there was plenty of water, and they were encouraged to drink as much as they could hold, but she'd only been able to spirit out a few bottles which could fit in her pockets. Even with careful rationing, they wouldn't last long.

By the time the landscape began to dim, its jagged edges blurring and the horizon pinkening, Wren was beginning to stagger. Her boots, slightly large anyway, had rubbed blisters into her feet, and she had foolishly forgotten to bring extra socks. If an infantry soldier didn't take care of his feet, she'd heard somewhere, he was a goner.

The confrontation with Daniel had distracted her; she should have focused on her objective, which was to escape into the future and not let herself get sidetracked by the past. Otherwise, her son might not have a future.

Well, crap, she thought, *you live and fucking learn.*

She had no idea how far she had traveled, no clue as to where she was, or even where she was going. Rest. That's what she needed. Unfortunately, she couldn't find another handy little bed like she'd found the first night. She'd waited too long to start looking, and dusk was hurrying deep shadows into the crevices and hollows, erasing familiar sights and scrambling her mind. Finally, the pain in her feet almost unbearable, she crawled into a cavelike cleft in the flank of a hill and collapsed.

*   *   *

"*What is the MATTER with you people?*" screamed Hunter, striding back and forth across the mess hall meeting room, face livid, the cords in his neck standing out. "I send fifty-two *trained soldiers* out to find one fucking *little girl* hiking alone across *open country* and *you can't find her!*"

Daniel had never seen Hunter in such a monumental rage. It was frightening and increased Daniel's uneasiness concerning his mother.

"Hunter?" interjected Meghan, the only person in the room who would dare to speak at that particular moment. "Maybe we shouldn't have concentrated on a two-mile radius. She might have gone farther last night than two miles."

Spinning on his heel, he crossed the room in two steps, towering over her until she cringed. Punctuating his remarks with sharp pokes to her chest, he shouted, "If I wanted your *worthless, useless* opinion, I would have *asked* for it! Did I *ask* for it? *Did* I?"

Daniel winced. He could see the little red curls which sprang out from her forehead and temples trembling.

"No," she said softly.

"Then *shut up!*"

"Now." He stalked back across the room. "The Alpha/Omegas will continue the search by night," he said, pointedly ignoring the answering groans from some of the men. "We will double up, four to a vehicle, and we will use night-vision binoculars."

Four to a vehicle, thought Daniel. *That must mean I get to go.* In spite of himself, he felt a little thrill. He'd never gotten to go on a Strike Force mission before. And here he was, just a recruit.

"Mind if I ask a worthless, useless question?" asked Big John sarcastically, his bulging arms clasped across his chest.

Hunter stopped pacing and glared at him. "What?"

"Won't we run the risk of bringing down heat on us? It's hunting season. The warden'll be keeping his eye out."

"All the more reason," said Hunter with a smug expression on his face, "not to have to worry about it. We've got enough people posing as hunters up at headquarters. He'll assume it's them and not give it another thought." He turned to his silent audience. "If the Strike Force can't find her tonight," he said, "we'll all depart tomorrow morning at first light and intensify the search. Now, I've got an announcement to make. Some bad news."

Waiting until the attention of the entire room was riveted to him, Hunter said, "I believe some of you know Pete Stanley. Well, last night the fat fed pigs and their storm troopers raided Stanley's camp."

The room seemed to draw a collective gasp. "Now, the government-manipulated liberal media *claims* the raid was bloodless, but we know better, don't we?"

Outraged jabbering broke out over the room, and Hunter quieted his troops. "This is just one more recent example of the blatant bullying of the little guy by foreign-controlled henchmen. *The heat is on*, ladies and gentlemen, and if we do not find this runaway, she will bring them down on our heads like all the demons from hell."

After a little more dramatic pacing, his hands clasped behind him, he said, "We will not give up until this woman is captured. Is that understood?" After pausing until a sufficient number of people had responded by nodding, he said, "Strike Force members will take a short dinner break and rest. Meet back at my trailer at 2100 hours. Dismissed."

As the meeting broke up, there was little talking. Daniel noticed that his bootlace was untied and squatted down to tie it. "*He never should have brought them two out here in the first place,*" grumbled somebody behind him. "*They're just gonna get us all killed.*"

"*You ain't a'kiddin',*" said someone else. "*He says he needs 'em for some kind of special mission, but I haven't seen 'em do a damn thing yet.*"

"*Well, that oughta tell you what kinda mission he had in mind for Elizabeth the Queen. Like Miss Meghan ain't hot enough for him.*"

As the two moved out of earshot, Daniel felt his face flush so hot that his ears burned. Is that what people thought? Is that what people really thought?

Because he didn't deserve it, is all. He'd done everything everybody else did without complaining, even when he was so tired he wanted to crawl off someplace and cry. And maybe his mom wouldn't win any prizes for Miss Congeniality, but she did her share of KP without griping.

Fuck it, he thought, shoving his way out the door so hard it slammed back against the wall. *They're just jealous because I'm accepted by the Alpha/Omegas and they're not.*

Who needed 'em, anyway? Bunch of weenies. Turning his cap around backward on his head, kid style, he strode off across the compound toward the men's barracks to start getting ready for the night mission.

A deep-throated growl stunned Wren wide awake, pulse throbbing. At first she did not know where she was. The darkness was as cold and absolute as a grave.

Struggling to sit up, she heard it again, sending her blood racing on electrified currents through icy veins. The instinctive, primal urge to run sent her floundering for the less-dark that was the way out.

The savage javalina was known to prowl this area, along with bobcats, cougars, foxes, and coyotes. Her hand came down on the walking stick. *Her spear.* She grasped the stick, thrusting it in front of her in a feral attempt to defend herself even before she'd become fully awake.

The throaty rumble returned, louder this time. Just as she scrambled to the cavelike entrance of her shelter, the truth dawned on Wren: This was no animal.

It was a Jeep.

In a flash of panic she almost sprang from her hiding place to flee for her life.

Imitate the animals.

She did not question the strange thought, because it brought with it an understanding that cleared her head. Instantly she ducked back into the cleft, pressing her body as far back in the rock fissure as she could. She dare not poke her white face out to look around. Pulling her camouflage sleeves over her hands and securing her cap on her head, she put her face down on her knees and froze, scarcely breathing.

Even night-vision binoculars would have a hard time differentiating her body from her surroundings. Like a fawn hidden away by its mother beneath a sun-dappled tree, she sat perfectly still.

Time crawled.

Little itchy places popped up all over her body, but she stoically endured the torture.

The growl drew nearer. Then nearer still.

Stop, start. Stop to look around. Start up again.

Her feet went numb, and then her hands.

Voices, floating on the wind like clouds across the moon, drifted to her . . . *"Any sign of her? . . . that clump of mesquites . . . a fucking witch or something? . . . of scrambled eggs . . . always hungry . . . the east . . ."*

Rustling, crunching footfalls from all directions crisscrossed just below her hideaway. Then they started up the hill. She opened her mouth, took short shallow breaths so they couldn't hear her breathe. Willed her heart to stop racing so that she wouldn't faint.

Started to pray, then stopped. The Cherokee did not ask for things in prayer, but gave thanks for what is.

Yeah, right. Like I'm going to give thanks for this train wreck. She squeezed her eyes shut.

"Mom?"

Her heart took a hard tumble against her rib cage. It was Daniel, standing about twenty feet away maybe from her hiding place, whispering loudly, "Mom? If you're out here, you gotta come back. It'll be all right. Nobody's going to hurt you. Mom?"

Joy flooded her body. He was all right. He was still alive. She could be thankful for that. It almost sent her scrambling for the entrance.

But in the next moment came the equally powerful thought: He was alive, all right, and she was hiding in a cave from him.

Thank you, Lord, that my own son has betrayed me. Thank you that I cannot trust him with my own life, she thought bitterly, fighting to suppress the shudders that possessed her.

He moved away. A very long time later, the voices faded and the vehicle rumbled back to life and moved on out of earshot. When she thought it was safe, she stretched out her deadened legs and rubbed them back to life. But she did not leave the crevice until dawn.

By the second morning after Daniel's mom had disappeared, camp morale took a nosedive. Each day that she remained missing increased the probability that she might bring the authorities down on them. The federal raid on the south Texas encampment had shaken everybody up.

Hunter placed the camp on high alert status, ready to hunker down and resist attack with full force for as long as humanly possible. Food and ammo were placed on severe rations; all target practice was suspended until further notice, and training exercises were curtailed.

The Strike Force, however, was ordered to keep searching in ever-widening concentric circles from the base camp.

The troops were on edge. Squabbles were frequent during breakfast, Daniel noticed with bleary eyes and hands made unsteady by exhaustion. Complaints first trickled and then flooded throughout the mess hall. Those who didn't fully understand why Hunter had brought in Daniel and his mother in the first place were the most dissatisfied about the situation; they felt their security had been put at risk for no good reason. Daniel found himself excluded from the ranks, and even some of his Strike Force buddies grew cool toward him.

After breakfast, Hunter emerged from his trailer in a most foul mood. When a binocular strap broke, he hurled the expensive piece of equipment into the wall, shattering the lenses. Slamming back into his trailer, he emerged a moment later with an M16 fitted with a high-powered scope, which he loaded into the Jeep.

Somebody stop him, thought Daniel helplessly. *He's going to hunt her down and kill her.*

But nobody said anything.

CHAPTER 25

WREN'S feet were a problem. The farther she walked, the worse they got, until finally she started to limp. As the day dragged on, the limping worsened. The pain soon consumed her every thought.

Until the water ran out.

The beef jerky actually lasted longer than the water, but she found herself unable to chew it after a while because she was having trouble making the saliva necessary to soften it.

By nightfall, her feet were throbbing so badly that she could barely stand. She clung to the sotol with both hands, dragging herself along like Quasimodo. Her throat burned, her stomach cramped, and her hands ached, rubbed raw from gripping the staff. She was unable to search for a good hideaway and just crawled beneath a skimpy juniper, where sleep eluded her.

All night it teased her mercilessly, dropping warm and comforting as a blanket over her, only to be yanked away by wind-driven noises, fierce pain, lonely cold, and malevolent, demonic nightmares, punctuated by the bone-chilling cry of coyotes running in the night, looking for prey.

After many hours of walking through the rough country with no food or water, by afternoon of the third day, Wren no longer remembered what had brought her into the desert in the first place. All she knew was that she had to keep heading north, north, always north. Why, she did not know. All she knew for sure was that she had to keep moving, and she had to be very, very careful.

Though Wren had tried to remove her boots the night before in an effort to examine her feet, she had been unable to. Her feet had swelled into the leather and melded with it, like hooves. They plodded along, heavy and ponderous, the pain seeming at times to amputate them from her body.

A couple of times Wren encountered the peculiar sheep fences which stitched like scars across the wild empty swelling sea of rock and shrub. Unlike fences used for cattle or horses, the strands of these fences were knit into twelve-inch squares, making it impossible to crawl beneath or through. Because they stood almost as tall as Wren, this made it much more difficult for her to keep going north, but she had to, that's all there was to it, and so she would find a way over.

Many times she had to stop and rest. Getting back up gave her vertigo; she'd stagger around until the dizziness passed, then find the sun and head north again.

Droughty wind from the southwest blasted her along as it parched everything in its path. By late afternoon on the third day, Wren's tongue was beginning to swell. She could no longer swallow. Light-headedness made her goofy sometimes, made her see things that weren't there. A house. Water.

Nothing. They were all nothing.

She was nothing.

At twilight, a strange and wonderful lavender haze feathered the rugged horizon, blotting the sharp edges as if a watercolor brush had moistened them with pastel hues of periwinkle, mauve, and amethyst. Even the thorniest plants assumed a soft corona, as though carefully backlit for a formal portrait. The beige soil warmed into tones of burnished rosewood, while the sky deepened from powder blue to ultramarine to fuschia to ruby, with cathedral shafts of light streaming from stained-glass clouds.

A high ridge lay due north, directly in her path. It seemed insurmountable; just to look up made her head swim. To go around it would make more sense, but Wren felt an overpowering urge to clamber to the top of it; it became an obsession long after the last drop of strength she possessed in her body was drained dry. Using the sotol for leverage and balance, she struggled over cantilevered rock ledges, ignoring the pain which continually screamed at her.

When she couldn't climb anymore, she crawled on her hands and knees, dragging the sotol behind, heedless of stickers and sharp rocks in her path, always heading due north.

At the summit, she finally gave out, her limbs collapsing under her, and gulped air down her swollen throat like a dying asthmatic, the muscles in her body quivering. Through the brush she could see the fire of the setting sun. Everything glowed bloodred.

And then she saw him. At first she thought he was a buzzard, attracted by her carcass as she lay dying, but then she noticed that his feathers shone black, so black that they gleamed purple. Perched on a low mesquite limb, he peered at her with his raisin eyes, first one way, and then another.

When he spoke to her, his voice was raspy and deep. It wasn't very attractive at all. *"I am Golana, here to guide you. You have climbed the steepest peak, the sanigilagi,"* he said. *"But you have far to go yet on your quest."*

"What quest?" she asked, and her voice croaked much like his.

"You have begun the vigil. Give thanks for what is."

"I think I'm dying. I failed in my mission, and now I am dying. I'm not very thankful for that."

"You must remove from your heart the conflict that has thrown your life out of balance. Until you are able to forgive, you will be blinded to your vision, and you will suffer for it unto three generations."

Wren thought about that. She supposed she should forgive Hunter for the bad things he had done. And maybe she should forgive Daniel for hurting her. "Is that what you mean?" she asked.

"I speak of forgiving yourself."

This bird, this crow or raven or whatever the hell it was, wasn't making any sense. "I haven't done anything wrong," she said with a sniff.

"You betrayed your mother. You abandoned her and broke her heart. And now your son has done the same to you. And his child will do the same to him if you do not break the repeating cycle."

Trembling, deep within the marrow of her being, shook Wren's body.

Her mother, her beautiful mother, the ugly duckling who was taunted, teased, and laughed at until she grew into a lovely swan. It had taken Wren many years to realize that her mother's mistakes had been made from misdirected love, never from a desire to hurt.

Wren, however, had deliberately done the one thing that she knew would hurt her mother the most.

And she had paid for her sin, many times over.

"*Never look to others as the source of evil,*" cawed the raven, "*because the potential to cause harm lies in the hearts of every one of us.*"

Wren wept, but no tears came out; there was not enough moisture in her body.

"*When we allow our fears to grow unchecked, they darken into shadows that can engulf us, push us to dominate others and to misuse our sacred power.*"

"I miss my mother!" cried Wren. "I'm so sorry I hurt her. Will she ever forgive me?"

The raven cocked his head. "*She has crossed into the spirit world, into the realm of the sacred sky vault, the Gulanlati.*"

"No! I want to see her!"

"*She's with the Nunnehi, the Immortals. She heard the cry of your heart, and she sent me to help you.*" Spreading his great glossy wings, he suddenly took flight, flapping them with slow arrogance up, up, up.

"Don't leave me alone!"

"*The Tsalagi say there are no accidents. Things are as they are. Be thankful.*"

The pain in Wren's battered and bruised body could not match the agony within—the suffering of looking into her own shadow. Darkness crept over her. Lying on her back, she searched for the North Star, but the clouds had thickened and there was no light, anywhere, save for a single fiery crimson strip along the horizon. Then it too was gone.

Wren dozed, quivering always on the edge of wakefulness.

The reckless, fickle November wind changed direction. Keening suddenly and with great force from the northwest, it rattled the mesquite beans like dancing skeletons, shaking loose mummified leaves with a crackle. Wren awoke with a start. Peering into the darkness, she said, "Is someone there? Golana? Is it you?"

She tried to lift her head to see, but could not, so she turned it to the side. She was alone.

"I can't see the stars," whined Wren aloud in confusion. "I'll lose my way without them."

"The eternity of the stars is within you. Walk the sky."

The thought was as clear as a voice in her mind, but when Wren turned her head again, she could see no one. A great sadness possessed her.

A muffled rumble of thunder shook the earth. Wren turned her face to the sky. Cherokee legend called Thunder the ruler of the heavens and earth. It seemed as if he was stomping his feet. The wind brought with it the scent of moist earth. Wren inhaled deeply and decided that there must surely be no more delightful smell in the world.

A fat drop of cold water slapped Wren's cheek. Startled, she tried to lick it with her tongue, but her tongue was too puffy to reach, Another smacked her in the eye. Then her cheek, and then the ruler of the heavens poured out his wondrous gift of water, blessed water, so much that she had to turn her head to keep from choking.

When she was strong enough to lift her arm, Wren took off her cap and let the rain soak into her dehydrated skin. She drank as much as she could, then unscrewed the caps on her empty water bottles and positioned them to catch more of the precious moisture. Shivering, water-soaked, her teeth chattering, Wren finally felt enough energy to crawl beneath a juniper, where she succumbed, at last, to the sleep of the dead.

When she awoke, the sun was high in the sky and all the clouds were gone, as if they had never been. Wren expected to find herself mucked in mud, but the thirsty ground had sponged up every drop like a greedy drunk, leaving behind only little pools collected in the rock hollows. She drank from them like an animal, then treated herself to a tiny breakfast of beef jerky.

Though her body ached and her feet were still a mess, Wren felt infused with a vibrancy that hummed through her veins. The morning light gave off a liquid amber glow that seemed to surround everything with a golden aura. Oddly enough, her teeth kept chattering even as her body felt hot.

The details of the night before were as clear to Wren as a vivid dream or a drug-induced hallucination that echoes in the vaults of the mind long after the dope wears off. That she had been close to death, she never doubted. The reality of what had happened was another matter.

In those long-ago days spent with Wren's grandmother, the elders had often spoken of a vision quest. Some actively pursued it with arduous physical stresses on the body, lengthy meditations, tribal chants and dances, and even the powerful medicine of the peyote. To be visited by a spirit guide unsought was considered sacred.

As Wren retrieved her sotol walking stick, struggled to her feet, and stood on the crest of the ridge at the edge of the sky, looking out at the sweeping grandeur of the solitary landscape before her, she knew that what had happened to her was powerful medicine indeed, a spontaneous healing, a spiritual cleansing. Something in her had turned, as if realigning her with the cosmos.

The dull pre-rain browns of the earth now gave off a luster of mahogany, cinnamon, and copper tufted with the hunter green of junipers. If she tilted her face just so, the plants seemed possessed of slight halos. Crisp desert air fanned her burning cheeks.

But the sun was high now, and Wren could no longer tell which way was north. She turned this way and that, but her head felt zingy, and nothing seemed right.

Now she truly *was* lost.

The sound of thunder drew her attention to the horizon behind her. She turned in that direction curiously, because she'd seen no clouds. Nor were there any in that direction, not even in the faraway distance. Squinting in the morning sun shimmer, she replaced her cap onto her head, and then saw, with a sizzle-shock to her system, not clouds but trees.

A tiny, distant clump of trees.

A *house.*

There could be no other explanation in this treeless expanse. Trees which stood out like that had been planted. They'd been watered. Cultivated.

People. Due north. She knew it.

Excitement zigzagging down her spine, Wren began limping, plunging down the far flank of the hill. The trees were miles away, no telling how far, but they were there and that was all that mattered.

If she had not climbed the hill, she'd never have spotted the trees.

She couldn't help letting out a delirious little giggle. Still, her feet, glued as they were to the heavy boots, refused to travel as fast as she might like. They had little pain-filled minds of their own.

As Wren placed one foot carefully down onto a rock ledge, an unmistakable sound froze the blood in her veins.

It was the *tch-tch-tch-tch* of a diamondback rattlesnake, stretched straight across her path, looping its sinewy body into a coil even as she stared, transfixed, into its cold black eyes.

Tch-tch-tch-tch. The rattler's forked tongue tested the air, feeling for her heat, so that he could strike her and poison her with his lies. Her skin crawled, for nothing terrified Wren more than the swift and deadly rattlesnake.

This one was enormous; at least six feet in length. Rattlesnakes were capable of striking the entire length of their bodies. The hypnotic sound of his mighty rattle filled the air.

"Are you going to talk like the others?" she asked.

He fixed her with his black and empty eyes. He would mesmerize her if he could, and then strike.

"So you *are* real. *Shit.*" There didn't seem to be a way to escape from this creature. The frenzied warning rattle seemed malevolent somehow, hostile. He meant her harm, and she couldn't run away because she was backed up to the rockface. She'd have to fight him, even though she was literally quaking in her boots.

Cherokee warriors often wore the revered rattlesnake skin into battle to give them strength and swiftness. Throughout their history, certain brave Cherokee women followed their husbands into battle and forevermore became known as *Ghigau*, Beloved Woman.

Taking a slow step backward, Wren raised the trembling sotol high over her head and brought it down with all her strength onto the snake.

But her ordeal had weakened her and the blow wasn't enough. The rattle struck with lightning speed just as she leapt aside, missing her by a whisper. Sidewinding his big whip-coiled body, he drew back for a second aim, but cold weather had slowed him just enough to enable Wren to be faster. Grabbing a plate-sized rock and screaming at the top of her lungs, she smashed the rock down right onto his head, once, twice—what the marksmanship instructers liked to call a "double-tap."

The head was severed. Even so, the body continued to slash back and forth, its mighty muscles striving to coil even in the death throes, until, at last, it lay at her feet. Panting, shaking, heart still hammering in her throat, Wren stared at the beast. Even touching it with the toe of her boot made her quiver. She wanted to recoil from it and hurry away, but there was one more thing she had to do.

Casting about for another rock, a sharper one that she might use as a tool, she hacked off the rattle from the tail of the snake.

A talisman, for strength and swiftness.

Clutching the rattle in her fist, Wren thrust it toward the sky and let out another yell—not of terror this time, but of triumph.

CHAPTER 26

C AM and Zoe stood on the front lawn of their house, facing what appeared to be an army of reporters, trampling Wren's flowerbed, aiming all manner of cameras, microphones, and tape recorders into their faces. He'd never realized before how predatory these people could appear from the other side. Up and down the street, vans and cars from various news networks blocked the curbs of other houses. The story, which had attracted national attention in 1980, was even hotter now, particularly in the light of the successful joint FBI/ATF raid on the south Texas survivalist encampment which had just transpired a few days before and was fresh on people's minds.

Someone signaled to him and said, "You can go ahead now, Mr. Cameron."

"Okay, thanks." Clearing his throat first, he said, "Um, before I answer any questions, I'd like to thank all the friends and family and people we don't even know for all the support and encouragement we've been given since this situation became public. My daughter and I have been on our own now for several weeks, and we didn't realize how much stronger we would feel just knowing that other people care." He glanced down at Zoe. She was nodding quietly. "Uh, okay. I guess I'll try to answer your questions now."

The assault of voices was almost simultaneous, but they soon sorted themselves out into some semblance of a pecking order.

"Did you know your wife was a federal fugitive when you married her?"

"Yes. It didn't make any difference to me."

"But aren't you a lawyer? Couldn't you get disbarred or something?"

"It is my understanding that the government has absolved me of any responsibility in this matter; now, whether the bar wants to consider this on the basis of ethics is up to them."

Whew. This was going to be tougher than Cam had imagined. Now he knew how some of his witnesses must feel as he grilled them in court.

"Why did you wait so long to notify the authorities?"

This one, he'd anticipated. "Because this is a renegade band of paramilitary survivalists. At least one of them, Jeremiah Hunter, is an ex-con and a known murderer. It was our decision not to go public at the time because we feared for the lives of my wife and son. For this reason I hired a private investigator to begin the search—"

"But wouldn't you have had more success with the FBI? And don't they do covert operations all the time?"

"They do, and you are probably right. Hindsight, as they say, is better than foresight."

"Isn't it true that you did not want to involve the feds because you knew your wife was a federal fugitive and you didn't want her to be arrested?"

Cam hesitated. There was only one thing he could say in a situation like this when the truth was required. "I'd rather not comment on that at this time."

"Your wife has been working as a high school chemistry teacher. Is she going to be fired?"

"She's been placed on indefinite suspension, pending the resolution of this whole thing. My wife is a very energetic, involved schoolteacher. Her kids love her. Frankly, I'd be stunned if they fired her for this."

"How's your little girl holding up?"

Cam squeezed Zoe's shoulders. "She's one hell of a trooper. I couldn't have made it without her."

"But Mr. Cameron, with all due respect, you have asked a child to carry around an enormous secret, and at the same time to basically hide her grief from her friends and family. Don't you fear long-term emotional problems?"

Let's go for the guilt trip, why don't we? Cam wanted to say. Instead, he said, "If Zoe were not the incredible human being she is, then I might. However, we've gotten her started with a counselor, one who specializes in personal trauma, and she's doing very well."

"Why has the FBI decided to go public with this?"

Stepping back from the phalanx of microphones with evident relief, Cam gestured to Sizemore, who took over. "My name is Special Agent Elliot Sizemore of the San Antonio office," he said smoothly. "I was the agent in charge of the raid on the south Texas compound. As you may know, Wren and Daniel Cameron were kidnapped from the front yard of their home four weeks ago. We believe they are being held hostage by Jeremiah Hunter at a survivalist encampment somewhere in this country. They could be anywhere. We'll be televising photos of Mr. Hunter and the Camerons, and it is our hope that if any of you have seen these people at any time during the past month, anywhere, that you would call the San Antonio field office of the FBI. Tell the switchboard operator that you have information regarding the Cameron case, and they will put you through to the agents involved in the investigation. We've lost a great deal of time here. We can't afford to lose any more."

"Special Agent Sizemore. If you find Wren Cameron, are you going to arrest her?"

Cam glanced at the imposing, stern-faced agent. *I'd like to know the answer to that myself,* he thought.

"That is a legal matter," said Sizemore, "and depends a great deal on what the federal prosecutor wants to do. We'll be talking it over with her and come to a decision very soon."

"But Mrs. Cameron didn't take part in the Community raid, did she? I mean, she wasn't shooting at you guys or anything, was she?"

Cam felt himself shaking his head, and stopped.

"We have no evidence of that, no, but the crime for which she is wanted is not related to the Community raid."

"What crime is that?"

"Bank robbery."

"What bank? When?"

"That's all the information I have for you at this time, ladies and gentlemen. Thank you."

"Was it armed robbery?"

"Are we talking about a situation similar to what happened to Patty Hearst?"

"What makes you so sure they were taken hostage by Jeremiah Hunter? Isn't it true that there were no witnesses to the kidnapping?"

Cam and Zoe, firmly escorted by Sizemore and guarded by a bunch of agents in dark suits and sunglasses, made it back into the house safely in spite of the throngs of relentless reporters who continued hurling questions at them like stones.

Closing and locking the door did not help. To his horror, they kept smacking up against the side of the house, looking for ways to infiltrate with their huge camera lenses. He went around closing all the drapes. The kitchen window, which was over the sink, had a pretty useless frilly curtain hanging, so he pinned up a thick towel. He felt like he was under siege from an invasion of body snatchers.

He was absolutely drained. "Zoe." She came to his side. "Would you make coffee for the agents, honey? I can't even think straight."

"Sure, Daddy. Do I use the big coffeepot?"

"Yeah. It's in the cupboard. Here, I'll get it down for you." He fetched the coffeemaker for her and went to join the agents, who were bustling around in the living room, setting up a recording device on the telephone.

It was an invasion, it seemed, from within as well as without.

"Agent Sizemore, do you think it would be possible to get those people to back off a little? I mean, this is my property. The least they could do is stand out on the sidewalk and quit trying to break through my windows."

Sizemore nodded. "Tell 'em to move back from the house," he told one handsome young agent. To Cam, he said, "I can't make them leave altogether, not if they stay on the sidewalk. They have their rights, too, unfortunately."

"I understand. No problem. I just don't want my little girl terrorized when she tries to go to sleep."

"We've got a lot of ground to cover," said Sizemore as the other agent went out the front door. "I suggest we get started."

"I've given you all the information I have," said Cam dubiously.

"I'm not talking about that," said Sizemore with a dismissing wave. "I'm talking about instructions for you on how to handle it if your wife or Hunter contacts you."

Cam gave a gloomy shrug. "They haven't yet. Why would they now?"

Sizemore leaned forward, giving him a shrewd smile. "Because it's a whole new ball game now, Mr. Cameron. This time the heat's on those boys, and it's going to change *everything*."

Steve Austin expected to walk into a room with bad fluorescent lighting and a big long table packed with feds who would proceed to grill him over the fire deep into the night. He'd brought an overnight bag to the San Antonio field office and instructed Patsy to stay near the phone; he might need a lawyer before the day was over.

Then he'd had a nerve-racking meeting with Buck Leatherwood in which he'd confessed all. The case was simply too high-profile. Leaks were almost guaranteed, and he didn't want his boss to be getting any surprises with the evening news. He was fully prepared to resign and help Leatherwood find a new security agency.

He should have known better.

All Leatherwood had done was smile, shake his head, and say, "Shit, Austin, I knew when I hired you that you were every bit as big a gambler as I am, but like me, you're not a foolhardy one. You only take those risks that you believe have every reason to succeed, or those that you're fully prepared to lose. And you've got heart. That's just the kind of man I want to entrust with my life."

Elliot Sizemore, however, was a different equation altogether. Austin knew a by-the-books man when he saw one. He'd dealt with them his entire career in the Bureau. They believed that if you followed all the rules, obeyed all the laws, kissed every butt higher than your own, then you could never be accused of making a mistake, never get a bad review, never get passed over for promotion, and retire happy.

There was some truth to that, if you were intent on the management track. But for the footsore street agent, such niceties didn't always apply. You had to get down and dirty and deal with the very people you were trying to put away. Sometimes you went undercover and *became* one of them. You had to work closely sometimes with streetwise cops who didn't have carpeting and bulletproof glass in their offices and didn't trust you because they assumed you did.

You had to make quick decisions, think on your feet, act on instinct. There were times the goddamned rules just didn't apply, period.

Throughout his long and distinguished career, he'd known many of both kinds of agents. Inevitably, the two types came to despise one another. In some ways, they each resented, and at the same time envied, what the other had.

And this *was* Sizemore's turf.

Austin was shown into a room that contained several unoccupied desks. Sizemore sat at one and gestured him over. He shook hands with Sizemore and sat in a stiff chair opposite the desk. Everything on it was neatly lined up, shuffled, cornered, and arranged, including a framed photograph of a cheerleader-beautiful blond wife and two precious little girls, all wearing matching outfits.

Austin stifled a groan.

"Thank you for coming," said Sizemore.

Austin inclined his head, thinking, *Like I had a choice.*

"I've thoroughly reviewed this case, Mr. Austin. I tracked down and read all the files on the Community case. I also interviewed Judge Bob Holden, who was the federal prosecutor at the time, and I interviewed Carla McGillis, who will be the federal prosecutor for the Cameron kidnapping case. I also spoke to the agents who were your superiors at the time of the Community raid, and I spoke to Agent Mike Martinez concerning your participation as SSG on the south Texas raid."

Austin had to give the guy credit. The files on the Community case were massive, and the agents involved long since transferred, promoted, or retired. "You've gone to a lot of trouble," he said.

Sizemore went on as if he hadn't spoken. "I gave transcripts of our interview the other day to Judge Holden, and he agreed that he did indeed intend to offer immunity to Lissie Montgomery for her part in the bank robbery in exchange for cooperating fully in bringing down Jeremiah Hunter and testifying at his trial. However, since she fled, her testimony was never used."

Austin sighed. "Correct."

"I'll tell you what Judge Holden said." Sizemore leaned forward.

"He said that her testimony was not needed due to the large amounts of evidence found at the scene. He also said that the only witness who reported seeing Montgomery during the raid itself testified to him in chambers that she was seen—"

"Holding one of the dying children in her arms," said Austin. He cleared his throat.

"Right. Anyway, Judge Holden said that, as far as he was concerned, the girl never should have been placed on the FBI's wanted list in the first place."

Austin sat up. "What?"

"Carla McGillis agrees."

Austin said, "It damn sure would have helped if somebody had mentioned this at the time! Do you realize what this has done to this woman's family? To her *life?*"

Bureaucratic fuck-ups. It reminded Austin why he'd gotten *out* of the Bureau in the first place. "I can't believe this." He wanted to hit somebody. Not Sizemore, necessarily. Just somebody.

"Well," Sizemore leaned back in his chair, "apparently it doesn't make any difference to Jeremiah Hunter. He'd have come after her anyway, sooner or later. Only difference is, *you* wouldn't have tried to play hero and we might've gotten the woman and her son home by now." He frowned at Austin.

"All right. I deserved that."

"If it were up to me," scowled Sizemore, "I'd string you up from the highest tree."

Austin chose to ignore the veiled reference to lynching.

"I cannot imagine what you must have been thinking." Sizemore's voice grew louder. "You could have gotten those people killed. What if they'd been there the other night? Our guys could have shot them by mistake!"

Not likely, thought Austin, but he had no intention of getting Bulldog Porter into trouble and so said nothing.

Sizemore launched into an SOP lecture.

Correction, thought Austin, *it is Sizemore I want to hit*. He tuned the guy out. When he dialed him back in, Sizemore was saying, ". . . and that's why we *have* Standard Operating Procedure in the first place. It's for our protection as well as theirs."

Trying not to fidget, Austin interrupted, "So what's my punishment in all this?"

"They think you showed a lapse of judgment in not reporting the Cameron kidnapping sooner. I agree. They also think you are the most knowledgeable person around on the subject of Jeremiah Hunter. I happen to disagree." Sizemore quirked an eyebrow. "Overhead wants you to consult on this case. Go figure."

"They want me to *consult?*"

With a frustrated shake of his head, Sizemore said, "What're they going to do, fire you? Personally, I thought disciplinary measures of *some* kind were called for here, but I was overruled. It seems you have a few friends in the Bureau." He glared at Austin, who said nothing. "They want you on board. Just stay the hell out of my way, Austin, understand?"

Austin couldn't resist a huge grin. For the first time in days, he was starting to feel hopeful again. It was even worth an ass-chewing. *Hang in there, Lissie,* he thought, *the cavalry's coming.*

During Wren's journey to the trees, her body seemed to take on a life of its own apart from her mind. She was hot, but every now and then, she'd be washed with uncontrollable shivering. And there was something strange about her eyesight; it was as though she were looking at everything through a star filter. Exhaustion dragged at her clunky feet, but she still felt high, so her mind pressed on even though her body wanted to fall down.

Her head had a hot-air balloon quality to it. It made her feel as if she were somehow detached from her surroundings and maybe even her body. So she had to be careful—she didn't want to float off into the sky.

She walked all day. At the crests of some ridges, the trees which surrounded the house were visible, and they helped correct her course from time to time, drawing her along as a target draws an arrow. At first it seemed as though nothing was changing, that no matter how far she plodded on, leaning heavily on her walking stick, the trees and their sheltered house weren't getting any closer. She'd just as well have been trudging along on some gigantic treadmill. It was discouraging, but what else could she do? She kept going.

Then the trees seemed to be getting closer. And closer still. She began to make out details. A rooftop. A windmill. That meant water.

Wren's bottles had only collected a half inch or so of water in them from the shower of the night before, and the farther she walked, the less evidence she saw of any rain at all. She couldn't help drinking the water—she was burning up!—and her body began to crave it as surely as any drug addict ever burned for dope.

By late afternoon, as Wren staggered to the top of yet another swell of monotonous, monochromatic land, the morning's high was fading fast; she was in a great deal of pain and beginning to wonder if she was going to make it at all.

And there it was, nestled in a small valley. Emerald City could not have looked more thrilling to Dorothy.

The buildings—a house, a barn, and a couple of outbuildings—were constructed of stone taken, no doubt, from the land itself, for they seemed to blend in like a natural part of the environment. The house had a wide front porch and a dormer window and a tin roof. The trees were slender and tall and had been planted to protect the house, its scruffy little lawn, and the outbuilding, as a windbreak. A fence had been constructed around the homestead, with a gate opening to a path which led to the barn. The trees—those glorious, blessed trees—had not yet turned their leaves, which was why Wren had been able to see them. An old pickup truck was parked outside the fence.

She could see a rough caliche road leading away from the house and winding through the brush and out of sight.

And carried on the wings of the wind was that most precious and soothing of sounds: the gentle splashing of water. No desert oasis ever looked more welcome.

She'd made it.

Withdrawing the rattlesnake rattle from her chest pocket, Wren gave it a little shake. Yes, indeed, she'd made it.

She plunged down into the valley, ignoring the pain which raged from her feet and the fever which scalded her brow. She'd made it, and the first thing she was going to do, by God, was get a drink of water. By this time, Wren no longer limped. She now lurched, stumbling over small rocks and soil so hard and dry that it had become slick in places.

The sound of wild laughter came cackling to her, and she was startled to realize that it came from herself. She didn't remember laughing, but there it was. And who cared? There was water. There was life. There was help.

Golana the raven was right. There were no accidents. Everything was as it was. She'd headed north because this place, these people, were waiting here for her. Whispering a prayer of thanks, Wren crabbed along until she finally reached the windmill with its high, round tank. The groan of the spindly windmill blade came to her in metronomic rhythm, keeping time to the song of the water which poured from a pipe and splashed into the tank. A big square rock had been placed nearby, which Wren gratefully used as a step stool.

The water poured cold and crisp into her cupped hands, but it was trouble getting it to her mouth, so she immersed one of her empty bottles and took a long, delicious drink. It was too much; it upset her stomach, but she didn't care as she splashed the stuff generously all over her hot face and head until her hands were numb with the cold. Then she refilled her bottles.

Wren halfway expected somebody to come upon her, to say, "Who are you? Where did you come from? I didn't hear a vehicle drive up," but no one did. She looked around for the ever-present farm dog to awaken from a nap beneath the porch and come flying out, sounding the alarm, but there didn't seem to be one around.

Finally, when she thought she might indeed survive, she clambered down from the rock, clasped her walking stick, and hauled herself up to the little gate in the fence. It opened easily, and she let herself in, lurching along to the front porch, wincing as she climbed the steps, thunking across the wooden porch to the screen door.

As she raised her hand to knock, Wren glanced toward the big front window and noticed that there were no curtains. She couldn't resist glancing inside.

Wren gasped. What she saw was a deserted house. What furniture she could seen was dusty cast-off fifties art deco tables and chairs and lamps, the cheap kind that nobody really wanted then and they damn sure wouldn't want now. Discarded cot mattresses leaned against the cold fireplace.

The wind whistled, hollow and cold.

"No." Wren stumbled backward, her hand over her mouth, flung her weary body over the side of the porch, and circled the house, peering into every window.

More junk. A few storage boxes.

"This can't be right!" she cried. "There's got to be a phone, *something!*" In a rage she smashed the thin glass window in the kitchen door, reaching inside to unlock it, and let herself in. The floor creaked beneath her limp, as if to say, "Get *out*, get *out*, get *out*."

The house was colder inside than it was outside. A layer of unwelcoming dust covered everything, and she sneezed. There was no phone, no food, no electricity.

A touch of spookiness tickled down Wren's back. She jumped and looked behind her.

There was nothing. There was no one. She was alone. It was the creepiest feeling she'd ever known in her life.

How could there be a whole home . . . just out in the middle of nowhere . . . abandoned? Did the land drive them away? Or was it the wind?

Wait—was that the sound of someone *laughing*? Wren was *positive* she heard somebody outside laughing. She hurried onto the front porch and looked around. There was no one there.

Okay, okay. Just calm down, she told herself. *Relax and let it come. The answers will come.*

Then she thought of it, and felt like an idiot. The pickup, of course.

As she dragged herself over to the truck, it was as though she were floating above everything, watching herself, and all the colors were starbursts.

The pickup truck was a 1958 Chevrolet Apache, painted the same chalky tan as the soil, with olive-and-brown camouflage splotches added and carrying 1989 license plates. The side mirror was tied on with twine. A large cammie-painted shooting platform had been clumsily constructed and welded onto the pickup bed. It held a gun rack—sort of a deer hunter's limo, she figured.

The interior was all metal. More twine tied the passenger door to the steering wheel. The key was in the dash—apparently there wasn't much risk of car thieves roaming about and lusting after it. It had a stick shift—no problem for a kid who used to hang out in Indian territory. Back in those days this would have been a good rig.

Please, please, just have a little gas, she begged, easing herself onto the split vinyl front seat. She had to open the passenger window so the sotol staff could stick out and the driver's-side window so that she could see the cracked side mirror.

Working the clutch was agony to her bleeding feet, and the engine was reluctant to start. "Please, please come to Mama," she whispered. Wren pumped and babied and prayed until, at last, came the awesome sound of the old pickup coughing and spitting to life.

For a few minutes she sat and familiarized herself with the configuration of the shifting pattern, then she took it out of neutral, rattled slowly across the cattleguard, and took off down the road, trailing a cloud of dust and crowing like a rooster.

Dizziness almost swamped her a time or two, and the shifting was rough, but the thing ran—glory be to God, it ran! She was going too fast, hitting each bump and bouncing nearly to the ceiling. Alarmed, she slowed down—it would not do to get a flat tire now.

But it was hard! She was almost there, almost there—she could feel her husband's warm strong arms around her, taste his mouth, smell her daughter's shampoo, oh hurry, oh hurry, oh please God hurry.

The road snaked through the endless brush, coiling and winding and switchbacking until she thought she'd go mad. Even worse were the sheep-fence gates she had to get out and open and get out and close; her head was on fire and she could hardly grasp the closures, but she didn't stop, she didn't dare stop, she was almost there—

Suddenly, the jouncing road took a hard left and the next thing Wren knew, she had pulled onto pavement.

A highway!

Which highway, she didn't know. Didn't care, either. Drive long enough, she'd find somebody somewhere, and if she ran out of gas, she'd get out and hitch a ride. There had to be truckers or ranchers or hunters or *somebody* traveling on this road. Maybe she should even try to flag somebody down.

Up ahead, a vehicle approached, the sunlight glancing off its black hood with blinding ferocity. Squinting, Wren wondered what she should do, then decided to do nothing. After all, they were going in the opposite direction. What *could* she do? Crash into them?

The old pickup groaned along like an ancient tortoise who knows where he's going but has forgotten why. The sun-glinting vehicle, a Jeep Cherokee, blew past Wren.

But not so fast that she didn't get a chance to see the bald dome and glittering sunglasses of the driver.

"No! No! No!" Grinding gears and pumping the clutch, she pressed on the accelerator, *willing* the old heap to speed up. In the side mirror she saw the Jeep brake, whip around, and burn up the road between them. She pressed harder, downshifting, and flattened it to the floorboards. Somebody leaned out of a passenger window of the Jeep and aimed a rifle at the old truck.

Immediately, Wren yanked the wheel back and forth as they fired the first shot, but there was no power steering in this tank; it couldn't respond the way she needed it to, but it tried. The shot whizzed past the passenger window.

C'mon, c'mon, she urged, scooting her butt forward as if that would help. "*C'mon!*"

The rear window exploded with the second shot, sending shrapnel shards of nonsafety glass flying, pinging into the back of Wren's neck, shoulders, and hands. Short little panicky cries came from somewhere inside her.

The third shot hit her right rear tire.

With a death screech of old rubber, the heavy rig lumbered off the side of the road, while the big hunter's platform pulled it inexorably over, over, over . . . and there was nothing Wren could do but cover her face with her arms as, with surprising gentleness, it came to its rest on the passenger side in a ditch, landing her in a bruised and dazed heap against the passenger door, gazing bewildered up through the driver's-side window, right into the pointed muzzle of Kicker's custom nickel-plated Colt .45.

CHAPTER 27

WHEN word came over the Jeep radio that Daniel's mom had been found, Hunter let out a war whoop and immediately turned the Jeep back toward the base camp. Daniel was pleased and excited that she was apparently all right, but queasy about what was going to happen to her.

He was also worn out and angry with her for causing all this trouble. They'd been searching for four days and three nights, with very little sleep, and the whole camp was on edge. The south Texas raid had scared everybody, and the high alert status and food rationing had only made things worse. Daniel was sick of being blamed for it, too, even though he hadn't done a damn thing. He was glad that things were finally going to get back to normal.

As Hunter pulled the dusty Jeep into the compound, Daniel could see that everyone was milling around, waiting to see what Wren's punishment would be. It was the first time Daniel could remember seeing the whole camp gathered together outside in one place. It reminded him of pictures he'd seen of public hangings in the Old West.

Hunter got out of the Jeep, but Daniel stayed where he was, his elbow casually propped on the open passenger window. Suddenly he felt a little ashamed; he didn't really want to face his mother. He just wanted to make sure she was okay. He probably wouldn't hang around for the punishment phase anyway.

As the sound of the Jeep returning Daniel's mother echoed

throughout the compound, the restless crowd grew quiet and still. Daniel looked away and began gnawing on a fingernail.

The Jeep rumbled to a stop and car doors opened and closed. Daniel glanced over. His mother's hands were handcuffed behind her back. Kicker, towering over her, held her by the elbow. Daniel was stunned at her appearance. Her cheekbones stuck out over hollow cheeks, and her eyes were sunken into dark circles. Her hair was a wild black cloud and her dirty fatigues hung on her like hand-me-downs. He could see that Kicker held her not to guard her as much as to keep her from falling; she could barely walk.

As Daniel watched, she shook loose from the man's grasp and hobbled over to stand in front of Hunter, her chin high and defiant. Even from the Jeep, Daniel could see her light eyes blazing proudly.

He'd never seen her like this before. She was . . . awesome.

Clasping his hands behind his back, Hunter gazed into her eyes for a long moment. Then he rocked back on his heels and paced a circle around her. She did not turn her head. Then he came to stand before her again, pursing his lips as if trying to think what to say.

Suddenly, his hand whipped out and struck her backhanded across the face. The crowd gasped. She staggered backward, regained her footing, and stood straight again. There was a tiny trickle of crimson at the edge of her mouth.

Daniel gaped in absolute horror. He had never seen a man strike a woman before, never once in his whole life. Not even any of Eric's lousy dads had ever beaten his mother.

Hunter must just be crazy with anxiety and fatigue, like the rest of them. Had to be.

Mom, he begged silently, *just tell him you're sorry. Say you're sorry and you'll never do it again. Do it, please.*

Hunter slapped her again, harder, almost knocking her down, but she would not fall and she would not submit.

There was no sound but the grieving keen of the wind.

Something in Hunter's eyes glinted, and Daniel felt an immediate knowing shock. Suddenly, Hunter clenched his fist and connected, *crack*, with his mother's cheekbone, knocking her onto her butt. After a dazed shake of her head, she began scrambling to her knees like a punch-drunk boxer who refuses to go down for the count.

Somebody, help her! cried Daniel's thoughts, but nobody moved.

Hunter lost it. His fists blurred as he went after Daniel's mom.

The next thing Daniel knew, he was springing from the Jeep, running, flinging himself between Hunter and his mother, and he was screaming, "*Stop it, you son of a bitch! You're killing her!*"

Without even knowing it, he had positioned himself on the balls of his feet, knees bent, springing on his toes, hands curved in front of his body, ready to fight to the death if necessary.

Hunter took a threatening step toward Daniel and said quietly, "Get out of my way, you little twerp, or I'll tear your heart out with my bare hands."

Daniel's heart was jackhammering out of his chest, but he would not move. He had never once defied Hunter. His adolescent body betrayed him with a hot red flush to his face and ears. "J-just leave her alone, Hunter! She's handcuffed—it's not fair!"

It sounded stupid, but it was all he could think of to say at the time.

Hunter's eyes narrowed. "Not fair? You say I'm *not fair*? After she put this camp through *hell*? She could have gotten us all killed," he bellowed, "and you say I'm *not fair*?" He took another step.

In a flash Daniel had quick-drawn his .45, thumbed the safety, and pulled a bead right on the man's heart. He could hear and otherwise sense a dozen other guns being drawn and aimed at him, but he did not lower the weapon.

With a smirk Hunter said, "Haven't I taught you anything, kid? You're never supposed to point one of those things at somebody unless you're prepared to use it."

"You hurt my mom one more time," Daniel said clearly, "and I'll kill you." His voice cracked on the word "kill." His hands were shaking. He struggled to stop them, while all through his mind, Daniel had this helpless slow-motion sense of everything having pinballed way out of control, and he was unable to stop it.

Big John stepped into the fray. "Hey, man," he said to Hunter, "back off. It's the kid's *mother*, for Chrissake. How would you feel, man?"

After pausing a beat, Hunter relaxed. With a heedless shrug he said, "I guess the bitch learned her lesson," spun on his heel, and walked across the compound through the murmuring crowd toward his trailer.

"You can put that up now, kid," said Big John to Daniel gently. "Gotta take care of your mom."

The gun seemed soldered to Daniel's hot hands. He had to practically unpeel them from it in order to jam the weapon back into the holster. Even then he missed a time or two.

"Don't forget the safety," said John. "You don't want to go shooting yourself in the foot. I've done it, and it's embarrassing."

Daniel rethumbed the safety. He couldn't seem to stop shaking.

Glancing up, he could see that everyone had turned away and gone on about their business, leaving his mother in the dirt like a ragged heap of old clothes.

They don't want to help her, he thought, *because they're afraid they'll make Hunter mad at them.*

His mother was mumbling something. Crouching down next to her, Daniel slid his arms under her shoulders and lifted her into his lap, but he couldn't make out what she was saying. There were little speckles of blood all over her.

"Oh, my God!" yelped Daniel, "he nearly killed her!"

Shifting his shades to top of his bald head, Big John stooped down next to Daniel and examined her. "That's from the rear windshield from this piece-of-shit hunter's truck she stole someplace," he said, a smile in the back of his eyes. "That dumbass Kicker shot it out. I told him if we just followed her long enough, that old heap would fall apart, but no, he just had to act like we were in some goddamned Hollywood chase scene shootout." With a heavy sigh he added, "Glass, kid. Just little bits of glass is all it is."

An ugly purple bruise was taking mottled shape on his mom's cheek, her lip was swollen and bleeding, and there was a split over her right eye trickling blood.

Hunter had definitely done that to her.

"She's real hot," he told John. "What's the matter with her?"

"Could be dehydrated," he said, laying a huge hand across her forehead. "Hell, that ain't it. She's burning up with fever!"

"What do we do?"

"Get her to the infirmary."

Daniel blinked. "What's that?"

"Oh, you know. Bandages, aspirin, shit like that."

"I didn't know we had one."

"Yep. Just don't got no nurse."

"Can you uncuff her first?" he asked plaintively.

Big John shook his big head. "I don't have a key, because I didn't cuff her in the first place. Hell, any moron could tell she was too damn weak to hurt a fly. Hang on. I'll go get the key."

While Daniel waited, he studied his mother's face. Her injuries were swelling rapidly, and although her eyes were closed, she kept muttering things that he couldn't understand.

Daniel was deeply confused. He couldn't help but feel bone-deep shame, but on the other hand, he could understand how frustrated and angry Hunter felt, especially after the south Texas raid. He'd just lost control, Daniel was sure of it. He couldn't imagine Hunter doing a thing like this deliberately.

She used to be so pretty, he thought, and fought back a sudden uncomfortable urge to cry.

Up close, he could spot sunlight glinting silver in a few gray hairs that had sprouted from her temples.

"Mom," he whispered, blinking furiously, "I'm sorry. I'm so sorry." At the sound of Big John's approaching foot-crunches, he cleared his throat.

It didn't take Big John long to get the cuffs off Daniel's mother, and her thin arms fell away. Daniel struggled to lift her. He could bench-press two hundred now, but picking up an inert human being was a different matter entirely.

Big John reached for her. "Let me help you, kid."

"I can do it!" snapped Daniel. Clumsily, he managed to stand, even to lift her in his arms, but carrying her across the compound proved more difficult than he had imagined.

"You're gonna drop her. Let me have her." John wrestled his mom from his arms and swung her into his like a floppy-headed doll. Daniel trotted along. "It's in that building over there," John said, indicating a small building similar to the one Daniel and his mom had first stayed in. "Open the door for me."

Daniel obeyed, and John deposited her on a narrow cot in the room. His mom said something like, "Trickster."

"What'd she say?"

"She's delirious. It's the fever. We gotta get some fluids into her." John rummaged around in a tall metal storage cabinet.

"Is she sick?"

"My guess is pneumonia. We had one of them freak showers last night that rains on one little spot and then moves on down the road somewheres else. She must have got caught in it."

Pneumonia. It was a very scary word. Daniel stared down at his mom. She looked so little, like a kid. She was so tired and everything. He worried that she wouldn't have the strength to fight it. "What can we do?"

"She needs penicillin. I'll get some."

"How? Town's forty miles away. And you can't call a doctor."

Big John slammed shut the cabinet door, his arms loaded down with a sterile water bottle, gauze, bandages, hydrogen peroxide, and antibiotic ointment. "I'll get it, don't worry."

"But how?"

"I got my ways. Now shut up and take your mother's boots off while I try to get some of this water down her."

Glad to have something specific to do to help, Daniel busied himself with his mom's bootlaces, then tugged at her feet. He pulled so hard her entire body moved down on the cot.

"What the fuck are you doing!" yelled Big John. "You made me spill water all over."

"I can't get her boots off."

John stooped down and examined the boots. "Her feet are swollen bad. We gotta cut 'em off."

"Her *feet?*" squealed Daniel.

"No, peckerhead, her boots." From a scabbard at his waist, he withdrew a savage-looking knife.

"Jesus," breathed Daniel, forgetting, for the moment, all about his mom.

"It's a beaut, ain't it?" John extended the blade so that Daniel could examine it. "Recon Tanto. Best combat knife made."

"How come the blade's black?" Daniel couldn't resist touching it.

"It's a carbon five blade. That's black powder epoxy on the blade. Protects it from the elements. Don't touch that—it'll slice a hemp rope in half. Your finger wouldn't be nothin'. Now step back out of my way."

Slipping the knife blade carefully into the ankle of the boot, he gave a sudden twist to his wrist and sliced upward. The knife cut through his mother's heavy leather combat boot like butter. Rapidly, he did the other, then replaced the knife in his scabbard. The boots fell away and clunked onto the floor.

"Oh, *man!*" Daniel almost gagged. Dried brown blood, mottled with the bright red of fresh blood, glued the socks to his mother's puffy feet.

Big John said, "We figured out she must have walked thirty miles."

For a long moment they stared in silence. Then, as if talking to himself, Big John said quietly, "Kid, you want to see courage? I'd say you're lookin' the wrong way."

"What's that supposed to mean?"

John cocked an eyebrow. "Nothin'. Just think about it, is all."

Daniel was still staring at him when his mom said, clear as a bell-tone, "Get that mangy coyote trickster out of here!"

They both jumped and looked down at her. "What coyote?" Daniel asked, glancing around the room.

"Don't you see him? He's standing right there in the doorway laughing at me!" Her eyes glittered strangely.

Big John laid a hand on his arm and murmured, "It's the fever talkin', kid. She's gonna say lots of crazy things. I gotta go pick up some penicillin for her now. She needs it bad."

"Well . . . what do I do?"

"Clean all her wounds with hydrogen peroxide. Soak some gauze in it—see? Dan! Listen up. See this gauze here? You soak it in hydrogen peroxide, see, just like this, then you dab it onto this dried blood. Just keep doin' it and the socks will come away from the skin. Don't try to pull the socks off. Use this pair of scissors."

Trying not to panic, Daniel listened, but he did not want to be left alone with his mother. He didn't know any first aid. He didn't know how to bandage her up, like Big John was telling him to do.

". . . use lots and lots of antibiotic ointment. And keep giving her little sips of water, as much as she'll take. See if you can get some aspirin down her. We don't have an IV around here. You gotta do it. I'll be back as soon as I can, okay?"

His big body shadowed the open doorway. "And kid . . . don't worry. Your mom's gonna be okay. She's tougher'n them boots over there. Okay?"

Daniel gave a reluctant nod. "Okay."

Then John was gone, and Daniel was left with what was left of his mother.

Rabbit dancing.

Wren knew she had a fever, and she knew it was making her see strange things, like a waking dream, but in her mind's eye she could see Rabbit dancing.

In the old Cherokee animal legend her grandmother had told her many times, a pack of wolves had captured a rabbit. In this waking dream though, Wren didn't see wolves. She saw coyotes.

Tricksters. Funny thing, though. Rabbits were tricksters, too.

The coyotes were planning to eat the rabbit, but the rabbit said, "Wait a minute! I've just learned a new dance. Would you like to see it?" According to the story, rabbits were known for their wondrous dancing, and so the coyotes formed a circle around the rabbit, watching while she patted her foot like a little drum. Then she sprang all around the circle, dancing and singing her song. . . .

Ahw'usti knew the song. She would sing it for Wren, but Wren could no longer remember the melodic Tsalagi words. It made her sad. She drifted.

Rabbit dancing.

There was something important about Rabbit dancing. Something she should remember. What was it?

She dozed.

Rabbit dancing.

A sharp jolt of pain from one of Wren's feet brought her to mumbling wakefulness, and then she remembered. There was Rabbit, dancing and singing and stamping her feet all around the circle, when suddenly, she took a giant leap and scampered across the field to her freedom.

"*Rabbit!*" she cried. "*Wait!*"

Someone was shaking her, and it was annoying. "*Quit it,*" she said, but they wouldn't stop. "*I'm trying to talk to Rabbit—*"

"*Mom.* Mom, wake up. You're delirious. There aren't any rabbits around here."

Daniel swam in and out of Wren's vision. "She was dancing right over there, Daniel," she said in an irritated tone. Her voice sounded slurred and her lips hurt real bad. "With the coyotes." She pointed vaguely toward the corner.

Daniel's face began to blur. "There's no coyotes, Mom. Quit talking crazy. You're scaring me."

"It's not crazy! They need the rabbits for the bombs!"

"Shshsh. You're real tired. You've got a fever. Big John went to get you some medicine. Here, take a drink of water."

"Oh, water! That sounds wonderful." She tried to lift her head, but it was so incredibly heavy. Daniel slipped his arm beneath her neck and lifted her. He tilted a bottle of water to her lips. It had a little dish-detergent spout, and that made it fairly easy to drink. She took three grateful sips, then shook her head. "I'm so tired," she said. "Why am I so tired?"

"You just need to get some rest."

"Daniel . . . son, are you crying?"

A large round teardrop rolled down his cheek. "Mom, I'm so sorry."

"Why?"

"I just am."

"It's okay."

He laid her head back gently to the pillow. "No, it's not." His nose began to run and he swiped his sleeve across it. "I didn't know Hunter would get so mad. He didn't mean it, Mom. He was just scared. We all were. We were afraid you'd bring the feds and they'd blow us all away or something. He didn't mean to hurt you—I know he didn't." More tears spilled.

She felt one land on her cheek, like a bitter raindrop.

Somewhere through the befuddled cloud of her mind, Wren's instincts thrust through a message: *You still can't trust him.*

Little jagged shards of memory, like the glass she felt prickling the back of her neck, impaled themselves into her thoughts . . . little rainbow pieces . . . escaping from the camp . . . walking forever through scrub and rocks . . . the strange night on the hilltop . . . finding the deserted house . . . running for her life down the highway . . . losing control of the truck . . . Hunter's face when he hit her . . . her son picking her up in his arms.

"You saved my life," she said in wonder.

"I just stopped him is all. I knew he didn't know what he was doing."

Wren searched her son's tanned, angular face—so much older now than it had ever been, and yet so very young.

Hunter had recognized the boy's adolescent anger and had tapped into the source, channeling the energy for his own purposes. Whereas Daniel's parents had tried to get him to somehow see his anger and learn to overcome it, Hunter had found a way to use it . . . by treating him like a man even though he was so far from it.

It was potent medicine. Not even his own mother could fight against it.

What could she do now?

It made her so tired . . . so very tired just to think about it.

Now here she was, right back where she started from. She wanted to die!

She was surrounded by coyote tricksters. How could she ever hope to—

Dance the Rabbit dance.

The thought was clear, burned crystalline by the fever.

Dance the Rabbit dance for the coyotes.

Coyote liked to watch Rabbit dance. Coyote liked to dance with Rabbit.

Tlage situn gali sgi sida ha.

The ancient words suddenly came clear to Wren.

On the edge of the field I dance about. Ha ha ha.

Sleep overshadowed her and she began to fade out, but struggled toward the light. This idea . . . she didn't want to lose it. Didn't want to sleep it away or wait too late and forget about it. It could work. She would make it work.

Groping for Daniel's hand, Wren said, "I want you to go get Hunter for me."

Alarm blanched his face. "Mom? What are you doing?"

"What you said makes a lot of sense. I can see now that you're right, son. I made a terrible mistake, and I can understand how Hunter would have been upset."

If the words sounded somewhat mechanical through her stiffening lips, Daniel didn't seem to notice. A look of tremendous relief lit up his eyes. "I mean, we all felt that way."

"I want to apologize to him. It's . . . the least I can do for all the trouble I caused." She swallowed painfully. "And for making him so mad at me."

"That's a good idea, Mom. It'll make everybody feel better. Just let me finish bandaging your feet—"

She shook her head, and the movement made her dizzy. She hung onto his arm for support until the wave passed.

"You need to rest right now," he fretted. "Big John says you're real sick. You can talk to Hunter in the morning."

"No. I want to dance now."

"Huh?"

She forced a laugh. "Silly me. Look what tricks the fever is playing on my mind. Ha ha ha."

PART IV

DEAD PAST

Trust no future, howe'er pleasant;
Let the dead past bury the dead,
Act—act in the living present,
Heart within and God o'erhead.

HENRY WADSWORTH LONGFELLOW
"A Psalm of Life"

The memory of what you have been
and will be
resides in the heart.

DHYANI YWAHOO
Voices of Our Ancestors:
Cherokee Teachings from the Wisdom Fire

The smile on your mouth
Was the deadest thing
Alive enough to have
Strength to die.

THOMAS HARDY

CHAPTER 28

WREN was too ill and exhausted to feel any fear by the time Hunter stood over her with iced calm, his muscular arms folded across his chest. Daniel, his nerves raw and exposed, hovered about in her peripheral vision. She could remember how that felt, how her very existence had once subsisted on Jeremiah Hunter's moods. A bad mood meant instant dread; it was just a matter of time before you said or did something to displease him and provoke his rage. Daniel's defiance of Hunter earlier had put him in an especially precarious predicament now.

She could sympathize in a remote, detached way, but was incapable of empathizing through the hot haze that made up her thinking processes. This was good, because this way, fear did not freeze up her thoughts.

"It was my little girl," she said to Hunter, her voice at best a raspy croak.

"What are you talking about?" Suspicion furrowed his brow.

"I never had a chance to say good-bye to her," she said, "and I was worried about her. She's just a little girl. I thought if I could see her, she'd be all right." From the corner of her eye, Wren saw Daniel's face flush red. She wondered if he'd given his sister much thought at all since this ordeal had begun.

As Hunter considered this, Wren could see that he believed her.

"Why didn't you say something about it?" he said. "Shit, we could go get the kid any time you want. I told you that from the beginning." He frowned at her, scolding her for forgetting his thoughtfulness.

She shook her head painfully. "No. She's better off with her father." When he started to protest, she said, "She wouldn't fit in here at the camp. All the physical activity and everything."

"You got that right," Daniel interjected. "She's the original couch potato."

Hunter grinned. "Like father, like daughter, huh?"

Wren, guessing correctly that Daniel must have badmouthed his own father to this man, felt a stab of anger at her son, but concealed it carefully. Still, she couldn't resist glancing Daniel's way. He avoided looking at her. She'd have given anything just then to reach over and bop him upside the head—not hard enough to hurt him, just hard enough to get his attention.

"So how do I know you're not going to pull this same stunt again?" demanded Hunter, oblivious to the undercurrents passing between mother and son.

"I got sick out in the desert," she said. As if to verify the truth of the statement, her body started an uncontrollable shivering. "And I guess the fever cleared my brain or something. It made me see that you've been right all along." Her teeth began to chatter. "I'm ready to help you now. I'll do whatever you want, as soon as I get back on my feet." Around clenched teeth, she said, "Th-thank you f-for rescuing me."

Hunter laid the palm of his hand against her cheek and over one ear. His touch was tender, and therein lay the inherent contradiction of Jeremiah Hunter. "Jesus, you *are* burning up," he marveled. "If I'd known you were sick, I might not have been so hard on you." He frowned, as if it were her fault. A typical Hunter forked-tongue apology.

But you didn't take the time to find out, did you, you son of a bitch? She smiled up at him, her split lip shortening the gesture.

As if seeing her for the first time, Hunter stepped back and surveyed her body. "You sure messed up your feet, didn't you?"

She nodded. "I should have known better."

"Yes, you should have." He glanced over his shoulder. "Dan!"

"Yes, sir," barked the frightened kid.

"You take care of your mother, you hear me?"

Daniel, who'd already been doing that, glanced at her in bewilderment and said, "Y-yes, sir."

"Get her whatever she needs. Where's Big John?"

"He went to get her some penicillin."

Hunter nodded. "Good. The quicker you can get her fixed up, the better. I need her. We've fucked around long enough." He glanced back down at Wren. "And clean up her face. She looks like shit."

The next few days passed in a blur of sleep and the painful changing of dressings on her feet. Her dreams, for the most part, were spotty and forgettable.

Daniel dragged a sleeping bag into the room and nursed her with surprising gentleness. Big John was a frequent visitor and helped her to the bathroom on many occasions until her feet were strong enough for her to walk on her own. Penicillin, aspirin, and lots of water and rest worked their wonders, and after a few days she returned to the women's quarters, where she was given light duty for a couple of weeks which would allow her to sit while working.

It was during this time that emotional reaction set in.

She had failed.

More than any other fact, this one haunted Wren. She had failed in her mission; she was still a prisoner along with her son, and there would be no further chance for escape. All the little escape games she had played with herself to keep herself going in the early weeks of their captivity had been only that, mind games, mental exercises which led nowhere.

Cam and Zoe—and even Daniel, as he had once been—invaded her thoughts like poison gas, sickening her with longing. She wondered if she and Daniel had been given up for dead, if Cam and Zoe were moving on with their lives as if their family would never be reunited.

Sometimes she wondered if that might not be the best thing for them all to do. There was no hope, anywhere. A line from a movie she'd once seen came to her and clung: a seasoned convict had said to a young con, "Hope is a dangerous thing in a place like this." She understood now just exactly what that meant. Hope was merely cruel, a femme fatale which flirted with you even though she had no intention of ever fulfilling your desire.

In her most desperate hours, Wren would listen for words of wisdom to come to her from her grandmother; she would long for the sacred to return.

But it never did.

Survivors of near-death experiences, she'd once read, who were dazzled by the unspeakable glories of the afterlife, often experienced deep depression once they were forced to deal again with the frustrating details and the mundanity of everyday existence.

But this was not even her normal daily life. It was a bizarre detour which seemed to have no end. She wondered how long-term hostages of hostile governments survived each monotonous day, how prisoners of war kept going.

One night, while staring up into the darkness of the women's barracks, longing for sleep because it was the only escape, a voice came to her mind, and it was her own.

All your life you have depended on others to direct your life. From your mother to Hunter to Agent Austin to Cam, you've allowed strong others to be your strength.

Now you stand alone.

You must depend on yourself, not your grandmother or anybody else, to save not just yourself but your son.

At the realization, a deep shock of fear spread from Wren's chest throughout her body, a chill just short of panic.

But how? she argued. *How can I possibly save anybody when I couldn't even save myself?*

You have the strength now, came the answer. *Within your own mind and heart, soul and spirit, you possess all you need or ever will need.*

And then, *You have survived. You will survive again.*

It was true, after all. Only a few weeks before, just the thought of doing anything concrete to save herself was petrifying. But that was before her life-changing desert trek. Now, she knew, she would be able to do what was necessary and she would not look back.

This was not hope. It was determination.

In that moment a great relief flooded Wren's mind and heart, and for the first time since being captured, she slept soundly and the demons held back, lost in the shadows.

* * *

Wren made her first move a few mornings later, after the prayer meeting. She walked up to Hunter and boldly said, "I'd like to go back into training for hand-to-hand combat. I think I'm ready now."

The meeting was just breaking up, and people were still milling about, talking. Four or five glanced over to see what was going on.

Hunter, who'd been admiring Big John's knife, glanced up and said, "Forget it."

Whereas once she would have flattened her ears and skulked away in disappointment, Wren knew that no bully respects a doormat.

"My skills are too rusty," she said. "I can never participate in a mission without more training."

He scowled. "What makes you think you're participating in anything?"

Scowling back, she said, "I don't think you brought me out here to peel potatoes."

"Why not? You're pretty good at it!" He laughed, and a half dozen of the others laughed with him, even though most of them had no idea what was going on.

Steeling herself against the inevitable embarrassment which washed over her, Wren looked Hunter straight in the eye and said, "It's a big waste of talent."

He regarded her coolly. Suddenly his hand whipped out and grabbed her shirt. Instinctively, she pivoted on the left foot and brought up her right knee for a power thrust to the vulnerable inner thigh, but he was ready for her, twisting his own body out of the way and behind her, folding his hard forearm against her throat as he did so in a deadly choke-hold.

Wren started to bring up her foot to smash it down on his instep or maybe kick the shit out of his shin bone or knee, but thought better of it and, instead, flailed helplessly.

She had gone far enough to prove her point and demonstrate that she had backbone. To go any further might undermine him (in his own mind) to the troops. Besides, her skills _were_ rusty or she'd never have allowed him to maneuver himself behind her. If he'd had a knife and this were a real confrontation, she'd be dead.

After holding her with uncomfortable pressure against her larynx just a split second too long, he laughed and released her. The people around them laughed, too. Wren was careful to smile. Any other expression would have signaled hostility.

"Talk to Smithy. He's the instructor. Or Kicker. Either one." To the onlookers, he shook his head and said, "Pathetic, isn't she?"

Grinning along with the others, Wren caught Hunter's eye, and cheerfully thought, *Fuck you, asshole.*

Steve Austin tried to stifle a yawn, but it was no good. He covered his gaping mouth with one hand and reached for a styrofoam cup of coffee with the other. Some of the agents who'd been gathered together for briefing by Special Agent Elliot Sizemore were taking notes, some simply listening attentively, and others, like him, were staring dully into space and trying to keep awake. The room was too warm and Austin's attention span too short.

For reasons not quite clear to Austin, Buck Leatherwood was growing increasingly uneasy about his safety. Recently he had related a sickening dream to Austin in which a bomb had gone off while he was giving a speech, and he'd watched parts of his body fly away. Though Austin kept a full entourage of security personnel assigned to Leatherwood at all times, the man seemed able to relax only when Austin himself stood at his side. Consequently, Austin had been taking Southwest Airlines more and more frequently from Dallas to Midland and other points on the map to be with Leatherwood.

It was an exhausting schedule, and at one point a resentful Patsy had accused him of being a rich white man's slave. The remark had provoked a rare argument between them and things were still uneasy. Being summoned to San Antonio by yet another authoritative white man hadn't helped matters any. And the more he sat here listening to Sizemore drone on about the importance of establishing probable cause of criminal activity before winnowing out informants from various survivalist camps and building the strong intelligence necessary to mount another raid, the more frustrated he got.

While it was true that a number of white supremacist camps had drawn FBI and ATF attention in recent years, Austin was convinced that Jeremiah Hunter was not interested in establishing a white separatist world, although he had probably done so already, in a way. Nor did he think that Hunter was particularly concerned with mounting some sort of concentrated attack on government officials above the county line or sabotaging IRS offices, as were some of the paramilitary survivalist groups.

In spite of his rhetoric to the contrary, Hunter was not about ideals, Austin was convinced, even those twisted by bigotry and paranoia. No, what Jeremiah Hunter was about was money. Austin was certain that Hunter had kidnapped the Camerons because he wanted to use Wren to help him commit a spectacular robbery.

But what kind? A Brink's truck was the natural choice. There had been successful armed robberies of the armored trucks before, involving millions of dollars and leaving the hapless driver/guards dead. But none of them had used explosives in any kind of major way.

Bank robbery was the next logical choice, but where? When? Austin had already had a long-suffering colleague of his cross-check the FBI data banks for recent unsolved bank robberies with elements of Hunter's known MO and had not been able to come up with a good match.

And what the hell was taking the guy so damn long anyway? Wren and Daniel had been held captive for six weeks now, and as far as Austin could tell, Hunter had not yet made use of either of them. *Could be*, Austin thought uncomfortably, *that it's taking him this long to complete the brainwashing process.*

Patty Hearst had proven that, given enough starvation, deprivation, and humiliation, even the classiest people could be coerced into committing crimes.

Sizemore passed out a sheet of paper containing a long list of survivalist camps which had provoked the concern of the FBI. Austin glanced over the list, then fixed Sizemore with a lethal stare.

The Camerons would be dead by the time they worked through this list.

"This is ridiculous." For a brief moment Austin wasn't sure if he'd said it or merely thought it, but by the look on Sizemore's face and the stares of the other agents in the room, he knew he'd said it loud and clear. Sizemore pursed his thin lips.

"We'll never find them this way—it's like looking for a needle in a haystack."

"This is standard procedure," said Sizemore, making no attempt to hide his annoyance. Clearly he'd put a lot of work in on his presentation, and he didn't appreciate being interrupted or, especially, having his judgment questioned. "This is not the Old West, Mr. Austin. We can't go roaring in, guns blazing, no matter how much some of us might enjoy that approach."

Austin ignored the jibe. "I'm not suggesting we go blazing into anywhere, *Special* Agent Sizemore," he said, drawing out the syllables of the title. "But my navy friends tell us that if we want to find a submarine, we don't go wandering all over the ocean hunting for it."

"Colorful picture, Mr. Austin. But I don't see—"

"We set off depth charges, make the sub rise to the surface on its own."

"*Disinformation!*" cried an intense young agent who sat next to Austin. Sizemore frowned at him.

"That's right," continued Austin. "We plant some story in the papers that isn't true, something terribly offensive to Hunter . . . like, say, that he's a homosexual."

"Oh God, they *hate* faggots!" said the young agent. The other agents in the room murmured and nodded their heads.

So much for the politically correct nineties, thought Austin wryly. *Maybe we should say he's got nigger blood in his family tree*. Aloud, he said, "Once Hunter gets wind of the story, he's bound to come crawling out of the woodwork to set the record straight. He'll contact somebody, somewhere—and that will be our connection to him."

Everyone turned expectantly to Sizemore, who, to Austin's disbelief, was shaking his head.

"I just can't authorize that kind of behavior," he said.

"*What?* Why not?"

"The Federal Bureau of Investigation, or the FBI, often goes by the motto, Fidelity, Bravery, and Integrity. The American people have to know that they can trust us. We can't generate lies."

Oh God, groaned Austin inwardly, *he's a fucking Hoover man*.

Austin thought rapidly. "Look. This story—nobody would ever have to know that we planted it. We've used the technique successfully in the past and it never hurt the Bureau's reputation."

"There's always a first time," said Sizemore sternly, "and it will not happen in this investigation while I am at the helm."

Exhaustion shoved Austin's frustration over the edge into rage. "Look," Austin's voice was deadly calm, "I don't give a flying fuck who's in charge, or whether the Bureau winds up *embarrassed*. All I

care about is the lives of two people. The longer we fuck around out
here with all this informant crap, the higher the risk that the
Camerons will be killed. In my opinion—there's no equation." Out
of the corner of his eye, Austin could see some heads nodding in
agreement.

"Well, Mr. Austin," said Sizemore coldly, "I don't remember
asking for your opinion."

Austin leapt to his feet and pounded the table with his fist, upsetting the coffee cup and spilling coffee in a wide brown pool across
the table. *"This isn't about personal opinion!"* he yelled. *"It's not a
power struggle, Sizemore, it's life and death!"*

"It may not be about opinion, but it *most certainly is* about
authority. You have no *authority* in this case, Mr. Austin. You are
here strictly as an *adviser*, and I am telling you, I will not authorize
such an action!"

The two men locked glares, then Austin spun on his heel and
stormed out of the room, leaving coffee to drip with agonizing slowness over the side of the table and onto the floor.

CHAPTER 29

"MR. Cameron? Cam!"

Cam looked up from the yellow legal pad upon which he'd been doodling an intense design of concentric circles and lopsided squares. His assistant, Jane Cooper, was standing in front of his desk. Her bleached blond hair had taken on a brittle cast in recent weeks and her makeup was starting to look patchy. She'd been with him a long time, from a young woman barely twenty and just out of legal secretary school to a thirty-something divorced mother of two.

"I don't know how to tell you this," she said, and her eyes instantly filled with tears.

Cam got to his feet, leaned across his desk, and touched her elbow. "Sit down, Jane. What's wrong?"

Still standing, she said, "I just thought I should tell you that I've started looking for a position elsewhere. I had to, Cam, once you put me back to part-time hours, and then when we had to change to a cheaper health insurance plan with a thousand-dollar individual deductible, well, with two kids, I just can't afford—"

"It's all right, Jane, my goodness, there's no need to explain. I understand fully. In fact, I'll write you up a letter of reference myself—you should be able to get a good job on that alone. Here, don't cry." He dug out a white handkerchief from his back pocket. It was neatly folded, but unironed and wrinkled.

She plopped down in a chair opposite him, tears running in black rivulets down her face underneath her glasses. "I'm so sorry, Cam! I feel like I'm abandoning you when you need me most."

"Nonsense." He came around his desk, pressed the handkerchief into her hand and put his hand on the back of her neck, squeezing the tense muscles gently. "You've got a family to support. You have no reason to feel guilty. You've worked your butt off for me through the years. You've never complained, and you hung in there with me when things started to decline much longer than most assistants would have."

"It's just . . . I kept thinking they'd find them, you know?"

"I know."

"And now I've got these bills—"

"When you leave, I'll give you fair severance pay."

"No, no! I didn't mean that! I know you can't afford it. You don't hardly have enough clients left to pay your own bills." Struggling to regain some composure, she lifted her glasses and swiped at her cheeks with his handkerchief.

"That's not your problem, Jane. Fair is fair." Staring at the back of her bent head, her disheveled brassy hair, Cam felt a wash of childish abandonment. He honestly did not know how he was going to function without her.

She blew her nose. "When you get on your feet, and when Wren and Daniel are home and everything, I'd be glad to come back and work for you again."

"Shoot, don't you worry about it," he said with false confidence. "I never paid you what you were worth anyway. By then you'll be earning more than me."

She looked up at him then, meeting his gaze with a tremulous smile, then impulsively threw her arms around his waist like a little kid. As he hugged her back, he thought to himself that some nightmares never end. They just go on and on.

Since there was little to do that day, Cam sent Jane home early and headed that way himself through rain-drizzled streets and cold just soaking enough to be depressing. Thanksgiving loomed; he had absolutely no idea what he was going to do about it. His parents were begging him to bring Zoe and come for a visit over the Thanksgiving holiday. He knew they meant well, but he didn't know if he'd be able to stand up to a barrage of unanswerable questions.

Now that Daylight Savings Time had been lifted and winter was closing in, the days were getting shorter and darker. It seemed as if Daniel and Wren had vanished a year ago. On this day, Cam got home even before Zoe and went around the house turning on lamps. This was the time of year that Wren loved; she was always filling the house with potpourri and scented candles and pumpkins and Indian corn. The house always smelled wonderful and put everybody in the mood for Christmas.

Now it smelled like an old damp sock, and neither Cam nor Zoe could even bear to think about Christmas. Looking around, it occurred to Cam that the two of them had generated an amazing amount of clutter, from scattered newspapers and magazines and junk mail to Zoe's shoes and books and assorted teenage crap.

And yet Wren had always kept the place looking, well, crisp, keeping up after the four of them. How the hell did she do it?

Nagged by a vague sense of guilt, he began picking things up and putting them away in a desultory fashion. It was an oddly thera-peutic exercise, and he pitched in a little harder, digging through the cupboards for furniture polish and dragging out the vacuum cleaner.

By the time Zoe got home, he'd even lit a couple of candles. The place smelled, well, homier. At the first expression of sheer pleasure that flitted across his daughter's wan face, Cam felt even guiltier. He couldn't let things just fall apart, after all. He had to hold things together for her.

Cam's gravest worry as he awaited the safe return of his wife and son was not even money, even though he'd lost Jane and was in the process of cleaning out his and Wren's savings and jacking up their credit cards in an attempt to avoid plundering the kids' college funds. No, his heaviest burden weighed barely a hundred pounds and faced him each and every day.

Though Zoe put up a valiant front, Cam knew that she was sinking daily into the quicksand of depression. In spite of seeing a counselor once or twice a week, her grades were still falling and she was isolating herself more and more from her friends. At home, she was uncharacteristically irritable and moody. He tried to tell himself that part of that was the inevitability of adolescence, but the truth was so much more than that, and he knew it.

Their grief had no end, no resolution. There was nothing they could actively do to combat it. They couldn't become victims' activists or help bring a perpetrator to justice or even put up fliers for their missing family members. Wren and Daniel were not likely to show up at a homeless shelter or a truck stop. Nobody was going to run into them on the street. They'd just been swallowed up.

Gone.

Phone calls from Steve Austin were becoming fewer and farther between. Cam called his office frequently, but his calls were seldom returned. Austin was avoiding him, pure and simple, because there were absolutely no leads they could follow to solve this case.

The only hope Cam had was so bizarre as to be almost laughable—if Jeremiah Hunter had truly kidnapped Wren and Daniel to help him commit a spectacular crime, then all they could do was wait for the crime to occur and hope that law enforcement didn't shoot his wife and son by mistake! And Cam, as a seasoned defense attorney, was not completely convinced that his wife and son wouldn't somehow wind up being charged with that crime themselves, as accessories.

It was a conundrum with no solution.

Sometimes Cam felt as if he were going crazy. He'd taken to sleeping in Daniel's bed. He was plagued by relentless migraines. Sometimes he'd start crying at unusual and embarrassing moments. Some whole days he wasted away, sprawled on Daniel's bed, staring up at the superheroes.

He was walking a tightrope stretched over limbo land, waving his arms in the air to keep his balance, with no net below, struggling against the gusting winds of change, praying for the end.

And he didn't dare look down.

The November wind whipped around the corners of the buildings with more bite than usual, and Wren ducked her head lower into her coat collar as she scurried past the mess hall and rock garden to the armory. On the outside, nothing distinguished the armory from any other building, with the possible exception of the padlocked door. The padlock was missing, which meant the gunsmith was in. Big

John didn't like people messing around with his guns unless he was there to supervise.

She knocked lightly a couple of times, then entered.

The smell of a gunsmith's workshop was like no other. The greasy scent of various gun oils combined with the memory-evoking tang of leather holsters and the faint acrid odor of gunpowder served notice that this was a unique world, a world of masculine power and a certain exclusivity. You either knew and understood guns, and liked and appreciated them, or you feared them. You either enjoyed the rush that firing a weapon could provide, or you recoiled in horror from it. You either wanted one of your own, or you didn't.

Wren wanted one of her own.

Gun guts lay strewn all over Big John's various worktables like a firearms slaughterhouse. It was chaotic. Dirty rags, mysterious-looking oily containers of different solutions, specialized tools and slender brushes similar to those she'd used to clean her babies' bottles littered the room. On the walls, pegboard racks sported almost every type of gun Wren could think of, though she knew there were thousands more available.

Oldies music danced from a boom box in the corner, which showed how privileged the big man was; it was the only tape player she'd seen in the whole camp.

Big John sat perched on a stool, hunched over a Browning 1911 .45 which was held upside-down in a padded vise grip. Bright overhead lights shone on his bald head. Gone were the ominous mirror shades, but she noticed he was wearing glasses. When the heavy metal door slammed shut behind her, he glanced up, his concentrated expression easing into a wide grin.

"Well, look who's here!" His smile was genuine. "It's nice to have a visitor. Grab a stool and stay awhile."

Wren threaded her way through the debris to get to the opposite side of the table where he was working. "What are you doing?"

"Aw, the grip screws are too long. They stick into the magazine well. I'm just replacing 'em."

She nodded, watching his large hands move with amazing dexterity to replace the tiny screws. After a moment she said, "Um, the reason I came was . . . I wanted to thank you for all you did to help me when I was sick. Daniel would have been lost without you. Me, too."

Without looking up from his work, he shrugged. "Always willin' to help a damsel in distress."

But Big John had done more than just help her. He had defied Hunter. Though Hunter had let such a transgression go this time, Wren knew it set a dangerous precedent. He'd taken a risk for her, and she appreciated it. She wondered if Big John knew just how well she understood.

Glancing around the workshop, she said, "I used to know a hell of a gunsmith. His name was Samson. This place really reminds me of him."

"What happened to him?" Releasing the .45 from the vise grip, he stuck a sausage finger up inside the empty magazine well and felt around.

"He died." Wren was feeling strange vibes, here in this place. It was true that she could almost sense the ghost of Samson and of carefree days before she truly understood just how much damage a firearm could do to the human body. But there was something more.

She got up and began a restless wandering, fingering various gun parts and lifting a leather holster to her nose for a whiff. Wren didn't like to admit it to herself—not after everything that had happened— but she liked guns.

Unlike some people who regarded it as a loathsome chore, she liked disassembling guns and cleaning them, liked the smell of gun oil.

And she liked to shoot. She liked the self-discipline that good shooting required. She liked going down deep inside herself to a place where no one else ever intruded, liked the challenge of beating her last grouping on the target, liked the power, liked the thrill, liked the sheer aggressiveness of aiming and pulling that trigger and knowing she'd hit the mark.

And yet she'd seen Samson's face explode in front of her very eyes, had felt his blood splatter onto her skin.

The thought distressed her. Here she was, just getting in touch with her Native American heritage and the gentle wisdom of so many of its teachings. How could she reconcile that with, with . . . *this*?

Needing to be busy, to be doing *something*, Wren picked up a

Smith & Wesson .38, checked the cylinder to make sure it wasn't loaded, took it apart, and taking her seat across from Big John, began to clean it.

"What the hell are you doing?"

Her body jerked at the reprimand, and she looked up at him as he sat across from her, his face incredulous.

"Don't you know? You been here all this time and you don't know?"

"I'm sorry. Know what?"

"Don't you know that nobody, and I mean *nobody*, touches my guns but me."

The weapons in this building did not technically belong to Big John, but Wren understood that she was trespassing on private territory. Sacred, even. Immediately she laid down the .38. "I didn't know. Nobody ever let me come here before."

He cocked his head. "Where'd you learn to handle a firearm like that?"

"Samson taught me. At the Community."

"Oh." He nodded. "I almost forgot that you were there with Hunter." His eyes narrowed. "Z'at what happened to this Samson guy? Feds blew him away?"

Wren's chin dropped as she ducked her head to hide the sudden tears that had sprung to her eyes. She *never* cried! It was not her way! What was happening to her? Blinking furiously, she took a deep and shaky breath, then glanced back up. "He was standing next to me."

She'd never said those words to a living soul except for Cam, who tried, in his own sweet way, to understand, even though they both knew he never really could.

Big John regarded her for a moment with a keen-eyed gaze. "You don't talk about it much, do you?"

Swallowing hard, she shook her head. Samson was at once all around her and inside of her; he was in the scent of gun oil; he was in the old songs on the tape player; he was standing beside her again.

Sixteen years vaporized. And oh, how she missed him.

Wren fidgeted her foot, rolled her eyes to the ceiling, anything to keep a tear from falling.

"I can always tell a real combat veteran," said Big John, his voice gentle.

She sniffed and swallowed but didn't look at him directly. Couldn't. Not yet.

"They don't talk about it much," he said. "Real memories . . . they hurt too much. If they talked about it as much as the fakes, they'd be cryin' all the time."

She nodded and met his gaze.

"C'mere," he said, getting to his feet and moving down the row between the tables. He picked up a blunt, black semiautomatic handgun with a short grip. "Ever handle one of these?"

"It's ugly," she commented.

Big John threw back his head and guffawed. He even had a laugh a lot like Samson's.

She smiled.

"I can always spot a true gun nut, too." Still chuckling, he added, "Traditionalists don't like it because the grips don't have all that fancy hand-checkering like some of the other autos or even the custom engraving and whatnot. And they're not satin-nickel finished or anything."

"Samson used to call it sex appeal."

"That's a good term for it. But here. Hold it and see what you think." After jacking back the slide to check for rounds in the chamber and making sure the magazine chute was empty, he handed it to Wren, butt first. "It's a Glock Nineteen compact nine millimeter."

She hadn't held a gun in her hand in sixteen years. Pointing it away from Big John, she hefted it. "My God!" she cried. "It's so light!"

He grinned. "And there you have one of the main reasons this gun has become so popular with police officers. It's made of a type of plastic called polymer."

"A plastic gun?" she frowned. "Wasn't there something about this gun being able to pass through airport security?"

"Buncha hogwash," he said. "It'll still show up on X-ray."

She examined it. "I can't believe how well the grip fits my hand—like it's custom made."

"Well, that is a rubber grip with finger grooves—I had to put that one on myself, but yeah, women especially like this gun."

She prodded around on the backstrap. "Where's the safety?"

"See that little extra thingie on the trigger?"

"Yeah."

"That's the safety."

"Wow." She mock-aimed at a target on the wall.

"So you can't go jamming it down the waistband of your jeans. You gotta use a special holster."

"Oh." *Crap,* she thought, *I like this gun. How can I steal it if I've got to have a special holster, too?*

"They're Austrian-made. People who love them swear by them. People who hate them complain that they sometimes jam, but I think that's mostly because of crummy ammo."

"How many rounds does it carry?"

"It'll still hold fifteen." He grinned at her. "Wanna try it?"

"You mean . . . down at the range?"

"Where else?"

"But . . . Hunter . . ."

Reaching for the gun, which she handed him, Big John took down a box of bullets and started to head for the door. "C'mon," he called over his shoulder. "You let me handle Hunter." Tossing his glasses on the table, Big John took his trademark mirrored sunglasses from a breast pocket.

Wren, her soul still disquieted, followed meekly behind. Somehow or another, she'd crossed over a line. It wasn't something she could verbalize; it was just something she knew. A part of her she'd thought securely stashed away in the past had come rushing out of the mists to confront her. It was scary and exciting and confusing.

It was reckless to go shooting without Hunter's permission, even if Big John accompanied her. It was risky for Big John, dangerous for them both.

She didn't care, though, that was the thing. She was itching to get her hands on that little gun and see how it fired; see, even, if she could still hit the target.

Was there a secret reckless part of her that she didn't want to face? A shadow of her school-teacher-mom self, separate from her sensible, eat-your-vegetables self?

Big John secured the padlock. As she followed him down the path which led to the gun range, the thought of Daniel suddenly pierced Wren's heart.

Maybe Wren the mother had more in common with her wayward son than she'd realized.

A bruising wind blustered down from a pale blue wintry sky as Wren and Big John headed down the final leg of the short journey to the gun range. The high desert air was crisp and mind-clearing. Wren was exploring a new world, and in spite of everything else, it was exhilarating.

The Cherokee believed that one's life must be in balance, that misfortune tended to follow when one's life was out of balance. Somehow, Wren knew, she was going to have to reconcile these two sides of her essential self. She was going to have to marry that part of her that echoed her grandmother with this other headstrong and wild side.

She had already explored one side. Now she was going to have to explore the other. And then, the gentle starwalker was going to have to find a way to get along with the rebellious gun nut.

Somehow Wren knew that if she didn't find a way to balance these two sides of her nature, she'd never discover a way to save herself and Daniel. She would merely flounder, looking for answers in all the wrong places.

They reached the gun range and selected a place. So eager was Wren for Big John to stick the bullets, one by one, into the magazine and load the magazine into the pistol so that she could take her first shot that she didn't even notice her gape-mouthed son standing in the next stall over, staring at her.

As soon as she took the loaded gun from the gunsmith, all Wren could see was the target, the gun sight, and her own steady hands, clasped around the grip like twins who've just been reunited after a long separation—ready to fire.

CHAPTER 30

DANIEL watched as his mother, her mouth set in concentration, eyes narrowed, assumed the stance, sighted, and fired five or six fairly quick rounds. Like Big John, he turned to look at the stand-up plywood target, which was placed about ten yards away.

Sunlight steamed through one large hole over the "heart" of the target.

"Aw! She just hit it once!" blurted Daniel, then said, "It's okay, Mom. You just need some practice."

Big John's laughter boomed across the range. Others, who had only been pretending to pay attention to what they were doing, openly stared.

"Kid, take a look at the size of that hole! What, you think she's carrying Hunter's cannon?"

Daniel squinted at the target.

"That's a grouping, Dan. All six rounds in the same goddamn hole." He laughed again.

Wren gave Daniel a wry grin. "No challenge." To Big John, she said, "Let's move it back to about twenty-five yards, give or take."

Still shaking his head, Big John complied. Nobody else was shooting. They'd all gathered at a near but respectable distance, watching Wren. When Big John had returned, she aimed and fired five more times.

Big John said, "Kid, run get the thing so we can take a close look."

Holstering his own .45, Daniel sprinted over to the man-sized target. There was the earlier big hole over the heart. Four more smaller holes were grouped around it within about a four-inch radius. One stood out about six or seven inches to the right. He lugged back the target.

"Look at that!" his mom cried in disgust. "Low and to the right."

"What'd'ya mean?" Big John gestured toward the target. "That's a hell of a grouping for your first damn time shooting in sixteen years."

"How do you know I haven't been practicing every day back home?" She examined her fingertips for gunpowder.

"Dan says you guys don't own any guns. Said you wouldn't have 'em in the house."

Still not looking at him, she shrugged. "There were kids around."

"Uh-huh."

His mom glanced up at Big John then, and a look was exchanged between the two that Daniel couldn't completely comprehend. There was affection in it, respect, and a certain understanding. Like they shared some kind of secret.

Daniel could not believe the change that had come over his mom since she got back from her escape attempt. This was a woman he'd never seen before. Shit, as far as he knew, even his dad had never seen her like this.

Hunter had been letting her work out with Kicker, and Daniel had watched her a few times. He couldn't believe how much stuff she already knew about hand-to-hand combat, and how quickly she learned new techniques. And now look! She'd even managed to impress Big John on the firing range! Nobody impressed Big John.

It was so weird.

One thing, though, he was beginning to understand why Hunter had wanted her back.

"I love this gun," she said to Big John. "It's accurate, it's light-weight, it's compact—it's just an outstanding firearm."

"It's yours," he said.

"What?"

"We'll have to get you fixed up with a holster. There are only a couple that'll work with a Glock."

"Because of that trigger-safety thing?"

"Yeah."

"What's going on here?"

The whole crowd seemed to flinch. Nobody had noticed Hunter approaching the gun range. People automatically stepped aside, the Red Sea parting for Moses.

Hunter stopped in front of Wren and Big John, his hands on his hips.

"Big John was giving me a lesson with the Glock," said Wren, her voice calm.

"You didn't tell us what a crackerjack shot she was," added Big John with a smile.

Hunter's face registered no amusement. "I also don't remember telling you you could place a firearm in her hands," said Hunter, reaching out for the gun without taking his granite eyes from Big John's mirrored shades. Wren placed it in his hand without argument.

"If she's gonna be one of us," said Big John slowly as the smile faded from his face, "she deserves the right to defend herself."

"And that's a right that *I* give to her, John, and *I* take away. You got that?"

Daniel glanced from Hunter to Big John. There was something else going on between the two men, something more than an argument about the Glock. He just wasn't sure what it was.

"She's earned the right, goddamn it," said Big John, his forehead and bald dome ruddy from wind, cold, and raw emotion.

"That's for me to say." Daniel could see the pulse pounding in Hunter's neck. "And I haven't said. When *I* say she can carry a weapon, she can carry a fucking weapon."

Hunter was quite tall—as tall as Big John—but Big John was much stouter. He folded his huge arms across his chest and stared down Hunter. "Fine. You don't want her to carry a gun, that's your business. But if I choose to bring her down here for target practice, that's *my* business. You don't like it, you can goddamn well *stop* me."

Daniel glanced at his mom. She was staring at her feet, saying nothing. There was nothing she could say, really; even Daniel knew that. In this male-dominated world she had no power. He wondered nervously if Hunter was going to punish her, but decided that this was something that was between Hunter and Big John.

The two men scowled into one another's eyes. Neither blinked. Hunter glanced away first, down at Daniel's mom. "I've got no objection to her practicing," he said after a moment, "but you will maintain possession of the firearm at all times, is that clear?"

Big John's lips stretched into a mirthless grin. "Perfectly."

Hunter's gaze met the mirrored shades again. "Practice is over." With that, he spun on his heel and left.

"Son of a bitch," muttered Big John.

"It's okay." Wren laid a soothing hand on his muscled forearm. "I have to be at the kitchen now anyway. Time to get ready for lunch."

"Come by the shop tomorrow morning," he said. "We'll practice again."

She nodded and turned to go.

"Mom?"

She turned back.

"That was good shooting."

"Thanks, son." She beamed at him, and Daniel felt a happy little thrill. It had been so long since he'd seen his mother smile. It was so great that she was finally starting to fit in at the camp. As he watched her walk away and head up the ridge toward the mess hall, he thought that maybe they could do stuff together sometime. He didn't mind hanging out with his mom once in a while. She was pretty cool.

Hell, it could be fun.

"*Hunter!*" Wren caught up with his rapid strides at the top of the ridge. Without looking over his shoulder or acknowledging her call, he slowed down a step or two, giving her time to catch up. When she reached his side, he still didn't look down at her.

"Don't be too hard on Big John," she panted, struggling to catch her breath and keep up with him at the same time. "I was telling him about Samson, and, well, I got a little choked up. He took me shooting to cheer me up."

He came to such a sudden halt that she stumbled into him. Still staring over the top of her head, he said, "Are you sleeping with him?"

"*What?*"

"You heard me. You two seem to be getting awfully cozy lately."

She stared at him. This was so typical of Hunter's single-minded, petty egotism that for a moment she was struck speechless. Finally, she said, "Don't be ridiculous. He's not my type. Too beefy."

This time he dropped his gaze and studied her face with intense dark eyes. "Oh yeah? What is your type?"

There was a time, Wren reflected, when such a look would have melted her at his feet. And the years had been good to him. He was one of those rare men who actually looks better as he ages, the lines in his face only adding character to the classic features, the gray in his hair mellowing youthful cockiness to quiet confidence, his sexiness more understated.

Too bad he was still the same old psychopath.

"What are you thinking behind those beautiful blue eyes?"

She dimpled at him. "I was just thinking that you, of all people, should know what my type is."

He smiled at her, his teeth flashing white and straight. "I don't know. Once I was out of the picture, you went and married that geek accountant."

Still smiling, she clamped her teeth down on her tongue, hard. In the next moment she tasted blood. Finally, she managed to say, "Let's not talk about him."

"You're right. Let's not." He put his hand to the small of her back and they started walking again. "I'm so glad you're finally starting to fit in around here. I knew you just needed some time to get adjusted."

She said nothing.

"Dan's a great kid."

"Thanks."

"He's young, dumb, and full of cum, but he gives it a helluva try. I'm real proud of the progress he's made."

"Yes."

"Everything's finally coming together, just the way I knew it would." They had reached the mess hall and stopped outside the door. "But we're only halfway there, Lissie," he said, his eyes shining. "I've got so many plans."

"I can't wait to hear them."

He nodded absently. "Not just yet. Soon, though."

"I guess I need to get to work," she said. "I'm supposed to help with lunch."

"Why don't you come to my trailer tonight?"

No! No! Not yet. I'm not ready yet. "Huh?" *Stall for time.*

"There's an old movie on satellite I know you'd like. *For Whom the Bell Tolls*, with Gary Cooper."

"I'd love to see it, but I'm, uh, supposed to be here tonight. Dishes after dinner. Set up for breakfast. I'll be late." She shrugged an apology.

His dark eyes held hers for a long moment. "Some other time, then," he said. "They show these things over and over."

"I'd, uh, like a movie," she stammered. "Especially Gary Cooper doing an Ernest Hemingway classic. It would be a treat."

"You're right about that." He grinned. "I'll let you know the next time they're showing it."

"Sure. I'll be looking forward to it. Um, I've got to get going." She pulled open the door to the mess hall. "See you later." She flashed a smile at him as the door closed behind her.

Inside, all the strength whooshed out of Wren's body and she slumped against the door. *Oh, Cam,* she thought as she clung to the doorknob with trembling hands, *if I don't do this, you'll never see me and Daniel again. Please, please forgive me.*

Bone-deep exhaustion tugged at her resolve. Her heart was pounding and the tight veins in her temples throbbed a hypnotic rhythm, like native drums in some ancient, sacred ceremony. She was dancing as fast as she could, and it seemed sometimes as if the drumbeat would never stop.

The decision to allow Jeremiah Hunter to seduce her was a cold and calculated one. Wren knew that a man with his twisted ego would never completely trust her until he believed he possessed her. Actually, *trust*, as most people understood it, did not apply here. Hunter, like most paranoids, trusted no one; however, in order for her to gain access to the information she needed, Wren would have to convince Hunter that he possessed her, body and soul.

Granted, he had already kidnapped and imprisoned her. And technically, he could have her anytime he wanted, should he decide to force the issue. But rape was not the way of Jeremiah Hunter; his weapons of choice in this power struggle were his movie-star good looks, charm, flattery, and lies—the ultimate con.

Sex, to Hunter, was a power thrust, a claim stake of ownership. And once the objective had been achieved, sex then became a weapon of manipulation and control. It had taken the virginal Lissie a very long time to realize that lovemaking, to Hunter, was always a performance and never an expression of love.

Buried in a back corner of the mess hall, peeling potatoes in solitary boredom while the others joked and jostled through meal preparation in the background, thoughts of that early roller-coaster ride through the carnival world of Jeremiah Hunter poked and prodded their way through the shell of forgetfulness with which Wren had long since guarded herself. Remembering made her feel sorry for the innocent and foolish young Lissie Montgomery. She wanted to stop her before things went too far. The irony, of course, was that Lissie wouldn't have listened to her if she'd had the chance. She wouldn't listen to anybody then, except Hunter.

It was painful now, remembering, but necessary if she was ever going to be able to go through with it. How different this virile grown man had been from the groping frat rats she'd dated on campus. How slow his seduction of her, how practiced. Though she yearned for him almost from the beginning, he led her along slowly and never even took her to his bed until she had dropped out of school and followed him to the Louisiana bayou and the Community.

Then he made love to her all night long with a slow, concentrated skill that left her breathless for him. It was several weeks before he began withholding sex from her in sullen rages whenever she did anything to displease him—which was often. And it was several months before he began openly flaunting his unfaithfulness to her, sleeping with other women sometimes, she suspected, just to break her heart.

By then, of course, it was too late to leave.

Potato peels unraveled into a paper sack at her feet like the years of her life. She could never peel potatoes without remembering how much Cam loved her mashed potatoes, how he always came and picked out bits of potato from the pot to eat raw, how she'd slap his hand and shoo him away. How very different the gentle Cam had been from Hunter. Even so, there were some bruises which were not visible to the naked eye, she reflected, and they took years to heal.

It took several years of marriage before Wren came to realize that Cam didn't just make love to her—he cherished her. Even now, dropping skinless potatoes into the water one by one, Wren could remember the morning she had opened her eyes and turned her head to gaze upon the familiar face of her sleeping husband—they'd been married about five years at the time—and thought with an acute sense of wonderment, *This man will never hurt me.*

It took that long for her to be able to trust this man who loved her and never said an unkind word to her. It had been a real revelation and marked a turning point in their marriage. And now here she was, making plans to betray him.

She was finished with the potatoes. Wren got to her feet and carried the sack of peels out behind the mess hall, beyond the rock garden, to a place easily accessible to critters far and near. There she dumped the peels. The wind was cold, but fresh and invigorating, and Wren sat down for a few moments to clear her head before going back into the close, smelly-warm mess hall.

Out of the corner of her eye, she spotted a wee cottontail, its ears pressed back against its head, creeping out from some hidey-place to nibble on the potato peels. Wren sat very still, and in a moment another rabbit crept out to enjoy the feast.

The Rabbit trickster. Dance, Rabbit, dance.

Too, too much was at stake here. *I'll treat it like any good whore does,* she thought. *I'll disconnect from my body. Treat it like a job—a means to an end. The bastard will never know the difference.*

And her precious Cam, she prayed, would never know at all.

Even so, with all her careful reasoning and planning, it came as a shock to her when Hunter appeared the very next evening at the women's barracks. He knocked at the door and politely announced himself, which was the courteous way to enter the women's barracks, so that if any were undressed, they could cover themselves. It was early in the evening. Some were reading, some taking care of little chores. Wren was doing what she usually did, lying propped up on her pillow, thinking.

Meghan had the bunk next to Wren's, and she immediately sat

straight up, green eyes shining. *She's all but wagging her tail*, thought Wren sadly. Lissie, all over again.

But Hunter hadn't come to see Meghan. Walking past her bunk, he stopped at the foot of Wren's bunk. *"For Whom the Bell Tolls* is showing again tonight," he said. "Wanna come to my trailer and watch it with me?"

Wren felt her cheeks flush hot as she glanced over at Meghan, whose beautiful young face openly registered all the old familiar expressions: surprise, disbelief, crestfallen disappointment, jealousy, and rage. But there was nothing Wren could say, nothing she could do.

Arranging a delighted smile on her face and ignoring the silent woman who sat next to her, Wren said, "Sure. Just give me a minute to put my boots back on." Then she got to her feet and hurried to join her one-time lover, her captor.

CHAPTER 31

WHEN Steve Austin stepped through the front door of his house, the garment bag he was carrying by a strap over one shoulder caught in the door frame and nearly dragged him back outside. Irritably he disentangled the bag, slammed the door behind him, and dumped the bag onto the entryway floor. He could not remember a time when he had felt so tired, with the possible exception of boot camp. Or maybe Vietnam, but even in those days he'd been so young, so incredibly strong and full of energy. All he'd needed back then was a good night's sleep and he was ready to go again.

The young man he had once been haunted him these days. So swift of step and flat-stomached and *hard*. He'd been hard all over back then. Unconquerable. Even the racism he'd encountered during his early days with the Bureau—as one of the first few token blacks to be recruited—hadn't fazed him. He was *hard* His mind was hard; his body was hard; even his prick could get hard in a heartbeat.

Now he was just plain tired. All he ever wanted to do anymore was sleep. If he sat still for too long in one place, he was likely to do just that, nod off, and it scared him. He wasn't ready to get old, to be old, to *think* old.

He was losing his patience. Time was he'd never have let that dickhead Sizemore get to him. Now everything seemed to bug him. Racial slurs that he used to ignore now pissed him off. Client demands he might have taken in stride now provoked him. He was angry all the time, at the whole world.

He was even pissed off at Lissie Montgomery for getting mixed up with a slug like Hunter in the first place, for running away instead of trusting the agent who was trying to help her, for trying to handle things on her own when Hunter showed back up, for endangering her family, for getting herself kidnapped. For staying lost while Austin was trying so goddamned hard to find her.

For maybe getting herself and her son killed.

And for making him feel like a total failure.

Austin wandered through the big, handsome den Patsy had decorated with African art and tribal artifacts they'd collected on a couple of trips to the continent. A fire crackled in the stone hearth beneath a pottery-crowded mantel. Shuffling wearily, Austin crossed over to the wet bar and got himself a beer, then headed into the kitchen, glancing around for his wife. The gravelly tones of Louis Armstrong wafted from the sound system, but there was no sign of Patsy.

Austin's trip to San Antonio had been brief, but long enough for him to regret some of the things he'd said during their argument. He could be a real shit sometimes. Patsy had her faults, but for the most part she'd devoted her life to him and the kids. She deserved a hell of a lot better than she got.

A better man probably would have thought to bring flowers, he thought, wincing to himself as he passed through the dining room and into the hallway which led to the master bedroom. He just never was any damn good at that romance stuff. When they'd first met, he'd been playing football for Grambling, but he wasn't one of the stars. Every big man on campus had the hots for the beautiful Patsy Shepherd. Some of them had plenty of money and wined and dined her properly. Austin didn't see how he could compete. A war veteran attending college on the GI bill, he was years older—centuries older—than those boys. Even though it was an all-black school, he'd still felt set apart from everyone and kept to himself, working hard on his studies.

In the end, she asked him out—to a Sadie Hawkins dance. Now, more than thirty years later, he still felt lucky.

The bedroom was Patsy's sanctuary, and it reflected her elegance and taste. Whereas the den was rugged and made any man feel welcome and comfortable, their bedroom was essentially feminine. Not frilly and fussy, but . . . soft. From the white handmade battenburg lace duvet cover to the pile of sumptuous pillows to the ecru lace panels draped seductively from the cherrywood canopy, Austin always felt as if he had been invited into his wife's bed.

He liked the way the bedroom made him feel; it was kind of exciting. But lately, all he'd been doing in that bed was sleeping. He sighed.

"*Steve? Is that you?*" Patsy called from the direction of the bathroom.

"Yeah, it's me." He plunked down on the edge of the feather-soft bed, a mere microsecond away from oblivion.

"Would you come here a minute, please? I'd like to talk to you about something."

Steve groaned. He really didn't want to fight anymore. "Can it wait till morning?" he asked plaintively.

"No." It was the no-argument no, the get-your-black-ass-in-here no.

God, he wished he hadn't sat down. Now he'd just have to get back up again. Loosening his necktie, Austin got to his feet, stifling a grunt as he did so. He kicked off his shoes and, taking another swig of beer, padded past the dressing area and walk-in closets to the master bath.

Before he could touch the doorknob, the door swung open, and Steve Austin choked on his beer.

Candlelight gleamed off his wife's long, nude, dripping body. Candles ringed the large oval tub, which frothed with bubbles. With a wicked little grin, she stood magnificent before him, her gleaming black hair swept off her face and twisted at the back of her head, her brown breasts voluptuous and inviting, bubbles still clinging to her curly pubic hair.

Reaching out, she took hold of his tie and tugged him into the room, where she proceeded to unbutton his shirt and pull off his tie and loosen his belt and zipper with painstaking slowness and care, pointedly ignoring his growing erection. Taking the beer bottle from his hand, she set it on the edge of the tub and pulled off his shirt, sleeve by sleeve. Then she pulled down his trousers and underwear and stooped in front of him, pulling them off his legs and teasing his balls with the top of her head.

He followed her into the tub, but when he tried to kiss her she pulled away, sat him down in the hot water, and positioned herself behind him, spooning his buttocks with her legs. Then, taking a big fluffy cloth, she massaged his tense back muscles, and he gave himself up to her ministrations gratefully, vulnerable in his neediness.

Nothing in his life had ever felt quite so good.

They stayed in the water until it grew tepid, then cold, and she worked over every body part he'd ever even fantasized about. After that, they dried each other off, and he took her to bed and made love to her with a passion he'd begun to fear was dead.

Afterward, instead of falling into the depths of the sleep that still called to him, Austin began to talk. He talked and talked, about Lissie Montgomery and about the Community and about Cam Cameron and about Jeremiah Hunter and about Elliot Sizemore and about how very, very tired he was.

"Oh, my silly man," she said finally when he had wound down to a stuttering halt. "You know I love you more than life itself, but sometimes you can't see your own hand in front of your face."

"What do you mean?"

She nestled up against his chest. "When I first met you, I knew you were an uncommon man. A special man. I knew then there would never be anybody else for me."

He peered down at her. "So why'd you go out with all them jocks?"

"Well, *they* asked me!" She giggled, and he grinned. "And you've lived an uncommon life, Steve Austin. No matter what, you've always been true to yourself, and that's not always easy for a black man in a white man's world."

He stared out over the top of her head and stroked her soft hair.

"So what I want to know is, why don't you be true to yourself now?"

"Patsy, I have no idea what you're talking about."

"If you think you can flush out Jeremiah Hunter, then why don't you do it? Who died and made Elliot Sizemore your master?"

Anger flushed hot on the back of Austin's neck. This was dangerously close to their last quarrel. "He's in charge of the investigation,
Patsy. You know that."

"Yes, honey, but he's not in charge of *you*. Not anymore. You're
retired from the Bureau. You can do what you damn well please and
there's nothin' he can do about it."

Austin blinked—once, twice. The heat faded from his neck. Patsy
was right. She was absolutely right.

She tilted her chin up and gazed into his eyes. "I'm right, aren't I?
You gotta admit it this time."

A new energy seemed to flow through Austin's veins. "Yes, my
lovely lady, you are absolutely right." He kissed her.

She kissed him back. "You're gonna find that girl. You will." She
took his hand and squeezed it.

Austin held Patsy's small hand in his for a long moment, twisting
the wedding ring around on her slim finger. No doubt about it. He
was damn sure a lucky man.

Hunter's trailer looked much like Wren had imagined it, and she
attempted to cover her nervousness by commenting on the books
and computer and posters. As long as he was in the room, she displayed no curiosity about the blueprints she spotted poking out from
under a pile of papers. And he did not leave her alone in the room.

He had not been lying about the movie, and when it came on, he
prepared a tray with cheese and crackers and wine and served it to
her with a flourish, taking a seat on the sofa beside her and draping
his arm casually about her shoulders.

She drank most of the wine.

Ingrid Bergman was luminous as the lovely Maria, whom Gary
Cooper, as Robert Jordan, the American who fought with the
Spanish guerillas in their civil war against fascism, called "rabbit."
Wren knew their brief love was doomed because she had read the
book many times. She had even torn out the page at the beginning
in which Hemingway had quoted John Donne with his "no man is an
island" lines. She had framed the page: "*Never send to know for whom
the bell tolls; it tolls for thee.*"

She could still remember some of Hemingway's words. In the

story, Robert Jordan had said, "No man has a right to take another man's life unless it is to prevent something worse happening to other people."

And he had said, "Today is only one day in all the days that will ever be. But what will happen in all the other days that ever come can depend on what you do today."

The Spanish Civil War was not Robert Jordan's fight. He joined the battle because fascism threatened everyone who valued freedom. He considered evil against the one to be evil against the many.

About love, he said, ". . . nothing could ever happen to the one that did not happen to the other . . ."

Thinking of these things, she almost lost her resolve.

Wren excused herself and went into the bathroom, where she sat on the lid of the toilet and squeezed her arms close to her chest. Her husband was with her now. He was *in* her; a part of her very breath. Once she crossed the line with Hunter, a fine and delicate filament between her and her husband would be broken; a crystalline strand so infinitesimal as to be invisible, but it was there and it would be broken forever.

Whether Cam ever knew about it or not would make no difference.

But what did her heartbreak matter when held to the scalding light of innocent deaths? If she did not do this thing—all of it—then people would die.

Wren got up from the toilet and ran water at the sink until it was very cold. She splashed her face and blotted it dry. Then she unbraided her hair. Taking a brush from the edge of the sink, she brushed her long luxurious hair until it sparked. Then she dabbed a little petroleum jelly on her lips and eyelashes to make them shine. Finally, she took three deep breaths to calm her hammering heart.

When she emerged from the bathroom, she could hear John Lennon's sweet ballad to his wife, "Woman" playing. In 1980, Wren had dearly loved the *Double Fantasy* album. After the FBI raid on the Community and the subsequent assassination of Lennon, she had not listened to it again. Now here it was once more, its haunting lyrics and melodies drifting like ethereal ghosts across the room.

Lennon had written the songs as a tribute to the long-married.

The irony was not lost on Wren. She didn't know if Hunter was oblivious to it or making some kind of sadistic point. Either way, he was definitely attempting to evoke the past.

He was standing in the middle of the little front room, waiting for her. She came to stand before him and looked up into his face. He took a strand of her hair and let it slide slowly through his fingers. "I never saw such beautiful hair," he whispered. "I had dreams about it in prison."

Deep in the dark pools of his eyes, Wren caught a reflection of something then which came as a shock to her.

Need.

For reasons beyond Wren's comprehension—maybe a sentimentality brought on by the movie—Hunter had dropped his customary guard. In that blink of a moment, Wren realized for the first time that her reason for being here went far beyond any expertise she might possess; it even went beyond Hunter's desire to claim ownership of her to the world.

He needed her.

Wren knew that Hunter's mother had died when he was quite young and that his alcoholic father had severely neglected him. She also knew that, for a time anyway, the young Lissie had loved this man as purely and completely as ever a saint loved a god.

This simple love of a young innocent for a godlike man—ungrounded and unreal and unlasting as it had been—was what he craved from her now. Even Meghan's petlike devotion wasn't enough. What he needed, apparently, only Wren could provide. Perhaps she'd touched on some sort of nerve those many years ago. Or maybe he'd built an elaborate fantasy.

Either way, this new knowledge was crucial. It meant that Wren was not, after all, powerless in this dangerous dance. The steps were intricate —one stumble could mean death—but as long as she continued to move in sync with him, she would, in effect, possess the power.

Placing the palm of her hand prayerlike on the side of his face, Wren said softly, "I've missed you."

With that, he swept her up in his arms as surely as a masterful Rhett Butler ever did a reluctant Scarlett, and carried her to his bed.

*   *   *

Although it was late, Cam was still up, juggling bills, when the phone rang.

"I hope I didn't wake you," apologized Austin. "I didn't look at the clock before I called."

"Don't worry about it. I don't sleep much these days anyway," said Cam, sitting ramrod straight as he always did when he received a rare phone call from Steve Austin. He prayed there was news—any news. By this time he would almost welcome a death announcement if it would just end this horrible waiting. "What's up?"

"No new developments."

"Oh." A simple word, filled with bitterness and despair and frustration.

"I have an idea, though. I thought it only fair that I run it past you, because it's something I would be doing independently of the official investigation."

Cam's mouth went dry. "Shoot."

"I want to release some disinformation to the press. About Hunter."

"What kind of disinformation?"

"I want to leave an anonymous tip with a friend of mine who works for the Associated Press. That Jeremiah Hunter is a homosexual."

"*Jesus.*" The word swept from Cam's diaphragm like a sigh. "He'll go ballistic."

"Yes. It's a deliberate attempt to flush him out."

"What does Sizemore say?"

"Sizemore says fuck off. Sizemore says we don't want people to think badly of the FBI for spreading rumors and lies."

"*What?* You've got to be kidding. Tell me you're kidding."

"I'm not."

Rage, long curdling within Cam's soul, seethed to the surface. "You mean to tell me he's more concerned with the reputation of his precious fucking Bureau than with finding my wife and son?"

"That's exactly what I mean to tell you."

His voice shaking, Cam said, "What does he propose to do?"

"Build a case through informants."

"But—he'd have to cover the whole country!"

"That's right."

"Well, why don't they establish a hot line and release mug shots and things to the media like they've done in other cases?"

"Because this is a kidnapping, not a bombing. It has lower priority."

"Not to me, goddamn it!"

"But to the Bureau."

"Look." Cam had already sprung to his feet. Now he began to pace. "You do whatever you goddamn well think will find my wife and son. Do it now. You have my support one hundred percent."

"I kinda thought that's what you'd say. If this were an e-mail I'd draw you a little smiley face out of punctuation marks."

Cam laughed. It's something he didn't do so much anymore. It was ironic that the subject of his family's disappearance would be the source of the joke, but what else could you do, save go insane?

"Steve . . . I just wanted to thank you for hanging in there with me."

"Oh, so *now* you call me Steve. I must be doing something right."

Cam couldn't help but grin. Austin was in a surprisingly good humor, and it was infectious. It gave him hope. Before, it seemed all they'd had between them was defeat.

"When's the shit going to hit the fan?" he asked.

"Just hide and watch."

"What do you think he'll do?"

"I think he'll get in touch with my reporter friend, who will then try to establish some sort of line of communication—an interview maybe, offer the guy some kind of forum. Meanwhile, we'll be tracing his call."

"Don't you need a court order for that? And the cooperation of the Bureau?"

"Don't worry your pretty little head about that. I have my ways."

"Okay. Is there anything I can do? I'm going nuts with this waiting and doing nothing. God, let me shuffle paper or something. Anything. I just want to help."

There was a pause. Cam could hear his heart hammering.

"I don't blame you, man," said Austin at last. "Let me think about it. I'm still trying to run a business here, and I've got too many irons in the fire. You know your wife better than anybody else. I'll send you some stuff to read over. See if you have any fresh ideas. In the meantime, keep the media pressure up. Talk shows. Whatever."

Cam's heart leapt. Finally, a chance to contribute, to make a difference, to *help*. He wondered what had gotten into Austin, but he wasn't about to question it. "I'd appreciate anything you've got," he said. "You don't know how much."

"It'll take me a day or two to get the stuff together, then I'll FedEx it to you. Which would be better, home or office?"

"Home. It's where I usually am, now."

"Hang in there," said Austin.

The two men said good-bye and hung up. Cam, too restless even to stay indoors, stepped outside and stared up at the full moon for a very long time. "*Wren, honey,*" he whispered. "*Stay alive. Whatever it takes, keep fighting. We'll find you, I promise.*"

He'd been telling her that, all along, but this time he actually believed it.

CHAPTER 32

WITH the first touch of Jeremiah Hunter's hands upon her body, Wren was plummeted into the past, when passion was new and each thrill of her body a discovery. As he lowered her onto the bed, he unbuttoned her shirt one-handed without breaking his kiss upon her lips. His other big hand was firm on the small of her back as he lifted her up and across the bed and into a comfortable position—a move the shorter Cam would never have tried. There were no awkward moments in bed with Hunter, a fact that inexperienced Lissie had taken for granted but that the woman Wren knew was based on years of practice with many different partners.

She busied herself unbuttoning his shirt and the cuffs of his sleeves—generic moves that did not call for the erotic, reminding herself to kiss back with some semblance of desire. This was a big man, a full foot taller than she; even his mouth was bigger than Cam's, which made his kiss decidedly different, yet still rendered familiar by the power of memory.

Naturally he had no problem unhooking her bra with one hand, and as his fingers slid smoothly over her breast, she gasped.

"What's wrong?" He lifted his head and scrutinized her face.

Her heart constricted. If she blew it here, she blew everything.

"Nothing. I just . . . forgot how . . . good you were," she said earnestly, praying the remark didn't sound as stupid to him as it did to her.

His face broke into a devilish grin. "Then let me refresh your memory." He lowered his mouth to her breast, tracing circles around the nipple with his tongue.

To Wren's dismay, the nipple responded by stiffening, as if it had a mind and a will totally disconnected from Wren's own.

Having sex with the man in order to survive was one thing; enjoying it was another.

She didn't know what to do with her hands. Well, she did know, of course, but she didn't want to do it. All along she had thought of this as a rape; once she began caressing his body, it would become a cooperation. She postponed the inevitable by struggling with his belt and zipper, trying to avoid thinking about the erection which sprang forth like the spear of a warrior.

He finessed her by sliding down her underwear and camouflage pants in one smooth move, licking her legs as he went, which he continued to do while he calmly untied and removed her combat boots. Then he stood and flung off his own clothes, finally looming over her in all the power and glory of his maleness, his penis held forth like a mighty sword, ruby-red and glistening. The room smelled of sex.

This was the point of no return, and Wren knew it. Before she could ask, he had delved into a drawer in the nightstand and removed a handful of condoms. He handed her one. "You put it on," he said huskily.

She did. Slowly, the way she knew he liked it. At some point Wren became disembodied, separate from herself, almost as if some alternate personality had emerged to take over and do what she herself dreaded. Memory and the experience of the long-married took over as well, and while Wren hid her own eyes like a blushing virgin, this new persona choreographed every move to perfection, a lick here, a bite there, now a silky stroke.

If the dance was rehearsed, Hunter seemed not to notice. Obviously he couldn't tell the difference between the mechanical movements of a captive courtesan and the freely given caresses of genuine passion.

Wren wondered how many men could.

For at least half of the little dance, Wren deliberately numbed her body until it was unfeeling, shutting it off from what it wanted to do, an easy enough exercise for a hostage lover. However, it was necessary to be convincing in her performance, and that alone created a certain physical ambivalence.

But when he buried his head between her legs and began the slow steps to Nirvana she remembered so well, her body began to make demands of its own, and there was nothing she could do but watch helplessly as the new Wren writhed and moaned at each step and responded in rhythmic counterstep.

When he rammed himself inside her at last, the old Wren deafened herself to his cries, while this brazen new being within tangled her fingers in his hair and moved her hips in synchronized time to his thrusts.

But afterward, while he slept, it was the same old Wren who crept into the shower, ran the water until it pummeled her with stinging darts, and scrubbed every inch of her skin with a rough cloth, scrubbed and scrubbed it raw, but it didn't help.

Nothing helped. She was still dirty.

"I want you to move in with me," he murmured as she slid back into bed beside him, clad in one of his tan T-shirts, which hung to her thighs, and a pair of his boxer shorts slung low over her hips. He took her in his arms.

"Okay," she said, her tone carefully neutral.

"Why are you wearing this?" he complained. "I want to feel you against me."

"It's cold. I'm cold." Her shiver was genuine.

"Then let me warm you up," he said, pulling her body over on top of his, where she could feel his erection already building.

Wren should not have been surprised at Hunter's penchant for having sex more than once in a night, but she was. The old Wren had eclipsed the new one in the shower, and there wasn't time to switch places again.

Thankful that the night's shadows masked her face, she dutifully pulled off her clothes, groped for another condom, and straddled him, guiding him inside her. Before she could make another move, a swift and terrible rage blindsided her, and she took it out on him, clawing him with her nails, biting his lip when he kissed her, and pumping him roughly until he came before he was ready.

A fine sheen of sweat coated Wren's body and she was panting like a long-distance runner, her hair hanging wild over her face, further shielding her true thoughts from him.

"Wow!" he cried. "That was a hell of a fuck! I bet that wuss accountant never tore off a piece from you like that."

Eyes narrowed to slits behind her curtain of hair, studying his silhouette in the darkness like a stalking tigress about to pounce, Wren stifled the urge to slap him with all the strength in her body. *Just be glad you didn't demand oral sex*, she thought. Aloud, she said, "I thought we agreed not to talk about him."

"You're right. You scrambled my brains, woman. Made me forget."

"Don't do it again." She rolled off him in spite of his yelp of protest and yanked the blankets up to her chin. "Kills the mood, okay?"

"Okay. Sure. Whatever you say." He chuckled. "Anyway, seems like you've picked up a few tricks since your sweet and innocent days."

She ground her teeth together. "Haven't we all."

"We're a team, Lissie," he said, his voice warm with the enthusiastic charisma that had the power to sway crowds and which Wren had once mistaken for love. "Just like the old days. We'll be unbeatable now. I want you with me every step of the way."

"Okay." If she sounded dull, he wasn't picking up on it.

"I knew you'd come around eventually."

"I thought you and Meghan were together," she said, as if that explained why she hadn't come around before.

Hunter shrugged. "She's a big girl. She knows when it's time to cut her losses."

Wren said nothing.

He stretched, appropriating most of the double bed with his six foot four inch body, languished, and farted loudly.

"Call of the wild." He goosed her. "Mating call."

She tried to think of something clever and cute to say, but the leaden weight on her chest was suffocating—the corpse of the old Wren, sitting on her heart.

Swinging his long legs over the side of the bed, Hunter got up and went into the bathroom, closing the door behind him. Wren knew his habit was to read and stay shut up in there for at least fifteen,

spectacular than she'd done in

the level of hatred in the camp
cate. This was his home office.
about the bank? Wren—more
n place—knew Hunter's weak-
ised, would harbor the funds of

ctrified Wren. Down went the
cketing down the hallway like a
king the floor, Wren dove for
g when the door to the bath-
stabbing through the adjoining
en's supine body like a prison

-hammering moment, Wren
ng as he stood naked in the

iswering flash of his teeth pro-
as she and her terrified son lay
van and he had said, "*Perfect.*"
ettled in beside her, arrangi
could be comfortable bu'
, Wren turned away f
her ears.   p
, her body as ter was
ligits on the   f my   had
reign snor   rican.
p a f headed
e door to   d her, if
d closely   entrance
ders   w full well
                             s in the field
                             y materials—
                             would be able

to make surgical strikes even more
the seventies.

Buck Leatherwood. Wren had see
toward the wealthy gun control adv
He had to be the target. But what
than anybody else in this godforsak
ness for banks. And this bank, she so
a very upscale clientele.

But what was he planning?

The sound of a toilet flushing el
pile of papers; out went the lamp. R
fleet-footed deer, her toes barely st
the bed. The covers were still settl
room opened, sending a shaft of ligh
bedroom and across the bed and W
stripe.

For a wild, dry-mouthed, hea
thought Hunter suspected someth
doorway, watching her watch him.

She smiled. "I missed you."

His face was shadowed, but the a
voked the memory of that first nigh
bound and gagged in the floor of the

The light snapped off, and as he
his tall body catercorner so that he
would be wadded up over to the sid
man at last and pulled the covers ove

I guess it's true, she thought grim
spring as she watched the bloodred
over, one by one, and listened to the
not her husband. *I guess I have pic
own since my sweet and innocent c*

Daniel had just emerged fr
toward the shower, rubbing
Hunter's trailer opened a
by Hunter. As Hunter d

sometimes as many as thirty, minutes. She'd seen the stack of *Soldier of Fortune* magazines beside the toilet.

After a moment Wren got up, slipped the T-shirt back over her head, and slunk out of the room on the balls of her feet, down the cramped hall past the tiny cluttered kitchen, and into the front room, where she risked turning on a lamp. Immediately, she darted over to the table against the wall and lifted up the pile of papers which rested on the set of blueprints she'd noticed earlier, taking care not to disturb the pile in any way.

In careful architect's printing, the building was labeled: LEATHERWOOD BUILDING.

Wren's breath caught in her throat. "Oh, my God," she whispered. Her heart seemed to swell against her diaphragm and she couldn't breathe. The building was a fanciful, futuristic all-glass structure shaped like a pyramid. Leatherwood's suites occupied the entire top floor. Glass elevators bulleted people up through an open central atrium two floors high filled with trees and plants and even a working waterfall.

Each of the seven floors was separately drawn, the spaces designated: café, meeting room, office, office, break room, restroom, storage. The second floor was an open mezzanine, accessible by escalator. The bottom floor contained a small, very exclusive shopping mall, fine restaurants, and a bank.

A *bank*.

Trembling overtook Wren's body. She glanced at the watch on her shaking wrist: ten minutes.

The third floor consisted of large rooms that were apparently booked for seminars.

People. There would be people everywhere.

Some terrorist bombs had taken down entire buildings. Wren had watched the news broadcasts with every other horrified American. *But he doesn't need me for that,* she told herself.

If he'd been stalking her for very long before he kidnapped her, if he'd been going through her mail, especially if he'd gained entrance into her house and gone through her things, then he knew full well that she'd been keeping up with the latest developments in the field of explosives. If he could get his hands on the necessary materials— and she had no doubt that he could—he knew Wren would be able to make surgical strikes even more spectacular than she'd done in the seventies.

Buck Leatherwood. Wren had seen the level of hatred in the camp toward the wealthy gun control advocate. This was his home office. He had to be the target. But what about the bank? Wren—more than anybody else in this godforsaken place—knew Hunter's weakness for banks. And this bank, she sensed, would harbor the funds of a very upscale clientele.

But what was he planning?

The sound of a toilet flushing electrified Wren. Down went the pile of papers; out went the lamp. Rocketing down the hallway like a fleet-footed deer, her toes barely striking the floor, Wren dove for the bed. The covers were still settling when the door to the bathroom opened, sending a shaft of light stabbing through the adjoining bedroom and across the bed and Wren's supine body like a prison stripe.

For a wild, dry-mouthed, heart-hammering moment, Wren thought Hunter suspected something as he stood naked in the doorway, watching her watch him.

She smiled. "I missed you."

His face was shadowed, but the answering flash of his teeth provoked the memory of that first night as she and her terrified son lay bound and gagged in the floor of the van and he had said, *"Perfect."*

The light snapped off, and as he settled in beside her, arranging his tall body catercorner so that he could be comfortable but she would be wadded up over to the side, Wren turned away from the man at last and pulled the covers over her ears.

I guess it's true, she thought grimly, her body as tense as a coiled spring as she watched the bloodred digits on the bedside clock flip over, one by one, and listened to the foreign snores of a man who was not her husband. *I guess I have picked up a few fucking tricks of my own since my sweet and innocent days.*

Daniel had just emerged from the men's barracks and was headed toward the shower, rubbing the sleep from his eyes, when the door to Hunter's trailer opened and his mom stepped out, followed closely by Hunter. As Hunter draped his arm over Daniel's mom's shoulders

and they headed together toward the mess hall, Daniel stopped dead
in his tracks and gaped.

"Better shut your mouth, kid, or you'll catch a fly," teased Hunter
with a grin, reaching out to chuck Daniel under the chin as the two
passed him. Daniel hardly noticed the good-humored gesture, so
intently was he staring at his mother. He expected her to avoid his
gaze, or at least avert her own, but instead she looked up and stared
him full in the eyes.

He didn't know what to say to her. He didn't know what to think.
He was, for once, shocked to his core. All he could do was stand there
like an idiot and gawk. He tried to read her expression and came up
blank.

She did not speak to him. Instead, she gave him a mysterious
little Mona Lisa smile as they passed him by. Her long hair was
unbraided, and it streamed out behind her in the morning breeze
like a shining flag. When Daniel turned to watch them walk away, he
saw Hunter lift his hand and stroke his mother's hair, almost as if he
were petting it.

The simple gesture smacked Daniel like a slap. He'd never seen
another man touch his mother in that way. While he was still
watching, his mom slipped her arm around Hunter's waist.

She slept with him! thought Daniel in disbelieving astonishment.
Hunter fucked my mom!

He felt a surge of . . . what? Outrage? Protectiveness? Jealousy?

For the first time in a long time, Daniel's thoughts turned to Eric.
Eric's mom had been married five times, and there were lots of
boyfriends in between husbands. Daniel's old friend had seen his
own mom go out with creeps and cool guys alike. In fact, whenever
Eric's mom had dated a sleazeoid, he had often helped Eric sabotage
the relationship. And if she dumped a cool guy, Eric would act like a
shit around the house for weeks.

But this was different. This was way different.

So what'd'ya wanna do? he asked himself as Hunter and his mom
disappeared into the mess hall. *Go back home?*

Home. The word didn't even sound right anymore.

He turned to continue toward the showers, and tripped over his
own big feet, almost sprawling headlong on the pathway. Someone
behind him laughed out loud, and he hurried on, staring at the

ground in humiliation. *Now the whole camp would know his mom was fucking Hunter.*

As if Daniel didn't have enough problems. Nobody liked him anyway. They thought he sucked up to the Alpha/Omegans. Truth was, he kind of did. But nobody messed with him because of Hunter. He had sort of adopted Daniel. *Like a father.*

The shower house was unheated. In spite of the hot water and steam, the place was freaking freezing, and he raced through, anxious not to be the brunt of any more baby dick jokes. As he toweled off and rapidly dressed in clean fatigues, he thought about the idea of Hunter-as-father. After all, Hunter and his mom had been together before. In a way. And now they were together again.

He had to admit, they did look, well, *right* together. A much better-looking couple than Wren and Cam.

He cut himself shaving, cursed, and stuck a piece of toilet paper to his face. He hadn't been shaving all that long, and the truth was, he didn't have to do it all that often, and it was a bona fide pain in the ass.

He didn't want to think about his dad.

He couldn't help it, though.

Daniel had never been able to understand his mom and dad being together. His dad was a nice guy and all that, but his mom . . . his mom was so pretty and everything. And his dad was such a *nerd.* What did she see in him anyway?

Maybe she just needed somebody nice to take care of her until Hunter got out of jail.

The thought stopped Daniel's razor in midair. Could that be true? Had she maybe loved Hunter all along?

And if that was true, then why did she fight so bad when they first came out here? Why did she try to escape?

Maybe she was playing hard to get, he thought in a weak attempt to joke his way out of his own confusion.

He remembered what his mom had said when Daniel had first brought Hunter to her, right after the escape attempt, when she was so hurt and everything. She said she'd done it because of his sister.

Just the thought of Zoe brought a guilty little stab to Daniel's heart lately. He didn't think he'd ever find himself even *thinking* this way, but the truth was that he missed her. She'd always been a pain in the ass and she always drove him crazy, but she was always there, too. When they were little, they'd played together all the time. She would set her doll house up with all these happy little critters she'd collected from McDonald's, and he'd dive-bomb them or attack the house with his toy dinosaur.

Daniel caught himself grinning in the mirror. He straightened up and went back to shaving. It was lonely out here sometimes. Whenever Daniel's parents weren't around to bounce off of, he and his sister used to have long talks about things. He missed that now.

Maybe Hunter *could* go get her.

Yeah, right. Talk about your natural disasters. He cut himself again.

He wondered if he was ever going to see his sister or his dad again. Something about seeing his mom *like that* with Hunter had put a stamp of finality on their stay at the Armageddon Army compound. Before, it had gradually come to seem like summer camp or something.

Now it seemed like . . . what? Home?

Swiping at his chin with the towel, Daniel buried his face in it for a moment. Funny how you could go to sleep one night and wake up to find your whole world had changed.

This whole thing with Hunter and Daniel's mom. They seemed happy. It *looked* right, it really did.

It just didn't *feel* right.

CHAPTER 33

AUSTIN decided to meet Marlene Swackhammer at a place they both remembered well, which was miraculously still there: a drive-in hamburger joint called Keller's, where carhops still brought out overloaded juicy hamburgers and bottles of beer to the car and people could pretend that nothing had changed in life, that the world was still sane. When Marlene careened up in the same old dented 1968 Mustang she'd always driven, he had to laugh.

She got out looking, as always, good enough to eat, with legs up to her neck and blond hair down to her hips. The fact that she was pushing forty would come as a surprise to people who hadn't known her as long as he had. She climbed into the car, pulling her legs in after her, reached over, and kissed him full on the lips.

"Hi, you sexy thang," she said, her shrewd brown eyes gleaming. "You sick of that Patsy girl yet?"

He grinned and shook his head. "Not yet."

"You can always have a little piece on the side," she coaxed. "Everybody else does."

"Marlene. Are you still dating married guys?"

"They're the only ones who don't want to lock me up and throw away the key." Cracking a window, she lit a cigarette. Glancing over at him, she winced. "And *yes*, I'm still smoking. Not that it's any of your business."

"It's gonna make you wrinkled one day."

"Aw, I'll never live that long anyway."

"Not if you don't change your evil ways."

"Life's too short, precious. My, my. Would you look at all those little tiny gray hairs. Got 'em anyplace else? I can check for you."

"You're wicked."

"And you, my sweet, are just entirely too angelic."

"And you're just dying to corrupt me, I'll bet." He signaled the carhop, who came over to the window. Near December, the weather in Dallas was raw and cold and windy and almost wet. Austin was surprised that people still came here, but the place was as crowded as ever. He started the engine and turned up the car heater. "Two burgers, with fries—"

"Onion rings for me," piped up Marlene.

"Okay. One fry, one onion ring, one Coke—" He glanced at her.

"What? You crazy? Get me a beer, baby."

"And a beer." The carhop left. Austin pushed the button to roll up the window and shook his head. "It's eleven-thirty in the morning. How can you stand a beer?"

"How can you not?" She lit another cigarette with the butt of the old one. "I guess Patsy cooks crap made out of celery and weeds and stuff. You look like you're in pretty good shape."

"Not according to Patsy." He grinned. "She'd kill me if she knew what I was having for lunch."

"I'll never tell," she said with a lascivious grin.

"Do you sexually harass every man you deal with like this?" He propped himself in the corner so as to get a better look at her. Mmm, hmmm. If he was younger. If he was single . . .

"Only if they're married," she said. She put a long-fingered, graceful hand tipped with ruby-red claws on Austin's thigh and lifted one eyebrow in a seductive question.

He covered her hand with his own and placed it gently on the car seat. "I'm too old for temptations like this," he said, "and I'm a lousy lay anyway."

"I doubt that," she said, then twinkled at him. "Austin, you restore my faith in mankind. Just when I was convinced that all human beings sucked, along came you. Patsy's a lucky gal."

"I know." He grinned back. "So how's work?" he asked. "Still your reason for living?"

"Shit. Back when we first met, I thought I could set the world on fire. Thought I could solve the world's problems. Win a Pulitzer. Now my greatest hope in life is that my hard work doesn't wind up collecting birdshit in some suburban cage somewhere." She turned her head to blow smoke out the window, and it made Austin sad to see such cynicism in one so lovely. Still, there was no better AP reporter in the business.

He'd first met Marlene Swackhammer when she was a young hot-shot journalist straight out of graduate school, dogging his shadow like the hound from hell when he was the agent in charge of a high-profile kidnapping case. She wouldn't be pawned off on the media rep. Eventually he found her to be a very rare thing: a journalist of integrity. Off the record meant off the record. If he asked her to hold a hot lead, she'd hold it. From him she demanded only the truth. She gained his respect, and from then on, they worked almost as a team on several major cases.

The carhop brought the burgers and Austin enjoyed his messy meal with Marlene. How that girl could eat the way she did and keep her figure was beyond him. Marlene tackled everything in life with great relish.

"So, good-lookin'," she said, licking onion ring crumbs off her slender fingers, one by one. On anybody else, it might look crude; on Marlene, impossibly sexy. "What've you got for me?"

"How 'bout a story from an anonymous source that's a bold-faced lie?"

"What, like I ever get anything else?" She pawed through a huge bulging tote bag and came up with a notebook and pen. Once the cap came off the pen, she was all business. "Tell me everything. I'll decide how it'll slide."

He did. He told her about Jeremiah Hunter and the Community and Lissie Montgomery; he told her about Cam and Zoe and Daniel and Wren and Hunter; he told her about Elliot Sizemore, and he told her about his plan. She took voluminous notes in this bizarre personal shorthand she'd invented years ago that nobody else could possibly decipher. By mutual unspoken understanding, she did not tape-record the conversation.

Marlene waited until Austin was finished before she began peppering him with questions. She'd followed the case with some interest after Sizemore gave the press conference at the Cameron home, "but I didn't know you were right in the middle of it, Austin. I should have."

She wanted to know what made the investigators so certain that Jeremiah Hunter was even behind the disappearance of Wren and Daniel Cameron. "Did you check out the FBI data base to see if they fit the profile of, say, a serial killer's MO?"

Austin told her he had.

"And you don't have any reason to believe the husband's got them cut up and stored in the freezer?"

"Doubtful." Austin grinned.

She probed him to learn if it was possible that Wren had left willingly.

"Cam and I discussed it at length," Austin said. "We both think there's no way, as do friends and family members who were interviewed after the case went public."

She asked a lot of questions about the raid that had yielded stolen armaments but no Hunter. At one point Austin had to order her another beer. In spite of the discomfort she was causing him, Austin respected her thoroughness; her questions were insightful and shrewd.

She wanted information about Hunter's family. Austin explained that his mother was long dead, and his alcoholic father had died ten years or so ago. No siblings, he reported, and cousins were spread far and wide. There were no close friends; even in high school he'd been—

"Don't tell me. A loner. You cop types are going to have to come up with some better word someday. We reporter types are getting sick of that one."

Finally, she seemed reasonably satisfied, though Austin suspected that a go-getter like Marlene was never really satisfied with anything she did.

"You want this bylined?" she asked as she crammed the notebook back into the overstuffed tote.

"Please."

She studied him for a moment, chewing the inside of her cheek. "You think he'll contact me."

"He might."

She nodded. "Gotcha." She leaned over to dig around in the tote.
"Marlene—"

She looked up.

"This guy is dangerous. What I'm asking you to do . . . could be dangerous. You want to back out, that's fine with me."

She snorted. "You think I'm scared of a limp dick like him?" Reaching into the bag, she pulled out a .357 magnum revolver.

"*Jesus*, Marlene!"

"Don't need six shots," she said. "I can get him in one." She stuck the heavy gun back into the bottomless tote as if it were a tube of lipstick, which she pulled out next. Flipping down the visor on the passenger side, she reapplied her flame-red lipstick in the mirror there.

He shook his head. "You're a bad girl, Marlene."

"The baddest." Leaning over, she planted a big red kiss on his cheek. "And don't you forget it."

Then she got out of the car, making sure her skirt hiked up a little too high on her slim legs, dazzled him with a scarlet smile, and sped away in her little black Mustang.

As Wren stood, staring at the wall, she sensed rather than saw her attacker rush her from behind. She stepped to the side, but she was not quick enough and he surprised her; he shoved the full weight of his body into her side, peeling her holster literally free from the gun belt. She countered by dropping her center of gravity even as she grabbed his hands with both of hers, squeezing with all her might, and pivoted as she did so, twisting his arm backward as she pushed her thumb into the palm of his hand and dug into the meat of his hand with both hers, causing his fingers to separate.

She had the advantage. The next step was to bring him facedown to the ground. But he surprised her. Stepping into her body as he pivoted, he shoved the heel of his other hand into her chin, snapping her head backward while bringing up his knee for a painful thrust to her groin.

With a sharp cry and a groan, Wren crumpled to the mat and drew her legs up against her body. She was panting and sweating. Kicker stood over her, grinning. He hadn't even broken a sweat. "You can't just practice the moves," he said. "It's not like learning to dance. You have to *feel* what you are doing."

"Yeah? Did I have to *feel* your knee as well?"

"Absolutely." He reached down and took her hand, giving her an easy lift to her feet. "It's the only way you'll remember."

Oh, I'll remember, you sadistic asshole, thought Wren. His knee had struck her right on the pubic mons—every bit as painful to a woman as a man's testicles being struck in the same way.

"Besides, I didn't hurt you. I wanted to, I could really hurt you." He held her gaze for a moment.

She said nothing.

"Now. Your mistake was in letting me get too close in to your body. The trick is to keep my arm elongated. Like this." He snatched her hand, twisting her wrist as he yanked her toward him like a reluctant dog on a leash. She went down immediately on both knees and one arm, but he kept pulling until her breasts hit the mat.

But she had a few tricks of her own. Throwing her body into an immediate shoulder roll, she sprang to her feet and confronted him face-to-face, bringing her leg up for a ferocious kick to his groin. Though he stepped aside quickly, the kick still landed with some force on the top of his knee and the vulnerable muscle which connected there.

"*Shit!*" He let go of her hand and grabbed his knee. "You bitch!"

Big John's booming laughter filled the workout room where Wren was training with Kicker. "Way to go, girl," he cried. "You're learning."

Wren was shaking in rage. If Kicker kept up these tactics, he'd sprain her wrist or cause some other sort of injury which could put her out of commission for weeks. But what was she supposed to do? Report him to the National Martial Arts Federation?

She removed her gun belt and handed it to Big John. "When do we get to practice defense moves with real guns?" she asked. "They've got to be heavier than these rubber ones."

"I don't know," he said, holding the door open for her as they left the building. "Hunter may not ever let you practice with a real gun. I just don't know."

She nodded her head in frustration. She'd been sleeping with Hunter for some days now, and he still had not taken her into his confidence about the mission, nor had he allowed Big John to arm her around the compound. It was depressing. What kind of game was he playing? Did he need a demolitions expert or not? And if not, then what the hell was she doing here?

Wren was sore all over. Kicker claimed to believe that the only way to teach hand-to-hand combat was to deliver the blows with enough force to "get your attention," and he would not allow them to wear protective padding. She suspected he was a closet sadist who just enjoyed hurting people. It was her fondest desire to hurt him badly enough one day that he would never touch her again.

"Ready to visit the gun range?" Big John said. "I can get the Glock in a flash."

She shook her head. "How about later? I could use a shower right now." *And some aspirin,* she thought.

"Sure." He smiled at her and ambled off down the path. Although Wren didn't want to get too close to anybody at the compound, she had to admit that Big John had been a lifesaver in more ways than one. He was kind to her, and he treated her with respect. Word of Wren's marksmanship had spread, and most of the others had become somewhat deferential to her—especially after she moved in with Hunter—but she couldn't call any of them friends. She didn't want to, either.

Climbing the rickety steps to the little trailer, she entered the front room. Hunter was at work at the table with the blueprints spread out in front of him. He was scribbling something in a notebook. The computer screen displayed a diagram. He glanced over his shoulder at her.

Wren stood rooted in the doorway. He had never gotten out the blueprints in front of her before. "I'm sorry," she said. "I can leave and come back later."

"No, no. Come on in." He waved her in. "It's time you knew the details of the mission. I'm going to need your help before long."

She hesitated. This was it. The spiderweb he'd been spinning from the start. One wrong move on her part could bring the whole thing down.

"C'mon. I won't bite."

She approached him slowly and stood to the side of his chair.

"Know what this is?" He tapped the blueprints.

"It says it's the Leatherwood Building."

"Right you are. Know what we're going to do to it?"

"No." Her heart began a slow drumlike thudding against her breast.

"We're going to blow it up. Well, not all of it. Just the most important parts."

She swallowed. "We are?"

"Actually, you are going to do the blowing, my dear."

"What do you mean?" Best to play dumb. Always best to play dumb.

"Let me explain. It's a brilliant plan—you'll see. Now, Buckwheat Peckerhead is going to be here—" he tapped his pencil against one of the seminar rooms on the north side of the third floor of the building "—giving a speech on some of his fascist ideas about gun control to a crowd of, oh, about a hundred people."

He glanced up at her. She nodded.

"And we, meaning me and some of the Strike Force members, are going to be down here, at the bank, here on the south side ground floor of the building."

Again he glanced up. Again she nodded.

"Now, you and a couple of assistants are going to blow up Mr. Peckerhead, his bodyguards, and anybody else who happens to be hanging around a little too close to the podium."

His bodyguards. That meant Steve Austin. Hunter glanced up at her. She nodded.

"Then, when the shit hits the fan and there's all this chaos and confusion on account of how there aren't any security people around to take charge, me and the boys will take advantage of those few minutes to rob the bank. I think we can be in and out in two, three minutes. The explosives, of course, will take longer, but that's your business."

Eyes shining, he looked up again. She forced a smile. "It *is* a brilliant plan," she said. "But aren't you afraid that the force of the blast will collapse the floor and bring everybody down on top of you?"

He shook his head. "See now, that's the brilliant part. I don't have to worry about that because I've got you, my love. And I know that you know little ways to accomplish this without blowing all the rest of us away at the same time."

"But if there's a structural weakness . . ."

He shook his head. "So what? They're on the north side. Me and the boys are on the south side. You and your compatriots—if you've done your job right—will already be waiting out in the van. Even if the floor caves in, it won't land on our heads."

But a hundred people could die, she thought. And that was not counting how many might be present in the area below: the mezzanine, the lobby, the restaurant, the shopping mall. Children could even be there.

"I've been planning this for months," he said gleefully. "We've still got a lot of work to do. More planning. Everything's got to be *perfect.*" He glanced up again, like a kid looking for approval from his mom.

If Hunter's plan succeeded, he would strike a symbolic blow for every gun nut who hated Buck Leatherwood—not to mention fear in the hearts of any gun control proponent who took a public position.

He would also get very rich in the process.

And the whole thing was all up to her.

Wren's stomach turned over on itself. Painting a bright smile on her face, she said, "You're right. It is a brilliant plan." It was just the kind of meaningless thing she used to say to the kids when they brought her their incomprehensible crayon drawings.

Hunter reacted in much the same way they had then. He wrapped an arm around her waist, gave her a squeeze, and smiled down happily at his brilliant plan.

CHAPTER 34

C AM slammed the car door, and then slammed the back door of the house for good measure, before stomping into the den and dumping his bags in a heap on the floor. Zoe got to her feet, gave him a sardonic smile, and said, "Way to go, Dad," before crossing the floor and giving him a hug.

"Where's the neighbor lady?" he asked irritably.

"You said on the phone you'd be home from New York by dinner, so she left and said to call if you were late."

"*What*? She told me she would stay until I got home."

"Daddy, I'm not a baby anymore, in case you hadn't noticed."

"I know, I know." Rubbing his palms over his eyes, he mumbled, "I got a headache."

"It's your punishment for walking off a nationally televised talk show right in the middle of a broadcast."

"Don't start with me! I already heard it all from the producer."

"I'm *kidding*. My goodness, sit down. I'll get you some aspirin. Have you had anything to eat?"

Plopping onto the couch, he shook his head.

"I'll heat you up some soup, then."

She stepped away, but he caught her by the hand. She entwined her fingers through his. "I'm sorry, honey," he said. "I guess I blew it."

"No way! That Spike Baxter was a sleaze, Daddy! He should have *told* you he was going to have that militia nut onstage with you."

"He told me it was a show about missing persons. I thought if I showed their pictures on TV and told our story, it would help to find Mom and Daniel. I shouldn't have gotten so mad. I'm a lawyer. I know how to keep my cool."

Perching on the edge of the couch, Zoe said, "Well, you weren't being a lawyer this time. You were being a human person."

He stared at his daughter. "A human person? Are you saying lawyers are *not* human persons?" Behind his aching, burning eyes, he could feel a smile forming.

She grinned. "I'd have to plead the fifth on that one."

He gave a weary sigh. "I'm just so tired." It wasn't what Cam wanted to say. Not to his young daughter, anyway. He needed to be strong for her, and here he was, in shambles.

She reached up and patted his shoulder. "I know, Daddy. It's okay."

He shook his head. "I looked like a blithering idiot on that show. I was screaming and there was that militia guy, sitting there like the sanest person on the planet. And *Baxter*! God, I wanted to kill him!"

"Don't feel so bad, Daddy. What he did was unfair. Every kid on the playground knows unfair when they see it. Grownups know it, too. He *wanted* to make you mad. Everybody knows that."

A corner of Cam's mouth went up in a half-grin. "So he wasn't being a human person, then?"

"Nope." Zoe sprang to her feet with the energy of a kid and quick-stepped into the kitchen. "Mom keeps aspirin in the kitchen, doesn't she?" she called.

Keeps. She had said *keeps* instead of *kept* or *used to keep*.

Leaning his head back onto the couch and loosening his tie, Cam closed his eyes and allowed himself a small smile at last.

It was the little things, after all, that gave him hope.

"Okay. Here's what we've got," said Hunter. Wren had followed him a short distance from the compound to a weedy area covered with scrub brush. He led her to a dead mesquite tree under which a large tumbleweed, maybe three or four feet in diameter, had lodged itself. Hunter grasped the tumbleweed by its prickly tangle of branches, hoisted it up, and moved it aside, where he anchored it with brown twine to the other side of the tree. A round white metal disk lay beneath where the tumbleweed had been, flush to the ground like a sewer cover.

Hunter pulled back the disk, which was hinged underneath. Beneath the disk was a tunnel heading straight down into the dark earth. As he eased himself into the tunnel, feetfirst, he flipped a light switch somewhere which revealed a ladder. He started down. Wren followed.

The well-like pipe down which they stepped descended about fifteen feet underground. In spite of the lights, it was very claustrophobic. At the bottom of the ladder, the pipe bent into an L shape, and Wren followed Hunter as he squeezed his body through the short bottom part of the L to emerge, at last, into a dome-shaped self-contained shelter.

"Ain't she a beaut?" panted Hunter as he stood upright. The ceiling was close to his head, but he could stand to his full height. "It's an ES10 fiberglass disaster shelter," he informed her. "Stealth entry for full covert use. Radiation resistant. No radar signature. No thermal signature to speak of. Impossible to find without ground intelligence. It's designed to completely support up to ten people for ninety days." He beamed happily.

"This is incredible," said Wren truthfully. Glancing around, she could see immediately that all the trappings which must have been included for the life support of people had been removed. This was no longer a shelter for human beings. It was a hiding place for explosives.

"We've got everything you need," he said. "Over here, a half-ton of ANFO." He pointed out a neat stack of fifty-pound sacks of farm-use fertilizer.

Ammonium nitrate, translated the chemist-Wren in her mind. *Commonly called "slurry."* All they needed to bring down a building was diesel fuel and a detonator.

As if reading her mind, Hunter said, "I don't have the diesel fuel on hand, but I can get it for you easy."

She shook her head. "Too big. Too uncontrollable."

"Well, that's what I thought. It's the reason I wanted you here. Not the *only* reason, of course." He winked at her.

She managed a smile.

"We've got plenty of det cord," he said, gesturing toward a box which rested near a couple of crates of grenades. "And over here, about fifty pounds of C-4. I can get more if you need it," he added.

Dear Jesus, thought Wren.

"Let's see . . . blasting caps . . . black powder . . . gelatin dynamite—I read someplace that's better than standard military dynamite because it doesn't produce fumes in storage."

"That's right," she said, then, aware of how much this man needed the approval of others, she added, "You've done a terrific job."

He shrugged, false modesty written all over his face. "Look here." He approached several wooden crates and prised up the top. Wren leaned over and peered in. It was full of AK47s.

"So . . . what's the plan?" he asked eagerly.

Wren had given a great deal of thought to "the plan" during the several sleepless nights she'd endured since Hunter had shown her the blueprint of the Leatherwood building. For the time being, stalling and delaying were her two best weapons. The longer it took her to get things ready, the more time she would have to think her way out of this nightmare.

Pursing her lips as if concentrating fiercely, she rummaged through the items for a while, then stood in the center of the shelter, hands on hips.

"These are great," she began, "but not specific enough."

He frowned. "What do you mean? This is what the military uses."

"Exactly. And what does the military do? Blow the hell out of things. Bridges. Tanks. And we're not trying to blow up a tank. We're trying to create a diversion."

Though still frowning, Hunter nodded. "Then just use smaller amounts."

"Still too unpredictable. Too much brisance." At the look on his face, she added, "It would shatter too much outward. That's what 'brisance' means."

"I know that!" he snapped, though of course, he didn't.

"Okay. First, I'll need Semtex H, for sure."

"Shit! You mean that stuff they used to blow up that airplane over Scotland?"

"Right."

"But you said these others were more powerful—"

"I said uncontrollable. You don't need much firepower to blow up an airplane. Depressurization takes care of that once you pierce the skin of the plane."

"Lissie. You gotta smuggle that stuff in from some Third World country."

Ignoring him, she went on. "And there's this new stuff I've been reading about. It's called Flex-X. You wouldn't believe this stuff." Uncomfortably, Wren realized that her enthusiasm was genuine. "It looks like leather. Comes in all kinds of colors. You can trim it and apply it to anything you want—the dashboard of a car, whatever. No fumes. Easy to handle."

"And?"

"And . . . extremely powerful. You could use it to cover, I don't know . . . a briefcase, maybe." She could see his eyes light up. "Then there's something called DEXS. Would you believe . . . you can apply it with a *caulking gun!*"

"Are you kidding?"

"Then there's Prima Foam. It's just like shaving cream and you can disguise it in a shave cream can."

He shook his head. "Man."

"Methyl nitrate is liquid. You can put it in a wine bottle or something."

"Like a Molotov cocktail?"

"Oh, no. Much more powerful."

Wren's heart was jerking in her chest. She was spouting off the names of explosives which were very new—some only recently developed by other countries. They would be extremely difficult to obtain in the United States and were usually controlled in other countries as well. Hunter would have to go outside his little clique to get his hands on them, taking a grave risk of encountering undercover operatives from the federal government.

The sensible thing to do would be for him to order her to use whatever was at hand and to custom-engineer the explosives herself to accomplish the task. After all, he *was* the "bigger is better" man. Even then the process could take weeks of dangerous trial-and-error experimentation.

But she could see that he was intrigued. Clearly, he liked the idea of wowing the bomb investigators with sophisticated explosives that alerted them to the fact that this was no dumb redneck they were dealing with, this was a *professional*.

She could almost hear the wheels of his mind burning rubber. The feds might even think a *foreigner* did it! They could get away clean and move on to the next target.

"Okay," he said. "We'll get you whatever you want. Make us a complete list—we're not about to go back out for more, okay?"

"Okay."

He studied her face. "We'll blow Buckwheat Peckerhead and his nigger bodyguard Steve Austin to hell and back—and anybody else stupid enough to be there listening to anything Peckerhead would have to say, too."

"And we'll get rich at the same time," she reminded him.

"Woman, when you talk like that, you turn me on," he whispered, pulling her close into his body and yanking her shirt out of her pants. Then he lifted her up as though she were weightless and positioned her on top of one of the crates of automatic weapons. Still standing, he unzipped his pants.

Wren felt like the unborn of the dead, imprisoned in the womb of hell. She could smell the black powder and other rank odors of destruction all around her, and the round walls seemed to be closing in, coffinlike.

And here she was, dancing with the devil.

CHAPTER 35

"T HERE'S no way this plan is going to work," stated Big John flatly.

Hunter had gathered the Alpha/Omega Strike Force members and Wren together for a closed meeting about the proposed "Special Op" to bomb the Leatherwood Building. Everybody except Hunter was scattered around on the exercise mats of the workout room. Hunter was standing over everyone at the front of the room, using a laser pointer to pick out details in the floorplans and building site transparencies he had prepared. Each transparency was neat and precise, everything clearly labeled. Obviously he'd gone to a great deal of trouble to put this little program together, and he did not appreciate Big John's remark. In the light of the projector which reflected upward to Hunter's chin and face, his displeasure was apparent.

"First of all," went on Big John, ignoring the scowl upon Hunter's face, "you're sending us out on the black market to pick up these contraband explosives—high-tech stuff that just shouts terrorist activity. There is a very good chance that we could encounter resistance from undercover federal agents."

With the exception of the whirring of the projector, the room was exquisitely quiet. Big John seemed not to notice, or if he did, he didn't care. "Second, your plan demands split-second timing in order to succeed. Anything goes wrong at any point of the plan by even as much as a minute or two, we're fried."

Wren sat perfectly still. Big John was absolutely right, but Wren would never be so foolish as to comment on it in front of Hunter. Apparently, neither would anybody else. No one else spoke up from the shadowy little audience.

"Third, with all due respect to our demolitions expert here, you can't possibly predict with complete accuracy what could happen with these explosives. You could have overkill or underkill. Even a timer could malfunction and the whole thing would be fucked."

Hunter's face had turned to savage stone. With the weird underlighting, Wren was reminded of a gargoyle. It turned her stomach cold.

"And fourth—"

"What's going on here?" asked Hunter. "I mean, what's *really* going on here?" His voice was deadly calm.

"What are you talking about?" asked Big John.

"That's what I'd like to ask you, John. What are *you* talking about? You know as well as I do that if you practice a Special Op a hundred times, it should go without a hitch. Allow for all eventualities and have a backup plan in place. I have done that already. This plan is foolproof."

No plan is foolproof, especially where explosives are concerned, worried Wren.

"I think there is something else going on here," continued Hunter. "Something more sinister."

Nausea gripped Wren's gut. Her mouth cottoned. *No,* she thought. *Please don't do this.*

"I always suspected that what happened to us at the Community was deliberately caused by a traitor, a treasonous blackguard in our own midst—one of our own, mind you—who betrayed us to the feds."

Ice surged through Wren's being. Paranoia gripped her: *Did he suspect? Did he know? Was he setting her up?* Trembling took over her body, and she struggled to stifle it.

"Is that what you are, John?" asked Hunter point-blank. "Are you a traitor, my friend? Are you selling us out for thirty pieces of silver?"

Big John got slowly to his feet, a hulking shadow monster in the darkened room. "Are you calling me a *snitch?*" he bellowed.

"I'm not calling you anything," replied Hunter calmly. "But I am asking you."

"Asking me *what?*" cried Big John. "I'm just trying to help you put together the best plan—"

"Maybe so. Maybe not. You may also be trying to talk us out of bombing a building, so that your coconspirator, that foreign agent Buckwheat Peckerhead, doesn't get blown away. A man could get a fucking medal for that, couldn't he?" he added, addressing the other Strike Force members.

A chilling murmur swept the room like hot wind passing over a dry grain field. Wren shivered.

"Because I just wanted to say, for the record, that if I ever dig under a rock and turn up a traitor in our midst, I guarantee you that justice will be swift." With that, Hunter aimed the laser pointer at Big John's head. The red dot appeared right in the middle of his forehead, striking an immediate and sickening resemblance to the laser sight of a gun.

Dinner that evening was an uneasy affair. Although Wren had cooked earlier for Hunter in the trailer, she had come down to the mess hall to pick up another plate of food and spend a little time with Daniel. In recent days he seemed to have accepted her relationship with Hunter and even to have grown a little closer to her.

It saddened her. Was he drawing closer to her as his mother—the person she had always been? Or was he drawing closer to this twisted image of herself that she now projected? In fact, she'd even caught herself a few times lately actually blending in with the other women—adopting their ferocity, cynicism, barely suppressed rage, blatant paranoia, black humor, submissiveness and deference to the men as traits of her own.

Was she the most talented and clever actress around? She wanted very much to think so. More worrisome was the thought that she was unconsciously *becoming* what she hated most, the very opposite of everything her gentle grandmother had ever taught her or been.

"What's going on with the AOs?" blurted Daniel, careening through her thoughts. "Everybody's in a bad mood, and nobody's hanging out with Big John."

"There was . . . a disagreement in the Strike Force meeting," she hedged, glancing over as she did so at Big John, who ate alone, sullenly shoveling food in his mouth.

"What about?" Daniel stuffed most of a roll into his mouth. Whatever table manners his mother had taught him seemed to have been left behind—back home, in the real world.

"I can't say," she said.

"It's about the Special Op, isn't it?" he stage-whispered, his eyes shining. "Everybody knows about it."

"Everybody knows what?" An alarm bell sounded somewhere deep in her brain.

"That you guys are planning to bomb the Leatherwood Building."

Dumbfounded, Wren stared at her son as he bit off half of a brownie.

"Nobody knows any *details*," he said. "But I think it's cool."

Dismay. Horror. Intense anxiety. One by one she had to deny the emotions that surged through her mind and heart beneath her pale, calm face. It took her two attempts to speak. "Cool? Why cool?"

"Well, it'll show Peckerhead that he can't mess with us."

Mind racing, thoughts scattering like pool balls on a blank green table, Wren said, "Then why not just assassinate Leatherwood?"

Shock etched the boy's face. "*Assassinate him!*" he cried. Several people turned to stare.

"Shshsh!" she warned. "Keep your voice down."

"Why would you want to assassinate him, Mom?" he asked plaintively. "I mean, bombing a building is one thing. Killing a man is another. Geez, you've really changed." He shook his head in disgust.

Relief flooded through Wren. Tears sprang to her eyes and she busied herself with her food in order to hide them. *My sweet boy*, she thought. *He's not completely corrupted! He still has a trace of innocence. The silly darling thinks Hunter's planning to bomb an empty building in order to make a political statement.*

It was all she could do not to shout for joy. "Of course you're right," she said evenly. "I guess I got carried away. You know, son, human life is a precious thing."

"I know." He drained his tea glass and swirled the ice around in it a moment, then filled his mouth with ice and began to crunch loudly. "You don't have to tell me that," he added in and around the ice.

Wren stared off into space. "Once you are responsible for the loss of human life," she mused, "you can never get their blood off your hands. Never."

"Earth to Mom. Earth to Mom. What's *with* you today?"

She patted his arm, allowing her hand to rest upon it for a few seconds. "Nothing. I'm just tired, I guess."

"Not sleeping too good, huh?"

Wren turned to look at her son. He glanced away and began to fidget. She could feel his leg jumping up and down next to hers under the table. For the first time it occurred to Wren that just as nobody ever saw her true emotions, it could be that more was going on beneath the surface with Daniel as well. Much more.

Now she knew for sure that the dark circles under his eyes were caused not by a growth spurt, but by sleepless nights. Apparently he hadn't adjusted as well to their situation as she had always assumed.

Could he even be . . . homesick?

"I do have trouble sleeping," she said softly, placing her hand back onto his arm, *willing* her strength to flow like some kind of electrical current into her son.

A look of raw vulnerability blanched across his face. He said, "Me, too. I miss . . . some people . . . sometimes."

"So do I," she coaxed. They were so close to making a connection. If she could somehow touch this boy where he *lived*, that genuine place of tormented doubt and sleep-depriving guilts, then she could save him; she was sure.

"Mom?"

"Yes?" She had to stop herself from calling him *baby*.

"Do you ever think of—"

The door to the mess hall crashed back against the wall with such force the American flag which was pinned up nearby came loose in one corner and dangled, cockeyed and surreal. Wren and Daniel both jumped almost out of their chairs, and conversation all over the room stumbled to a halt. Jeremiah Hunter stood in the doorway in a towering rage, the cords on his neck superimposed like purple ropes. In his hand was clutched a half-crumpled newspaper.

"I'm gonna *kill* whoever did this to me!" he screamed.

Wren felt the blood drain from her face. Her fingers clutched Daniel's arm like claws. *Oh, dear sweet Jesus help me*, she prayed. The drumbeat of her heart pulsed in her brain, and she knew how a rabbit felt when it was caught in a snare.

"Who the *fuck* told an AP reporter that I was a queer? You better talk now, because if I have to ferret you out of here, I'll make you pay."

Wren blinked. Her mind seemed incapable of grasping what her ears had just communicated to her.

"Ouch." Daniel gently disentangled her hand from its grip on his arm.

Still the drumbeat sounded.

Hunter's burning gaze swept the room. Not a soul in it stirred.

"Fine," he said. "So the gutless coward chooses not to reveal himself. I'll call the fucking reporter and *find out* who's spreading lies about me to the media."

Big John lumbered to his feet. "Hunter, man, get a grip. Don't you *see* what's going on here? You can't call up that reporter—that's exactly what the feds have in mind! It's so obvious, man! It's a disinformation plant. They *want* you to contact this guy so they can trace you right back here."

Hunter folded his arms across his chest, muscles straining against the fabric of his fatigues. His eyes narrowed. "You telling me what I can and cannot do?"

"Somebody's got to!" cried Big John. "You're losing it, man. You keep this up, we're all gonna fry."

Hunter smirked. "You know, John, that's exactly the kind of thing I expected you to say. Seems to me like you've got an awfully *familiar* working knowledge of how the feds think. I especially like that word. Disinformation. Most people would think *mis*information. *Dis*information sounds like just the kind of thing a *fed* would say."

Wren's heart constricted with fear for Big John. She fought the desperate urge to yell at him to shut up and sit down. Nobody here at the so-called Armageddon Army had yet seen the full extent of Hunter's self-delusions.

Nobody had yet seen him murder in cold blood a man pleading for his life.

She glanced over at Daniel. Bewilderment and confusion, his affection for Big John, and his loyalty to Hunter all warred for dominance on his face. She put her hand back onto his arm and gave it a soft, reassuring squeeze.

"In fact," continued Hunter with ominous calm, "I wouldn't be the least bit surprised to find out that you were the son of a bitch who lied to that reporter about me."

"What?" Big John's eyes bulged. His customary mirrored sunglasses were folded into his chest pocket.

"After all, who has unlimited access to town? Who usually makes the trips to collect the mail and stock up on supplies?"

Everyone in the room knew that any one of the Strike Force members was likely to make the town runs; they also knew that Big John took over the chore more often than not.

"And I've been meaning to ask you, John. Just exactly where did you pick up your knowledge and skills with firearms?"

A hot red flush spread across Big John's bald head. His voice seething with barely concealed rage, he said, "In the military, man. In the war. Just like you."

Hunter shrugged. "For .45s and M16s and M14s, maybe," he said. "But not for the nine-millimeters and all the other types of weapons we've got here."

People in the room were beginning to scrutinize Big John with the same suspicion in their eyes that was mirrored on Hunter's face. Only Daniel appeared to be completely lost.

Wren couldn't bear it anymore. She stared at the table, at the cold, uneaten food, at anything but these two men. The drumbeat pounded at her temples.

"And what about all those trips to the hunting lodge? There's phones there."

"It was my turn, man, you know that."

"Oh, yes. You're quite a team player, my friend. Quite a team player. You even make little side trips, just to help out."

"Side trips . . . ?"

"Like the time you *volunteered* to go get penicillin for Lissie? She didn't *need* penicillin, John. She's a strong girl. All she needed was rest."

Wren felt Big John's troubled gaze turn to her. Anguish convulsed her heart. Swallowing hard, she fought dizziness and glanced up just long enough to plead, *please forgive me*, with her eyes.

Something about the look on her face signaled to Big John that he was in far worse trouble than he had imagined. For the first time the dark shadow of fear crept over his eyes.

Hunter placed his hands on his hips and regarded the big man over the heads of the silent crowd. "Trust is a delicate thing. I used to think I could trust you, John. I really did. Now I'm not so sure."

"What're you talkin' about, m-man?" John glanced around himself uneasily. "C'mon, you guys. It's me, remember? I been here from the start. From the beginning, in the joint. I ain't no fed. Think about it. It doesn't make any sense. It's cra—"

"Tomorrow at dawn we'll have a tribunal," pronounced Hunter. "Alpha/Omegans only will serve as this man's judge and jury. The final decision will rest with me. Kicker, Preacher—throw him in the hole."

The two men sprang to their feet. Big John, electrified into action, fought as they grabbed his arms. Chairs, meal trays, food—even a table—crashed to the floor as he struggled and kicked. Other men jumped up to restrain him as he bellowed like a freshly gelded bull.

As they dragged him screaming from the building, bile arose in Wren's throat and she swallowed miserably, trying not to vomit.

"Mom?" She glanced up. Beneath his tan Daniel's face was yellow-pale. "What's going on?"

She shook her head. What could she say? How could she possibly prepare him?

She should have known this would happen. It fit the pattern. It was just like the Community. Big John—just like the hapless hunter in Louisiana—now presented a threat to Jeremiah Hunter.

Big John was a dead man.

And just like before—once Hunter wielded his swift and terrible power, once he determined life or death for another human being, once he began to rule the others by fear rather then inspiration—then nothing would ever be quite the same again.

CHAPTER 36

ELLIOT Sizemore managed to track down Steve Austin at home in his study, where he was sorting through a briefcase full of Buck Leatherwood's hate mail.

"You son of a bitch," Sizemore said over the phone.

Austin grinned. "You must have me confused with somebody else, because my mama was no bitch."

"You went behind my back to plant that story about Hunter."

"I cannot deny that. Neither can I confirm it."

"Bastard."

"Now, we've already discussed that."

"*Who the hell do you think you are?*" yelled Sizemore. "I specifically told you—"

"Look, Sizemore. First of all, you can scream at me all you want but what are you going to do? Huh? Fire me? And second, since you were so worried about the reputation of your precious Bureau, then I have now removed that worry. I am no longer affiliated with the Bureau, and anyway, Marlene will go to jail before she'll ever reveal who gave her that tip."

"I'll have your balls for dinner, Austin! I'll—"

Austin carefully replaced the receiver back in the telephone cradle. He was out of the Bureau now. He no longer had to put up with that kind of crap.

After a few thoughtful moments, he put through a call to Cam. "Caught you on *Spike*," he said with a devilish grin.

"Oh, God; I looked like an idiot. Forrest Gump on steroids."

"Aw, it wasn't so bad."

"If I thought I could win, I'd sue the son of a bitch."

"Don't worry. I did some checking. Phone calls to the program switchboard are two to one in your favor."

"They are? How'd you find that out?"

"Well, I'm just that good."

Cam chuckled. "Thanks. I've been beating myself up about it."

"I figured you were. Say, man, the important thing is getting out the word on your wife and son. You accomplished that, and that's all that matters."

"I've just felt so . . . *impotent*. A total limp dick, wandering around the house wringing my hands. I can't stand it anymore. I've got to find a way to get involved, do what I can to help find them. I won't be able to live with myself if I don't."

"Listen. Every time I've been over to your house, I've observed a well-adjusted, bright young lady who's showing some pretty remarkable courage. You have *not* been doing nothing. I don't want you thinking that way."

"I don't know . . ."

"I've seen families torn apart by situations like this. I've seen other kids in the household, especially teenagers, feeling resentment of the missing kid for stealing all the attention. Then they feel guilty for feeling that way. Before you know it, they're acting out, getting into all kinds of trouble. You've been a steady presence for that child, and you've kept her on an even keel. Somehow you've let her know that she has value, too. You've done an incredible job, Cam, you really have."

There was a considerable pause. Finally, Cam said, "I never thought about it that way."

"Now you have."

"Thanks. I appreciate your help more than you'll ever know."

"Don't worry about it. Say, did you catch the little item in the paper about Hunter?"

"I did. He'll go ballistic. I just hope he doesn't take it out on Wren or Daniel."

"Don't worry. I have a hunch they're not the ones who'll be the target of his rage."

So said Austin to the distraught husband and father, but the truth was he'd taken a risk with this planted story, a big risk, but considering the alternatives they had going at the time, one well worth taking.

Daniel did not understand what was going on at the compound. He'd never seen everybody so worked up. Almost everybody he knew had been angry and upset when his mom ran off, but this was worse. Way worse.

As he lay in bed that night, staring up at the dark and cold ceiling, he thought about it. For one thing, when his mom escaped and the feds hit that compound in south Texas, everybody had been united, banded together to bring her back and prepare for a possible raid on their own camp by the feds. But this was different. The thing with Big John had divided people. Some immediately started mouthing what Hunter had said and spreading rumors about how Big John was probably an informant for the FBI and stuff.

Others, like Daniel, could not believe that Big John would ever do anything like that. If it hadn't been for Big John, Daniel's mom might have died. He didn't believe for a minute that Big John had used that solitary trip to town for penicillin as some kind of excuse to meet with the feds. Daniel thought that was crazy, and he couldn't understand why everybody couldn't see that.

But then, not everybody had seen—up close, anyway—just how sick his mother had been. No one but Daniel and Big John had seen her pus-encrusted, bloody feet, for one thing.

Well, Hunter had.

Daniel couldn't understand what had made Hunter so mad. Big John was just trying to keep him from running off and doing something when he was mad that he might regret later. He was saying just the same kinds of stuff that Daniel's dad was always saying to him when—

The thought brought Daniel up short. For a brief, powerful moment, he felt his father's presence so strongly that he halfway expected to look down to the foot of his bed and find him standing there. The thought gave him the creeps. He rolled over onto his side and punched his hot pillow, but he did not look down toward the foot of the bed.

The truth of the matter was that Daniel missed his dad. He missed his calm strength and his quiet common sense. Lately, people had been running around half-cocked. They were all so paranoid. At first Daniel had believed everything they told him, about computer chips being planted in newborn babies so the government could track their every move as they grew up, and about sophisticated machines the government possessed which could detect how much money you had just by driving past the house, and about the UN raid on the country, how they'd come in on giant black helicopters and round everybody up and take away all their guns and put them into work camps. He had believed it all.

Until Big John.

This he could not believe.

What really scared Daniel was how fast everybody, or most of them anyway, seemed ready to believe anything Hunter said, or anything they heard from each other. They'd been living and working and taking instructions on the gun range from Big John for months and months—since long before Daniel had come to live here—and yet they refused to question what they knew in their hearts was wrong.

Why? He couldn't understand.

Only a couple of guys on the Strike Force, and Daniel himself, and maybe his mom, felt frightened for Big John. They were worried that the rumors would get out of hand. Daniel wasn't sure what was supposed to happen if they did. He didn't want to think about it.

He spent a restless, dream-tossed night and woke up long before dawn. When he couldn't get back to sleep, but still felt exhausted, he decided to take a shower.

It was crystal-cold out, and the wind howled down from the hills like a wounded coyote. Daniel shrugged on his coat, gathered up a fresh pair of cammies, clean underwear, and socks, and stepped out into the wild dark.

As he took the trail from the men's barracks to the showers, he passed the little building where he and his mom had spent their first few nights. As he hurried past, a sound slipped in with the keening wind. A different sound. He stopped, reaching underneath his coat to unsnap his holster as he did so. Heart racing, he listened.

The sound was coming from inside the building.

Pulling the .45 from its holster, Daniel stepped closer and bent his head at an angle to the wind so he might hear better. He shivered.

It was a man, sobbing.

Chills crept beneath Daniel's coat, up the back of his neck and into his scalp, where the skin crawled. Putting his hand to the door-knob, he tried it, but the door was locked. Instantly, the sobbing ceased.

Shaking from head to foot he said, "H-hello?"

"Daniel?"

The muscles in the back of Daniel's neck relaxed, and he rehol-stered the .45. "Big John? I didn't know you were in here."

"You shouldn't be here, son. You could get into trouble. They'll think you're trying to get me out or something."

"I would if I could, Big John," said Daniel bravely.

"I know you would, son, but you better run on."

"Big John? What's going to happen to you?" Daniel waited. "Big John?"

"I'm not real sure, kid, but whatever it is, you gotta promise me somethin'."

"Sure, Big John. What is it?"

"You gotta promise me you won't get mixed up in it. Don't try to stop them, no matter what they do."

"I don't understand."

"Promise me."

Daniel hesitated. "Okay." He felt extremely uneasy.

"One more thing."

Daniel nodded, forgetting that Big John couldn't see him.

"Take care of your mom. Okay? Stick with her and do whatever she says. Okay?"

"Yes, sir," said Daniel, fighting a sudden urge to cry.

"What're you doing here, you little runt?"

Daniel jumped and yanked his body away from the door. Preacher stood right in front of him, aiming an AK47 at his stomach.

"N-nothing. I was just talking to him."

"Well, get the fuck out of here before I blow your head off."

Daniel didn't have to be told twice. He ran all the way to the showers. But no matter how long he stood beneath the hot water, he could not seem to stop shaking.

By the time he got dressed and shaved, a blustery gray dawn had crept across the silver-frosted hills and touched the camp. Daniel hurried over to the mess hall, which had been turned into a sort of courthouse. The tables had been folded up and leaned against the wall, and all the folding chairs had been laid out in aisles and rows. The room was filling up fast. Coffee was available, but no breakfast. Stomach growling, Daniel poured himself a cup, added a generous dollop of cream and sugar, and went in search of his mother.

He found her huddled in a chair on the back row nearest the wall, lips pursed with grim intensity, eyes shadowed underneath by purple smudges. When he took his seat beside her, her face seemed to light up. Knowing how much she loved him sometimes made Daniel feel bad, because he knew he was usually a pretty crappy son. He reached over and gave her an awkward pat on the shoulder. Hunching up her shoulder, she pressed his hand against her cheek for a moment.

The gesture made him feel strangely bereft inside, and he wasn't sure why.

Being here, with the Armageddon Army, had made Daniel feel, for the first time in his life, like he actually *belonged*. His whole life he'd felt like a misfit, but here, it was as if all the misfits of the world had gathered together with one common cause and one common purpose.

Some things were exciting, too, like hanging out with the Alpha/Omega Strike Force. Listening to their war stories. Eavesdropping when they talked about Special Ops. More than anything in the world, he wanted to one day be on the Strike Force.

And Hunter. There was no question that Hunter was the coolest dude Daniel had ever known, bar none. He was a war hero, and he could do anything. Sometimes, he made Daniel feel like he could do anything, too.

But this, this *tribunal*—whatever the hell that was—just didn't make any sense to Daniel. He could not understand for the life of him how Hunter could say the things he'd said about Big John. And to throw him in that, that *place* all alone in the cold and dark, and put an armed guard on him? What was that all about?

Daniel was terribly confused.

He glanced over at his mom, but her face was blank. It occurred to him that her face was nearly always blank now. The only time he saw her really smile was when she was talking to him. Otherwise, she usually had absolutely no expression at all on her face.

Recalling what she'd been like before they came to the compound, Daniel realized how weird that was. As he was pondering that, the tribunal started.

A cafeteria table had been placed lengthwise in front of the crowd. Seven chairs were arranged around it in a semicircle facing the audience. Hunter sat in the middle. A chair was placed to the side of the table. The door opened, and two heavily armed Strike Force members brought in Big John with his hands handcuffed behind his back. They led him to the chair and he sat down, his hands still cuffed behind him. He was wearing his mirrored sunglasses. The guards took their places beside Hunter and the other Strike Force guys, three on each side. Hunter rapped a wooden gavel on the table, like a judge, and everybody in the room grew quiet and attentive.

"The proceedings of this tribunal will come to order. Preacher will act as secretary. The charges against Big John are as follows: treason, conspiring with the enemy, conducting counterespionage against his own troops, and willfully endangering the members of this Armageddon Army compound for his own financial gain. What do you plead to these charges, John?"

"I plead you're a certified nutcase, asshole. They never should have let you out of prison."

"Let the record show that John Fritz, otherwise known as Big John, is acting in his own defense."

"Defend this, you son of a bitch."

Daniel craned his neck to see around the side of the chair where John was sitting. Sure enough, he was giving Hunter the finger behind his back.

"Gentlemen of the court, I think we can say at this point that John here is showing no remorse for his crimes."

"May it please the court," said Kicker.

"You may speak."

"Do we have any proof of these allegations?"

"We do."

Daniel's gaze jumped over to Big John, just in time to see the big man's jaw drop. He looked over at his mother. She was staring at her hands in her lap.

Hunter got to his feet and pulled out a briefcase, which he opened. "Let the record show an address book which was confiscated from John Fritz's footlocker after his imprisonment." He held up the small cheap booklet. It was black. "Inside are the names, addresses, and phone numbers of *known federal agents*," he said, his voice rising dramatically.

"*You lying cocksucker!*" screamed Big John as he leapt to his feet. "You're setting me up!" Two Alpha/Omegans jumped up and each grabbed a huge arm. They then wrestled him back into the chair and stood over him, panting. Big John's face—all the way to the sweaty dome of his head—was lobster-red.

"Kicker?" said Hunter in loud, deliberate tones. "Would you read the first name in this book?" Still standing, never taking his eyes off the outraged Big John, he handed over the booklet.

Kicker took the book from Hunter and fumbled through to the As. After studying the first inscription, the expression on his face twisted from one of disbelief to one of amazement. He looked up at the crowd.

"Steve Austin," he said. "It says Steve Austin right here."

Tumult broke out. Every person in the room knew who Steve Austin was. Hunter had made certain of that.

"*LIAR!*" bellowed Big John. "*You motherfucking LIAR!*" He struggled mightily to get out of his chair, which tipped over and crashed to the floor.

"Mom?" Dismayed and confused beyond belief, Daniel turned to his mother. She was watching the whole thing with that same goddamned blank expression. What was the matter with her? "Mom? Is it true?"

Barely moving her lips, she murmured, "Shshsh. Say nothing."

What the hell was *that* supposed to mean? Hell, if he hadn't promised Big John, he'd . . . he'd . . . well, he wasn't sure what he'd do. Why did he have to make that stupid promise?

But his mother said for him to keep his mouth shut. He promised Big John he'd do whatever she said, so shit, he'd keep his damn mouth shut. Crossing his arms over his chest, he slumped down in his seat and watched.

"Preacher?" said Hunter. "Would you verify that this is indeed Big John's address book?"

Preacher took the booklet from Kicker and thumbed through it. "It's his, all right," he said. "He showed it to me when we first got here. Has a system of stars for girls which are . . . I mean, it's his."

Never taking his eyes off Big John, Hunter said, "Please pass the book around for everyone in the tribunal to examine freely."

As each member of the Strike Force studied and flipped through the address book, the room grew so quiet that all that could be heard was the ragged panting of Big John, placed securely back in the chair, a .45 held to his throat.

When they had all examined it, Hunter said, "Now. If you will be civilized and *watch your language*, John, as there are ladies present at these proceedings, I am going to give you another opportunity to speak in your own defense. What say you?"

Chest heaving, muscles working in his cheeks, veins prominent on his bulging arms, Big John's voice, when he spoke, was different this time. It was plaintive, almost pleading. "Hunter, man, that's my address book. It's true. *But I did not put no federal agents in there*—I swear to holy God I didn't! I swear on my *life*! You gotta believe me, man. I would never turn you guys in. There's no amount of money in this world that could ever make a rat out of me. Surely you know that, man. We were together, inside, man, remember? Cellmates. You never saw me rat out anybody in there, did you?"

"Of course not, John. That's why I invited you to join the Armageddon Army. But people change. They get corrupted. The pig feds have unlimited funds. They shell out untold millions of tax-payers' money to any ratfink who'll talk. I guess they got to you. It makes me sick." He shook his head.

"No, no, I—"

Hunter held up a hand. "You've had your say. Now it's time for the tribunal to have theirs. Men, I believe it's time to take a vote. Preacher, what say you?"

"Guilty."

"Kicker?"

"Guilty."

And so on down the line. Daniel watched helplessly as, one by one, Big John's closest friends turned their backs on him. Daniel was the son of a lawyer, a man who defended guys like Big John every day of his life, and if there was one thing Daniel knew for sure, it was that this was no court, and Hunter was no judge.

For the first time in his entire life, Daniel thought he understood his dad and why he did what he did. *If Dad were here,* he thought desperately, *they'd never get away with this.*

But Dad wasn't here. His dad would never be a part of proceedings like this because this wasn't even a real trial. Leaning over close to his mother, Daniel whispered, "Mom, this is a kangaroo court. It's not real. Can they do that? I mean, isn't Big John an American?"

With a sharp shushing noise, his mom grasped his arm and squeezed until he yelped. He got the message and said nothing more.

Suddenly, the verdict was in, and it was unanimous.

Guilty.

Hunter, still standing, pronounced sentence to the audience. "It troubles me a great deal to have to pronounce this sentence. Like all of you in this room, I, too, have loved this man. But I believe we are all in agreement that treason must be punishable by the fullest extent of the law, because, in this case, to tolerate anything less could result in the deaths of everybody sitting here today."

Daniel's gaze burned into the Alpha/Omegans' faces. Not one of them was looking at Big John.

Hunter rapped the gavel onto the cafeteria table. It was a sound which would haunt Daniel's nightmares for the rest of his life.

Hunter said, *"Death, by firing squad."*

"NOOO!" Somehow Daniel found himself on his feet. "You can't do this! Not to *Big John!*" Anguish pierced every syllable. A reflection of light caught his eye, and he glanced over at Big John. The man had swiveled in his chair and was fixing a stern gaze straight onto Daniel, his glasses reflecting the condemning stares of the people watching him.

Remembering his predawn promise to the big man, Daniel sat down and said nothing more.

After a brief scowl in Daniel's direction, Hunter said, "I will excuse that outburst, this one time, because the boy is young and doesn't know any better. I will trust *his mother* will keep him in line."

Everything else happened in surreal time—super-fast slow motion, if such a thing existed. Before Daniel had time to think or even react, Big John had been led out to the gun range, of all places, and tied to one of the targets.

Although mass gatherings outside were usually forbidden, this time everyone followed meekly behind the Strike Force as Hunter led them down to the range and barked out instructions like a drill sergeant.

Daniel couldn't believe it was happening. It was too unreal. He kept thinking something would happen to stop it, but nothing did. Nobody said anything, not even his mom. If it hadn't been for his promise to Big John, he'd have done *something*—thrown himself in front of his friend—anything to stop the insanity.

For a while he believed fervently that his mom would stop Hunter, but she didn't even try. Daniel didn't know why Big John had made him promise to obey his mom; how could he possibly respect her when she seemed willing to stand by and watch a good man die for *nothing*?

They took off Big John's sunglasses and tried to blindfold him, but he wouldn't let them. "I want to stare all you sons of bitches in the eye," he said. "And I hope to God you never forget it." Then he spat on the ground.

Hunter was going to give the command to the Alpha/Omegans.

"Don't look," mumbled Daniel's mother, tugging at his sleeve, but Daniel couldn't help it; he was frantically hoping that maybe they'd miss or something, that maybe Hunter had put blanks in the guns just to give Big John a bad scare, that maybe he'd shout *halt* at the last minute—something, *anything*.

But in the end, all of the bullets fired from all of the guns, and they all found their mark, just like the big man had taught so well. One big shot, it sounded like.

And as the echoes reverberated off the cold, barren hills, Big John slumped at his post, dead.

"Bury him," ordered Hunter to the Strike Force as he turned his back to walk away. "Someplace where he won't be found and deep enough so the coyotes don't dig him up."

CHAPTER **37**

THE night Big John was killed, Wren's grandmother, Ahw'usti, visited her in a dream.

They were sitting in Ahw'usti's house in Oklahoma, making buffalo grass dolls. Although Wren loved listening to Ahw'usti's stories, she hated making buffalo grass dolls. The work was tedious and tiresome and Wren thought the dolls were silly. Ahw'usti was determined that Wren should learn the art, for she feared that it would die out with the Cherokee elders.

"It is important for you to learn *kano helvhi,* the old ways," said Ahw'usti. "Without the old ways our people will die."

"Oh, Ahw'usti," said Wren, "the people won't die just because nobody makes these stupid dolls anymore."

"But a part of them will die. It is the same part which longs to dance to the drumbeat around the fire beneath the stars."

"I don't want to talk about dancing!" snapped Wren. "I'm sick and tired of dancing."

Ahw'usti was shocked. "Can you be weary of the turtle song?" she cried, referring to the habit of Cherokee women dancers of strapping turtle shells filled with pebbles to their legs for the rhythmic sounds they made as the women danced, one-two, one-two, while drifting sparks mesmerized the watchers and smoke from the fire curled into the night like a mystery.

Wren threw down the doll she was working on. "I'm weary of all of it! I've danced and danced and I just want to stop!" She sprang to her feet and strode across the room to leave.

"*Una tse lidv-u nato tivhi!*" cried Ahw'usti. "You think you are alone because no one else dances? It is not true. We must *una tse lidv-u nato tivhi*—think with our *heads* and not our *feet!*"

Wren stopped and turned to stare at Ahw'usti. She said, "I cannot outdance the coyote. He has great power and I am merely *agehya*—woman."

Ahw'usti shook her head. "His power is *nigvnhdiha*." She made a wave of dismissal. "He puts it on each day with his guns. Your power is *adanvto*; it flows from within you like a great *uweyv*. Who can stop the river?"

"He can," said Wren, hanging her head miserably.

"*Vyoho wayigi!*" insisted Ahw'usti. "Not true! How can you believe these lies? What you are knowing is *unayehisdi*. There is a reason for this great fear. It is that you are in the presence of terrible *usonvi*. But it is not this evil enemy which gives you fear." She folded her hands in her lap as if that was all there was to say on the subject.

"He is *gadaha!*" spat Wren. "I cannot wash myself clean of his filth." She shuddered.

"If you take on his hatred, you too become dirty," said the old woman quietly.

Wren blinked at Ahw'usti.

"In order for *ala sdi*, for you to fight him, you must find the balance of living *duyugodv*," she said, holding both hands palms up, "squarely, with *truth*. Do not try to live with his lies; he puts them on with his guns. Do you want him to *asda wadv stodi?*" Ahw'usti narrowed her eyes at Wren.

"I don't live with his lies!" yelled Wren defensively. "Every day I put on the *adutivtodi!*" She was referring to the stoic face of the Cherokee, the mask worn to hide their feelings during times of trouble. "And he is not going to rule over me. He will *never* rule over me!"

"You live with his anger," said Ahw'usti, ignoring Wren's near-hysteria. "This terrible rage can be *ali so qui lvdi*—a great weight on your heart, little one. This anger can cloud your *agowadvdi* so that you can no longer see the way in which you should go. Then his put-on power rules you, don't you see? Or has your own anger blinded you to the truth?"

"I don't *care* anymore!" howled Wren. "Old woman! *You* are blind! I am tired! I am so *tired!*"

Wren started to run. For some reason, Ahw'usti's house had many, many rooms, and a very long hallway. Although Wren ran and ran, she couldn't seem to get out of her grandmother's house. Finally, she flung open one door, only to find herself back in the same room with her grandmother! But when she turned to rush out, her grandmother commanded her, *"Gatogv!"*

Gatogv. Stand still.

Wren obeyed.

"If you want to *asquadv*—to triumph—over this evil, this *usonvi*, then you must stand still. Allow the *Gulan Lati*—the Great Spirit— to speak to you in the stillness, *ada toli stodi.* You will not win this battle over evil with your strength, but with your *gohu sdi-gesv*, your *intelligence.*"

"He is evil," said Wren weakly. "He plots death."

Ahw'usti shook her head. "It is not the evil which is your enemy, my child. It is your own *unayehisdi*—your own fear! It is only after you face *this* enemy—the enemy within—that you may allow your- self *gananvdisgi*—the war whoop of triumph!"

Then Wren's grandmother did a strange thing. She jumped to her feet like a young girl and began to dance in a circle, singing, *"Tlage situn gali sgi sida ha; Ha nia lil! lil! Ha nia lil! lil!"*

On the edge of the field I dance about.

"Ha nia lil! lil! Ha nia lil! lil!"

"Ha nia Wake up, wake up, Lissie!"

Someone was shaking her. She resisted for a while, but she kept being shaken. Like coming up from a great depth, she rose to the surface and gradually opened her eyes. The shadow of Jeremiah Hunter loomed over her.

"Jesus," he said irritably. "You woke me up talking gibberish in your sleep." He plopped back onto his pillow. "Shut up. I need my rest."

But there would be no more sleep for Wren that night. Once Hunter resumed his snores, she eased out of bed and shut herself up in the bathroom—the one place where she could be alone and reasonably certain he would not wake up, grow suspicious, and come check on her.

Her mind was crystal clear, almost supernaturally so. Her grandmother would say the stagnant creek had encountered a fresh, clear-flowing stream.

Death to life.

The shock of Big John's death had stunned and bereaved Wren more than she would have thought possible. Even more debilitating was the horror she'd seen on Daniel's face—the terror, the desperation, the terrible disappointment when she did nothing to stop the death of his friend.

What her young son did not know—could not know—was that the Armageddon Army was entering a new era. Once the Pandora's box of suspicion was opened, none of them would be safe.

And once Hunter demonstrated his total lack of regard for human life, no one dared challenge him.

Overcome with emotion, numb over her own powerlessness, Wren had staggered through the rest of the day suffused with nothing more than the simple desire to sleep.

Now she thought she knew why. In spite of the emotions which still ebbed and flowed within her heart, her mind was clear and clean and strong.

By dawn, twenty-four hours after the condemnation of Big John to his death, Wren had a living plan of action.

Over the course of the next few weeks, changes, some subtle, some not so subtle, took place in the camp. Big John's absence was, of course, the most dramatic. No one else in the compound came close to possessing his expertise in firearms; now if a weapon developed a problem or was in need of repair, it was usually left in the armory with all the other unrepaired weapons and replaced with a working one. Kicker was put in charge of the armory, but he had little interest in it and was often careless.

Wren used this carelessness to make her first move; she stole the Glock 19 Big John had set aside for her. Later, she took a special holster for it and, at another time, a box of ammunition and a spare clip. Stealing what she needed actually proved easier than hiding it. Though she was no longer under guard, or even watched as closely, this was still not a place for privacy. The best she could do was a hollowed-out spot beneath a large stone in the rock garden, the Glock wrapped in plastic bubble-pack. It was hardly weatherproof, but fortunately for Wren, the Glock was known to be especially weather resistant, and rain was seldom a problem in this rugged area anyway.

Big John's absence had other, less noticeable, ramifications, none of which came as a surprise to Wren. Any idealistic innocence which may have been possessed by members of the rank and file died with Big John. Fear and suspicion—a hallmark of the group anyway—now grew deadly. Hunter's ease in dispatching a valued member of the Strike Force served notice to one and all that any of them could be next. Therefore none dared speak out against anything Hunter said, or otherwise draw attention to himself.

Not everyone in the Armageddon Army had been as quick to condemn Big John as the Strike Force had, and some of them still reeled from it privately. But then not all the "Army" was composed of hardened convicts, which seemed to have been a prerequisite for membership in the elite Alpha/Omegans. Wren suspected that Hunter had recruited that entire inner circle while still in prison. Consequently the Strike Force had an even healthier fear of the consequences of arrest, less respect for human life, and—most important of all—greed, and lots of it.

Most of the Strike Force members were in this whole thing for the money, Wren had observed. While it was true enough that they adhered to Hunter's paranoid philosophy, the real reason they put up with him was that they wanted their cut. And like most cons, they were addicted to the thrill that committing crimes provided them, and nothing was more thrilling than the ultimate Big Take. Every true con, Wren had learned, lived for the Big Take. It was the all-consuming fantasy.

For Hunter's part, his behavior over time was predictable as well; the déjà vu for Wren was sometimes almost spooky. As he grew more involved with the planning of the crime, discussing the details endlessly with his team, working on charts and blueprints, calendars and clocks, rehearsing and so forth, Hunter's behavior began to fit several familiar patterns.

The murder of Big John climaxed the first: Hunter took any criticism of the plan as a direct threat to his power. Therefore, after Big John's death, Hunter was allowed total freedom to make his plans without anybody cluttering them up by pointing out any weaknesses or mistakes.

Then, as the plan took more concrete shape, Wren noticed the next element setting in: Hunter's absolute, wildly optimistic conviction that they were going to succeed, get away with it, and go on to bigger and better crimes. It was a rush as addictive as any drug, and it was contagious. Everybody on the team grew more confident by the day.

Except Wren, of course. But then, she had worries of her own. Fortunately for Wren, another aspect of Hunter's precrime nature began to manifest itself. As he grew more preoccupied with his scheme, he gradually lost all interest in sex. The relief of being released from a situation which had amounted to daily rape gave Wren the freedom to concentrate fully on her own plan.

Unlike Hunter, she anguished over the possibility of failure.

But the hardest thing of all for Wren to handle during those days after Big John's death, beyond missing his friendly smile, was the impact on her son. Daniel retreated into a sullen, silent place unreachable by Wren or anybody else. More than anything else, Wren longed to comfort the boy. She knew what he'd seen that day had been the most traumatic event of his life. She knew he needed to talk about it, needed to work through it with someone who cared. Daily she worried about her son's long-term emotional stability, but there was nothing she could do about it. She simply could not risk anything going wrong at this point.

Too many lives were depending on her, and Daniel's, precious though it was, was only one.

So each day, as Wren awoke in Hunter's bed and prepared Hunter's breakfast and helped Hunter with his plan to bomb the Leatherwood Building, she put on her *adutivtodi*, the mask. No one gazing upon her face could see into her soul and read the bitter truth which resided there.

"Okay guys, listen up," said Wren. "I've been working with these explosives for several days now." She was standing by the overhead projector in the workout room. The Strike Force team, including Hunter, was arranged on the mats in front of her. She held up something which resembled a piece of brown vinyl. "This Flex-X is terrific," she said. "I've never seen anything like it. My original plan was to cover a briefcase with it and leave the briefcase somewhere in the second row. Sometimes people leave their briefcases behind after a seminar."

"Pass that around," said Hunter.

"Will it blow up?" Kicker's whole body seemed to cringe at the thought.

"Not without a detonator." She handed the material to Hunter, who examined it.

"But I understand that one Mafia kingpin got a little surprise when he went for a ride in his freshly upholstered car," she added. The whole room erupted into laughter and whoops. Wren grinned wickedly. "Anyway, I have rejected that plan for several reasons. In the first place, Steve Austin's much too sharp to overlook something as obvious as a briefcase. In the second place, I have no intention of making this a suicide mission."

Hunter chuckled, winked at her, and passed the Flex-X on to Preacher.

"And third, I really don't have the materials here to do a professional-looking job of covering a briefcase. I tried. It looked like one of Daniel's third-grade science projects."

"So what're we going to do with it?" asked Hunter. "That's expensive shit, and you would not believe what I had to go through to get my hands on it."

"Don't worry. We'll save it and wait for just the right moment some time in the future. You never know."

Leaning back on his hands, he nodded approvingly.

Wren went on. "Okay. There's no doubt that C-4's powerful stuff, but the good thing about Semtex-H is that it's made with a formula containing powdered RDX, PETN, and plasticizers, but—"

"What's RDX and PETN?" Hunter bugged her to show off her chemistry acumen so the others would see how smart he'd been to bring her in.

"PETN stands for Pentaerythrite Tetranitrate, a very powerful explosive," she said, responding to the cue. "RDX actually stands for Cyclonite. It's usually used in combination with PETN. Anyway, *as I was saying*, the Czechs developed Semtex-H. What sets it apart

from other explosives is that they added plain old vegetable oil to the formula. It's sort of like jelly. You can just smear it wherever you want to."

"Which is why it is damn near impossible to get ahold of," added Hunter importantly.

Wren reached for the Flex-X, which was being passed back up to her. "I thought about taking one of those little leather boxes that you can get at Radio Shack for sound systems, you know? They're usually spotted under the podium. I was going to hollow it out and put the explosives in there."

"And blow ol' Peckerhead to kingdom come!" cried Preacher. "I love it."

"Mmmm. Well, the problem is, again, Steve Austin. The Leatherwood Building is his stomping grounds. It's Leatherwood's home office, after all. And the podium is a very vulnerable spot—in fact, the Secret Service takes its own podium along every time the president gives a speech. It's covered with Kevlar."

"Like a bullet-proof vest?" cried Kicker. "Huh."

"That's right. And, like the Secret Service, I'm sure Austin positions men on or around the podium area. There's no way we could sneak in an extra box like that. He'd spot it right away."

The men nodded to one another.

"I tried to think of some way we could infiltrate the staff, like, man the coffee machine or something, but again, that's just too obvious. Then I hit on something that would not be so obvious."

She paused for effect. "Potted plants."

"What?" Hunter raised a skeptical eyebrow.

"Potted plants. To be placed entirely around the stage and the podium. First of all, Austin would use potted plants of some kind around the podium as a matter of course anyway."

"How do you know?" asked one of the men.

"Plants, arranged in a semicircle around the podium, act as a barrier between the speaker and the audience. If anybody tries to approach the speaker through the plants, it is inconvenient and obvious enough to alert security. It looks like decoration, but it's SOP for protection."

"What do you know about it?" mumbled Kicker, just loud enough for all to hear.

Hunter's voice cut through the air like a whip. "She reads, asshole. And she's a hell of a lot smarter than you. Go on, Lissie."

Wren cleared her throat. "The explosives would be packed beneath the potting soil, so if Austin happens to look inside the plants, he'll see nothing suspicious."

"I got a question," said Kicker. "What about dogs?"

"You're right, and I thought of that. I'm sure that before every important speech, Austin calls the local PD to have them send in the bomb dogs to check out the room—maybe the whole building. So we'll plant a decoy explosive at the airport. Something relatively harmless, and we'll set the timer for hours in advance so it won't go off. The idea is not to hurt anybody."

"What is the idea?" said Preacher, stifling a yawn.

Wren ignored him. "What we do is we call in a bomb threat, right? Just before we're ready to deliver the plants to the conference room. Naturally, the local PD responds by bringing out the dogs. The dogs find the explosive. Bomb squad takes care of it." She gave them a small grin. "But we've told them to expect three or four explosive devices, not just one. Dogs'll be there for hours. The PD'll tell Austin he's got to wait, but the speech is already scheduled. People are showing up. Too late, right? I think they'll go ahead with the program. Without the bomb dogs to sniff out the place first."

There was a moment of silent contemplation, then Hunter got to his feet and gave her slow applause. She bowed.

After Wren had taken her seat with the others, Hunter said, "Okay, folks. I think it's time for the run-through."

The shock of his words took everybody by surprise, but nobody more than Wren. Naturally she knew that no special op—or crime—was complete without a run-through on site. But she had not set foot off the compound since the night she and Daniel were grabbed off the street, bound and gagged, and brought here as hostages, except for her brief escape. Now Hunter was the most wanted felon in the country; everybody was looking for her and Daniel, as well. Wren knew that from the CNN news reports she'd managed to sneak in from the satellite dish while Hunter was in the shower.

It was reckless. It was insane. It was typical Hunter. And of course, nobody dared object.

"I'll be in the van," said Hunter, oblivious to the stunned silence that had followed his announcement. "Wren will be in disguise. You'll all be wearing business suits and carrying briefcases. Here's a Spiegel catalogue." He tossed it onto the floor. Wren reached out and picked it up. "Pick out whatever you want to wear, and I'm talking serious business suits. I'll need exact sizes from all of you. You've gotta look sharp. I'm not going to have you walk into a classy building like that looking like a bunch of slobs."

Wren flipped through the catalogue. It was the first time she'd seen women's clothes since arriving at the compound. It was like gazing at a brochure advertising rocket trips to an alien planet.

She didn't even know if she could still speak the language.

"Kicker and Preacher—you'll accompany Lissie up to the conference room where Leatherwood will be giving his speech."

"Won't somebody spot us?" asked a doubtful Preacher. "Austin'll have security everywhere, won't he?"

"I've picked a day when Leatherwood's going to be out of town—in fact, out of the whole state," said Hunter with his usual cocky assurance. "Austin will probably either be with Leatherwood or at his Dallas offices. Security will be minimal. You'll all be fitted with wires. Anything goes wrong, you can let me know. Okay. You other four guys will case out the bank. And I mean the vault—everything."

"How'll we do that?" asked one.

Hunter smiled. "Why, you'll open up a safety deposit box, dickhead. The rest of you, mark the positions of all security cameras, tellers, officers, the works. I want to be able to put together a detailed map when we get back. We'll also put the building under surveillance for a day or two to mark the bank's routine. Any questions?"

Of course there were questions. Hundreds of them. Nobody asked.

Wren wasn't paying much attention anyway. She paged the catalogue, looking at cheerful winter suits in crimson wool and black leather, at cashmere sweaters and silken lounging pajamas in holiday colors of berry red and pine green, at suede boots and black stockings with seductive little garter belts and matching bras designed for maximum cleavage.

Christmas. When had the season come? Had it blown in with the blue north wind? Had it clung to the cedars like clumps of mistletoe?

Did it drift into the winter sky like smoke from the hunter's lodge fireplace?

Wren stared at the smiling models. She'd missed Zoe's thirteenth birthday, which came right after Thanksgiving. Fighting down a wave of despair that threatened to wash over her, Wren thought instead about the people in the Leatherwood Building.

The Leatherwood Building would be filled with men and women just like the ones in this catalogue, bustling about the busy mall to the sounds of piped-in carols, buying festive baskets filled with scented pine cones and cinnamon, filling shopping bags with toys and other gaily-wrapped goodies, stopping in at the bank for more cash, drinking spiced cider and hot cocoa in the little restaurants . . . while in their happy midst, death would come creeping, dressed in business suits and carrying brown leather briefcases.

CHAPTER 38

"**D**ADDY, are we gonna have to move?"

Zoe popped this question to Cam as he was stretched out underneath the kitchen sink, the cabinet ledge digging into his back, trying to attach a new U-piece to a leaky pipe, in the dark, where there wasn't enough room to fit both his elbows, much less the pipe wrench. Why she insisted on broaching life's most difficult issues when he was deeply engrossed in something else was something Cam would never be able to figure out.

"Just a minute, sweetie. I'm almost finished here. Would you mind holding that flashlight a little lower, please? Right there. That's it. Thanks." The heavy wrench slipped and banged painfully against one of his knuckles. Blood mixed with sweat and began to sting. "*Fuck, fuck, fuck,*" he muttered.

"What?"

"Nothing. Zoe, you've got to hold the flashlight still, okay? It's not a goddamned strobe light!"

"I *am* holding it still!"

I hate thirteen, he thought. *Why can't they just skip thirteen and jump straight from twelve to fourteen? Not that it's all that much better.*

The phone rang. Zoe sprang to answer it, taking his light with her.

I hate plumbing. I hate pipes, I hate sinks, I hate toilets, and I hate

*things breaking when I'm too fucking broke to hire somebody to
fix them.*

After a little more yanking on the wrench, he called to Zoe to turn
on the water in the faucet for him. But Zoe was nowhere around,
and Cam was forced to drag his body out from under the sink, unfold
it, and stretch stiffly to his feet. There he had to turn the water
on and then get back under the sink to make sure the pipes held.
Miraculously, they did.

Too ill-tempered to clean up his own mess, Cam left it and went
into the bathroom to wash his hands. Already his back was shaped
roughly like the pipe he'd just replaced, and he could feel a mam-
moth headache coming on.

The truth was that Zoe's question had frightened Cam more than
he cared to admit, even to himself. Three, four months ago, he'd
have laughed at the question, reassured her, and changed the subject. But three or four months ago, he'd had a wife bringing in a large
chunk of the family's income. They always paid the mortgage and
some of the bigger bills from her paycheck because it was regular and
predictable. Since he was self-employed, most of his income after
overhead tended to come in lumps and stretches. If the law practice
was going well, they set much of it aside or splurged on new appli-
ances or vacation trips. If the practice was slow, they'd do the best
they could.

But that was three or four months ago. The money they'd set
aside was pretty much gone, and he'd had to refinance the mortgage
recently. If Wren did not return within the next few months, Cam
faced the very real possibility that the house might have to be put up
for sale.

Staring at his haggard expression in the mirror over the sink, Cam
wondered if his little worrier had thought up the scenario on her own
or if he had somehow revealed to her the extent of their situation.
He'd tried not to, but Zoe was a sensitive child. Now Daniel, Daniel
he could have fooled. The absent smile which flitted across his lined
face lasted only briefly. Cam stared into the mirror as his haunted
eyes stared blankly back at him.

Time was when he practically counted the days until the boy
could leave home for college. Or juvie hall. Whichever came first.

Now he missed his son with a ferocity he could never have

expected. Missed his free spirit and his lopsided grin and his offbeat sense of humor and his big feet and his goofy friends. Missed his gift for mimicry; how many times had he and Wren escaped the room after scolding him for some school infraction, only to double over, suppressing howls at Daniel's bull's-eye imitation of the offended teacher?

As each day passed with no word about his missing family, Cam felt rage curdle in the back of his throat and swell up beneath his diaphragm, choking off everything but the blind desire to hurt the ones who'd robbed him of them. Every night that he laid awake, listening to his daughter's sobs in the next room, it was all he could do not to find a gun somewhere, load it, and take off in search of the bastards who had broken her sweet, tender heart.

The self-obsessed act of an egomaniac had shattered their lives. If Cam lost his law practice—which he was in danger of doing—and they were forced to move into an apartment or small rental house, then they would have truly lost everything.

Well, maybe not everything. Cam and Zoe still had each other. If he'd lost Zoe, too, he didn't think he could have hung on.

Cam bent over and splashed cold water on his face, rubbed a limp towel over it, composed his expression, and went in search of his daughter. He found her stretched out on her bed, flipping through a fan magazine for teen heartthrobs. And although her favorite actor was featured on the cover, he noticed that she didn't seem to be reading any of the articles. He sat on the edge of the bed and patted her shoulders. They were stiff and tight. Zoe, too, paid a physical price for the stress they were under.

"I'm sorry I snapped at you."

"It's okay, Daddy." She flipped through a few more pages.

"I really hate plumbing."

"I know. But we can't afford a plumber."

"No." He sighed. "Listen, I don't want you worrying about losing the house."

"Why not? My friend Rudy had to move into an apartment after his dad lost his job. He couldn't find another one, and their unemployment checks ran out."

Cam frowned. "I thought Rudy's dad was working now."

"He is. Out at the golf course. He keeps the grounds. But he used to be an engineer making war planes, and they're just not making as many war planes as they used to. It's all he could find. Rudy says they used to be sorta rich, but now they're poor."

"Well, they're not exactly poor, but their standard of living has been substantially reduced. It happens sometimes."

"Is it going to happen to us?" She carefully studied a photograph of a rock star in the magazine, as if the question didn't matter at all.

Cam hesitated. At this point he could not promise this child anything. He couldn't even promise her that she would see her mother and her brother once again. "Zoe . . . I'm working very hard to make sure that doesn't happen. I've signed on as a public defender for the county. There's not much money in it, but the work's steady. That should help."

"Will you make enough money to keep the house?"

"I don't know, honey. That's the honest truth. But we will be able to stay here until spring for sure. I just don't want you to worry about it right now. Let's take this one day at a time."

"*Spring?*" She sat straight up and nailed him with those eyes. "Are you saying that Mom and Daniel may not even be here by *spring?*" With each word her voice rose.

"No, no! I'm not saying that at all! I'm just saying that—"

"*I thought they'd be home for Christmas!*" she wailed, her eyes blurring with tears. "They won't even be home for *Christmas?*"

"They might." Cam struggled to keep his voice calm. He'd learned that the worst thing he could do was react when she got upset like this. "You never can tell. They might."

"Why don't you ever tell me the truth? *They're never coming home at all!*"

Zoe leapt off the bed and dashed from the room, slamming the door so hard that it sounded like a shot, leaving her weary father all alone with the unicorns and teddy bears, groping for a tourniquet that he might apply to the gaping wound in his heart.

Though it was only the first week in December, the Leatherwood Building was decked out for Christmas as if Santa himself maintained an office in the complex. Very un-Christmassy Texas sunshine poured in the bronze-tinted glass walls all the way up to the third floor, casting a warm golden glow over everything. The second

floor was an open mezzanine accessible by escalator as well as either
of two glass elevators; the waterfall frolicked forth from some mysterious source just beneath the mezzanine. Silvery background music
of Christmas carols played on harp, mandolin, acoustic guitar, and
flute harmonized with the merry plash and play of the water.

Tiny incandescent lights glittered like stardust everywhere. A spectacular twenty-foot very realistic artificial blue fir Christmas tree
dominated the center of the lobby. Twinkling pinpoints of white lights
shimmered off the ornaments: the entire tree was done up in hundreds of Victorian handcrafted angels; the whole effect was luminous.

The irony of the Christmas angels was not lost on Wren as she
stumbled to a halt and gaped at the magnificent scene, so designed
as to draw the eye heavenward. She and her two "assistants" had
entered the building ahead of the others; they would drift into the
first-floor bank at staggered intervals.

Wren had been rendered virtually stupefied by a steady visual diet
of drab desert camouflage and the monotonous landscape of grays
and browns. She was hungry for color, starved for music, ravenous for
evidence of the human spirit on the wing. When the soul feeds on
fear, hatred, and anger, she had learned, all the colors gradually turn
gray, the music fades to black, and the very air grows heavy and
hellish. A spirit so crippled soon withers from lack of use, stalls, spi-
rals into a downward tailspin, and disintegrates.

It was easy to forget, in an environment like that, the simple
splendor and radiance of the human spirit unfettered. It was easy to
overlook the generous capacity for compassion present in the human
soul, the sheer contagious gift of joy.

She was reminded now, here in Buck Leatherwood's building, the
building where her companions were plotting death. Were she to
carry out the plan to its fullest extent, Wren would bring it all down
in a single moment of speechless horror into a massive pile of broken
glass, dust-clouded rubble, dead bodies, blood, and angels.

Kicker's sharp nudge at her ribs shattered the spell. Crossing the
polished floor on wobbly heels, Wren stepped onto the escalator,
fighting the almost overpowering urge to scratch her scalp, which
itched madly beneath the short blond wig under which she'd stuffed
her voluminous dark hair. Black sunglasses covered most of her face,

Jackie O. style. She stared at her feet and avoided making eye contact with anyone.

At the top of the escalator, Wren and her dapper-dressed colleagues casually strolled the promenade, disappeared behind an exit door, and took the stairs to the third floor. Preacher scouted the corridor behind the stairwell exit door and they emerged, one by one. The rooms were laid out just as they recalled from the blueprints. It didn't take long to find conference room C. The door was locked.

Kicker turned his back and used his body as a shield for Wren and Preacher while serving as lookout at the same time. There was little traffic, and Wren stood ready with an open briefcase stuffed with meaningless papers to drop, should anyone happen by and wonder why they were all standing there.

From an inside pocket of his suit coat, Preacher withdrew a pick gun, which he had adapted by attaching the pick gun holder to the controls of an electric toothbrush, rendering it handy and rechargeable. Covering his hands with his body, he inserted the pick gun into the lock, manipulating a small tension wrench into the same spot, and squeezed the trigger, making an annoying buzzing noise as the motor drove the needle against the bottom of the tumblers in sharp and rapid motions. At the same instant, with a delicate manipulation of the tip of his finger, he turned the wrench about one-eighth of an inch. Quickly, using a screwdriver instead of the wrench, he retracted the bolt.

The door swung open.

Slipping into the room, Wren and Preacher shut the door behind them and locked it. Amber light flooded the room from the floor-to-ceiling slanted windows. Thick copper-tone carpet absorbed the light and their footfalls as they made their way up to the stage area. Wren felt as if she were walking in a bottle of champagne. It gave her a dizzy feeling.

It was a large room, plenty big enough to hold at least a hundred people. Tables covered with white linen cloths at the back held shining coffee and tea machines big enough to serve all the people. The stage was flanked by the American flag on one side and the Texas flag on the other, hanging limply from poles. Walls paneled in mahogany behind the stage gave it the somber air of a courtroom.

The only judge, however, would be Wren's conscience.

Two steps led to the small stage area, which was about ten feet square. The podium was standard, the sound system box underneath as she had anticipated. Had she used another box, it would most certainly have been spotted by security.

"Does anybody know yet when Hunter is planning this shindig?" asked Wren.

Preacher shook his head.

"Okay. If it's before Christmas, we'll ring the podium with poinsettias. If it's after, we'll use some other potted plants. Lots of green."

"No flowers?"

"Nah. Too fragile. We'd have to keep them cold someplace, and they might wilt before we could get them here."

The first row of seats was uncomfortably close to the stage, only ten feet or so. This worried Wren. For her plan to work, she would need some sort of baffle to absorb the major force of the blast. It would have to be chosen with care, too, or the baffle itself could become a flying missile.

Preacher was watching her think. "What's wrong?"

"Um, I need another prop," she said, "for backup."

"Like what?"

"I don't know," she said. "A piece of furniture, maybe."

Wandering the room, he called from a distant corner, "How about this?" He was standing next to a head-high TV stand on casters. The stand was constructed of metal, complete with a metal back that supported the TV, a VCR, and other equipment on three adjustable shelves.

Wren went to examine the TV stand. "Can you move it up by the stage, say, over to the right? Hell, he may want to show a propaganda tape anyway. And there's an outlet in the wall up there too."

"Sure." He started pushing the unwieldy structure up the aisle toward the stage, where he parked it a few feet to the side. "How's this?"

"Can you turn it a little? Catercorner to the stage?"

He lugged it back and forth. "Like this?"

For the first time that day, Wren smiled. "Yeah!" she called, and added, "*Perfect.*"

CHAPTER 39

"THE run-through was an unqualified success!" announced Hunter to the team as they assembled in the workout room two days after returning from Midland. "But then, I knew it would be."

The mood in the room was ecstatic, euphoric . . . and dangerously overoptimistic. At least, that's the way Wren read it as she listened to the men around her discuss all the ways things could go right with the final plan to bomb the Leatherwood Building, kill the despised Buck Leatherwood, wreak deadly revenge on Steve Austin, and make off with a fortune.

"Front and center, guys," said Hunter. "I'm ready to reveal the target date."

Instant attentive silence fell over the room.

"Ground zero: December fifteenth. That gives us two weeks."

"Two weeks!" cried Wren. "I can't possibly be ready by then!"

All eyes turned to her, and the silence which followed her remark was an uneasy one. Hunter was giving her one of those smiles she knew so well, the one which never reached his eyes.

"But my dear," he said, "Leatherwood's propaganda speech to the gun-control apes is scheduled for that day. Period. You'll have to be ready, that's all. You will be ready."

She was shaking. How typical of the bastard to hinge the whole thing on explosives and then not tell his demolitions man when he had to be ready. (Or she, as the case may be.) Hunter's compulsive need to be in absolute and complete control could ruin the whole plan, that is, if he were to allow for failure, which of course he did not.

The truth was that Wren wasn't worried about Hunter's plan—she was worried about her own. Now if she didn't have everything she needed, there was no time to get it. She would simply have to make do.

"Fine," she said, giving him a bold and fierce gaze. "Then if you are going to put these time restraints on me, you're going to have to loosen up in other areas."

"Such as?" He cocked his head.

"Such as giving me free rein in the underground shelter."

He tightened his lips.

"As it is, I have to wait until you are available to accompany me, or at least track down a guard. You're going to have to let me come and go as I need to. And I may have to be down there late nights, after lights-out. I need the freedom to set my own hours and work alone in peace." Without breaking eye contact, she added, "Otherwise there is no way I can be ready. Period."

She knew she had him by the short hairs. As it was, they were short-handed without Big John. The others were needed for all the exhaustive rehearsals Hunter liked to stage, as well as their usual duties around the compound.

"Fine." He folded his arms across his chest.

Hiding her elation, Wren added, "And I'll need to make a trip into Midland."

"No way. What, are you crazy?"

"Not by myself. I understand that. But I need to purchase pots. Lots of them. I need to experiment with various thicknesses to see which is the best to house the explosives as well as have room for the plants. Make it El Paso. I don't care. But the nearest little town will never have what I need. A large gardening supply house would. We could find one easy in the city."

"What difference does it make?" he snapped, irritation all over his face. "A pot is a fucking pot. You're putting a fucking bomb in it. Who cares how thick it is?"

She regarded him without fear. "Do you want maximum effect or not? You want the force of the blast directed upward or out into the crowd? You know so much, *you* go buy the goddamn pots!"

No one except Big John had dared speak to Hunter like that, and everybody in the room knew what had happened to Big John. But Wren was protected by the shield of Hunter's dependence on her for the success of the operation. He simply couldn't do it without her.

After a long pause of crackling tension, he said, "Make it Odessa. Whatever you need, it better be there because you are *not* going to Midland. And you will be accompanied by Kicker and Preacher every step, you got that?"

She nodded.

"One step out of line . . . I'll kill you myself. Is that clear?"

It was a bluff designed to keep her under control and reestablish his power in front of the others. Wren knew that, at least until after the operation, she was safe. Unless, of course, she blew herself up.

"Very clear," she said.

After that confrontation, and in the following days, every sinew in Wren's body existed in a constant state of alert. Her hands were steady, but her nerves were raw. In spite of the danger, she preferred to work in the underground shelter because of the silence and privacy. True to his word, Hunter left her alone. Though he did send Strike Force team members on surprise checks, this presented no problem to her because they had only a rudimentary understanding of explosives. It was easy enough to fool them.

Wren was limited in the amount and size of practice detonations she could set off. Though she had enough material to blow up every boulder in sight, she couldn't take the chance of attracting the attention of a vigilant game warden or sheriff's deputy. Fortunately, she could explode pots to her heart's content; nobody lived near enough to hear or feel the smaller devices.

Hunter visited her wombish laboratory only once (he was probably afraid of being blown up) to request that she pack lots of steel nails and other sharp objects into the malleable claylike explosives, for maximum shrapnel damage. When she assured him she would, he clapped his hands together like a little kid on Christmas morning.

Under cover of darkness, Wren moved her gun and ammo to a

more accessible place, and crept around the camp like a commando, gathering up other odd items that she needed.

The detonators were the trickiest part. Knowing that Hunter knew just enough about explosives to be highly dangerous, she had to install convincing detonators. Remote radio beams or burn-down fuses weren't practical. And though she knew how to set the explosives so that each one would set off the other in a millisecond, this was not what she wanted to do. However, she had to make it *seem* as if that was the intent. To her way of thinking, that left electronic as the only way to go.

Setting them up was no problem—it was the timers that scared her. Each one in each pot would have to be set on the agreed-upon time for the explosion. But part of Wren's plan involved a very delicate and difficult process—rigging the timers so that they would not detonate at the agreed-upon time, but much later, long after the building had been cleared and hopefully after the bomb squad had removed them and encased them in protective bomb-proof barrels.

Even scarier than that was Hunter's determination not to launch the bank robbery until after detonation. He and the bank team would be waiting out in the van for Wren, Preacher, and Kicker to return. There they would all wait for the room to fill and the speech to begin. As soon as the explosion occurred, they would all rush the bank, with the exception of Hunter himself, who would stay behind to "coordinate the operation" by monitoring radio communications, driving the getaway van, and keeping an eye on Wren.

So there had to be some kind of explosion. If there wasn't, Wren would be killed on-site, for certain, which would leave Daniel back at the compound, at Hunter's mercy. She racked her brains to think of some way to accomplish the required detonation without hurting anybody.

Finally, Wren had to face the simple truth concerning explosives: there were no guarantees. She would have to take the risk that someone might be hurt, perhaps seriously. She didn't want to, but there seemed to be no choice in the matter. All she could do was make every effort to ensure that didn't happen and trust the rest to the Great Spirit.

Placing a large block of wood in the bottom of one of the pots, which was thicker than all the others and so would help direct the impact of the blast upward and away from the people, she smeared just enough Semtex-H over the top of the wood to make it appear as though the whole thing was Semtex. Then she added just a bit of black powder. She set two detonators in this one and wired them together so that if one failed, the other would work, and set the timer for the "real" time. Finally, she outlined the rim of the pot with a black marker so that she would make no mistake in placement.

This was the poinsettia which would be set on the floor off to the right side of the stage, just behind the heavy metal TV stand.

There was nothing more Wren could do. She believed she'd thought of everything.

If all went according to plan, Wren should be able to disable her guards before leaving the building by a back way not visible to the van. She gave a great deal of thought to trying to track down a phone and call 911, or alert a security guard.

The problem with that was that the plan called for everyone to wait some time after setting out the poinsettias before the room filled and Leatherwood took the podium. The explosion itself would be the signal to assault the bank. If she called too soon and the police came while everyone was still in the van, the Strike Force could conceivably get away. And even if they didn't, they would not have committed a crime at that point, unless a case could somehow be made for conspiracy to commit murder. Wren was not willing to take the chance that Hunter could be released somehow to come wreak revenge on her and her family.

They had to be caught in the act.

If Wren and her guards did not return to the van as scheduled, Hunter could get suspicious and send somebody into the building as recon. This worried Wren a great deal, but she finally decided that was a chance she was going to have to take. For one thing, she still had to disable two armed, well-trained martial artists.

However, there was one thing she could count on which could come in handy, and that was the collective greed of everyone involved. In their zeal to commit the crime for the money, those waiting in the van might be unwilling to veer from the plan, no matter what went wrong. Hunter, especially, would be unwilling to abort the mission no matter what.

By the time they heard the signal to launch the assault on the bank, Wren should be well on her way to the compound in whatever car she could steal and, should all go well, have time to get Daniel out before the others realized that everything in Midland had gone terribly wrong. (That part of the plan was somewhat shaky, too, but she still had time to work on it.)

It was a good plan, and Wren had thought of everything. Unfortunately, there was one element she'd neglected to factor into the equation: Jeremiah Hunter.

He brought Daniel along.

The others on the team were as stunned as Wren. "No way!" cried Kicker. "He's a baby! He'll fuck everything up."

"I will not," asserted Daniel. "And I am not a baby."

"He'll be in the van with me," said Hunter. "I'll keep him out of trouble."

Wren stood rooted in shock while the others, mumbling resentfully among themselves, loaded weapons and poinsettias into the back of the van. She was so dismayed she didn't even try to hide it. "He's too young," she said, her voice tinged with desperation. "He'll panic and get somebody killed."

"I already told you," said Hunter, his eyes a mystery behind dark shades, "he's staying in the van with me. What's to panic? Kid won't even see any action."

While the others continued to grumble behind her, Wren knew she would never be able to change Hunter's mind. She should have known. Although Hunter had given her free rein with explosives, he would ensure that he maintained ultimate control over her. That's all Daniel was: an insurance policy. Hunter knew that Wren knew if she did anything to blow this operation, Daniel was as good as dead.

Silently, she turned away. Wren had two choices: repair the timing devices tonight in the motel room so that Hunter's original plan would go off without a hitch, and thereby make sure Hunter did not kill Daniel, or go through with her private plan and run the terrible risk that she would be forced to sacrifice her own son so that others might live.

The decision was made already, of course; she'd decided that back before she made her escape attempt. But Daniel's life had been

close to her son and murmured, "Daniel, do you remember what I told you the very first night we were at the compound?"

He frowned. "No."

Peeking through the door toward the other room to make sure Hunter was not near, she said, "Remember, I told you that *nothing is what it looks like.*"

"What are you talking about? You're gonna *bomb* that building full of people!"

Grabbing his face with both her hands, Wren forced her son to look her straight in the eye. "Daniel. I said. Nothing is what it looks like. If you don't remember anything else, remember that." Suddenly, impulsively, she reached over and kissed him. Then she jumped to her feet and left the room so that Hunter would not discover her in there alone with her son.

It took a few minutes for the hammering in her heart to slow down. It took even longer for Wren to shut down every emotion, so that she could focus everything on the task at hand.

She did not speak to her son again.

Once events were set in motion, there was no turning back. A flight bag containing an explosive device was dropped off at the airport. The bomb threat was called in from a pay phone an hour later.

After an agreed-upon interval of time, Kicker and Preacher, dressed in green coveralls with *Friendly Flowers* stitched across the back and wearing matching caps, carried in the poinsettias. Wren, wearing a frizzy red wig, dark shades, and a boxy black blazer (which hid the Glock well), over jeans, a white T-shirt, and black leather boots, waited in the van and later at the foot of the escalator for the all-clear to melt through the crowd and slip into conference room C.

Stuffing her fear into the same dark corner which held her love for her son, Wren moved with lightning speed to arrange the poinsettias, placing the last one carefully on the floor behind the TV stand. Secreted in her pocket was a pair of tiny snips used to clip the detonator wires. If the men left her alone, her intention was to clip the wires on all the bombs except the one behind the television stand.

As it was, she dared to clip wires on only two of the devices closest to the podium before pocketing the snips—just as Preacher turned back from stepping out of his coveralls. Underneath, he was wearing jeans and a flannel shirt. Kicker was wearing jeans and a University of Texas Permian Basin sweatshirt.

"Let's get the fuck out of here," he said. They left conference room C and moved casually down the corridor, heading for the stairwell. Up ahead, Steve Austin rounded the corner. The other two men did not recognize him right away, but Wren did. Before Austin could see them, she grabbed both men and ducked into a janitor's closet.

"*Have you lost your mind?*" cried Preacher, reaching for the doorknob.

"Touch that knob," she murmured quietly, "and when you step out the door, you can get acquainted with Steve Austin, up close and personal."

"Shit."

"Are we gonna get blowed up in here?" whispered Kicker nervously.

"Don't be stupid. They're not set to go off until the room is full and Leatherwood's at the podium," mumbled Wren.

"Let's get out of here," whined Preacher. "I'm claustrophobic."

"We can't!" she stage-whispered. "We've got to wait until Leatherwood gets here. That way we'll know Austin's with him." Actually, Wren had already decided that this would be the best way to handle her own problems. In a barely audible voice, she said, "Tell Hunter we're going to have to cut off radio transmission for a while and not to worry about it."

Kicker nodded and muttered the message into his hidden mike.

"Now turn 'em off," she whispered. "We can't take a chance on that kind of noise."

Kicker and Preacher, accustomed to following orders, did so.

After a few long minutes, Preacher said, "Jesus, Kicker, ever hear of a thing called *deodorant*? It's a new invention. You oughta try it someday."

"Shut up," said Kicker, a man of few words.

"I hate this. Can we go now?"

"Shut up," said Wren.

In the close darkness of the closet, her mind was galloping in a headlong search for some way to get rid of the two ex-cons she had come to think of as the stooges.

"Are you sure them bombs is set right?" worried Kicker. "How do we know they won't go off accidentally?"

"They won't go off accidentally," murmured Wren, "and anyway, if they do, then you won't have to worry about it anymore."

"Yeah, Kicker, you won't have to worry about *anything* anymore, not even deodorant." Preacher giggled.

"Shut up."

Wren edged her way around the cramped room, feeling for some sort of weapon. The Glock was her last resort, to be used only in self-defense. She didn't want to kill anybody, just get away.

Besides, it would make too much noise.

After a few more nervous minutes, Kicker said, "What time is it?"

"It's five minutes past the last time you asked," said Wren. "You're worse than a little kid."

"When are they set to go off?"

"Relax. We've still got a good half hour."

"Oh, good. That makes me feel just *loads* better."

"Stuff it, Kicker," said Preacher.

"Well, why the fuck can't we just leave?"

"Why the hell can't you just shut up!" whispered Wren loudly as she groped her hands over a shelf. "We won't have to bump into Austin—he'll just follow the racket and open the door himself!" Her hand closed around an aerosol can.

"I don't see why we can't just can't leave," persisted Kicker. "He doesn't know who we are."

"Oh yes, he does," lied Wren. "Your pictures are all over the news." She slipped the can into her pocket.

The announcement brought a stunned silence to the cramped space.

"Sometimes I get to watch CNN in Hunter's trailer," she said, warming to the lie, "and the entire Strike Force is on the FBI's Most Wanted List."

"No kidding!" said Preacher. "You mean we're celebrities?"

"The federal government thinks so."

"Cool."

"You moron!" cried Kicker. "Don't you know what this means?"

"It means we're bad guys."

"No, fuckhead, it means the cops'll shoot us on sight."

"Huh-*uh*," said Preacher. "They'll just arrest us is all."

"Now, that just shows how much attention you've been paying in our meetings. The pig feds don't want their conspiracy with foreign agents exposed. Most Wanted means, Most Wanted Dead."

"Oh. *Shit*."

"Tell you what," said Wren. "I'm the one wearing a disguise, right? I mean, they're not looking for a redhead."

"Right," they said doubtfully.

"So why don't I take a peek around? Just a peek. When I see that it's all clear, I'll give you guys the signal."

"I don't know," said Preacher, his voice edged with suspicion. "Hunter won't like it."

"Well, Hunter's not standing in here next to a room full of explosives now, is he?" said Wren. "And I notice he made it a point to wait out in the van, where nobody might see his face and recognize him."

"She's right, Preacher," said Kicker. "He's makin' us take all the risks."

Wren waited for their brain gears to shift. Her heart was pounding.

"Okay," said Kicker. "Just a quick peek."

"I'll be right back," she promised. Slowly, she eased open the janitor's closet door a crack. When she could see or hear no one, she poked her head out and glanced around. Finally, she slipped out of the door, closing it just hard enough to mask the sound of the *click* of the lock.

"Suckers," she whispered. She knew that as soon as they realized the door was locked, they'd start raising holy hell . . . or would they?

After all, she had no way of knowing if Preacher was packing that mean pick gun. He could have them out of there in about ten seconds.

Either way, a head start was a head start.

As she hurried down the corridor, she glanced at her watch. Five minutes to detonation.

Flinging open the door to the stairwell, she started down the stairs. She had just reached the landing when the door above slammed back against the wall.

"You *bitch*!" cried Kicker. "You left us in there to *burn*!"

To Wren's shock, he sprang down the stairs in two long leaps, arm outstretched to grab her. She dodged him and sprayed him straight in the eyes with disinfectant.

Bellowing, he covered his eyes with his hands.

Preacher had reached the same step as Kicker. Before she could spray him, he'd knocked the can out of her hands, but she was ready, bringing the Glock up to smash the steel slide against the side of his head. When he staggered, she hit him again with all her strength on the temple of his head, splitting the skin. He went down like a stone.

Recovered somewhat from the disinfectant spray, Kicker lunged at her. Pivoting to the side, she used his downward momentum to give him a hard shove forward. He stumbled to his knees, and Wren virtually leapt over him for the stairs.

A hand clasped over her ankle and nearly brought Wren down. She grabbed at the rail with her right hand, but it was holding the Glock, so she had to settle for jamming her elbow between the rail and the wall for support.

Then she whirled and answered Kicker's move with a hard kick straight to the face. She could feel the toe of her boot connect— *crack*—with Kicker's chin. His head snapped back and he loosened his grip on her ankle. Yanking her foot away, she scrambled down the stairs a few steps and whipped the Glock around, aiming it at his head.

He started to cry.

"Please, please don't kill me," he blubbered, sobbing, cowering into the corner with his hands over his head. "Pleeeze."

"Big, big man," she said in disgust, lowering the pistol a fraction. "You bullies are all alike." Then she kicked him, hard, on the chin again and he slumped to the floor, unconscious. Heart pounding, chest heaving, Wren stuck the Glock back into its holster. "What can I say, Kicker?" she said. "You gotta *feel* what you're doing."

Trembling, she emerged from the exit door into the second-floor mezzanine. Walking rapidly, she smoothed down the red wig. She was running out of time. Frantically she looked around for a phone or someone from security, but she couldn't find either one. A quick glance at her watch told her she had two minutes to detonation.

Hurrying openly now, Wren made her way down the escalator and walked out of the building at a fast clip, where she broke loose and ran for the van.

A slight trembling suddenly shook the building, and Wren could hear screams and sounds of breaking glass coming from inside. Just as she reached the van, the doors opened and the Strike Force team bailed out and dashed into the building even as some people were scurrying out. Racing around the back of the van, Wren yanked open the driver's side door and jammed the Glock beneath the jaw of Jeremiah Hunter.

"Let Daniel out!" she ordered.

"Mom!"

More people emerged from the building.

"*Now!*"

Over the radio that Hunter was monitoring, Wren could hear Steve Austin's voice crackle, loud and clear, *"This is Number One! Execute Emergency Code Black!"*

Hunter cut his glance over to her. "You lousy stinkin' bitch," he said. "You set us all up, didn't you? I should have known."

His eyes were cold as death.

Without moving the gun barrel from Hunter's throat, Wren cried, "Daniel! Get out! Hurry!"

"Too late, bitch," said Hunter.

Then he brought up his left hand from its position on the steering wheel, striking the inside of Wren's wrist with such force that it not only shoved the gun away from his face, but caused her trigger finger to involuntarily straighten off the trigger. Before she could react, he had smashed his right fist into her face, knocking her to the ground.

Then he floored the accelerator, ducking his head below the van window, and threw the gearshift. The van shot down the street. The last glimpse Wren had of her son was his bewildered face staring ghostlike through the passenger window as the van screeched around the corner and vanished.

Sirens screamed in the distance. Staggering to her feet, Wren ducked between a row of cars. Gunfire erupted from within the building.

Wren started to run.

CHAPTER 40

THE concussion from the blast knocked Steve Austin off his feet where he was standing at the rear of the stage and onto his back. Ears ringing, his mind was still saying, "Huh?" even as his body—conditioned to instant reflex by many years of training—took over.

Within the first two seconds after the explosion, Austin had gotten to his feet, flung his body over the prone form of Buck Leatherwood, and begun to move toward evacuating his client. Leatherwood, though dazed, seemed all right for the time being.

Two other of Leatherwood's protection detail were already scrutinizing the crowd for any behavioral clues which might reveal their attacker, or anyone who might be prone to further violence against their protectee.

Within the next two seconds, Austin realized that the panic in the room was far out of proportion to the size of the bomb. A fine white powder from gaping ceiling tiles and sheetrock dusted everything. One of the large windows, the one nearest the stage, had been blown out, probably more from shrapnel than from the force of the blast itself. Most of the broken glass was outside, on the sidewalk three floors below, not on the people nearby.

The portable podium had been knocked off the stage to the floor, but the TV stand to the side of the stage seemed to have taken the brunt of the force. It had been upended and the TV, VCR, and other electronic equipment scattered around on the floor like kids' toys. Some people's chairs in the front row had been overturned, but everyone Austin could see was ambulatory—they could have knocked their own chairs down in the panic to get out. Everyone was scrambling for the door at the back of the room. None of them was rushing the stage, drawing weapons, or firing at his client.

"This is Number One!" he barked into his radio. "Execute Emergency Code Black! Repeat, all personnel, Code Black!"

Austin's next step, along with his associates, was to gather Leatherwood up and get him the hell out of there. Within five seconds after the explosion, Austin had hauled Leatherwood to his feet, placed his own body as a shield between Leatherwood and the commotion behind him, and bent the man over at the waist, literally shoving his head down with one hand as he and three members of his team basically ran him in a mad rush out a private exit door behind the stage and down the corridor toward a preplanned exit.

Other security people ran with them, weapons drawn and aimed behind toward the meeting room, and still others had secured a private stairway (elevators were too vulnerable after a bombing) and were standing by for Leatherwood's dazed dash down the stairs.

Less than two minutes later, as they dove for the limo, Austin's radio crackled: *"Number One! This is Number Six. Recommend Code Red. Repeat. Recommend Code Red."*

Austin knew that the announcement of Code Black meant to alert the police and fire departments and notify the entire security team to begin evacuating the building. Code Red signaled the possibility of gunplay. Immediately, Austin stumbled to a halt and handed over his charge.

"Affirmative," he said as the entourage scrambled through the open limo door. "Go with Code Red. Number One responding."

Normally, Austin would have flung his body into the limo practically on top of Leatherwood while the tires smoked. The emergency announcement from Number Six immediately activated Plan Two, which meant that Sandra Dodge would take over the evacuation team and get Leatherwood to the safe house. Like most members of the protection detail, she was a trained paramedic, more than qualified to handle any injuries which were not critical.

The last thing Austin saw as the limo screeched away was Dodge, winking at him over Leatherwood's head. Cool as a cucumber, that one. As Austin sprinted for the private exit door of the building, he said, "Number Six, this is Number One. Give me a location."

"This is Number Six. Room One-A."

Austin's heart skipped a beat. Room One-A was security code for the bank. Weapon in hand, he flung the door back and took off down the corridor toward the lobby at a dead run. Unlike every cop on television and in the movies, Austin did not carry the gun at right angles to his head, pointed toward the ceiling, where it could panic the already frightened people who were trying to leave the building. Like many police officers he carried it safely down close to his thigh, arm straight but relaxed, gun pointed at the floor, ready to draw a bead in a microsecond if necessary.

He emerged into a lobby of chaos. Terrified shoppers, most of whom had no idea what had happened but had heard a bomb was involved, thronged toward the lobby doors. The only thing which prevented a stampede was the hard work of his security people, diligently directing everyone safely out, even physically restraining those who were panicked. Dodging through the crowd, he spotted Number Six, Mohammed Fusch, and his three team members spaced around the bank doors, which opened into the lobby. Their guns were drawn but held out of sight of the crowds of people who streamed past.

Taking his position beside them, Austin could see that a bank robbery was in progress. All the bank employees were stretched out facedown on the floor. Some wept. All the robbers were armed with automatic weapons.

"Shit," he whispered to Mohammed.

Mohammed murmured, "They've already shot out the cameras."

"Hold your fire for the time being," said Austin in a low voice. "Too many people. Those autos can go wild and kill civilians."

The team members nodded.

Austin studied the faces of his team. Experienced professionals, all of them. Some in his firm had been recruited from the retired ranks of the Secret Service and the FBI. Mohammed had once been a double agent for Israel's crack intelligence outfit, the Mossad. They were the best that Leatherwood's money could buy, and Austin was damn glad to have them assembled here now. He knew they would, every one, come through for him.

"How many?" mouthed Austin.

Mohammed held up four fingers. Austin counted three robbers. He raised his eyebrows. Mohammed pointed toward the vault. Austin nodded. As he did so, one of the robbers joined the other one in the vault.

Sirens sounded in the distance.

"*Shit!*" screamed the robber nearest the door. "Cops already!" He yelled into his chest, "*Hunter! Cops! Hunter!*"

One of the others looked out of the window. "He's gone!" he cried. "The son of a bitch is gone!"

The one nearest the door ran to the window to look for himself. "Fuck! What do we do now?" Sprinting for the vault, he shouted, "We gotta get out of here! Hunter took off!"

Both men were waving their loaded weapons around frantically, and the situation was getting more volatile by the moment. Austin had no way of knowing if they intended to spray the bank people with gunfire as they were leaving out of sheer frustration and revenge, or worse, take hostages. He could sense the situation rapidly spinning out of control.

The other two emerged from the vault carrying heavy-laden plastic trash bags, their weapons clasped underneath their armpits. They gathered with the other robbers, and a loud argument ensued.

Austin flattened himself against the wall and, as clearly as he dared, said, "Number One to all units. Emergency. Bank robbery in progress. Get everybody down. Gun! Gun!"

The ripple of response took a few moments of confusion, but then, like a wave, the hundreds of people still making their way out of the building started to hit the floor. There were screams and some panic, but his brave security people darted about, getting everybody down, one by one and group by group, which made their own bodies even more exposed to stray gunfire.

The argument inside the bank reached a fever pitch. One of the robbers shouted, "*Fuck this, man!*" He whirled and fired two blasts into the ceiling. The people on the floor cowered. "I got nothin' to lose, man," he yelled, "and I'm takin' *hostages!*"

Austin nodded to his team. "We can't wait for the police," he murmured. "On my signal." He held up three fingers, then two, then one.

The five-man team, counting Austin, burst through the bank doors in the classic FBI SWAT "quick entry" style: two flanking the doors as they entered at a rush, guns drawn; three staggered behind. As Austin screamed, *"Security! Drop your guns!"* the two team members just inside the door swiftly began "running the walls"—surrounding the robbers at forty-five degree angles—while the others entering the room zigzagged into stair-steps, taking "buttonhole" positions left, then right.

The robbers opened fire.

Austin could see their gun muzzles breathing heat as he rolled to the side for cover, returning fire. He could hear the wave of screams well up all around him from the horror-struck people cringing on the floor of the bank in front of him and the floor of the lobby behind, blending with the excruciating roar of glass windows coming down, while all the time, over everything, the deafening thunder of gunfire and the sickening *smack* of bullets hitting too close to home.

Mohammed took a direct hit and went down, as did two of the robbers, both of whom had been hit in the legs. It took Austin several bloody moments to catch on that the robbers were wearing bulletproof vests.

"Armor! Armor!" he screamed to his team, but nobody could hear him. He saw another one of his people—Cindy Thomas—spin into a fall. A hot poker jabbed Austin in the left arm, knocking him backward. Ignoring the pain, he scrambled behind a desk and sprang up just long enough for a heartbeat's aim: a groin shot. He fired twice, then ducked back behind the desk, but his legs were too long; he'd unwittingly braced himself by extending one out to the side of the desk, and another searing blast of heat blistered that exposed leg.

And then it was over.

Though people were still screaming, the thunderstorm of gunfire had stopped. Through the smoke and smell of gunpowder, Austin could see one of the robbers cowering on the floor in a little wad, his hands up. The Hefty bag he'd been clutching was riddled with bullet holes.

"Don't shoot! Don't shoot! Don't shoot!" he was crying.

Haltingly, Austin raised himself a little higher behind the desk. One of the robbers lay across the prone but apparently uninjured body of one of the bank customers. The robber's head was a bloody mess. The other two were hollering in pain, holding blood-drenched hands over their wounds.

A couple of people started to get up.

One of Austin's team members, Pedro Rodriguez, shouted, *"Lie down! All of you!"*

All three surviving robbers pitched forward in unison, facedown to the floor.

Austin exchanged glances with Pedro. Under any other circumstances it might have been funny. As he got to his feet, his left leg buckled beneath him and he had to grasp the desk for support. Most of the people who'd been screaming had stopped, but now the wail of sirens filled the air.

While one security team member, Gunther Stoltz, covered the robbers, Pedro kicked away their weapons and then ran to check on the team members who were down.

"Put your hands behind your neck," commanded Austin, adding wryly, "I'm talking to the robbers. You move one *muscle*, and I swear to God I'll blow your head off."

"I'm hurt!" cried one. "I'm bleeding."

"Well, pardon me if I don't fall apart in sympathy," growled Austin. He noticed several of the people who were still stretched out on the floor chuckling. *Something about nearly getting killed makes you want to laugh, cry, and have sex all at the same time*, thought Austin. "Is anyone hurt?" he asked, scanning the bank customers. They all shook their heads no.

"I think Mohammed is going to be all right," reported Pedro, who was checking over Austin's wounded people. "I'm not sure about Cindy. She's lost so much blood already." He whipped off his belt, hiked up her skirt, and fastened the belt tightly around the downed woman's thigh.

Into his radio, Austin began barking orders to his people outside to get the cops and ambulance personnel into the building immediately.

"This is Number Seven. What about the people out here who are on the floor, sir?"

Austin said, "Make sure no one got hurt, then leave them where they lay for the time being. We've got to get our wounded out in a hurry, and I don't want a massive traffic jam at the front doors. Number One out."

"Affirmative. Out."

To the people in the bank, Austin said, "If you good folks don't mind, I'd appreciate it if you'd just stay where you are until the police give you permission to move. We've got some badly wounded people here, and we need to get them to the hospital. The ambulance is here already. And the police will want to take your statements before you leave. I know you've been through hell, and I really appreciate your cooperation."

One of the bank vice presidents turned her head and said, "Thank you—all of you—for saving our lives."

"You're welcome," said Austin, and then he collapsed.

Wren had learned to hotwire cars, not from her paramilitary captors, but from a bad boy cousin who liked to show off for her. The industrial business district side street she was on was close enough to the Leatherwood Building that she could hear what sounded like every cop car in town careening past, sirens blazing. She knew what she was looking for: an unlocked older model vehicle that would not be likely to be outfitted with an automatic burglar alarm and other high-tech devices designed to keep out criminals like her.

Selecting a blue '79 Buick Skylark, Wren crawled behind the wheel, ducked her head under the dash, and went to work. It took only a few seconds to get the car started. Still, it was broad daylight, so Wren waited a few moments to make sure she was not being observed before driving away. More police cars and a news van sped past. She kept going at a reasonable rate of speed in the opposite direction.

The image of Daniel's face, drawn with fear as he stared out the passenger window of the van at her as Hunter drove away, was everywhere.

Wren couldn't escape from it, but she couldn't let it cloud her mind either, so she looked past the face as best she could and tried to think what to do next while she tried to ignore her throbbing cheekbone. Before leaving the compound, Wren had stolen a couple of hundred dollars from Hunter's private stash in the trailer, but it wouldn't get her very far. She was too vulnerable in a stolen car, but she couldn't rent one without a credit card. Bus tickets could be too easily traced.

There was only one place Wren could think of where Jeremiah Hunter would feel safe now. But it was a long way away, in another state, and the journey would be fraught with the peril of getting caught by the law. Wren was certain that Hunter could evade capture as long as he wanted; it was herself she worried about. She was afraid that she'd get caught before she could get there to rescue Daniel.

She had to be the one to save him—there was no question about that. Any move by law enforcement would get Daniel killed, period. She was the only one. But any rescue would require planning and supplies. More than she could afford on two hundred bucks. She needed time to think.

One thing Wren had learned in her months of living with cons was that there were places in almost every city where nobody asked questions; places where people tended to have no past or future either, for that matter; places cops tended not to venture into unless invited.

Midland was a city which had never fully recovered from the oil field crash. It was littered with sleazy motels located well out of sight of financial meccas like the Leatherwood Building. Transients tended to rent rooms by the week in these places, and they paid with wads of crumpled cash. Seldom staying long enough to set up residence, they moved on, seeking jobs or cheaper housing or marks for their con jobs or some other sort of respite for the restless wandering of their souls.

Wren checked into a filthy fleabag of a place. It cost ten bucks for the night. While signing a fake name at the register, she made sure her blazer fell open just enough to reveal the Glock, a habit she continued whenever anyone approached her.

Nobody bothered her.

The first thing Wren did after checking in was go to a public phone booth outside the motel and call Cam. When there was no answer at his office even though it was the middle of a workday, Wren was alarmed. Her fingers shook as she dialed her home phone number. A razor-cold wind sliced through the thin blazer, making her shake even harder.

She had less than two minutes.

"Hello?" His voice, sure and strong as ever, sounded as though it were two feet away.

A powerful rush of emotion swept over Wren, buckling her knees and weakening her resolve. It was all she could do not to burst into sobs.

"Cam?"

"Wren! Oh, my God, where are you?"

"Darling, I can't talk long. Please listen carefully."

"Okay."

"Hunter forced us to take part in the Leatherwood robbery."

"What Leatherwood robbery?"

"Turn on the news after we hang up. You'll see. Anyway, I think the police got most of the others, but Hunter escaped with Daniel."

"How'd you get away?"

"Long story. Best told later." Wren was freezing. Tilting the receiver on her shoulder, she rubbed her hands together and stuck them under her arms.

"Where are you?"

"I can't tell you that, sweetheart. I just wanted you to know that I'm going to find Daniel and bring him home."

"Call Steve Austin. He's working for me, Wren."

"He is?"

"He is. Call him. He'll know what to do."

"I can't, Cam. If the police get within five miles of Hunter, he'll kill Daniel. There's no doubt in my mind."

"How do you know he won't kill you?"

She hesitated. "I'll be all right."

"Wren—"

"Trust me. Please, please trust me."

Now Cam hesitated. "All right."

"Please know that I did everything in my power to keep anybody from getting hurt at the Leatherwood Building. They had Daniel. They wanted me to blow the whole place up, but I didn't. I rigged the bombs so they wouldn't go off. I hope and pray no one was hurt."

"What are you talking about?"

"I have to go. My darling, I love you more than life itself."

"I love you, too," he said, his voice breaking.

"Is Zoe all right?"

He cleared his throat. "She's doing fine. Don't worry about us. Just please be careful."

"I will. Please tell her I love her. And Cam—"

"Yeah?"

"Nothing."

"What?"

"I just . . . I just wish *we'd* had a chance for a honeymoon, you know?"

"We will. When you get home."

"See you later," she said, and was hanging up when she heard Cam shout, "*Wait!*"

She put the phone back to her ear. "What?"

"When you see Daniel. . . . Tell him . . . Just tell him how proud I am that he's my son, okay? And that I love him."

She nodded into the phone. Throat aching, she said, "I will, I promise."

Hanging up was hard to do. She leaned her head against the cold glass of the booth. Dizziness spun her around and she sat down right in the middle of the phone booth.

Oh, Cam, she prayed, *I hope you got my message.*

She also hoped she'd hung up before the feds could get a trace—that is, if they still cared enough about finding Wren and Daniel to bother with phone traces. There wasn't anything on the tape (she was sure they had Cam recording all his phone calls) which could get Daniel hurt.

The secret code was up to Cam.

Breathing deeply to calm her ping-pong heart, Wren thought about what Cam had said, that Austin was working for him. *Call him*, he'd said.

There was only one place Steve Austin could be at this time.

Impulsively, Wren got to her feet, dialed information for the number, and then called. The phone rang many times.

"*Hello?*" The voice was male, panting. Obviously no receptionist.

"Is this the Leatherwood Building?"

"*It is.*" Suspicious, now.

"I'd like to speak to Steve Austin, please."

"*That won't be very easy,*" said the voice, angry now. "*The ambulance just took him to the hospital. He was shot. Who is this?*"

Instantly, Wren hung up the phone. Groping her way to the room like someone blind, she shut herself up in the chilly semidarkness, connected every lock she could find, kicked off her boots, and crawled beneath the sour blankets, where at long last she allowed herself that luxury of the desperate and frightened everywhere the world over: a few hopeless sobs, and the endless repetition of the one universal cry of the human heart for which there was seldom any answer: *Why?*

Like the Wolfman who changes into a fierce and wanton creature with every full moon, the shadowman of Jeremiah Hunter had emerged from hiding behind its genial mask at last to reveal a man possessed by demons to wreak a terrible revenge on Daniel's mother.

Nothing else seemed to matter to him.

"That little bitch fucked me over the first time, too," he snarled. "I should have *seen* it! I should have *known!*" Whipping in and out of freeway traffic, Hunter said, "She was probably working for the feds this whole time, from the first day you guys came to the compound." He gave Daniel a look of unharnessed paranoia.

Daniel chose not to remind Hunter that he and his mother had been kidnapped.

"What's going to happen to the Alpha/Omegans?" he asked timidly. Anything to distract the guy.

Hunter shrugged. "They're pros. They'll land on their feet."

That made no sense whatsoever to Daniel, but he was afraid to say anything else. Hunter found a radio station broadcasting news reports from the Leatherwood Building:

"... *apparently no serious injuries as a result of the blast, which was set to go off just as controversial gun-control advocate Buck Leatherwood was scheduled to make a speech. Leatherwood was not hurt. However, in what appears to be a related crime, a bank robbery was halted in progress by building security. After what is reported to have been a 'hail of gunfire,' one of the robbers was killed and two injured. Three security guards were also wounded. Police spokesmen on the scene ...*"

They were whizzing along on Interstate 20, on a barren stretch that connected Midland with her sister city, Odessa. Whipping the wheel sharply, Hunter pulled over to the side of the highway on a broad weedy area, yanked open the door, leapt out, and began kicking and pounding the van, screaming and cursing, his face so contorted by rage as to be virtually unrecognizable to Daniel.

"I'll kill her!" he screamed. *"I'll kill 'em all!"* Through the windshield, he glared at Daniel for one blood-stopping moment, then strode around the front end, jerked open Daniel's door, grabbed the boy's collar, and yanked at him as though he intended to drag him out and pummel him right there. But the shoulder harness and seat belt held Daniel fast, and when a passing car slowed, its occupants gaping, Hunter let go.

When he stepped back, though, he had Daniel's .45 in his hand. "You're too young to be playing with guns," he said. "You might hurt yourself."

Dismayed, Daniel realized that he'd forgotten all about the weapon. He could have possibly escaped, but he hadn't even thought about it.

Some warrior he was.

Chest heaving, Hunter stood there for a moment in the icy wind and seemed to come to a decision. As he got back into the van, he said, "We gotta ditch this van. Feds'll have it traced in no time." Then he drove straight across the scruffy bar of ground separating I-20 east from I-20 west and headed rapidly in the opposite direction.

Daniel's neck hurt where Hunter had grabbed him. Everything was happening so fast he could hardly assimilate it all. "Where are we going?" he said. Hunter might whack him for asking, but he had to know.

Hunter turned his head and smiled at Daniel. It was a spooky smile, and it gave him the creeps. Hunter said, "I just figured out the best way to find your mom."

Suddenly Daniel was having trouble breathing.

Still smiling, Hunter said, "We'll just pay a little visit to your dad."

"She won't be there!" cried Daniel, his voice rising in desperation. "She'll know better than to go there!"

Hunter shrugged. "Maybe so. But there's no way she can resist calling him." Glancing back at Daniel, he said, "He'll know where she is. Count on it. And he will tell me; I'll make sure of that." He reached down and caressed the Desert Eagle which rested innocently on the van seat next to him. Then, giving Daniel a suspicious glance, he took the Desert Eagle and placed it on the floorboards between his legs. The .45 he stuck under one leg as he drove.

Terror unlike anything Daniel had ever known rose in the back of his throat, choking him. He couldn't breathe. He thought maybe he was going to pass out.

He'd been so scared the night they'd been kidnapped, but compared to this, the abduction was nothing but a practice run.

Of course, then, he'd had his mom with him.

What a lionheart she'd been, all along. It made Daniel want to cry, just thinking about it.

Remember, nothing is as it seems, she'd told him time and time again. But he'd been too pigheaded, too immature, to see what she meant.

He'd thought this guy Hunter—*this guy!*—was brave! How could he have been so *stupid*?

Brave men did not run away and leave their buddies behind to die.

Sadly, Daniel wondered which of the Strike Force team had been killed. He supposed he was going to have to face the fact that they were probably all scuzz, but that didn't mean they didn't have their likeable sides.

Trying to calm himself by taking deep breaths, Daniel thought about his dad and Zoe. If there was just some way he could warn them! Some way he could stop Hunter!

But he was scared; he didn't know what to do. God, what a wuss he was.

All those guys back at the Armageddon Army, all those guys with their big guns and their uniforms and their war games . . . Daniel had thought they were all heroes. With the bitterness of hindsight he realized now that bravery had nothing to do with the size of a man's gun.

It had to do with the size of his character.

Sounds like something Dad would say, he thought ruefully. *And I wouldn't listen to him, either.*

Miserably, he stared out the passenger window. *What would Mom do?* he found himself wondering. *What would she want me to do?*

He wasn't sure what she'd done back at the Leatherwood Building, but he was pretty sure she'd sabotaged the whole thing so that nobody would get hurt. For the first time he thought about Preacher and Kicker. They'd been with her. What happened to them?

Somehow she got rid of 'em, he thought, stifling a grim smile. *Way to go, Mom.*

She never let them know what she was thinking; he'd noticed that much anyway. Not before she escaped and not before the special op.

Okay. He could do that much.

And she thought things through; she didn't panic.

Okay. He could try.

She watched for opportunities.

He could do that.

And she never let the bastards know just how scared she really was.

That was going to be a lot tougher.

Thing was, on the night they'd been abducted, Daniel had been so scared, mostly for *himself.* Now, for the first time (he was ashamed to admit, even to himself), he was scared for others. He was scared for his family—all of them, even his mom, who was out there dodging and hiding.

And that kind of fear—the kind of fear you have for someone you love—was so much worse than just fear for yourself. If Hunter did anything to Daniel's dad or Zoe, Daniel would never forgive himself.

He'd think of something.

It was a six-hour drive from their west Texas location to Daniel's hill country home on the outskirts of San Antonio. Twice during the trip Hunter ditched the vehicle they were in and stole another. During one such theft Daniel noticed that Hunter forgot the Desert Eagle, leaving it behind on the floorboards. Naturally he had no intention of pointing that fact out to Hunter; as it was, Hunter had brought along a pump-action shotgun and Daniel's .45.

At one point, a highway patrolman whizzed past, going in the opposite direction. There was nothing Daniel could do but watch him disappear. Once they pulled through a drive-through window at a highway McDonald's. Daniel wanted desperately to give the young clerk some sign of the terrible danger he was in, but he didn't dare. Hunter was still sitting on the .45. Daniel knew Hunter wouldn't hesitate to shoot anybody who got in his way.

Dusky winter darkness crouched in the branches of the live oaks as

Hunter and Daniel approached the little town Daniel had called home his whole life. It looked like some kind of alien planet now. As they cruised through the town square—already deserted, even though it was still early evening—Daniel stared at the red-and-green holiday lights that festooned every lamppost, twinkled from the branches of every lacy wintry tree, and outlined every business.

He'd been so bored here, he recalled, his mind dulled by anxiety and fatigue. He'd thought the place was so podunky. He and Eric couldn't wait until they could get out. They used to throw rocks at the lampposts and try to bust out the lights. Run from the headlights of the investigating cop cars and jump over people's fences to hide. Anything for a little excitement.

What Daniel wouldn't give now for just one of those days back again. He knew in his heart that they were gone forever, and the knowledge left a yawning hole inside, as if someone he loved had died.

They passed his dad's law office.

Sudden panic shocked Daniel from his stupor. They were almost there! They were almost at his house and he still didn't have a plan! He glanced over at Hunter. The man's expression hadn't changed the whole trip; it was twisted onto his face like some terrible birth defect: the hatred, the madness, the lust to kill.

The Chevy sedan Hunter was driving now took a slow, malevolent turn down a quiet, tree-shadowed street, creeping forward: a steel-clad animal, wild and feral, stalking its prey.

They were two blocks from Daniel's house.

Do something!

Frantically, Daniel searched for one of those cop cars that used to annoy him and Eric so much, but of course, there were none around.

Hunter turned the Chevy down the alley behind Daniel's house, moving slowly, searching for the right one. Daniel spotted his dad's Volvo, parked in the driveway behind the house. Hunter saw it at the same time and pulled to a stop behind it without turning into the drive itself—all the better for a quick getaway.

"*Nooooo!*" yelled Daniel, lunging across the seat, diving for Hunter's throat, the .45, anything he could get his hands on. Instinctively, Hunter threw up his arm to block the attack, slamming it into Daniel's nose.

Daniel felt blood pouring down his face, but he didn't care. He'd gone into a frenzy of punches and kicks, landing blows where he could. Hunter's head hit the glass of the driver's side window; Daniel could hear the glass crack. He rammed his elbow into Hunter's crotch—a glancing blow at best in the cramped space, but effective. Hunter bellowed. The car was rocking on its wheels as the two men struggled, their cries muffled by the rolled-up windows and the winter cold, which kept all the neighborhood people buttoned up in their warm houses.

Daniel groped for the gun, but Hunter was quicker; he came up with Daniel's ear in one hand, securing the boy, and the pistol in the other, which he began to beat savagely against Daniel's head. With a great yell, Daniel tried to evade the blows, but Hunter had a good grip on his ear. Finally Daniel yanked his head away. He felt a tearing sensation and the warm dribble of blood down the side of his head.

Sobbing from pain and frustration and hysterical fear, Daniel reached up a tentative hand to inspect the damage. The ear was partially torn away—nothing serious, just a half inch or so, but it hurt like hell and Daniel knew he was licked. His vision was blurred and he felt off balance.

"You little shit," said Hunter. "I oughta shoot you right here. Only reason I don't is that you're bait, you got that? *Bait*, dickhead. Because I know that wherever your shiny little ass is at, your mama won't be far behind." He shoved open the car door. Training the .45 at Daniel's head, he backed out of the car and gestured for Daniel to scoot across the seat and get out.

Tears streamed down Daniel's face, mixing with the blood. "Please don't hurt my dad," he begged. "Please don't hurt anybody. I'll do anything you want. Just leave them alone."

"What a little panty-ass you are," said Hunter. "Look at you, blubbering like a little girl. You disgust me." He shoved Daniel forward with the gun. "Now shut the fuck up and get us inside that house before I blow your whiney little head off."

Daniel's feet were leaden, and he kept staggering to the right for some reason. The garage door was open. As they walked in, Daniel had to put his hand out and balance himself on his mom's Blazer. He kept feeling as if he were going to pitch over to the right, like he was standing on a sinking ship.

In a way, he was.

The back door was unlocked. Of course. It was a small town and everybody knew everybody else and the big bad world was somewhere far away, like in the city or some other country. Not here.

All the smells were familiar. They enveloped Daniel in a cloud of memory. At long last he was home, and his heart was breaking.

They walked through the utility room just like Daniel had done a hundred times before, maybe a thousand. With a wild sort of recklessness he looked everywhere they passed for some kind of weapon, but there wasn't anything. Even the detergent was stored neatly away in the cabinets.

Into the kitchen. Through the dining room. And there they were, just like always, sitting side by side on the couch, watching TV, their backs turned to the door. So exposed. So vulnerable.

"*Dad!*" cried Daniel. "You should have locked your door! You should have known he'd come!"

"What?" Cam and Zoe both jumped to their feet and whirled to face Daniel and Hunter.

Horror froze Cam's face. "Daniel! My God, son, what happened to you?"

Hunter said, "We had a little altercation in the car. Dan here didn't seem to want us to pay you a visit. But I convinced him you'd be very hospitable. Still, the kid's right. You should have locked your door. Not that it would have stopped me."

Cam ignored Hunter. "Son, are you all right? You're covered in blood. Your ear—"

"I'm okay, Dad." Daniel made a soothing gesture with his hand.

This wasn't the way he'd fantasized about seeing his family again. Against his will, more tears overcame him. "I'm so sorry, Dad. I'm so sorry." He sobbed openly.

"Oh, shut up, for Chrissake!" yelled Hunter. "I'm sick of your little weenie weeping!"

"You don't have anything to be sorry for, son," said Cam, his voice strong as he reached out one hand to push Zoe behind him. "You haven't done anything wrong."

Struggling to get himself under control, Daniel swiped at his face with his sleeve. To his amazement, he found himself actually hoping there might be some feds around, keeping an eye on his dad. Somebody who could stop Jeremiah Hunter. Somebody who could protect his family.

"What do you want, Hunter?" His dad stood very erect, fixing Hunter with a steel gaze. "She's not here, if that's what you thought."

"But you know where she is, don't you?" demanded Hunter.

Cam didn't blink. "No. I have no idea."

"You're lying."

His dad *was* lying; Daniel could tell. Yet he betrayed no nervousness or self-doubt. He stared down his sworn enemy like a man.

He was splendid.

He's not a nerd after all, wondered Daniel. *Look at him! He'll never back down, no matter what.*

Daniel had never been more proud.

For a long, charged moment the two men stood facing one another across about ten feet of space, and it might have been ten miles as far as Daniel was concerned. Jeremiah Hunter didn't even have the right to be in the same room with Daniel's dad, and that was the awesome truth.

Then Hunter said, "Fine. If that's the way you want it." And he shot Cam, point-blank in the chest, with Daniel's .45.

Zoe's high, keening wail of anguish was the last sound which throbbed in Daniel's ears as Hunter dragged him at gunpoint out to the car.

The last thing he saw was the blood of his father, pouring out his life in shimmering crimson pools, all over the living room floor of their home.

PART V

PERSONAL SECRETS

All personal secrets have the effect of sin or guilt.

CARL JUNG

He! Hayuya haniwa.
"In truth you were conceived."

CHEROKEE SAYING

Death will always come out of season.

OMAHA CHIEF BIG ELK

CHAPTER 41

WREN awoke deep in the night with a sickening sense of unease, a foreboding separate from anything she'd known at the compound.

No. Not foreboding.

A *knowing*.

Something was desperately wrong somewhere, but she didn't know what, with whom, or where. All she knew was that she had to find Jeremiah Hunter and she had to find him fast. Daniel's time was running out.

There would be no more sleep that night. A glance at her watch told her it was midnight. Her stomach growled; she hadn't eaten all the day before. There was a candy machine a few doors down. Wren dug around through Hunter's money and gathered up some quarters. She slipped outside the room and walked a few doors down in bone-aching cold.

The vending machines were located in a shadowy area around the corner that stank of urine. The place made her scalp crawl. Hurriedly she dropped in a few quarters, and was trying to find a knob—any knob—that would pull, when she felt a hand on the back of her neck.

A throaty, greasy voice purred, "Hey, pretty lady. You made a mistake coming out here all by your lonesome. A boy like me just wants to have some fun."

Wren spun around to the right, jabbing her elbow into the man's ribs with all her strength and bringing up her left knee for a quick power thrust to the groin. When the man doubled over, she brought an elbow down in a hard jab to the base of the skull. The man fell to the ground. By the time he had rolled over, she had the Glock jammed up against his forehead.

"And a girl like me just wants a goddamned Snickers bar, asshole," she growled. "This baby's cocked and there's no safety release and I'm in a bad mood. Just give me an excuse."

"Don't shoot! I'm s-sorry," he whimpered, palms out in supplication.

"Are you going to mess with any more poor defenseless women who have no choice but to be out alone late at night?"

"No! No! I swear!"

"Because this is the nineties, pal. You never know what you're going to find out there."

The man was trembling all over. Wren stepped back and eased around the corner, still aiming the gun at the man. Before she had reached her room, she could hear the sound of sneakers hitting the pavement in the opposite direction. *Hell with it,* she thought. *I'm getting out of here.*

As she headed the stolen vehicle down darkened roads leading out of town, it occurred to Wren that it might take her a while to assimilate back into polite society.

Avoiding the interstate, she took back country roads to the small town of Big Spring, made famous (or infamous) by Jon Voight in the gritty 1969 film *Midnight Cowboy.* The movie's other star, Dustin Hoffman, had said Voight's biggest problem was faking a Texas accent, but then, Wren had never heard a faked Texas accent that didn't sound faked.

In Big Spring she wolfed down a Big Mac and fries at the local McDonald's. At a truck stop she gassed up the car and washed it. Then she parked it in a fairly nice residential area where it was more likely to be reported than stripped. After locking it, she took off on foot—her little way of saying, "I'm sorry I had to borrow your car without your permission. I tried to take good care of it. Thanks for the loan."

Using a city map she'd bought at the truck stop, Wren walked a good three miles to the bus station. The vigorous walk helped to keep her from freezing, but the relentless wind tormented her with an almost demonic fury. She even had to hold on to the red wig she was wearing for fear it would blow off.

To her dismay, she discovered that the bus station was closed. She'd forgotten about small towns. For two hours she had no choice but to hunker down in the lee of the building amidst a tangle of bushes. By the time the building opened, Wren was blue with cold, so stiff she could barely move. In the restroom she tidied herself up and put on the dark glasses. Then she bought a ticket and a cup of coffee, which she nursed in the warmest corner of the building she could find.

She didn't think she would ever feel warm and safe again.

A television had been set up in a corner of the building to pacify waiting passengers. Wren stared at it blindly, sipping her coffee and working out what she had to do next. She had already bought the ticket, but there was still time to change her mind.

Even after all she'd been through, nothing frightened Wren more than what she was about to do. Every step she took which brought her closer was filled with greater dread.

There would be no mind-changing, though; Wren knew that. The truth of the matter was that she was desperate. There was simply nowhere else to go.

"... *was shot by the fugitive in his home while his daughter looked on in horror. Hunter is considered armed and extremely dangerous and is believed to be traveling with a hostage. Federal officials are also seeking this woman, Wren Cameron, whom they wish to question as a potential witness. If you see either of these people, do not approach them. Call the following toll-free number and report the sighting to the authorities.*"

As she sat in the west Texas bus station, staring in staggering disbelief at the news program, Wren's picture suddenly filled the TV screen. They'd used a photo from the faculty section of the yearbook from the high school where Wren taught. It was not a very flattering photograph, but it was a good likeness.

Still reeling from the news about Cam, frantic for word of his condition, Wren barely reacted to the cold shock of seeing herself flashed across national television as a wanted fugitive. It was too much to take in all at once. Still, she froze in her seat, scared to even glance at another person, terrified they'd recognize her.

Nobody was paying any attention.

On legs tingling with alarm and anxiety, Wren approached the ticket salesman to ask if they might turn to another channel. She wanted to see if any of the other networks were providing any more comprehensive coverage—it was the only way she had of finding out what had happened to Cam.

Wren's bus was just pulling into the station when she learned that Cam was in the intensive care unit of a San Antonio hospital and was listed in critical condition.

The bus trip was never-ending. They stopped at every little windy dot on the map, picking up and delivering far more parcels than passengers. Wren's fellow passengers were just the kinds of people you'd expect to see on a cross-country bus, trampled and weary and preoccupied with the woes that prevented them from flying in the first place, sprinkled with the occasional soldier and fresh-faced college kid.

At every stop, Wren anguished over the possibility of being spotted by someone and arrested. It never happened. Most people— even police officers—didn't study faces enough to recognize one in a disguise as dramatic as Wren's.

Screaming harpies of agony plucked at her composure with every short white highway line licked up by the big bus. At war with herself over her resolve to find Daniel now that Cam lay in a hospital near death, the psychic battle lasted for the entire journey. The only thing which kept her sane was the certainty that she was doing what Cam would want her to do.

When Wren finally climbed stiffly down off the bus, she hired a taxi to take her to a brick-paved shopping village she knew in the center of town. By this time it was late afternoon. "The Little Drummer Boy," performed by the Mormon Tabernacle Choir, swelled over an amplified stereo sound system as winter dusk prompted holiday lights to blink on, one by one. Window displays celebrated the joy of the season; some featuring Hannukah menorahs; some elves and Santas and antique toys all spread out in the Victorian splendor of wine-red velvet gilded with gold.

The homes to which these shops catered were stately; they whispered old money, class, dignity, bigotry, and snobbery. The fabulous light displays which bedecked them turned an enclave of wealth and taste into a virtual fairyland. By dark, Wren knew, cars from all over the city would come trailing through, filled with children, just to look and delight.

It was a perfect excuse for Wren to drag her feet, strolling slower and slower with each step. Her heart was all crowded up into her throat, and the closer she got, the harder it was to swallow or even breathe.

Ghosts danced on the grave of her past.

At the house she sought, Wren could go no farther than the sidewalk in front. She thought she might faint and sat down at the base of a splendid pecan tree which still littered the grass with its luscious nuts. No suburban noises rattled the calm winter night at the dinner hour. Smoke from various hearths and homes drifted into the night sky while the radiance of holiday lights warmed passersby, folks walking pedigreed dogs, mostly, who smiled and nodded at Wren as if she were a member of their private fraternity of privilege and safety.

With trembling hands Wren removed the wig and the tight skullcap beneath it, liberating her wads of dark hair, which tumbled to her shoulders and down her back in waves. Packing the disguise into one of the blazer's deep side pockets, Wren rubbed her fingertips over her scalp with relief, then looked for some other way to postpone the inevitable, but there was none.

She had to confront not only who she had been, but what she had done.

Pushing herself slowly to her feet, Wren crossed the expansive lawn to the front door. Heart throbbing at her temples, Wren's cheeks were flushed hot while her fingers were so numb with cold that she could barely feel it as she pressed the doorbell, though she could hear its melodious chimes sounding from deep within the great house.

He opened the door himself.

For a heart-struck moment they regarded one another over the wasteland of time and space and pain and guilty wrongs and grievous loss, for he was an old man now, and she, aged beyond her years.

There were no words to speak, and neither one made a move to reach across that span.

Not at first.

Twenty years had whitened his hair and dragged deep lines down his face. Brilliant blue eyes, now masked in shock, gazed down at her. She knew those eyes because they were her own, but she could not read them now.

Dangerous tears shoved their way into Wren's ephemeral composure. She dare not cry, she wouldn't cry, but how could she speak without the threat of it?

She couldn't. At last, over the tumult and crowding of too many riotous emotions to bring under control, Wren said, "Daddy, please forgive me. I . . . I have no right to be here, I know." It was too late; she couldn't help it, and the tears coursed down her hot cheeks even as she tried so hard to fight them off. "I have no right to ask for your help, and if you don't want to give it to me, I'll understand. But . . . but I don't have anywhere else to turn, and I don't know what else to do."

And then she stood, shivering in the cold wind of her own mistakes, while behind her, cars full of happy families drove aimlessly past.

Daniel, deadened by psychic shock, spoke not a word during the perilous interstate trip undertaken by Jeremiah Hunter. Though the entire country was looking for them, Hunter had contacts in the murky underworld survivalist network who provided food, supplies, gasoline, ammunition, and "safe" vehicles for the long drive. Some asked no questions; others accepted his explanation that he'd been entrapped by the feds in order to fan the flames of hatred toward militias and all independent-minded people everywhere who loved the Constitution of the United States of America.

The country-plain wife of one of the men stitched up Daniel's ear with a sort of crude gentleness and gave him a bottle of aspirin to take along for the pain while three kids sat at the same kitchen table doing their home-school lessons. When she asked what happened, Hunter told her Daniel had been shot at by a fed, but that the bullet had only grazed him, thank the Lord. When she inquired about news reports that Hunter had shot Daniel's unarmed father point-blank, he assured her it was a damn lie cooked up by the liberal media to manipulate public opinion in favor of gun control. Since Daniel made no effort to dispute Hunter's version of events, he was believed.

Some offered to put Hunter and Daniel up indefinitely, but Hunter assured the well-meaning, if misdirected, people that they had to be moving on, that they were expecting Daniel's mom to meet them at a predetermined location.

At no time did Daniel make any attempt whatsoever to recruit a confederate to his side. Hunter's powers of persuasion were too great, his celebrity too enticing, and anyway, Daniel feared for the life of anybody who chose to cross the man.

At any rate, he couldn't think; he had retreated into a dream-like state, as if his mind had suddenly detached itself from his body and drifted up above someplace so that it could watch him as he moved through an unreal world. Over and over again, the video kept replaying: the deafening blast of the gunshot, the spurt of his father's blood as he collapsed, the piercing scream of his little sister as Hunter dragged Daniel out and left her behind to watch her daddy die.

Daniel knew that his dad was dead; not right then, maybe, but soon after. Hunter's aim had been dead-on, and the .45 was a hideously powerful weapon. His dad couldn't possibly survive such a terrible trauma to his body, and now he was dead—or would be soon—and he had died before Daniel could tell him just how much he loved him and how very, very much he needed him.

The last leg of the journey was a meandering series of breathless hairpin turns up, up into the Ozark Mountains to a cabin where an uncle of Hunter's had once made bootleg whiskey and hunted deer illegally with packs of dogs. Shock was starting to wear off by then. As Daniel became more and more aware of his surroundings, he grew more and more frightened.

Hunter was traveling deep into hillbilly country.

Dense forest crowded right up to the road, impenetrable to any who did not know their way. What houses were visible were virtual shacks held together by little more than baling wire and bubble gum. Junked cars, old tires, furniture spewing stuffing, headless dolls, too many vacant-eyed kids, and other remnants of the human soul rendered threadbare by poverty and hopelessness littered their weedy yards.

This was the true backwoods; perhaps the original birthplace of suspicion and distrust, where major life decisions were often based on nothing more substantial than superstition, and where feuds between neighbors tended to be solved by either a shotgun or an arsonist's match. Doing time was a family legacy in many of the homes.

The woods at night were blacker than the bottom of a well. Spooks roamed throughout—restless, dissatisfied spirits longing to find a home—and it was said that a man could get lost in there and never be found.

Daniel knew all this because Hunter had held the boy spellbound on many a night at the compound with tales from his mountain boyhood, of running through the woods to the baying of the hounds hot on the bloodtrail of an out-of-season buck, of the particular madness of being liquored up with homemade moonshine, of joyriding in fast cars too close to the edge of the world, of closing a fist over the pulse of life in the ghost-blue rays of a full moon and feeling it stop, of the thrill of that first kill.

Those stories had rung in Daniel's ear like the call of adventure, had seduced his boyish heart into believing this man came from someplace magic.

That maybe it somehow made him magical.

Now Daniel knew that it had only made him insane.

They found the lost cabin down a one-lane logger's road so rutted the pickup chassis thumped loudly against each crusty bump as Hunter fought the wheel, the headlights sweeping past hostile tree trunks that lined the road like a fence. Hand-painted wooden signs nailed to the occasional tree shouted: KEEP OUT and NO TRESPASING!!!

They reached a tumbledown, ramshackle building with a rusted tin roof and walls which had never seen a paintbrush. The shack had been so long a part of these woods that vines covered the outer walls on two sides. Wood rot had long since caved in the porch. Daniel was fervently glad it was winter, because he could well imagine the bugs which must have taken it over. That is, until he spotted the outhouse.

Hunter had brought several kerosene lanterns, and when he lit one, yellowed newspapers thumbtacked to the front room walls sprang to life, proclaiming: *"Sandy Koufax Helps Dodgers Skunk Yankees 4–0"* and *"Shocking Nude Photos of Liz & Richard in Their Cleopatra Love Nest!!"*

Daniel had never heard of Sandy Koufax, but he supposed Eric had since he collected baseball cards. But he knew who President Kennedy was, and when one of the small headlines announced an upcoming Friday afternoon press conference for the president, Daniel realized how old the newspapers were.

The shack was bitterly cold, so cold Daniel could see his breath. There was a soot-blackened wood-burning stove, but when Hunter tried to light it, the room filled with choking smoke. They were forced to crawl into sleeping bags which had generously been provided by the survivalist underground, but it was not enough and Daniel couldn't seem to stop shivering.

He kept hearing that gunshot, seeing that blood, listening for his sister's scream. When he dropped off into a restless doze, he only dreamed it all over again.

Daniel didn't see how his mother would ever be able to find them here, and anyway, he didn't think he wanted her to.

Watching one parent die in front of his eyes was enough.

Hunter had the pickup keys and both guns. He didn't seem to mind when Daniel went out alone to the butt-freezing outhouse. Apparently he had no fear that Daniel would make any attempt to find his way out of these woods alone.

Sometime deep in the night, it started to rain. The roof might as well have been nonexistent for all the good it did. It was the kind of winter rain that cuts through the soul and freezes by morning, and the incessant drip-drip monotony of it did something to Hunter's mind—crazed him even worse, if such a thing were possible.

Any little thing could set him off into a roaring rage. With his three-day beard and wild, feral eyes, he finally looked like the terrorist he really was. No wonder Daniel's mom had changed her name and hidden for all those years; it wasn't the feds she was scared of, it was this man. *Nothing is as it seems,* she'd told him—or tried to— but he'd been far too smart to pay any attention to her.

On the afternoon of the third day, Hunter found the moonshine. By nightfall, he was seeing feds behind every tree, jumping at every *plop* of rain into every tin pan, shooting at shadows, and ranting about the New World Order.

"*Boooy!*" he yelled, his face inches from Daniel's. "Don't you know they can see everything we *do*? Look at this, just look!" He leaned over, dropped his pants, and pointed at his white buttocks. "See that? That's a microchip they surgically implanted in my butt when I was in the army." Pulling the britches up clumsily and missing a belt loop, he stage-whispered, "It's how they know where I'm at. They're comin' to get us, but they won't take me alive, you know *why?*"

Daniel shook his head. He was crouched on the filthy floor in the same corner where he'd huddled the first night, his sleeping bag pulled up to his chin. He had not spoken since his father's death. He was afraid of doing or saying anything which could set Hunter off, but this . . . this scared him more than anything he'd seen yet.

Hunter put the barrel of the .45 to Daniel's head right at the temple and pulled back the hammer. The *click* of the cock made Daniel jump. In spite of the cold, he was sweating, and he could smell his own fear.

"They're not gonna get me," said Hunter, his breath foul and his eyes so maddened that Daniel had to look away, "because I got me a hostage. And when your mama gets here, I'll have me *two* hotsages. I mean hostages. And when I decide to go, I'm taking *everybody* with me, do you understand, boy?"

Eyes squeezed shut, throat constricted, Daniel nodded.

Hunter pulled the trigger.

Daniel leapt to his feet.

Laughing, Hunter waved the smoking .45 at a gaping hole in the front wall.

Feeling a miserable sensation between his legs, Daniel looked down. He'd wet himself. Still convulsed with a violent case of the shakes, Daniel ran outside into the relentless rain and wondered if he'd really died, after all, and gone straight to hell.

The years stretched between them like the fine, fragile, incandescent strand of web spun by a spider from the bough of one tree to another, weighted down by beads of heavy dew left by the long night which threaten at any moment to sever the bond.

Her father's eyes neither condemned nor forgave her, but his silence was more terrifying than any words he could have spoken.

Wren's tears humiliated her. Lifting her chin with what few remaining remnants of pride she could muster, she turned to walk away.

"Lissie! Wait!"

She turned back.

"Come in out of the cold, for goodness' sake," he said.

She hesitated. "Are you sure?"

"Of course. Of course. It's freezing out here. Where's your coat? Don't you have a coat?"

"No, Daddy, I don't have a coat," she said, trudging through the door like an old, bent woman. Her father closed the door behind her and Wren gazed around the handsome room. "This place never changes," she said. "It's exactly as I remember it." Her stomach clenched from nerves, and she couldn't look him in the eye.

Suddenly, her father touched her shoulder awkwardly, and the next thing Wren knew she was burrowed into his chest and he was holding her tight and they were both bawling like babies.

"Mother's dead, isn't she?" she said.

Surprise blanched his face. "How did you know?"

She shrugged. "I can't explain it."

He nodded, then shook his head at almost the same moment, musing as if to himself, "You always had that spooky way about you." A ghost of a smile glimmered across his face. "Margaret always called it *the knowing*."

Wren found herself smiling back, but it was a sad smile they shared.

"The cancer got her," he said softly. "I told her and told her to quit smoking, but she was afraid if she did, she'd get fat." He gave a helpless little shrug.

"That sounds like Mother." She still seemed unwilling to look right at him. "Daddy . . . I'm so sorry. So very sorry. About everything."

"I know. Me, too."

"I never meant to hurt you. And I wanted to come back . . . so many times."

"I know. These things happen. Sometimes you have to do things in life that other people don't always understand."

His comment came as a complete surprise to Wren. The last thing she'd expected from her father was any sort of sympathetic understanding. Still, she felt the compulsion to explain herself. "If I could start all over again . . ." She stared across the room. "I would do it so very differently."

"No, you wouldn't," he said. "You had a path you had to take."

She felt her jaw go slack and gaped at the old man in spite of herself.

He gave another little shrug. "As far as I'm concerned, you've been punished enough for whatever mistakes you made when you were still a foolish girl."

For a long moment, she regarded him. "Daddy, I don't understand you. I thought you would be so angry with me."

"I was. At first. But after that FBI agent came to talk to me, I understood then."

"What agent? Understood what?"

"Agent . . . Houston? Was that it? He told me about the bank robbery, and how you were helping the government."

"You mean Agent Austin?"

"Yeah. That's the name. Austin."

"He told you?"

"He did."

"Did Mother know?"

Robert shook his head.

Glancing at him from beneath her lashes, she said, "Wouldn't have made any difference if she had, would it?"

" 'Fraid not, kiddo." He gave her a lopsided grin.

"Oh, Daddy," she said, flinging her arms around his neck. "It's been so long since anybody's called me kiddo."

They shared a can of Campbell's chicken noodle soup (made with milk, just the way she had liked it as a child) and saltine crackers. It was a feast. Afterward they retired to the den and sat in front of the fireplace while an old cat he called Macy dozed peacefully in his lap. For hours they talked, catching up on family news, and then about the scary stuff, the serious stuff that had finally brought Wren home.

"I need money, a car, and supplies," she said. "A backpack and camping gear. And ammunition. For this." She reached inside her jacket and pulled out the Glock. Her father recoiled from it.

"You know I don't like guns, Lissie," he said sternly. "I don't like the idea of you carrying one."

"Daddy, this isn't the same thing as sneaking out of bed and creeping downstairs to watch John Belushi and Dan Ackroyd on *Saturday Night Live* like I did when I was in high school. It's a matter of survival. You don't seem to understand the danger I'm in."

"I understand. I understand that's what the police are for. Why don't you let them help you?"

She sighed. Gazing into the fire, she said, "How can I make you understand? This man . . . he's crazy, Daddy. Extremely paranoid. If he even suspects that the FBI or anyone else is out there in those woods, he'll kill Daniel on the spot. It's as simple as that."

"And how do you know he won't kill you, kiddo?"

She held up the gun. "That's what this is for."

He cringed. "Put that thing away. Do you know how to use it?"

"Yes, Daddy. I know how to use it."

"Because that's all a handgun is good for, you know." He sniffed. "The bad guy can just take it away from you and use it on you himself."

"He won't take it away from me. I won't let him get that close."

"My, but you've sure become a cocky little thing," he said.

She didn't respond to the accusation, but it amused her all the same. *Cocky.* Well, maybe so.

"I still don't like it, Lissie. You are asking me to help you do something that could get you killed, and I—"

"And if you don't help me, I can promise you that you will never have the opportunity to meet your grandson. Hunter will kill him, I'm telling you."

"I don't know," he fretted. "Are you sure you can find your way in the mountains? You could freeze to death up there. You could get lost in the woods."

"I won't get lost." She grinned. "Not if you buy me a compass."

Wren knew that all this talk about trekking about through the woods was worrying to her dad. About the most wilderness he'd ever seen in his life was the rough on the edges of the golf course at the club.

And the thought of guns, she knew, frightened him. "Daddy, I know there's so much about all this—about me—that is strange to you—"

"You can say that again."

"But please. I really need your help. You've got to trust me that I know what I'm doing." Glancing at him from beneath her lashes, she added, "I'm all grown up now, you know."

"I know," he murmured, his voice almost a sigh.

"I'll make you a complete list," she coaxed. "The store people will help." She bit her lip. "Daddy, here's the thing: I've got to leave tomorrow, and I'm going whether you help me or not. I'm going if I have to crawl naked through the snow."

He regarded her for a long moment, then quirked one eyebrow. "Well, we certainly wouldn't want you to do that," he said. "Now would we?"

CHAPTER 42

IT was nine o'clock, and one of the intensive care unit nurses and Zoe's next-door neighbor, Sandy, had been trying to convince her to go home—or over to Sandy's, anyway—and get some sleep, but Zoe was prepared to put up far more of a fight than either of them expected. Planting her feet, she crossed her arms over her chest and refused to budge.

"I'm not leaving my daddy alone," she said. "I can sleep here, in the family waiting room. If you won't let me see him but once an hour for five minutes, then wake me up once an hour so I can go spend my time with him."

"You can't help him, sweetheart," said Sandy, a plump, pleasant-faced mother of three who kept kids in her own home during the day. She was the motherly type, not cool like Zoe's mom. "He's in a coma. He doesn't know what's going on."

"Yes, he does. I know he does. Just because his body doesn't wake up doesn't mean his mind doesn't." She set her chin resolutely. "If he doesn't hear from me, he'll worry about me." To the nurse, she added, "We worry about each other now that my mom and brother are gone."

The nurse and Sandy exchanged glances. Sandy said, "Well, do you think she'll be all right here alone?"

"I'll keep an eye on her," said the nurse, a pretty young blonde whose name tag read *Maria*. "My shift ends at six, and I'll talk to Sam when he gets in for the next shift."

"Are you sure?" Sandy was a worrier, but her kids were immature, too. They were so used to having Sandy around to look after them every single solitary waking second of their lives.

"I'll be fine," assured Zoe. "You better go on."

Sandy rummaged around in her huge purse. "Do you need some money? Here's ten dollars. You might want to get something to eat in the cafeteria. Now, don't go down by yourself. Go with an orderly or a nurse or someone like that. And don't talk to strangers. And—"

"It's okay," said Zoe patiently. "Thank you for the money. I'll pay you back."

"Oh, you silly child." Sandy dabbed her eyes with a damp, wadded-up Kleenex tissue. She enfolded Zoe in her flabby arms and hugged her close to her generous bosom. "Poor, poor baby."

She was sweet, really, but Zoe had to take her in small doses; too much time around Sandy made Zoe feel suffocated. She would have preferred her grandma, but her daddy's folks were out of the country on a cruise, and she didn't want to bother them unless . . . well, she didn't want to bother them. Daddy had told her that they'd been saving up for this special senior citizens cruise for like *centuries*. There was supposed to be big band music and all that kind of corny stuff on the ship, and they were so excited about it and everything. She didn't want to spoil their trip unless . . . well, she didn't want to spoil their trip.

Sandy finally left, but not without bringing Zoe a Coke and a candy bar, some gum, and a *Seventeen* magazine. She really was a sweet lady, but Zoe was relieved when she was gone. There were lots of cool articles in the magazine that Zoe was interested in, like "Best Friend Envy," "How to Flirt With the Coolest Guys," and "Quiz: How Shy Are You?"

But when she opened the pages, the words made no sense and she had to read the same paragraphs over and over. Then she couldn't remember what she'd read. Dropping the magazine to the floor, Zoe stretched out on the couch with a starched white hospital pillow. More than anything, she wished she had Fluff Dawg with her. Fluff Dawg was the same ratty old softie she'd slept with since her third birthday, but Zoe had been too embarrassed to admit that to Sandy, and so hadn't asked for him.

She tried to doze, but every time she did the same creepy thoughts snuck into her brain: *What if he dies? What if he dies and you're all alone? What if Daddy dies and Daniel dies and Mom dies and you don't have anybody else in the whole world? What if your entire family dies and you have to move out of your house and maybe out of town because you have to go live with Grandma and Granddad, who are really nice but their house smells funny and they haven't had teenagers in forever and ever? What will you do without your family? What will you do if you are all alone in the world? Even* Seventeen *doesn't have an answer for that.*

Then Zoe would have to slap herself—well, in her mind anyway— and tell herself, say, *Stop it! Daddy needs you, and that's all that matters right now. Think about this later. Think about it tomorrow.*

Maybe she was going crazy. Maybe she was having that post-traumatic stuff they were always talking about on TV. Maybe Maria would know somebody she could talk to. Hospitals probably had lots of people to help with stuff like that.

Zoe sat up, fluffed the pillow, retrieved the magazine, paged through it some more. Maria appeared at the door.

"Hey, kid," she said with a smile. "You've got a phone call."

"I do?" Zoe frowned. None of her friends would be calling her here at the hospital in San Antonio, because it would be a long-distance call from their town. "Who from?"

"Your Aunt Lissie. The hospital switchboard transferred the call to the nurses' station."

"But I don't have an aunt . . . Oh, my God! Oh, my God! It's Mo—my Aunt Lissie!" Still babbling, Zoe dashed from the room and sprang down the hall like a deer in flight, skidding past the nurses' station altogether, doubling back, and landing, breathless, beside the counter.

"Slow down, little one," smiled the nurse behind the counter. "These floors can be awful slippery. Come around here—you can take the call back there, in the office."

"Thank you, thank you, thank you!" cried Zoe, charging past the bemused nurse to the paper-crowded desk and the phone receiver, which she plucked up but was then too out of breath to speak into.

"Zoe? My darling! Are you all right?"

"I'm fine!" squeaked Zoe, and then, to her horror, she burst into tears. "J-j-just f-f-fine," she sobbed.

"Oh, my brave, brave girl! You've been so alone, haven't you?"

Zoe wept, helpless at her lack of control, furious with herself because she didn't want her mom to worry.

"How is Daddy? The TV news doesn't say anything about him anymore."

"He's in a c-c-coma." Zoe snuffled. "They won't let me see him but once an hour for five minutes. They already operated on him, and they said the bullet missed his heart by a quarter of an inch."

"Oh, my God."

"And he bled and bled, and that's why he's so sick now, they said."

"Is somebody there with you, sweetheart?" Her mother's voice, her precious mother's voice, was so very soothing.

"Sandy was, but I made her go home. The nurses said I could sleep here."

"Good. I know that will make you feel better. You know, your daddy can sense that you are there. He may not react to you, but he knows."

"That's what I told Sandy. She didn't believe me."

"Don't you worry about it. You just keep doing whatever your heart tells you to, my precious girl."

Zoe made a Herculean effort to get herself under control. She didn't know when she might be able to speak to her mom again, and she didn't want to blow it. "Mom? That Hunter guy, he really beat Daniel up bad."

"Oh, no."

"He was bleeding all over, and his ear was, like, hanging."

"*What?*"

"Okay, okay. It was hanging just a little. But it was bleeding a whole bunch."

"You know why, don't you?"

"Why it was bleeding?"

"No, I mean why Hunter beat Daniel."

"No." Zoe took a tissue from the box on the desk and blew her nose. "Well, Hunter said something about Daniel not wanting to pay us a visit."

"He probably fought Hunter to keep him away from you and your dad. He loves you both very much, you know. He misses you."

"I miss him, too," said Zoe mournfully. In a whisper, she said, "Mom . . . when are you coming back?"

"As soon as I can, darling. I'm going to get Daniel tomorrow."

"You are?"

"Or the next day. No later."

"Do you know where they are?"

"I have a pretty good idea. Now, Zoe, I need you to do a couple of things for me."

Zoe sat up straighter. Her mother needed her. "Yes, ma'am."

"Okay. Now, do you know if your daddy has a little device on the telephone so that he can record calls?"

"Yeah! He played that tape for me from when you called. It made me feel a lot better."

"Honey . . . did Daddy say anything to you about a secret code? On the tape?"

"Secret code? No! He didn't say anything about that! What secret code?"

"I was afraid of that," mused Wren. "All right. What I need you to do is get hold of Mr. Steve Austin—Daddy said he was working for y'all or something?"

"Yeah. I've got his phone number, but he's in the hospital. In Midland."

"I know. I know. You're going to have to be very clever. Get hold of him somehow. I don't think he's injured that badly, and he'll want to know this. Play that tape for him and he'll figure the rest out."

"Mom? Can't you just tell me what it is and save a lot of trouble?"

"I wish I could, darling, but you never know who may be listening."

Zoe pondered this. It didn't make any sense to her.

"Now. The second thing I want you to do," said her mother, "well, it's sort of spiritual."

"Spiritual?" They hadn't been to church in *years*. "You want me to pray?"

"Well, certainly, honey. That wouldn't hurt a bit, but I'd like you to talk to your daddy every chance you get, and tell him that I'm okay and that I'm bringing Daniel home soon."

"Oh, *that*! Mom, I've been doing that anyway!"

"You have?"

"Every hour. I say the same thing in his ear, over and over. I say, 'Daddy. It's gonna be all right. Mom's okay and she's bringing Daniel home soon.'" She waited for a response, and when she didn't get one, she said, "Mom?"

"I'm here, darling. You just overwhelm me sometimes. I've missed you more than you can ever imagine."

"Yeah, I can, too." Zoe gave a rueful chuckle.

"My brave girl. You've been through so much. You're such a hero, you know."

"I am? A hero?"

"Absolutely. A superhero."

Zoe marveled at that.

"I'd better go, honey. I love you so very much."

"Me too." Zoe couldn't say more; the tears were too close to the surface again.

"I'll see you soon."

"Okay. Mom?"

"Yes?"

"Be careful. You're pretty brave, too."

"What can I say? We come from pretty good stock. When I get home, I'll tell you all about it."

And then it was over. Her mother's voice—her lifeline, her heart— was gone and she was alone again.

"Thank you," she said politely to the nurses as she walked on leaden feet back to the waiting room. They smiled her way, but they were busy.

They were all busy. One of the patients had a problem. Zoe glanced over at her daddy's bed. He seemed to be sleeping peacefully enough for a guy in a coma. So it wasn't him who had the problem. She looked back toward the nurses. They all had their backs turned.

Zoe crept past the beepers and signals and tubes and wires which connected critically ill patients with their watchers and tiptoed around to the other side of her father's bed. Stooping low so that she wouldn't be readily visible, Zoe laid her head on the pillow beside his ear and began to whisper, *"Daddy. This is Zoe again. It's gonna be all right. Mom's just fine—she really is. I'm not just saying that this time. I talked to her and she's bringing Daniel home soon. So you have to be strong and you have to fight so we can all be together again. I love you, Daddy."*

So intent was Zoe on her chant, her mantra, to her sick father that she did not notice Maria staring at her jean-clad legs, which were visible beneath the bed. Maria glanced at Mr. Cameron's monitors; his blood pressure was going up, the first positive response she'd observed yet. After a moment Maria turned away and pretended that she hadn't seen anything at all.

The phone call to Zoe almost finished Wren. All her carefully constructed defenses came tumbling right down the moment she heard her daughter's brave, tearful voice. But Zoe was counting on her—they all were—and she was not about to let them down.

That night Wren slept in her old room. Her mother had long since converted it to a guest room, one of those impersonal *Southern Living* kinds of rooms that reflected more taste than personality. But the view out the front window was the same, the settle creaks of the old house the same, and the kaleidoscopic shape-shifting Christmas colors that danced across the ceiling from the holiday lights up and down the street were the same.

It was strange, to be the same and yet so different. Strange to feel so alien in a house that had once formed the nucleus of her universe. Strange to know her father and yet not know him.

Still, there was something Wren did know, and it gave her strength. In the crescent moon that formed her life path, she had passed through the dark side and emerged once again into the light; her life now was in balance, the light and the dark. She now felt peace in a soul long troubled, and in spite of the difficult journey ahead, there was new power flowing through her veins with her lifeblood, power not just from her ancestors and from Gulanlati, but power from the rightness of her life choices.

Wren had discovered that the brave know a secret the coward can never learn: a sacrifice made for the many was a sacrifice made for the one. The web of life connecting us all was made stronger by every act of unselfishness, and for every act of self-indulgence, a little part of us all was destroyed forever.

Wren slept well that night for the first time in many weeks. The next morning, after her father left to begin running her errands for her, she found a glistening raven's feather on the porch just beyond the back door. The raven, Golana, was sacred to the Cherokee. That crows were plentiful in this part of Texas at this time of year did not detract from her belief. She took the feather as a talisman of good luck and put it in her pocket along with her rattlesnake rattle.

It took longer than Wren had hoped to prepare for her journey, but it was important that she forget nothing. She suspected that Hunter would keep Daniel alive at least until she arrived, and to find herself unprepared could be disastrous. After all, she was going to the Unuk'sutii—the den of the rattlesnake—a place where one could be found who was so evil that even to follow in his footsteps could lead to death.

But this was no longer the trembling child Lissie; she was now Ghigau—Beloved Woman—a warrior in her own right. She would fight Uk'ten, and she would defeat him, for she was not just any warrior; she was the fierce little wren willing to fight to the death to drive the wicked hawk from her nest.

And she would use her enemy's own strategy against him.

When all was ready and it was time to leave, Wren and her dad clung to one another. How strange, too, that Wren should learn to depend on her father just after she'd learned to stand alone. Families should be interdependent, she thought as she inhaled the familiar scent of him; so should the family of man.

"Spend Christmas with us, in our home," she told him. "And you'll meet the rest of your family."

"I'll look forward to it," he said, wiping his eyes as he handed her the keys to his Cadillac. "Don't dent the car." The last thing she saw as she backed out of the drive was his dear crooked grin as he waved good-bye.

The drive was very long, but the transportation luxurious. For the first time since leaving the compound, Wren was able to relax and not worry so much that she might be spotted by highway troopers. She kept to the speed limit and tried not to panic every time she passed one of their distinctive marked cars lurking on the side of the highway.

Getting to the mountains was the easy part. Finding Hunter's uncle's cabin nestled deep in the surrounding woods was much tougher.

Many years before, in the early blooming days of their romance, Hunter had promised Wren that they would one day honeymoon in that cabin. It had not occurred to him, of course, that a decrepit old hunter's shack might not be viewed as paradise by a young bride. Still, even Wren had found herself warming to his enthusiastic descriptions of nearby mountain streams, the abandoned old church in the woods with its spooky graveyard, and other rugged charms.

Though, like most of Hunter's promises, this one had vaporized under the light of day, Wren still remembered much of what he'd told her about the surrounding countryside. At a roadside tourist trap, she bought a topographical map; map-reading was one of many skills she'd picked up in her paramilitary training.

Wren dared not seek directions; mountain folk were clannish even with feuding neighbors where outsiders were concerned. There was no doubt that the most casual inquiry would somehow be telegraphed along the crawling forest grapevine and alert Hunter to her nearby presence.

After studying the map over a thick, succulent barbecue sandwich, Wren did ask about the weather. Country folk were always eager to discuss the weather. She learned that several days of rainfall had lightened, but an encroaching cold front was fast cloaking the mountain in the kind of mist that spawned dreadful folk tales about death and dismemberment deep among the dark trees and lost mountain trails.

Wren wondered if they were trying to scare her, if they were having some fun at the city girl's expense, but as darkness crowded against the steamy cafe windows, she wasn't so sure. Driving gradually became a spectral nightmare; she was forced to a crawl because she couldn't see beyond her own headlights, and once she turned her father's Cadillac into the trees, Wren felt herself being swallowed.

Still, Wren refused to allow herself to be daunted. Her backpack was well loaded. Her dad had spared no expense. And her son was out there somewhere, in the shrouded tangle of woods on the side of the mountain, alone with a maniac bent on vengeance. As she had done before in the desert, she kept going.

Outside the cossetted comfort of her father's automobile, the gloom was Stygian. Thoughts of *Sunoyi anedohi*—night travelers who prey on the vulnerable—and scary tales her grandmother once told of the lost souls of the unburied dead, lurked in the back of Wren's mind, but she shook them off as best she could, because it was taking every ounce of concentration she could muster just to find her way.

Once, she thought she heard the cry of the *dedonsk*—owl. In Native American tradition, such a call always signaled the approach of death. Wren had heard many stories from her grandmother's people about the owl; even those who claimed not to believe could still relate instances where they had seen or heard owls just before experiencing great personal tragedy.

She told herself it was her imagination.

With her next step, the toe of her hiking boot caught on something solid on the ground before her and flung her headlong. Shielding her penlight with the palm of her hand, Wren peered through the ghostly mist to see what had brought her down.

A broken tombstone.

The name on the tombstone was *Daniel*.

Now, for the first time in days, Wren's newfound confidence suddenly and completely abandoned her, leaving her quite alone and very much afraid.

CHAPTER 43

AUSTIN shifted his weight in the hard hospital bed. He'd found there was no comfortable position, but he was too hardheaded to take the pain medication prescribed for him because it fuzzed up his mind. He was figuring out, the hard way, that Tylenol, while great for the occasional headache, was crap on gunshot wounds.

Austin had other reasons to be gloomy. Cindy Thomas had died on the operating table, leaving behind a four-year-old son. She'd told him when he hired her that the reason she'd left the Secret Service and the presidential protection detail in the first place was so that she could have more time with her little boy.

And what'd she do? thought Austin. *She came to work for me and got herself killed.*

He was heartsick, awash with guilt. Ned Thomas, Cindy's young husband, had come to see Austin in the hospital to tell him that Cindy wouldn't have lived her life any other way—or chosen to die in any other manner. He told Austin not to blame himself—and then the guy had the dignity and sensitivity to donate Cindy's organs so that others might live.

The talk with Cindy's husband helped, no doubt about it. Without that talk Austin might have dropped over the edge into the black abyss of depression. But it wouldn't bring back that little boy's mama, and Austin knew a day would not pass for the rest of his life that he didn't think about that.

Buck Leatherwood, true to character, had set aside a trust fund for the child's college education and privately matched Cindy's life insurance payout dollar for dollar. He also took care of all the hospital bills not covered by insurance for all three of his wounded security force members, in spite of Austin's protest that he could pay for his own.

Leatherwood gracefully refused to blame Austin for any of what happened, saying that if assassins could get to the president of the United States, they could get to him. He also reversed his previous hard line on various security measures which had been suggested by the reports prepared by Guaranteed Security Associates, Inc. Metal detectors and other devices were already being installed.

"No use innocent people getting their heads blown off just because I choose to shoot off my mouth in public," he said angrily. "This is my fault as much as it is yours. If I'd done what you said in the first place, none of this would have happened."

Austin wasn't so sure about that, but he appreciated the gesture and felt relief at the implementation of better security for the Leatherwood Building.

Mike Martinez had come by and given Austin a complete rundown of the explosive devices the ATF had dismantled. "It was weird, Steve," he said. "The two devices closest to Leatherwood had already been disabled. The others were rigged—and this is the weird part—the timers looked like they were set to go off the same time as the one behind the TV stand, but the detonators were actually timed for much later than that. In other words, even a bomb expert would have thought these were armed and ready to go, but once that little explosive went off, there was ample time to evacuate the building and contact the bomb squad before anything worse could happen. And another thing. They said the placement of the small explosive device—the one behind the TV stand that did go off—had to be deliberate."

"I'm sure they were all deliberate," commented Austin wearily.

"No, I mean it was placed behind a baffle."

"What's that?"

"It's a block of sorts. A protective device—like wearing a lead shield when you're getting X-rayed, man. So nobody would get hurt.

The firecracker boys tell me that the whole scene was a work of genius."

No, thought Austin. *It was the work of Lissie Montgomery. Or Wren Cameron. Or whoever the hell she is.*

With a heavy sigh, Austin picked up the remote bed control and adjusted the height of his head a little. Maybe that would help with the pain.

"Can I get you anything, honey?" fretted Patsy, ever vigilant to his needs.

"No, I'm fine, thanks." He stared at the ceiling. Lissie was still out there. And so was Hunter. With Daniel. That poor kid—no telling what he was going through with a psycho like Hunter. Once his little party got thwarted, and once he figured out Daniel's mama was responsible . . . Austin shuddered at the thought of what he might do next.

"You're worried about that woman, aren't you?" asked Patsy. "And her son."

Still counting ceiling tiles, Austin nodded.

The phone rang. Naturally Patsy dove for it. She was screening his calls and supervising his meals, and it was beginning to drive him crazy. When a big smile crossed her face, he relaxed.

She said, "The switchboard says one of our daughters is on the line. I told her you'd take the call." She handed him the phone.

"Hello?" He could hear a *click*.

"Mr. Austin?" said the reedy voice which was not one of his grown daughters. "This is Zoe Cameron."

"Zoe!" He sat up. "Ouch. Forgot myself there. Okay. Better. Now, how's your dad?"

"He's in a coma. They said the bullet missed his heart by a quarter of an inch."

"Oh, child. I'm so sorry."

"His condition hasn't changed, but it hasn't gotten any worse, either, so we think that's good news."

"It is, it is. Your dad's a tough old bird. He'll make it."

"How are you doing?" she asked politely. "I heard you got shot, too."

"Aw, I'm too mean to kill," he said. "I think the doctors are about ready to kick me out of here." He smiled. "I'm so glad you called."

"I'm supposed to give you a message. From my mom."

"*From your mom?*" Patsy's eyebrows shot up. Austin almost dropped the phone.

"She called me. Here at the hospital. And she called my dad. I mean, before he got shot. Daddy taped the call, and Mom wanted you to listen to it."

"Did she say why?"

"She said there was secret code on it and that you would understand."

Austin frowned. He wondered if being forced to spend so much time with these paranoid creeps had gotten to Lissie. She seemed to be getting a little paranoid herself.

"Did she say anything else? About me, I mean."

"No, but well . . . I think she thinks that you can help her, Mr. Austin. You know she's afraid to involve the government because of what happened at the Community."

But I was in charge of that raid, thought Austin. *Why would she trust me?*

Maybe because nobody else would get the so-called "secret code." Maybe because he'd been helping Cam. Who knew? He was glad of it anyway, because it gave him an opportunity to get involved, to do something, to make retribution for sins of the past.

Austin made a writing gesture in the air with his right hand in Patsy's direction. Instantly a pad of paper and a pen appeared. He blew her a kiss.

"Okay, sweetheart, shoot. Whoops! Bad choice of words."

She giggled. It was a good sign.

And then he could hear that voice, that clear and strong Texan voice he remembered so vividly from the past. It was so amazing just to hear her again that he missed most of the conversation and had to request that Zoe replay it. This time he took notes.

"Secret code, huh?" he said wryly. "Who does she think she is, a code talker?"

"What's a code talker?"

Austin chuckled. "In World War II they used men from the Navaho Nation to send out important communiqués in the Navaho tongue regarding troop movement to the Allies. The Japs were never able to break the code."

"Cool! Was Mom doing that here?"

"Hardly," said Austin. "Listen, kid, I sure do appreciate this." He really did, too. Just having something concrete to do, a *contribution* to make, had gotten his blood pumping. "You take care of your daddy, and I'll come see him just as soon as I blow this pop stand."

"As soon as what?"

"As soon as I get outta here, sweetheart. You're a brave young lady," he added seriously. "It's been an honor to know your whole family."

"Well, there's still time to change your mind," she said. "You haven't met Daniel yet."

Austin laughed and they hung up.

Instinctively he patted his pajama pockets. "I need my address book. Where's my address book?"

Patsy shook her head and rolled her eyes heavenward. "Well it's not in your PJ's, dummy," she said. "It's in the pocket of that bloody suit the nurses had to cut off of you when they brought you in here all shot up full of holes."

"Aw, it wasn't that bad." He reached his good hand out, and she placed her own in it. Closing his fingers around hers, he said, "How do you put up with me, woman?"

"I wonder that myself sometimes." Grinning, she brought up her other hand, which was holding his pocket-sized address book. "Now get busy and find that woman. You've been layin' around here in this bed doin' nothin' for too too long."

The graveyard of the old abandoned mountain church had long since been overtaken by vines, underbrush, and pine seedlings. Vandals had knocked down most of the tombstones and even stolen a few. All the graves were at least a hundred years old; once Wren forced herself to look, she learned that Daniel Jenkins, the mountain man whose gravestone had tripped her up, had died in 1854, followed by simply "wife" in 1855.

There wasn't anything left of the church itself but a burnt-out foundation; she speculated that vandals had been responsible. If it had happened while folks still worshiped here, they'd have made all sorts of sacrifices to rebuild their church, which was the hub of frontier community life. She wondered if they'd outgrown the building and moved on down the mountain to a more spacious and civilized location.

Mist still swirled around her as she explored the site in the dark. Although the shock of seeing her son's name engraved on a tombstone had almost done her in, the realization had gradually dawned that this graveyard was a crucial landmark for which Wren had been diligently searching. As she remembered from Hunter's descriptions, the cabin of Hunter's uncle lay just a few hundred yards to the east.

After a brief rest, to collect her nerves as much as anything else, Wren headed east. Hiking through the forest in the midst of a fog-draped night was a hell of a lot harder than crossing the desert, Wren reflected in frustration. In spite of other hardships, the desert gave you vistas; it gave you horizons; it was mostly flat; and it very thoughtfully provided snakes that actually warned you before they struck. Poisonous woodsy snakes were silent and deadly, not like the audacious rattler with its arrogant noisemaker.

Of course, it helped if one had enough water with one when one was sojourning across said desert, she thought wryly.

The Armageddon Army, and the Community before them, had taught Wren well. She moved with slow precision and great stealth. Those veterans who'd actually seen real combat duty in Vietnam had learned well from studying the tactics of the courageous Viet Cong guerilla fighters.

You become one with the night. You wait and you wait and you watch. And then you pop up in unexpected places.

Wren had no intention of charging the cabin, gun blazing. In fact, she had no intention of doing anything at all for at least twenty-four hours—after she'd had ample opportunity to reconnoiter the setup. She would observe their routines and their movements during daylight hours as well as at night.

The mission was clear: get Daniel safely away. Her mission was not to kill Hunter unless in self-defense—much as she might want to. Any attempt to get revenge on Hunter would only jeopardize her true mission: getting Daniel home safely.

Any surprise encounter with the enemy on his own territory would put her at serious risk, which would not help accomplish the mission, especially if Daniel was hurt. Surprise ambush was a possibility, so she had to plan ahead of time for that. *It's not like I can call in artillery*, she thought grimly.

On the other hand, if Zoe got through to Steve Austin, and if Austin heard the tape and understood it and took the kind of action Wren thought he might take . . . But Wren couldn't wait around for that hopeful eventuality. Not if Hunter was hitting the moonshine, which she knew was very probably the case. The stuff made him crazy and he knew it. He just didn't care.

Poor Daniel.

A sense of urgency nipped at the back of her mind, but Wren refused to give in to it. If she hurried, she would make some mistake that could get them both killed.

The gloom of night was just beginning to fade when Wren finally made it to the clearing that sheltered the old cabin. Wren took advantage of the added light to secure a good position with adequate cover. Then she made herself as comfortable as possible and settled in for a very long wait.

Once the moonshine ran out, Hunter no longer raved or shot at imaginary feds, but his mood turned savage and watchful. The .45 he kept strapped in the holster around his waist, the pickup keys were in his pocket, and he slept with the shotgun, so Daniel's options were limited.

From time to time it occurred to him that he could walk out while Hunter slept. After all, the man wasn't a machine; he was a human being, albeit a crazy one. And although Daniel had no idea where to go to get help, he thought it possible that he'd learned enough survival training to at least stay alive until he stumbled onto somebody, somewhere, who could help.

The problem was Daniel's mom. Hunter seemed convinced that she knew about the cabin and would come looking for it in order to rescue Daniel. And Daniel had to admit, in that respect anyway, the loony tunes was probably right. Daniel's biggest fear was that his mother *would* come and, in searching for him, get herself killed. He simply could not take that chance. He didn't see that he had much choice but to wait, keep an eye out for his mom, and see if maybe they could sneak out while Hunter slept or something.

While he waited, he tried to anticipate what his mom would do.

He didn't think that, after the disaster at the Community, she would bring law enforcement with her. So she would probably come alone. He knew she was armed now, but he didn't know if she would have thought to bring a backup weapon so that he could maybe help out if necessary. A shotgun would be the best thing, but she wasn't likely to drag a big heavy gun like that through the forest.

What really worried Daniel was how his mother was going to manage such a feat without anybody to help her. She was so alone out there, especially now that Daniel's dad . . . Well, he'd learned the bitter truth lately that there was nothing wrong with depending on other people once in a while, as long as you were capable of standing alone when necessary.

After all, Jeremiah Hunter didn't need *anybody*, and look where that had gotten him!

Every time Daniel thought about his own behavior over the previous weeks, he just wanted to dig a great big hole and stick his head in it. He'd been such a complete and total moron.

Sometimes, when the rain was *dripdripdripping* into the water-filled pans they'd set out, and Daniel would move around, dumping out the old rain water to make room for more, total misery would set in. He'd start by thinking about Big John, and he'd get so sad. Maybe Big John had committed some crime or other and, okay, maybe he had been taking part in planning another one, but he wasn't all bad. He had helped to save Daniel's mom's life, and Daniel would never forget that about Big John. Never.

And there was no way Big John would ever have driven off and left the other Alpha/Omegans behind to die.

Daniel made a decision: if he ever got out of here alive, he would see to it that somebody went and dug up Big John and gave him a decent burial in a real cemetery.

Then Daniel would get to wondering if they'd already had the funeral for his dad, and that's when he would just lose it. He'd have to go out to the outhouse and sit over that stinking shit hole and bawl. It was the only privacy he had, and anyway, if Hunter knew Daniel was out there crying, he'd probably just shoot him and get it over with.

Once the relentless rain let up, this godawful spooky cold fog pressed in around the shack, unnerving Daniel even more than the rain and setting off Hunter to shoot at every single little sound out there in the sunless gloom of the fog-veiled woods. It wasn't booze that made him trigger-happy this time, Daniel observed, it was plain old meanness. The militia men had given Hunter literally hundreds of rounds of ammunition for the .45 as well as the shotgun, and he was in no danger of running out.

Another thing about Hunter which Daniel began to notice with some surprise was that he seemed jumpy. *Scared.* He was scared of Daniel's mom! He'd pace around the shack from window to window, peering out, squinting into the shadows. Sometimes, Daniel could hear him muttering under his breath, saying things like, *"I know you're out there, Lissie, you little bitch. Creepin' around like the little sneak you are. Why don't you bring your ass out in the open and fight like a man?"*

Big tough guy.

One thing was definite: Hunter sure wasn't so handsome anymore. His scraggly beard was mostly gray; he looked like Yasser Arafat, and his eyes were burning as if with fever. It scared the shit out of Daniel just to look at him, and he didn't dare make eye contact. The law of the jungle applied here; even a look could be interpreted as a direct challenge.

Daniel's job was to cook the food on their little camp stove, do whatever he was told before he was told to do it, and to stay the hell out of Hunter's way. Like a kick-cowed dog, he soon learned to tuck his tail and do just that.

By late afternoon of the third day, Daniel was beginning to doubt that his mother would be able to find them after all. He didn't think she'd ever been here before. It would be a miracle if she could find this place based on comments made by Hunter two decades ago. Daniel didn't know what to do. After the incident where Hunter had almost shot him in the head, Daniel lived in absolute fear of the man. He was completely mercurial at this point and could take it into his head at any time just to blow Daniel's head off and say something like, "Whoops. I was aiming at the door, there."

Daniel was constantly on the lookout for an opportunity to get his hands on that shotgun. One pull of the trigger and he'd be free, plus his mother would be safe. But there was no way. Hunter kept it zipped up in his sleeping bag when he was asleep, and when he was awake, he took it with him if he had to go outside.

While Daniel was cooking beans for their supper that evening, Hunter's silence, which had lasted the day, suddenly began to get to Daniel. It was creepy. He worried that Hunter might be suicidal—and he knew there was no way he'd be left behind if Hunter decided to take his own life. When Hunter took out the .45 and started toying with it, pretending it was a six-shooter and he was a stud cowboy who could do all those fancy tricks, Daniel's stomach grew queasy. Twice he dropped it to the floor and Daniel just about peed in his pants again.

Then Hunter said, "I know you're a federal agent."

Daniel said nothing. He had not spoken to Hunter since the man took his daddy's life; besides, it was much safer that way. He stirred the beans. Slowly and carefully.

"I know you and your little bitch mama infiltrated the Armageddon Army so that you could destroy us. Only reason she crawled into my bed was so that they could monitor me better. Through that chip that's in my butt."

Suddenly, Daniel was possessed of a ludicrous desire to laugh. A hysterical desire to laugh. *What a way to go*, he thought. *I died laughing.*

Oh God, oh God . . . he was going to get himself killed right here over the bean pot. Knocking the spoon on the edge of the pan, he laid it down on the floor and walked slowly out the door to the edge of the forest to pee. But he didn't unzip his fly. Instead, with his back to the shack, he put both hands over his mouth and guffawed until the tears streamed down his face.

After he'd gotten himself under control, he wiped his face and muttered, "Man, you are such a total nutcase. It'd be funny if it wasn't so pathetic." Then he cleared his throat and walked back into the shack.

Wren could not believe what she had just witnessed. Daniel was standing not six feet away from her, but she dared not reveal her presence at this time because it was still daylight and they were too close to the shack to get safely away before Hunter would come after them. She had to make her move under cover of darkness.

Hunter's continued mental deterioration was a source of great worry to Wren. He was too unpredictable—explosive, in fact. But she knew he was armed with weapons she herself could not have carried on a long hike through the woods in the dark. For all she knew, he had an AK47 in there. She had to take a chance on waiting, and it was the longest day of her entire life.

She'd heard her boy sobbing in the outhouse, and it had wrenched her heart, but seeing him now filled her with such pride. Only the truly courageous can see the humor in a life-threatening situation; more than one war hero had saved his buddies' lives by making them laugh in the face of danger.

This ordeal had certainly made a man out of Daniel. It saddened her more than words could express, because it was far too soon. When she got him home, he would be a different kid, but Wren could see that it wouldn't all be necessarily bad.

As darkness gathered in the tangled branches of the trees and crept over the clearing, the tattered shreds of mist began to wrap themselves around the shack and surrounding forest like a winding gravecloth. There was something depraved, something malevolent about the deep obscurity of the encroaching gloom, as if Satan's minions themselves crouched on the branches, poisoning the close, suffocating air with their lust for blood.

Exhaustion played tricks on Wren's mind. Once or twice she thought she saw Daniel emerge from the cabin, only to discover that it was Hunter. She could tell from his movements that he was sober now, too. Had he stayed drunk, his reactions might have been slower. As it was, he seemed edgy and on the alert. A great unease settled in her spirit. From this time forward, any mistake she made would be fatal.

Everything dimmed with the approaching moonless night. Soon Wren was blinded altogether. Her skin prickled. Goose bumps.

And then she heard it, this time for sure: the call of the owl.

Her mind. All in her mind.

She heard it again. There was no mistaking it.

Foolish superstition. Indian folk tale. Owls hunted at night. No biggie. Don't get distracted.

A shapeless form clunked out on the caved-in porch. Wren

strained her ears. The devilish fog had beclouded any source of light which might have filtered down from the night sky to the clearing.

It thunked into the mud, *suck, suck, suck,* heading straight toward her. Her pulse pounded in her brain.

Daniel?

"I know you're out there, Lissie. I'm going to murder your baby boy and drink his blood. What do you think of that?"

She opened her mouth so that he couldn't hear her breathe. Short, wild pants. A deer listening to the baying of the hounds.

Shoot him, screamed her mind. *Blow his fucking head off!*

Jamming back the slide to cock a Glock was a noisy business. Fortunately, Wren had thought to do that before leaving the car, even though it made the weapon more dangerous to carry. She withdrew the gun now from the holster at her hip and grasped it in trembling hands.

Do it.

Sudden self-doubt tormented her. What if something went wrong and she missed somehow? What would happen to Daniel then?

Pulse pounding madly in her throat, she hesitated.

Suck, suck, suck. Clunk, clunk.

He was gone.

Couldn't take a deep breath. Wanted to but couldn't. Sweating in the cold. Shivering from the sweat.

I blew it, she agonized. *I had my shot and I blew it. He was right. Hunter was right all along.* Aiming a gun at somebody and pulling the trigger to snuff out a human life *were* two different things.

Oh God, she thought. *When push came to shove, I didn't have it in me. Now what's going to happen to us?*

She had to get Daniel away somehow. It was their only chance.

Daniel, come out. I don't think he's going to give you another night.

The relentless fog-soaked night dragged on. She waited. Waited some more.

Dozed.

The sound of running water jerked Wren awake. The Glock had slid from her grasp and landed barrel-down in the mud. She yanked it up, wondering with sickening fear if it would jam if she had to pull the trigger.

Because if Wren had to pull the trigger, one jam and they'd both be dead.

The water stopped. She peered into the maddening dead dark night.

"Mom?"

The whisper sent chills swarming over Wren's body. She didn't move; it could be a trick.

"*Are you out there, Mom?*"

Was it Daniel? *Was it?*

"Daniel."

The name popped out almost against Wren's will. She clutched the Glock tighter in sweaty palms and extended it blindly in front of her.

Sucksucksucksuck.

"Where are you?" came the whisper.

Heart thundering, Wren got to her feet. It was now or never, either way. With exquisite care she eased out of her hiding place. Glock at the ready, she took a step that sounded like a gunshot to her hypersensitive hearing.

He came stumbling in her direction, and Wren knew then that it was Daniel for sure, because if it had been Hunter, he'd have simply fired a shot her way. They fumbled for one another, and then his arms, so manly and strong now, enfolded Wren in a bear hug so tight she couldn't breathe.

He was shaking from head to foot.

"You came," he murmured against her ear. "You found me. You came."

Placing a warning finger against his lips, Wren hugged back, wondering how in hell she was going to get them out of there.

The sudden shock of brilliant yellow light blinded Wren.

Heart suspended in midair, she leapt to the side even as she shoved Daniel in the other direction. A blast shattered the night; mud splashed into Wren's face, stinging her eyes, making it worse, even as the light went off, plunging her into the blackness again.

"*I'll find you, you little bitch, and I'll kill you, and then I'll kill your brat kid, and then I'll go find your other brat kid and kill her too, you know why? Huh? Because you failed to learn the single most important rule: never point a gun at anyone unless you're prepared to use it!*"

A demonic laugh echoed off the trees and the light strobed on again, full in her face, but she was ready. This time, by God, she was *ready*, she had on her sunglasses, and all she had to do was aim the Glock straight at the brilliant yellow circle and pull the fucking trigger and pray to holy God that it went off because it was the one and only chance she would ever have—*BLAMBLAMBLAMBLAM-BLAM*—how many times did she fire did she get the son of a bitch or not?

Panting heavily, hands shaking violently, Wren rolled to the side and up on her knees, Glock straight out in front, ready to empty the whole goddamned magazine because she was getting real sick of Jeremiah Hunter.

Silence.

Ragged breathing. That would be her own. Swallow, get it under control, shake the hair out of the eyes, wait. It hadn't been so hard to pull the trigger after all, when her son's life was at stake.

Gurgling. The final gasps of a dying man.

One final comment.

"Shit. I didn't think you had the balls."

They couldn't find the pickup keys, and Daniel was terrified that Hunter had dropped them down the shit hole. He wanted out of this place so bad.

"Daniel."

His mom was standing beside him while he rooted through Hunter's sleeping bag. He turned to look at her. In the soft glow of the kerosene lamp, she looked young again.

"I just wanted to say—" she looked off someplace over his head "—how very sorry I am."

He rocked back on his heels. "What for?"

She sighed. "I promised myself that there would be no more secrets between us. I owe you that much."

"Mom—"

"No. Let me get through this before I chicken out."

"Mom, wait! I know what you're going to tell me."

"I don't think you do, son."

"You're going to tell me that Hunter was my real father."

She gasped, a sharp intake of breath like he'd stabbed her. "You knew?"

He shrugged. "I started figuring it out when you two were . . . together . . . at the compound. There was just something about it that got me to thinking."

"I didn't mean to lie to you all those years. I just didn't know how to tell you, you know, about who Hunter was. And Cam was so good—"

"Did he know?" The question came out more sharply than Daniel intended.

Wren nodded. "From the beginning. I was four months pregnant when we met." She gave him a weak smile. "We fudged a little bit on our real anniversary date."

Daniel stared at his hands.

She touched his chin, forcing him to look into her eyes. "As far as your daddy was concerned, honey, you were his kid from the very beginning."

Tears choked Daniel's throat. "He didn't hate me?"

"Oh, Daniel." Wren got to her knees so that she could look into his eyes directly. "Why would he hate you? You are your very own person. Just because Hunter was bad does not in any way mean that you have to be, too."

"He was always worried that I'd be a delinquent or something."

She smiled at him. "That was based on your behavior, honey, not on your heritage. Besides, I think you've dipped pretty heavily into the Montgomery gene pool. I've got a lot of exciting things to tell you about that. You're one-eighth Cherokee, you know."

Daniel turned away from his mother and put his hands over his face.

"What's wrong? What is it?"

"The only *real* father I ever had was Harry Cameron," mumbled Daniel, "and now he's *dead,* and I can't even—"

"But he's not dead, Daniel. He's very sick, but he's not dead."

Adrenaline shot through Daniel's body with the force of an electric current. "Dad's not dead? He's not dead?"

Beaming, she shook her head. "We're going to go see him. As soon as we find those pickup keys."

"This is great! This is terrific! He's not dead! He's not dead!"

Daniel leapt to his feet, grabbed his mother up into a bear hug, and twirled her around and around. "I'm going to find the car keys!" he cried, racing out the door and bounding over the broken porch. As he dropped to his knees beside Hunter's body, iron arms clamped around his body from behind and a steel fist mashed his lips against his teeth.

Before he could react, he was picked up and bodily carried into the trees like an armful of firewood. Electrified, he fought with all his might, even as a low voice in his ear said, "I'm a *friend*, kid, a *friend*! Settle down. We're here to help you and your mom. Stop it! I am a *friend*."

Chest heaving, sucking air through his nostrils, he looked around wild-eyed at the man who was in front of him. He was covered head to toe in camouflage, right down to the face paint. Scary shit.

He didn't look like a fed, though.

"Steve Austin sent us," murmured the man. "We're here to rescue you and your mom. I'm Pedro. This is Gunther."

Daniel had calmed down. The other man, Gunther, tentatively removed his hand, and Daniel grinned at Pedro. "Sorry, amigo," he said. "But I'm afraid you're too late."

CHAPTER 44

MUFFLED sounds moved back and forth and in and out. Sometimes they made no sense and sometimes they made too much. Somebody said *be a vegetable* and somebody said *blood pressure* and somebody said *Mom's coming home.*

He was so tired. So heavy. So tired.

Asleep.

Awake.

All the same.

Wanted to speak. Tried to. So tired.

Flurry, noise, confusion, piercing squeal, *shhhhh!*

"Cam, my darling, we're home now and we're safe."

"Dad. This is your son, Daniel. I love you, Dad."

Strong grips, one on each hand. One large and strong. One small and strong.

Safety.

Love.

He squeezed back.

The doctors said that Cam's recovery was miraculous. He gathered that Steve Austin was responsible for much of the good stuff that came afterward. Leatherwood's Learjet, for one thing, had flown Wren and Daniel back from Arkansas while Austin's men drove home her dad's Caddy.

There was so much to take in; most of the time he just slept. He slept when he didn't want to and he slept when he did. The worst was when he slept during a conversation.

But each day he got a little bit stronger and slept a little less. Once they changed his medication, he was much more alert.

Wren and Daniel had to be away much more than either of them wanted. The federal authorities had an endless supply of questions for them. Cam believed that without Steve Austin's pull, the feds would have been much more suspicious of Wren's part in the Leatherwood Building bombing. In spite of the fact that no one in the immediate area was seriously hurt, and even though Buck Leatherwood refused to press charges, she had still broken several laws—not the least of which appeared to be conspiracy to commit murder—and was fair game for prosecution. Fortunately, her testimony as a witness against the bank robbers was far more important to the feds than her hide, and she was able to make a deal that cleared her record once and for all.

Most of the country was still reeling from news reports that traced the flow of money which had supported Hunter's compound through a complicated maze of dummy corporations and fraudulent bank accounts to its source: the right-wing political/religious group, United for a Stronger America. The baby-faced boy wonder who ran the organization, Paul Smith, had denied any wrongdoing and hired one of the country's most notorious defense attorneys. Even so, the political fallout had left the organization severely weakened.

Austin was still worried about the other members of the so-called Armageddon Army, who had fled to the four winds after the death of their fearless leader and capture of the Strike Force. He talked to Cam and Wren both about going into the federal witness protection program, but Wren refused to consider it.

She said she was done with running.

Cam was more concerned about his son than his wife. Wren was tough, she could take care of herself, but Daniel was a kid who'd been through a relentless ongoing trauma for weeks on end. Cam fretted about the long-term effects this would have on the boy.

But Wren shrugged off his fears. Though she put the boy in post-trauma stress counseling and hired a private tutor to help him get caught up in school, she assured Cam that Daniel was stronger than he could possibly imagine.

One thing was for sure: Cam had never seen the kid so affectionate. He guessed some kids needed a little shock from time to time to help them appreciate what they truly had going for them.

Sadly, the friendship with Eric went by the wayside. Daniel told Cam that he'd outgrown his old friend.

But there was one remaining chore Cam dreaded above all. There had to be a full circle; he was never again going to keep anything from his wife, even if she never spoke to him again.

Confessing his secret to his wife was the toughest thing Cam had ever done. "You need to know," he began hesitantly late one night when no one else was around and they finally had some privacy. "I've kept it from you all these years. I was afraid you'd hate me . . ."

She put the palm of her soft warm hand against his cheek. "I could never hate you. I don't think I could even be mad at you again."

"I'll remember that next time I leave the toilet seat up."

They smiled at each other, then Cam said, "When we were first together . . . I mean . . . when you first told me about who you were . . ." He stopped. Sighed. Started over. "I'm an attorney. I defend the Constitution all the time, or at least, people whose constitutional rights have been violated. I couldn't . . . I couldn't marry you without . . . It was important that . . . I just . . . I had to do the right thing, Wren. God, this is hard. Quit looking at me like that."

"I know about Steve Austin, Cam. I know you called him and told him about me years ago, before we were married. That you knew where he could find me if he wanted to—even though you knew I was pregnant. And I know you kept it from me all those years because you thought I'd feel betrayed."

He nodded, glancing away from those laser-beam eyes. "I thought you'd hate me. I just couldn't bear the thought."

"You want to know a secret?"

He looked back.

"I couldn't care less. I almost lost you, Cam. We almost lost each other, our family. . . . Nothing else could possibly matter as much as us, being together, you and me, our little family. Now and forever."

She kissed him.

"That's a pretty good secret," he said, his whole face relaxing as a smile broke through the clouds. "I think I'll keep it."

PART VI

THE BEAUTY PATH

Our sacred duty to one another is to build community on a foundation of right action. . . . Thus we build a strong community. . . . We are the beauty path. The Peacekeeper that all peoples await is a seed within each of us.

DHYANI YWAHOO
Voices of Our Ancestors: Cherokee
Teachings from the Wisdom Fire

CHAPTER 45

IT was January fifteenth—Christmas Eve for the Cameron family. They had unanimously agreed to postpone their celebrations until Cam could be home and well enough to enjoy it.

Wren sat on the couch facing the fireplace, a child on either side of her. The kids' granddad, Robert, sat adjacent to them in a comfortable rocker. Cam was all propped up against the hearth in a sea of pillows.

"I'm going to tell you some of the things I learned in my vision quest," she told them, using her hands to gesture gracefully as she spoke, in the ancient storytelling tradition she'd learned at her grandmother's knee.

"The Cherokee *elo*, or philosophy of life," she explained, "is to live so as to benefit others and place the world in harmony. In this world, we are all connected, like a delicate spider's web. You pluck one strand, the entire web trembles."

"Didn't I read that somewhere?" asked Zoe.

"Something like that. It's attributed to Chief Seattle, but we don't know for sure if he really said it."

"Don't be such an encyclopedia," complained Daniel to his sister.

"Well, at least I can read one, butthead."

"So go brag about it at the Nerd Convention."

"Guys." Wren exchanged a glance with Cam. It said, *It sounds so great to hear them fighting and name-calling again, doesn't it?* He winked at her.

"Anyway." Wren took a small sip of unspiked eggnog. "In this world, we all depend upon one another, so if we as individuals see a wrong and do nothing to right it—then the wrong harms all of us."

"It's not easy to do the right thing when everybody around you is doing wrong," said Cam. "It's not even easy to do the right thing when nobody else wants to do it. And it's *really* not easy to do the right thing when you know it could hurt someone you love." He smiled at Wren. The crackling fire behind him cast a ruddy glow over his face.

Wren nodded. "Sometimes you have to forgive yourself for that. I had to forgive myself for the people who died at the Community."

"Well, they weren't so innocent, Mom," commented Daniel. "After all, they were armed and they were aiming at federal agents, trying to kill them. Even the kids. The agents didn't know."

Wren's father sighed. "I blamed myself for not being there more for your mother when she was growing up."

"But we all have to take responsibility for our own actions, Daddy," said Wren with a firm hand gesture. "The mistakes I made were not your fault."

A log popped and settled, sending a flurry of crimson sparks into the air.

"I learned something too," volunteered Zoe in the ensuing quiet. "I didn't have a vision quest or anything, but I learned that even though we depend on each other, sometimes we need to be able to be strong by ourselves. Otherwise, we won't be able to do the right thing when we have to."

"That's the main thing I wanted to tell you kids," said Wren eagerly. "Anytime we find ourselves at the crossroads of life, and we don't know what is the right thing to do, or we are afraid to do it . . . Ahw'usti—or Gulanlati, the Great Spirit—or God, or whatever name you want to give it—is right here," she said, tapping her chest, "inside of us, bringing wisdom and courage."

"Well, somebody sure gave a dose of it to Zoe," said Cam with an earnest smile. "If she hadn't had the wisdom and courage to get the bleeding slowed down by the time the ambulance got to the house the night I was shot, I wouldn't be here now."

"I saw it on TV," said Zoe. "*Rescue 911.*"

Everybody laughed, the echoes of it resounding from one corner of the room to another in a familiar family chorus.

It was a good sound.

Acknowledgments

Not everyone who helped with this book knew he was helping. It is a writer's job to observe; when spending time with paramilitary survivalists, I did just that. Every word in this book, apart from the storyline, is accurate and based on months spent talking with and listening to individuals who are involved in such activities and their sympathizers, as well as reading through the vast network of various newsletters, magazines, books, and other communications made available by these underground militias.

What I read and heard and viewed on homemade videotapes worried me a great deal; I could see there was a mounting wave of rage, fear, and hatred being fed and nurtured by those who stood to profit from it, and I feared for the effect it may all be having on those members of our society who cannot separate rhetoric from fact, and who, quite frankly, may not even be sane.

Ordeal was two-thirds complete when the horrific explosion brought down the federal building in Oklahoma City, causing the deaths of nearly 200 people, a dozen of them children. (As I write this, two suspects are being held in prison and a trial is pending.) Like many Americans, I grieved as though I'd lost loved ones in that federal building myself, and in a way, I think we all did.

Many of my questions on matters of procedure were answered by friends of mine who are agents in the Federal Bureau of Investigation. They asked that I not mention them specifically in the acknowledgments, and I honor that request.

I'm deeply grateful to my friends, Monty and Lisa Harkins, for allowing me to explore their sheep and goat ranch near Sanderson, Texas, which provided the setting for my fictional paramilitary compound.

I did receive some technical assistance from my friend, Texas Ranger John Billings, who read the manuscript and kept me from making a fool of myself. I am grateful.

I would also like to thank Wilma Mankiller, who at this writing has just retired as the first female Principal Chief not only of the Cherokee Nation but of *any* major Native American tribe. She gave her blessing to the project and became a sister to my soul in so doing. I am thankful beyond words.

This book could not have been written, period, without the generous assistance of my dad, Ken Henderson, United States Marine Corps, retired, Vietnam veteran, former high-risk security expert, and rogue explorer and outdoorsman. He is not unsympathetic with the complaints of the more moderate element of the survivalists and militiamen, and did more than anyone in helping me understand the pathways of logic which can lead to extremist views. His expertise on explosives, domestic terrorism, weaponry, hand-to-hand combat, and survival skills were absolutely invaluable to me. I flat out adore the guy. Thanks, Dad.

I also owe more than I can ever repay to my good friend and cyber-buddy, John Bailey, of the Interagency Task Force located in Klamath Falls, Oregon, for his careful reading of the manuscript, his superb suggestions on technical matters regarding personal security, weaponry, martial arts, and the like, and his smiling e-mail messages.

My husband comes from a proud and distinguished military family. His father, Leroy Mills, served in the navy in the Pacific in World War II. His older brother, Travis W. Mills, served two tours of duty in Vietnam in the Special Forces (a *for real* war hero, as opposed to the Jeremiah Hunters of this world). His younger brother, Lieutenant Colonel Richard W. Mills, is currently still on active duty in the Army Special Forces and will soon accept a post with the War College.

And my husband, Kent Mills, a member of the 101st Airborne Division, served in Vietnam as a platoon leader and brought home a

Bronze Star. The perspectives of these men in general, and my husband in particular, enabled me to enter a world I found very foreign at first: that of the combat veteran and true military man. Without my husband's help, some of the scenes in this book couldn't have happened.

My husband, my dad, and the men in my husband's family (along with my brother, Brad Henderson, also a Vietnam veteran, and my step-dad, Leon Lewis, who fought in World War II) have taught me the true meaning of what it means to be a man, and what courage it takes every single day . . . just to do the right thing.

DEANIE FRANCIS MILLS
January, 1996

·   A NOTE ON THE TYPE   ·

The typeface used in this book, Transitional, is a digitized version of Fairfield, which was designed in 1937–40 by artist Rudolph Ruzicka (1883–1978), on a commission from Linotype. The assignment was the occasion for a well-known essay in the form of a letter from W. A. Dwiggins to Ruzicka, in response to the latter's request for advice. Dwiggins, who had recently designed Electra and Caledonia, relates that he would start by making very large scale drawings (10 and 64 times the size you are reading) and having test cuttings made, which were used to print on a variety of papers. "By looking at all these for two or three days I get an idea of how to go forward—or, if the result is a dud, how to start over again." At this stage he took *parts* of letters that satisfied him and made cardboard cutouts, which he then used to assemble other letters. This "template" method anticipated one that many contemporary computer type designers use.